"[AN] INTELLIGENT AND PULSE-POUNDING THRILLER . . . Hougan demonstrates fine command of his material. His familiarity with the ways of spies permeates his novel. Better yet, his writing is punchy and spare, his characterizations lively."
—*Publishers Weekly*

Dunphy looked out the window at what might have been a SwissAir postcard: cerulean skies and umber mountains, plastered with snow. It was a beautiful world at 35,000 feet.

But it was a dangerous one on the ground.

Adjusting the pitch to his seat, he sat back and closed his eyes. *It's too big,* he thought. *Whatever it is, it's just too big. We'll never get out of it.* He opened his eyes and looked out the window once again, thinking: *It doesn't matter how much I find out. What do I do with it—go to the police? Go to the press? They'd have me committed.*

"A penny for your thoughts," Clem suggested. . . .

These guys are gonna kill us.

"A SKILLFULLY SKEWED TAKE ON CONSPIRACY MANIA."
—*Kirkus Reviews*

KINGDOM COME

Jim Hougan

BALLANTINE BOOKS • NEW YORK

A Ballantine Book
Published by The Ballantine Publishing Group
Copyright © 2000 by James Hougan

All rights reserved under International and Pan-American Copyright Conventions. Published in the United States by The Ballantine Publishing Group, a division of Random House, Inc., New York, and simultaneously in Canada by Random House of Canada Limited, Toronto.

www. ballantinebooks.com

Library of Congress Cataloging-in-Publication Data: 2001116600

ISBN 0-449-00321-3

Manufactured in the United States of America

First Hard Cover Edition: January 2000
First Mass Market Edition: July 2001

10   9   8   7   6   5   4   3   2   1

Some people get better and better,
even as they stay the course.
This book is for them.

Jeff Bale
Kevin Coogan
Gary Horne
Pallo Jordan
Norman Mailer
Ron McRea
Robin Ramsay
Ben Sidran
Judy Sidran
Scott Spencer
Joe Uehlein
Carolyn, Daisy, and Matt

"Events seem to be ordered into an ominous logic."
Thomas Pynchon, *V.*

PROLOGUE

Major Angleton floated through the moonless heavens above Sant' Ambrogio, suspended in the night air by nylon cords and a canopy of black silk. He could see a line of fire burning along the forested ridge above the town, and wondered whether lightning or bombers were its cause. There was little else that he could see, still less to be heard, and only the wind to feel.

> To build the city of Dioce whose
> terraces are the colour of stars.

As he drifted lower, the smell of wood smoke came at him from the nearby fires, a whiff of hyacinths and the fragrance of scrub pines. The pines were shadows, swelling against the dark hillside, until, quite suddenly, he was among them, falling past them, flying laterally across the face of the hill. And then, with a shock, he was on the ground, staggering forward on his heels, pulling against the chute, rolling it up. The air was cool.

The major's destination was a large and crumbling villa set amid ruined terraces on the slopes above where he'd landed. A soft yellow light spilled from the villa's windows, gilding the untended vineyards that sprawled in every direction. Major Angleton unholstered his .45 and began walking up the hill until he felt the crunch of gravel underfoot and knew that he was in the courtyard. Crossing to a shuttered window, he peered between the slats. The man whom he'd been sent to

1

find, reviled at home and hated in Europe, a poet of inestimable talents and a violent baiter of the Jews, sat at a worm-eaten library table, surrounded by books. He was writing by the light of a kerosene lantern in what appeared to be an enormous leather diary. Behind him, hanging askew from the cracked plaster wall, was a painting of Poussin's, a small and wonderful oil in a cheap wooden frame.

A soft breeze brought the scent of wisteria with it, and Major Angleton realized that he had been holding his breath, though he didn't know for how long. The hand with the gun was clammy with perspiration.

Leaving the window, he went to the villa's door, sucked the cold night air into his lungs, pushed the door open, and stepped inside. The poet looked up, shocked to find an armed man so suddenly in front of him. Then his eyes focused on the soldier's face, and his shock turned to incredulity. "Jim?" he asked.

Angleton nodded.

"Well . . . are you here to arrest me?"

Angleton shook his head. His mouth was dry. "Helmsman," he said, dropping to one knee and lowering his eyes. *"Maestro di color che sanno. . . ."*

8 May 1945
FROM: 15 Army Group
            92 Division
            OSS, X-2

TO: Commanding General
            Mediterranean Theater of Operations

SIGNED: Maj. James J. Angleton

American civilian writer EZRA LOOMIS POUND, reference FBI cable 1723, indicted for treason by grand jury, captured by Italian partisans 6 May at Sant' Ambrogio. Held MTOUSA Disciplinary Training Center for confinement pending instructions on disposition. All security measures taken to prevent escape or suicide. No press. No privileges. And *no interrogation*.

-Ω-

1

Dunphy huddled beneath the warm sheets, half-awake, his back to Clementine. He could feel the coldness of the room beyond the bed and sensed the gray London light seeping through the windows like a cloud. The time was anyone's guess. Early morning. Or late. Or afternoon. *Saturday,* in any case.

He mumbled something about getting up (or maybe not) and listened for her reply. "Mmmm," she murmured, then arched her back and rolled away. "Dream . . . "

He sat up with a low grumble, blinking himself awake. He swung his legs from the bed, pinched the sleep from his eyes, and got to his feet. Clementine whimpered and purred behind him as he shivered his way across the cold floor to the bathroom, where he brushed and spat. Filling his cupped hands with water from the tap, he lowered his face into the cold of it. "Jesus," he gasped. And again.

"Christ!" he whispered, and taking a deep breath, shook his head like a dog.

The man in the mirror was thirty-two years old, broadshouldered and angular. An inch over six feet, he had green eyes and straight black hair. The eyes glittered back at him from the surface of the mirror as Dunphy, dripping, pulled a towel from the rack, then buried his face in the raised letters of white pile.

Dolder Grand.

And that reminded him: he'd promised Luxembourg that he'd send a fax to Credit Suisse, inquiring about a wire transfer that had gone awry.

4

There was no point in shaving. It was the weekend. He could jog to work, send the fax, do a bit of paperwork, and take the Underground back to the flat in time for lunch. Returning to the bedroom, then, he pulled a ragged sweatshirt from the dresser and dragged it over his head.

Clementine remained in a fetal position, the sheets and covers bunched inefficiently above her knees. There was a quizzical look on her face as she slept, her lips slightly parted. Dunphy stood for a moment in the still, cold air of the room, wondering at her immaculate complexion, the paperwhite skin brushed with pink and framed by a cascade of dark curls.

It occurred to him to make love to her then and there, but the cold had had its effect. Shivering, he pulled on a pair of sweatpants and white socks and jammed his feet into his running shoes. As he tied the laces, his eyes never left the soft parabola of hip beneath the sheets.

Clementine shifted, turning onto her back. Dunphy stood. Maybe later—unless, as seemed likely, she'd returned to her own place.

A sigh ran through him as he went out the door.

Running was important to him. Though his life in London was a good one, it was suffused with a low-voltage anxiety that never really went away. He lived with a constant static charge of tension and a slight adrenal drain—the consequence, he knew, of spending his days in the cheap suit of a false identity.

So he ran.

He ran five times a week, about ten kilometers a day, following the same route from his apartment in Chelsea past the houseboats at Cheyne Walk, along the Embankment and across the Albert Bridge. This was the unpleasant part of the run. Even on Saturday mornings, the air was heavy with diesel fumes, the streets choked with trucks—*lorries,* he reminded himself—and cabs. There were a dozen streets to cross before he reached the Embankment, and, all in all, it was a dangerous way to stay in shape. Even after a year in England, Dunphy instinctively looked to the left for cars—which, of course, bore down upon him, horns blaring, from the right.

The middle of the run was lovely, though. It took him into Battersea Park, along the south bank of the Thames, and past the park's improbable pagoda. There was a sort of wildlife refuge among the trees, too pretty to be called a zoo. It held spotted deer and sheep, and a herd of wallabies that looked for all the world like prehistoric rabbits.

In the early morning stillness and gloom, the wallabies reminded him of the statues on Easter Island, immobile against the hillside, gazing down at him with stony indifference. Dunphy smiled as he strode past the beasts, moving easily and with the virtuous feeling that the passing miles gave.

This was the midpoint of his run, the place where he usually returned home the way that he had come. Today, however, he continued on through the park to Chelsea Bridge, across the Thames, and on to Millbank, heading toward his office in Gun House.

It was bad tradecraft to run the same route every day but, then again, this was London, not Beirut. Running through the park, Dunphy was entirely at ease, not only with himself, but with the person that he was pretending to be.

A light mist settled on him as he ran, soaking his sweatshirt, but never quite coalescing into rain. He was listening to the sound of his breathing and thinking about Clementine.

He'd seen her for the first time only three months before, standing behind the cash register in a used bookstore on Sicilian Avenue, the one with the funny name. *Skoob.*

And though Dunphy was not one to hustle clerks in bookstores, he'd known at a glance that if he didn't talk to her (or as Merry Kerry would put it, if he didn't *chat her up*), he'd never forgive himself. It wasn't just that she was beautiful, or that she had the longest waist he'd ever seen. It wasn't *just* that, he told himself. There was something else, a sweet vulnerability that made him feel guilty for the cover story that he'd given her, and for the fact that when she whispered his name, it wasn't really *his* name, but an alias.

He'd make it up to her, he told himself, though he couldn't say how. Coming upon Grosvenor Road, with his mind adrift in the Eden between Clementine's navel and her knees, Dunphy glanced to the left and, striding out into the street, set off a fugue of horns and shrieking brakes that startled him into a reflexive sprint. A column of cars, taxis, buses, and trucks, approaching from the right, slammed on their brakes and, shuddering to a stop, erupted in curses.

Dunphy waved ambiguously and kept on running, irritated with himself for succumbing to distraction. You have to be careful, he thought. In the business he was in, it was easy enough to get blindsided.

2

Dunphy knew exactly when his skin began to crawl.

He was seated at his desk in front of the computer, writing the letter to Credit Suisse, when the phone began to ring: the short, sharp, angry bursts that tell you you're in England, not the States. Lifting the receiver to his ear, Dunphy heard Tommy Davis's voice quavering against a background of airline departure announcements.

British Airways, flight 2702—

"Ja-ack?" Tommy asked.

It was then, just then, that his skin began to move. Ever so slightly.

—departing for Madrid.

"Ja-aaa-ck?"

Christ, Dunphy thought. Three syllables, and his voice rising at the end. We're in for it.

Syrian Arab Airlines—

It didn't take a genius. Even if Tommy had sounded normal, there was no good reason—no happy reason—that he should be calling. Their work was finished, and Tommy had been paid. That should have been the end of it.

"Jack! For the love of Jay-sus! Talk to me! Are ya there, old son?"

"I am, Tommy. What's up?"

"There's a wee problem," Tommy said, his voice a broad Irish brogue, flat with understatement. "I've only just heard about it myself. An hour ago."

8

"I see," Dunphy remarked, holding his breath. "And what would this small problem be that it's taken you to the airport?"

"You can hear for yourself," Tommy replied. "They're talking about it on the Beeb." Dunphy's skin stopped crawling, got to its feet, and walked quickly away, leaving his carcass behind, stripped to the nerves in the swivel chair from Harrod's.

A deep breath. He blinked twice, sat up, and brought his lips close to the mouthpiece. His posture was suddenly perfect, his voice low and cold.

"I don't happen to have a radio in the office, Tommy. So what are we talking about? What's the subject?"

"Our professor."

"What about him?"

"Well, the poor man . . . I'm afraid he's been injured."

"He's been injured."

"Well—he's dead, then."

"Was it an accident, Tommy?"

"An accident? No, it wouldn't be. Not under the circumstances. Not with his balls cut off—I shouldn't think so."

"His *balls*—"

"I have a plane to catch. If you need me, I'll be drinkin' in Frankie Boylan's bar. You can reach me there."

And then the line was dead, and Dunphy didn't feel well.

Francis M. S. Boylan was a hard man who'd done a turn in the Maze for a string of bank robberies that he and Tommy had committed. Whether or not those robberies were politically motivated (the police described them as "fund-raisers for the IRA"), Boylan had taken the time to put aside enough of the loot to buy a small business. This was a bar on the south coast of Tenerife, overlooking the nude beach at Playa de las Americas. Tommy and his pals went to see him whenever their problems became unmanageable—which is to say, when they could not be solved by lawyers, guns, or money (or a combination of the three). Simply stated, the Broken Tiller was a hideout in the Atlantic, a hundred miles off the coast of Africa, two hundred miles south of the Rock, a hole in the twentieth century.

Fuckin' hell, Dunphy thought. The *Canaries. Tenerife.* His *balls*.

His stomach clenched, turned over, and clenched again. The Beeb was on it.

He let his eyes have their way with the room. It was a third-floor walk-up, a seedy redoubt amid the grime of Millbank. He liked it. The view through the window, spotted with rain, was gloomy and depressing: a wall of brick, a patch of gray sky, a peeling and faded billboard. ROTHMANS CIGARET E , it said.

Dunphy had quit smoking nearly a year ago, but there was, he knew, a stale packet of Silk Cuts in his top desk drawer. Without thinking, he found one, lighted it, and inhaled. For a moment, nothing happened, and then he felt as if he was about to levitate. Then he coughed.

There was no reason to panic, just because Tommy had. Looked at in an objective way, it was a matter of fact that Dunphy had paid Tommy to install an Infinity transmitter on the professor's telephone. This had been done, and it had worked for more than a month. Admittedly, or at least *seemingly*, the professor had then been murdered, but there was no reason to believe that his death was in any way a consequence of Dunphy's eavesdropping activity. Obviously, he told himself, he was in the midst of a terrible coincidence.

Awkward, yes, but . . .

These.

Things.

Happen.

Except, as Dunphy well knew, they did not happen in England, or if they did, they did not happen in quite this way. If the professor had been done by professionals, by the SAS or some such outfit, there would have been two in the derby and one in the chest—and that would have been the end of it. But if Tommy was right, the poor bastard had been castrated—which meant that it was a sex crime, or something like it.

He watched the soot stream down the windowpane until the phone rang for the second time, jolting him into focus. He didn't want to answer it. His stomach was a small balloon, filling slowly with air, wobbling toward his throat. The phone shrieked and shrieked again. Finally, he picked it up and held it in front of him, as if it were a snake.

"Hullo?" He could hear the *beep-beep-beep-beep* of a public phone, the sound of coins dropping, and then, "Get out."

It was Curry, Dunphy thought, though he barely recognized the voice, which came at him in a strangled continuum of real-time burst transmissions. "Go-home!/Do-it-now!/Do-you-understand-me?"

Jesus, Dunphy thought, he's at a pay phone, and he's got a handkerchief over the mouthpiece. "I think we need to talk," Dunphy said.

"*Go home.*"

"*Which* home?"

"*All the way* home."

"What?!"

"Flaps up. Do it now. Don't bother packing, and don't go to your flat. I'll have a housekeeping team there in half an hour. They'll ship your belongings in a couple of days."

Dunphy was stunned. "It's Saturday," he said. "I'm wearing sweats! I—I don't even have my passport. How am I supposed to—"

"You heard the news? I mean, you heard the fucking *News at Ten*?!"

"Yeah . . . sort of. I mean . . . my Irish friend just called and—Jesse, I have a life! Fahchrissake! I can't just—"

"You were supposed to clean up!"

"We *did* clean up. I mean, *he* did—my man did. I told him to go over there—when was it? The day before yesterday."

"They found a device."

"A *what*?!"

"I said, the *police* found a *device*." There was a pause, and Dunphy could tell that Jesse Curry was hyperventilating. "Listen to me, my friend. There are people—policemen— who are trying—even as we speak—to find out whose *device* it is. They're making 'in-*kwy*-ries,' and I think they have a name. Do you understand what I'm saying?"

"Of course."

"Well, then, just how long do you think it will take MI5 to find that mick son of a bitch of yours, and then to get from him to you? One day? Two?"

"They won't find him. He's already out of the country."

"Good. That's just where I want you to be. Don't go back to your flat. Just take the first flight out."

"How the fuck—I told you, I don't even have my wallet! I *ran* to the office."

"I'll have a courier in the Arrivals lounge. Terminal 3, just outside the Nothing-to-Declare. He'll be holding a cardboard sign." Curry paused, and Dunphy could hear the wheels spinning in his head. " 'Mr. Torbitt.' Look for him."

"Then what?"

"He'll have everything you need: passport—"

"Cash—"

"—ticket to the States, and a suitcase full of someone else's clothes. Probably his own."

"Why do I want someone else's clothes?"

"When was the last time you saw someone cross the Atlantic without a suitcase?"

"Look, Jesse—"

Beep-beep-beep. The pay phone wanted another coin.

"Go home!"

"Look, I don't think this is such a great idea!"

Beep-beep. "Just do it."

"But—"

Beep-beep. "I'm outa change!"

There was a clatter on the other end of the line, a strangled curse, a distant harmonic, and that was it. Jesse Curry was gone.

Dunphy sat back in his chair, dazed. He took in a lungful of smoke, held it for a long while, and exhaled. Leaning forward, he stubbed out his cigarette in the ashtray and stared at the wall.

Don't go to your flat. I've got a housekeeping team—

A *housekeeping* team. *What about Clementine? Was she still asleep? Would they cart her out with the laundry?* Lunging for the phone, he tapped out his own number and waited. The ringing came in extended, noisome bursts punctuated by long intervals of crackling, dead air. After a minute that seemed like an hour, he hung up, figuring she'd gone to her own place. Should he call her there?

Dunphy shook his head, muttering to himself that Clementine was too important to handle on the fly. And, anyway, the operation was crashing and there were things that had to be done—now and by him. In the end, he would do his own housekeeping. He'd take care of his own "disposals."

With a sigh, he touched the trackball next to the keyboard and clicked on *Start*. Clicked again on *Shut down*, and a third time on *Restart the computer in MS-DOS mode*. Then he leaned over the keyboard and began to peck out the cybernetic equivalent of a lobotomy.

CD/DOS

It gave him the same sickening thrill that a skydiver feels as he steps, for the first time, into the air. Here goes, here comes—nothing:

```
DEBUG
G=C800:5
```

The computer began to ask a series of questions, which Dunphy answered in a perfunctory way, tapping at the keyboard. After a while, the hard disk began to grind. An age passed as Dunphy smoked, until at long last, the grinding stopped, and the command line blinked:

FORMAT COMPLETE

The machine was brain-dead, its cursor blinking dully. Dunphy was perspiring. A year's work, lost in the ozone.

And, then, to make certain that it stayed in the ozone, he ran a program called DiskWipe, overwriting every byte on the hard disk with the numeral 1.

The computer was the main thing he had to deal with, but there were other details, including some letters that were waiting to be sent. Most of the correspondence was trivial, but at least one of the letters was not. Addressed to a client named Roger Blémont, it contained details of a newly opened bank account on Jersey in the Channel Islands. Without the letter, Blémont would not be able to get at the money—which, as it happened, was rather a lot.

Dunphy thought about that. Making Blémont wait for his money would not be a bad thing. Not necessarily, and probably not at all. They were, after all, ill-gotten gains intended for a bad purpose. *Still,* he thought, they were *Blémont's* ill-gotten gains and—

He didn't have time to think about this shit. Not now. The world was falling apart all around him. So he tossed the letters into his attaché case with the vague idea of mailing them from the airport. Removing a battered Filofax from the top drawer of his desk, he dropped it into his attaché case and got to his feet. Then he crossed the room to a scuffed-up filing cabinet that held the detritus of his cover—business correspondence and corporate filings. For the most part, it was paper that he could safely leave behind.

But there were a few files that Dunphy considered sensitive. One contained pages from the previous year's appointments book. Another held Tommy Davis's bills for "investigative services." A third file was the repository of receipts for "business entertainment," including his regular meetings with Curry, some lunches with the FBI's Legat and the DEA's mission coordinator for the U.K. Scattered among the four drawers of the filing cabinet, the sensitive files were easily and quickly retrievable because they were the only ones with blue labels.

One by one, he took out the flagged dossiers, making a stack, five or six inches high. This done, he took the pile to the fireplace and, squatting beneath the battered antique mantel, set the files on the floor. As he pulled the phony fire logs out of the way, the possibility occurred to him that no one had put a match to the grate in more than thirty years—not since the Clean Air Act had put an end to the city's pea-soupers.

But what the hell. There was a distinct possibility that he would soon be indicted for wiretapping and, perhaps, as an accessory to murder. There was the espionage issue, as well—not to mention money laundering. If, then, he should also get nailed for air pollution, what the fuck?

Dunphy reached into the chimney, fumbled around until he found a handle, and, straining, yanked open the flue. Gathering the files together, he leaned the manila folders against one another on the grate, creating a sort of tepee, then lighted the structure at its corners. The room brightened. Fire, Dunphy thought, is nature's way of destroying evidence.

He warmed his hands for a moment, then rose to his feet. Returning to the desk, he removed its top drawer and set it on the floor. Then he reached inside, felt around, and retrieved a kraft-colored envelope. Unfastening its closures, he extracted a microcassette of used recording tape.

Tommy had given it to him the day before. It was the last of eleven voice-actuated tapes, the take from a five-week-long electronic surveillance. Dunphy had meant to give the tape to Curry at their next meeting, but now . . . what to do? He could melt the cassette in the fire, send it to Curry in the mail, or take it to Langley and let the Agency decide.

The decision was a difficult one because the surveillance had been off the books, an out-of-channels operation of the chief of station's. Dunphy himself hadn't listened to the tapes, and so had no idea what might be on them, or what might be at stake. And he didn't want to know. To his way of thinking, he'd been a middleman and nothing more: he'd hired Tommy to wire the professor's flat, and he had taken the product to Curry twice a week. It was a favor for the chief of station, and that was all.

Still . . . Jesse Curry did not strike Dunphy as a stand-up

guy. Not exactly. In fact, not at all. Indeed, Dunphy thought, surrendering to his paranoia, Curry struck him as the sort of prick who felt most at ease in the company of fall guys.

Which was not what Mother Dunphy had raised her son to be.

So Dunphy shoved the tape recording into a Jet-Pak, stapled it closed, and addressed it to himself:

> K. Thornley
> c/o F. Boylan
> The Broken Tiller
> Playa de las Americas
> Tenerife, Islas Canarias
> España

He slapped a two-pound stamp on the envelope and glanced around the room.

What Curry didn't know wouldn't hurt him.

Or so, at least, Dunphy theorized.

3

To reach the airport by train, Dunphy needed exactly one pound fifty. He found it in the bottom drawer of his desk where, for months, he'd been dumping one-, five-, and ten-pence coins. The drawer contained about twenty pounds in change, he figured, but anything more than the exact amount would be less than useless because, of course, his sweatpants didn't have pockets. For a moment, he considered dumping the coins into his attaché case, but . . . no. The idea was ludicrous.

He took just what he needed, then, and walked quickly to the Underground station on Liverpool Street. Dressed as he was in battered Nikes and tattered sweats, he felt conspicuously American. And, under the circumstances, very jumpy.

The train rumbled under and through the city for fifteen minutes and then surfaced with a clatter in the bleak suburbs to the west. A prisoner of his own distraction, he noticed nothing about the ride until, for reasons no one bothered to explain, the train rocked to an unscheduled stop near Hounslow—where it sat on the tracks for eight minutes, creaking and motionless in a soft rain.

Dunphy felt like a jack-in-the-box, coiled in on himself, ready to go through the roof. Staring through the filthy glass windows at a sodden soccer field, he was half-convinced that the police were walking through the cars, one after another, looking for him. But then the train gave a lurch and started moving again. Minutes later, he was lost in the flux of the Arrivals lounge at Terminal 3.

He saw the courier from twenty yards away. He was a tall, muscular young man in a cheap black suit and motorcycle boots—a Carnaby Street punk with a pitted complexion and jet-black hair cropped so short it seemed to be a shadow on his scalp. He stood without moving in a crowd of greeters and chauffeurs, just where Curry had said he would be. The way he stood, stock-still, with his eyes flicking from side to side, made Dunphy think of Wallace Stevens' "Thirteen Ways of Looking at a Blackbird" where

> The only moving thing
> Was the eye of the blackbird.

Dunphy came closer. The courier held a small, stenciled sign in front of his chest: MR. TORBITT. Holding the sign in the way that he did exposed the kid's wrists, and Dunphy saw that each was dotted with a crude blue line—the work of an amateur tattooist (probably the kid himself). He knew that if he looked closer he'd find the words *Cut Here* scratched into the skin on each wrist.

Which is to say that the courier was perfect: London's Everyboy.

And that made Dunphy smile. Where in the name of Christ does Curry find them? he wondered. Kids like this. So ordinary as to be invisible.

"Jesse said you'd have something for me."

The young man swung around with a smile, exposing a tangle of gray teeth. So much for the National Health.

"Ah! The guv'nor himself," he said. "That's your kit over there, and there's this lot, as well." He handed him a large manila envelope that Dunphy knew contained money, tickets, and a passport.

"Ta."

The young man bounced on the balls of his feet and flashed his gray grin. "Have a nice fucking day," he said. And then he was gone, his head bobbing through the crowd like an eight ball without spin.

Opening the envelope, Dunphy checked the ticket for his flight number and glanced at the Departures board. With an hour to kill, he went looking for a newspaper and soon found one. CHELSEA CARNAGE! KING'S COLLEGE PROF SLAIN!

He could feel his stomach floating lazily up to his chest. The story was front-page, and it was dramatized by a four-column photograph of police and passersby gawking at a stretcher being loaded into an ambulance. The stretcher's burden was unusually small, about the size of a large dog, and covered by a stained white sheet.

According to the article, Professor Leo Schidlof had been found at 4 A.M. by a drunken law student in the Inns of Court. The man's torso—the word gave Dunphy pause—was lying on a patch of lawn near the Inner Temple.

Dunphy looked up. He knew the Inner Temple. Indeed, he knew the patch of lawn. The temple was a small, round church in the heart of London's legal district, not far from Fleet Street. His own solicitor kept offices around the corner, in Middle Temple Lane. Dunphy went past the church once or twice a month on the way to see him.

It was spooky looking, as most anachronisms are.

Which should have been enough to set the scene, but Dunphy couldn't stop himself. He was in denial, and the more he thought about the Inner Temple, the longer he could keep his eyes off the newspaper article.

The temple was thirteenth century, or thereabouts. They'd built it for the Knights Templar. And the Knights, of course, had had something to do with the Crusades. (Or maybe not.)

Dunphy paused and thought. That was it. He didn't know any more. And so he turned back to the article, hoping for another monument to divert him. Instead, he got police sources, "*unidentified* police sources," who said that the King's College professor had been dismembered, apparently in vivo. A strip of skin, about three inches wide, had been flayed from the base of his spine to the nape of his neck. His genitals had then been removed, and his rectum "surgically excised."

Dunphy's eyes skittered from the page. Jesus, Mary, and

Joseph, he thought. What the fuck is *that*? And where are the poor man's legs and arms? The story made him woozy. But there wasn't much else. The police were unable to say how "the torso" had come to repose in the place that it had: the lawn was enclosed by a wrought-iron fence not far from the Thames Embankment.

And that was that. The article ended with the information that Schidlof was a popular lecturer in the psychology department at King's College, and that he had been writing a biography of Carl Jung at the time of his death.

Dunphy tossed the newspaper into a bin and went to join the long queue at the TWA counter. He didn't want to think about Leo Schidlof. Not yet—and maybe not ever. Schidlof's death wasn't his fault, and if Dunphy had anything to say about it, it wouldn't be any of his business. In any case, he had his own problems. Nudging the suitcase forward with his foot, he opened the manila envelope and took out the passport, intending to memorize its details.

But to his immense unhappiness, no memorization would be necessary. The passport was in his own name—his *real* name—which meant that his cover was broken and the operation, *his* operation, was ended. There was a single stamp on the passport's first page, admitting one John Edwards Dunphy—*Dunphy!* for chrissakes—to England for a period not to exceed six months. The stamp was a forgery, of course, and indicated that he'd entered the country only seven days earlier.

Seeing his cover so casually broken took his breath away. For a little more than a year, he'd lived in London as an Irishman named Kerry Thornley. Other than Jesse Curry, the only person who knew enough to call him by his real first name was Tommy Davis. Tommy was too much a Kerryman to fool about Ireland. Within a week of working with one another, he'd sussed out the fact that his newfound friend and sometime employer, Merry Kerry, was in fact a dodgy American businessman named Jack.

Meanwhile, Dunphy's business card identified Thornley as chairman of

Anglo-Erin Business Services PLC
Gun House
Millbank
London SW 1

This false identity had covered him like a second skin, keeping him high and dry in the immunity of its folds. Because Thornley was notional, a fiction generated by a computer in the basement of Langley headquarters, Dunphy could not be made to suffer the consequences of Thornley's actions—which meant that Dunphy, as Thornley, had been free in a way that Dunphy, as Dunphy, could never be.

Losing his immunity so suddenly left him exposed at the very moment that he felt most in jeopardy. Unconsciously, he began to sag into himself, the wisecracking Irishman—Merry Kerry—giving way to the more restrained and worried-looking American, Jack Dunphy.

It took another twenty minutes to reach the head of the line, and by the time that he did, his feet hurt and his head was pounding. It was just beginning to hit home that, in the space of a single morning, he'd lost nearly everything he cared about, including Clementine.

Clementine! Jesus Christ, he thought, what about Clem?

4

Nine hours later, Dunphy signed into the Ambassadors Club on the second floor of the B concourse at John F. Kennedy International Airport. The club was nearly empty. Dropping his suitcase next to a worn leather couch, he grabbed a handful of pretzels, ordered a Bushmills from a wandering waitress, and went into a booth to call the hello-phone at the watch office in Langley.

The phone rang twice, as it always did, and then a young man's voice came on the line.

"Hello."

Some things never changed. "This is . . . " He hesitated, as he always did when the rules called for him to use his crypto. It was embarrassing. Grown men, playing with code names. "Oboe," he finished. "Do you have anything for me?"

There was silence at the other end, and then, "Yes, sir. I have you down for an eight A.M. at headquarters."

"That's . . . Monday."

"No, sir. This is for tomorrow."

Dunphy groaned.

"I guess someone's eager to see you."

"I just got in," Dunphy complained. "I don't have any clothes. I'm jet-lagged. I don't even have a place to stay."

"I can recommend a couple of—"

"Tomorrow's Sunday, for Christ's sake. Nobody'll be at the office. They'll be—" Dunphy fumbled for the word. "They'll be *worshipping*. *I'll* be worshipping. I'll be worshipping all day."

22

"It *says* Sunday, sir. Eight A.M. Maybe you could make a later service."

"Don't fuck with me, kid."

"I just relay the messages, sir."

Dunphy hung up and dialed the 800 number for Marriott. He took a room for the weekend at the hotel near Tysons Corner and then called Hertz. That done, he got the international operator and gave her the number for Clementine's flat in Bolton Gardens.

"Kerry?"

He was tongue-tied.

"Kerry? Where are you?"

"Hey, Clem! I'm . . . "

"Where are you?"

"Traveling. Something came up. A last-minute sort of thing."

"Oh, well . . . in that case, where are you?"

This was a highly focused girl. "I'm in the States. New York. JFK. The Ambassadors Club. Booth Two."

"Testy, aren't we?"

"Yeah, well, it's been a long day."

"Then . . . when will you be back?"

"That's just it. I don't know. It could be . . . a while."

"Ohhh, noooo!"

"Yeah, but—listen, I can't stay on the phone—I have a connection to make. What I need to know is, did anyone come by the flat this morning?"

"Not when I was there. Are you all right?"

"Yeah, of course I am. Why?"

"You don't sound right."

"Why not?"

"Well, for one thing," she said, laughing, "you've acquired an American accent."

Dunphy rolled his eyes and slid back into a well-practiced brogue. "I can't help it, darlin'. I'm a natural mime. But this is the important part, now, and you must do what I ask, and I'll explain everything later."

"Fuck!"

Dunphy was taken aback. "Why 'fuck'? I haven't said anything yet."

"Because 'explain everything later' always means there's trouble."

"Yes, well, what I'd like you to do is, uh, just . . . stay away from the flat."

"What?!"

"Stay away from the flat until I can see you."

"Why?!"

"Just stay away, Clem. It's important."

"But I have things there! Why can't I go there? My makeup is there! Is there someone else, then?"

"Don't be stupid."

"Then why do I have to stay away?"

"Well—for one thing—because *I* won't be there. And, for another . . . "

"Yeah? *What,* then?"

"Because it's dangerous."

"It's 'dangerous'?"

"Clem . . . trust me."

When Dunphy hung up, he reentered the club room, found a chair, and sat back to count his losses and brood. He watched the planes take off. And other planes land. And when the waitress came by, he ordered the second of what became too many Irish whiskeys.

No one had ever walked out on Clementine before. He was pretty sure of that. You'd have to be nuts.

5

Dunphy swung the T-bird into a right turn off the G. W. Parkway at the Chain Bridge, looping around the exit ramp onto Dolley Madison Boulevard. He pointed the 'Bird west and drove on for a mile, then turned right into a long arcade of trees leading to the gatehouse at the edge of the CIA compound. A huge black security guard emerged from the guardhouse with a clipboard and a smile. "Mawnin', " he said. "You have an appointment?"

"John Dunphy. I'm running a little bit late."

The guard checked the clipboard, walked to the back of the car, noted the license-plate number, and came back to the driver's window. "I'll need to see your rental papers," he said, nodding at the Hertz sticker on the windshield. Dunphy gave him the papers and watched as the guard began, with meticulous and painstaking strokes, to copy the information onto his pad. It was as if he was drawing the letters, rather than writing them.

Not that Dunphy was in a hurry. The air was clear and cold and bracing—just what he needed. All in all, he liked being at headquarters. It had the feel of a small college in upstate New York. A complex of architecturally indifferent, more-or-less-modern buildings, it had been set down, invisible from the road, among a hundred acres of grass and trees, hidden cameras and dipole antennas.

"Thanks," the guard said, returning the papers. "You know where to go?"

"No problem."

"You can park 'most anywhere today."

"Great," Dunphy said, putting the car in gear.

"Hardly anyone here on Sundays."

Dunphy nodded, pretending interest.

"Makes you wonder," the guard added.

Then the gate lifted, and Dunphy let the T-bird roll forward.

Driving through the parking lot, he marveled, as he always did, at the high percentage of Corvettes and the weird mix of bumper stickers.

| REAGAN IN '84 | GREENPEACE | FREE O.J.! |
| BUSH IN '85 | SAVE THE BALES! | |

He drove past the Nathan Hale statue, parked his car in the space marked DIRECTOR, and got out in front of the headquarters building.

Entering the lobby, he found a fragile blonde waiting in the atrium astride the CIA seal, an eagle embossed on the marble under her feet.

"Mr. Dunphy?"

He winced, provoking a quizzical look.

"Jack Dunphy?"

"Yeah," he said. "Sometimes."

"Just clip this to your lapel," she said, handing him a laminated yellow tag, "and I'll escort you."

Dunphy did as he was asked, but he wasn't happy about it. Everyone at headquarters, from the janitors to the inspector general, was required to wear an identification tag, conspicuously displayed. The tags were color-coded, as were the halls in each of the buildings: a colored stripe ran down the middle of every corridor so that security officers could tell at a glance if someone was where he wasn't supposed to be.

You could go virtually anywhere with a blue tag, but a red tag restricted you to the A building, and a green tag was even more confining. It meant that you could enter only those corridors in the A building whose floors were marked with a green line. A yellow tag was the most restrictive of all, because it meant that you had to be escorted everywhere. It was reserved for visitors and the press—people who didn't belong—and wearing it was like dragging a bell. People looked away, as if you were the scene of an accident.

But the blonde's presence made up for the insult implied by the yellow tag. As she walked, her ponytail swung like a metronome in perfect counterpoint to the roll of her buttocks. It occurred to Dunphy, who gave considerable thought to the matter, that her ass would be most aptly compared to a valentine sprayed with tweed. It was a wonderful thing to behold, and clearly, it was no accident that she'd been assigned to escort-duty. If she'd wanted, Dunphy would have followed her to hell and back, and never have complained.

Which was saying a lot, given the way he felt. In Olympic terms, he supposed the judges would rate his hangover a 5.6, and not much more. But, still, he did not feel well. He was wearing the same sweatshirt and gym socks that he'd worn in London on the day before. The stores wouldn't open until ten, and the suitcase that he'd been given was stuffed with GWAR T-shirts, a pair of worn-out Doc Martens, and blue jeans with holes in the knees. It just wasn't him. Not now, not then, not ever. In any case, it wasn't just clothes that made the man: there was a faint blush in Dunphy's eyes, he needed a shave, and the back of his head seemed to weigh more than the front. Call it a 5.9.

Dunphy's escort led him through a maze of pale blue corridors in the B annex until, finally, they reached a small reception desk. A young security guard in a black uniform, epaulets bright with braid, got to his feet, gesturing to a cloth-bound register on the desk. "If you'll sign in . . . your friends got here a while ago."

Dunphy bent over the register and did as he'd been asked. The names above his were *Sam Esterhazy* and *Mike Rhinegold*: 7:50 and ".

The guard turned his back to them and tapped the keypad on the door's cipher lock. There was a soft click, and the door sprung open on silent hinges.

The moment it closed behind him, Dunphy felt worse. He was in an anechoic chamber, or "dead room"—a windowless, fluorescently lighted cube that rested on unseen, but enormous, springs. Impossible to bug, it amounted to a thickly carpeted vault of conical foam baffles deployed in such a way that they absorbed and neutralized every disturbance of the air. Not a signal, resonance, or echo left the area, whether its origins were human, mechanical, or electronic.

Because the room was entirely without resonance, everything that was said within it sounded empty, hollow, and false. *Flat.* It was a place in which even Mother Teresa would have come off as a phony. Dunphy had never been in a room like this before, but he had heard about them. Most embassies had one, and Moscow had three. He'd been told that it was impossible to play music in such a room. The Juilliard String Quartet had tried in a test at the Bureau of Standards; within seconds, the musicians had fallen, laughing, into dissonance.

But Dunphy didn't feel like laughing. In fact, a wave of nausea surged through him as he stood in the room, looking at his interrogators.

Seated at a long conference table, they were curiously, unpleasantly alike. Improbably tall, and equally gaunt, they shared the same unhealthy gray complexion, as if they'd been camping in a mine shaft. They combed their hair into low pompadours, short on the sides, and were dressed in shiny black suits, white polyester shirts, black wing tips, and string ties with turquoise bolos. Each of them carried a large catalog case packed with kraft-colored file folders. They seemed to Dunphy like a malignant version of the Blues Brothers. His stomach heaved, and he felt light-headed.

"Mr. Dunphy," said one.

"Mr. Thornley," said the other.

Fuck all, Dunphy thought. I've had it.

Esterhazy and Rhinegold removed various items from their briefcases, arranging them with care on the table: two legal pads, two ballpoint pens, a package of Virginia Slims, and a Bic lighter. Each.

Despite the way he felt, Dunphy chuckled at the choreography. "You guys have a lot in common, y'know that?"

They looked at him, blankly.

"Excuse me?" said the older man.

"How do you mean?" asked the younger guy. They seemed perplexed, as if the idea had never occurred to them.

Dunphy began to explain, but their humorless expressions made him change his mind. "Never mind," he said. He was irritated that they didn't introduce themselves—though he could tell by the monogram on the younger guy's cuff links that he was Rhinegold.

He assumed that they knew everything, but *everything*, about *him*: who he was, who he'd pretended to be, and more. That was what all the files were about, or so Dunphy supposed. They had a need to know. And he didn't. Those were the rules.

Esterhazy removed his wristwatch and placed it on the table so that it would be in sight throughout the interview. This done, he and his partner lighted cigarettes, exhaled thoughtfully, and looked at Dunphy with a sense of expectation.

Dunphy sighed. I am, he reflected, in the presence of

Two.

Major.

Geeks.

"Let's start with your alias, Mr. Dunphy."

"Which one?"

"The Irish cover. Can you tell us to what extent Mr. Thornley's identity was backstopped?"

Dunphy began to talk, and as he did, he listened to himself, and to the sound of his words in the peculiar room. It seemed to him that his voice originated from a point just outside his body, the words forming an inch or two in front of his lips. From the other side of the table, questions floated toward him, curiously empty of inflection, and impossible to read.

It was a strange, informational waltz, and Dunphy tired of it very quickly.

* * *

"So," Tweedledum said, "your principal responsibility was to establish commercial covers—"

"And banking facilities—"

"—abroad."

"Right."

"And how did you do that?" Tweedledee asked.

"Well," Dunphy said, "every situation is different, but basically, I'd pick a venue, depending on the client's needs, and then—"

"What do you mean, pick a venue?"

"The place where the incorporation would take place. There are a lot of possibilities, and they're all different. Some are more respectable, and more expensive, than others."

"For example?"

"Luxembourg, Liechtenstein, Switzerland."

"They're more respectable?"

"Yeah, compared to Panama, Belize, and Vanuatu, they're a lot more respectable. Panama's *funky*. You see Panama on a letterhead, and the first word that comes into your mind is *cartel*."

"And then? . . ."

"I'd fill in the forms to create a new company, or if the client was in a hurry, or didn't care about the name, I'd just take one off the shelf." Before they could ask him the obvious question, he explained. "I spent half my time drawing up corporations, so I always had a couple of dozen of them, waiting to go. That way, if a client walked in off the street and needed something right away, I could give it to him—there and then—wherever he wanted it."

"And what would he get—actually?"

Dunphy sighed. "Well, *physically,* he'd get a large envelope. And in it, he'd have two copies of the Company's Memorandum and Articles of Association. Plus the undated resignations of the founding directors and secretary—"

"Who were? . . ."

"Locals. Liberians, Manx, whatever. They were people

who made their names available for a small fee. They didn't have any real connection to the firms. They were just names. And let's see . . . what else? There'd be some blank stock transfers, a certificate of nontrading—and, of course, all of it was embossed with stamps and seals and tied together with red ribbons. Once the incorporation fees were paid, the company was live."

"And then what?"

"Then they'd need a bank account."

"And how was that set up?"

"They'd give me a deposit. And I'd open an account in the company's name. Mostly, I used the Midland Bank in St. Helier—Channel Islands."

"So you controlled all the accounts."

Dunphy laughed. "Only for a few days. Once I sent the paperwork to the client, they'd take my name off the account. Not that it mattered. Most of the time, I opened these accounts with less than a hundred pounds. It wasn't like I was *tempted* or anything."

"Most of the time."

"Yeah. There were exceptions. I had a couple of clients that I'd done a lot of work for, and sometimes they gave me some fairly substantial checks to deposit. But those were exceptions—and they knew where I lived. So to speak."

"Like who?"

"Like us." Rhinegold and Esterhazy looked puzzled. "I set up half a dozen companies for the Agency, and each time, there were substantial deposits up front. So what? I'm gonna skip out?"

"But you did the same thing for individuals. And private firms."

"Of course. That was my cover. That's what Anglo-Erin Business Services *did*. Publicly."

"And this was entirely confidential."

"It was supposed to be," Dunphy said.

"But . . . ," Esterhazy prodded.

"I was tasked—indirectly, of course—by half a dozen agencies."

"Such as?"

"DEA, IRS, Customs—" Dunphy paused for breath and continued. "—ISA—"

Esterhazy waved him off. "And how did that work?"

"I kept my eyes open. If something hot came in, I was supposed to keep the station apprised. Jesse—the station chief—would pass it along to the appropriate agency. Or not. It was up to him."

"When you say 'hot'—what would be hot?"

Dunphy mused. "Well, for example, it would be hot if Alan Greenspan walked in off the street to set up a company on Jersey with Saddam Hussein, using the Moscow Narodny Bank as the registered agent."

Rhinegold's eyes dilated.

"That would be very hot," Dunphy added.

"That happened?" Rhinegold was on the verge of levitation.

Dunphy shook his head. "No. That was just an example. A hypothetical example. I never had anything *that* obvious."

"Who did you report to at the Embassy?" Esterhazy asked. "Who did the tasking?"

"Jesse Curry."

"And these other agencies were privy to your cover?"

"They didn't know me at all, or if they did, they thought I was a foreign asset: Merry Kerry—that sorta thing. In practical terms, all they really knew was that, every so often, the Agency came up with something interesting from Anglo-Erin. And passed it along."

"Was it profitable?" Rhinegold asked.

"In what sense?"

"Did Anglo-Erin make a financial profit?"

"It was starting to when I was pulled out."

Dunphy wished that he had a cup of coffee. And a pair of goggles: the room was thick with cigarette smoke, and totally unventilated. His head felt as if it were encased within the nucleus of a positive ion. A large, beige one.

"—and you would set up these corporations for? . . ."

"Whoever paid the freight. I had American clients. Some Mexicans, a few Italians. Coupla Turks, a Franco-Lebanese. One guy from Buenos Aires set up thirty-five entities in eight jurisdictions. God knows what he was up to. Guns, coke, or emeralds. All three, probably."

"And you'd provide the Agency—and, through it, other agencies—with copies of the incorporating documents?"

"That, and the bank data, and anything interesting that I might pick up over lunch or a pint of bitter. And if a company was owned by bearer shares—which it usually was—and if I knew who held them—which I usually didn't—I'd put that in the pouch, too."

"Clients came to you—out of the blue?"

"Sort of. Some of it was word-of-mouth—my fees were unbelievably reasonable. And I advertised."

"Where?"

"*Herald Tribune. Economist. Sunday Times.* A lot of places. The receipts are at the office."

"Well," Esterhazy said, "I'm afraid the contents of that office are no longer available to us. We're told they're in custody of the Metropolitan Police. And, I suspect, MI5."

"I see." He'd been expecting this, but now that it was a fact, he suddenly felt worse. In fact, he suddenly felt like shit.

A girl brought sandwiches and coffee at eleven, rolling her eyes at the cigarette smoke. Esterhazy announced that "We'll take a short break now," and Dunphy nodded, grateful for the coffee.

He did his best to get a pastrami sandwich down, but the meat had a purple hue, and it made his stomach queasy. Pushing the sandwich away, he made a half-assed attempt to engage his interrogators in small talk ("How 'bout them Wizards?"), but neither of them was interested.

"I don't follow sporting events," Esterhazy said. Rhinegold shrugged.

"Sports are a waste of time," Esterhazy added. Rhinegold grunted.

Maybe it was the acoustics.

As they lapsed into silence, Dunphy watched his companions take small plastic bags from their catalog cases, placing them on the table. Each of the Baggies contained at least a dozen tablets and half a dozen capsules, which they spread out in front of them in a sort of pharmacological phalanx.

"Vitamins," Esterhazy remarked.

"This one's a nicotine neutralizer," Rhinegold explained, holding a fat pill between his thumb and index finger. One by one, they swallowed the tablets, pills, caplets, and tabs with tiny sips of coffee.

And then, apparently refreshed, they returned to the subject at hand.

Time did not fly.

"Can we assume that your cover was meticulously maintained?" Esterhazy paused, flipped a page of his legal pad, and looked up.

"Of course."

"There wouldn't be anything in your filing cabinets that would identify you as Jack Dunphy, or connect you with this Agency?"

"No. Nothing. The files supported the cover, that's all."

"A telephone bill or—"

"I never called home from the office. Not from my apartment, either. If I had to make a call to the States—as Jack Dunphy—I'd use a pay phone. Same with reaching Curry."

"Did you use a computer?"

"Yeah. An Amstrad."

"I'm embarrassed to ask this, but, you didn't leave any sensitive files—memos, reports, anything like that—you didn't leave anything on the disk?"

"No. To begin with, everything on the disk was encrypted. Strongly encrypted. I used a one-hundred-forty-bit algorithm—"

"PGP?"

Dunphy shook his head. "RSA. And when I left, I wiped it."

Rhinegold leaned forward, wrinkling his brow. "When you left London, Jack—you didn't take anything with you? I mean, everything was more or less left as it was?"

Jack? "I took my attaché case," Dunphy said. "I had my address book in it. Otherwise, I'm out a lot of clothes—"

"A disposal unit went through your apartment last night. It's 'broom-clean.' You'll have your clothes and your personal belongings by Friday at the latest."

Dunphy held his breath, saying nothing.

"What we need to be certain of is that there is nothing in London, at the office or elsewhere, that would connect you to . . . well, to yourself. No—"

"Pas de cartes. Pas de photos. Pas de souvenirs."

"What's that supposed to mean?" Rhinegold asked, his voice heavy with a mixture of suspicion and resentment.

"It's a saying. It means I didn't leave anything behind."

"You said you wiped the disk on your computer. What would MI5 find if it examined that disk with the special utilities they have at their disposal?"

"It's a reformatted disk. It's a tabula rasa."

"You can retrieve data from a reformatted disk—even if the data is encrypted," Esterhazy said. "All the DOS function does is eliminate the addresses. The data are still there, if you know how to find them."

Dunphy shook his head. "I ran a low-level format, using debug, and then I overwrote everything with DiskWipe. I might as well have passed a permanent magnet over the thing. There's nothing left."

For the first time, Esterhazy looked impressed.

"Brain-dead," Dunphy added.

Rhinegold smiled.

* * *

"Why did Curry come to you for the surveillance on Professor Schidlof?"

"You'd have to ask Curry."

"It wasn't something you usually did."

"It wasn't something I *ever* did. I didn't know the first thing about it."

"And so you hired this man? . . ."

"Tommy Davis. Actually, we were working together already."

"How so?"

"I used him as a courier. He had good connections in Beirut—which was useful, because I had a pretty lucrative clientele there. Tommy could get in and out, even during the bad old days, no problem. What's important here, though, is that he had a reputation as a good wireman. And I could trust him. When Curry tasked me with the surveillance, I went to Tommy."

"And he's still in London?"

Dunphy shrugged, suddenly uncomfortable. "I don't think so. I think he left town."

Rhinegold and Esterhazy fixed him with a stare, but Dunphy was unmoved. If the Agency had taught him anything, it was how to sit quietly or, failing that, to

Deny everything.

Admit nothing.

Make counterallegations.

Finally, Esterhazy broke the silence between them. "Because it's important," he said, "that we find him before the Metropolitan Police do."

Dunphy nodded. "I see," he said.

Rhinegold's brow furrowed, and he cleared his throat. "You see, Jack, a listening-device was found on the professor's telephone line."

"I know," Dunphy said. "Jesse mentioned it."

"And . . . well, the police think it had something to do with the, uhh, incident."

"Right."

"Which is absurd, of course."

"Of course."

Silence again. Rhinegold drummed a pencil on the table. Esterhazy frowned, stubbed out his cigarette, and shook his head.

"I should think you'd be more helpful," he said. "Because— well, frankly, this is not such a great thing for you."

Dunphy looked puzzled.

"Careerwise."

"Nothing I could do," Dunphy said. "Nothing I *can* do."

"Still—"

"What's done is done," Rhinegold said. "The point is that the device connects Professor Schidlof to Mr. Davis, and Mr. Davis connects to you. And so on."

"And so forth."

"And so on. It's hard to say just where it might stop."

"It's the kind of thing that could go right to the top," Esterhazy added.

Dunphy nodded, then tilted his head to the side, raised his eyebrows, and let them fall. A soft and apologetic *tsk* fell from his mouth. "I see the problem," he said, "but . . . I don't know where Davis is. I just *don't*."

The older man frowned. Shrugging, he changed the subject. "Tell us about the professor."

Dunphy grunted.

"Why was he under surveillance?"

Dunphy shook his head. "I wasn't told."

"But you listened to his telephone conversations. You must have some idea."

"Nope."

"Surely—"

"I don't. And you're wrong about my listening to his telephone conversations. All I did was sample the tapes we made to make certain there was something on them before I passed them along to Curry. From what I was told, and from what I read, the guy taught at King's College. I think the paper said he was in the psychology department. Something like that."

Esterhazy leaned forward. "Tell us about that."

"About what?"

"About Professor Schidlof's interest in psychology."

Dunphy looked from one interrogator to the other. Finally he said, "How the fuck would I know about that?"

"Well—"

"I'm telling you, all I know about this guy is what I read in the paper."

"You weren't curious about the person you were bugging?"

"Curious? About what? A psychology teacher? I don't think so. The only thing interesting about this guy, as far as I can tell, is, he was butchered."

"Butchered?" Rhinegold asked.

"Yeah."

"Why do you use that word?"

"As opposed to what?"

"Killed."

"Because he wasn't just 'killed.' He was torn apart. Arms, legs—they castrated him. You want *my* opinion? The cops oughta go down to the grocery store, and ask everyone in the meat department where they were the other night! Because this wasn't just a killing. It was like . . . like a *dissection*."

Dunphy's interrogators frowned. "Yes, well . . . I'm sure it was horrible," Rhinegold said.

Esterhazy looked away, and the room fell silent for a long moment.

Finally, Dunphy asked, "So what's the connection?"

"Connection?"

"Between the surveillance and the killing."

"There *was* no connection," Esterhazy answered. "Why should there have been a connection?"

"Well, it's certainly an amazing coincidence, then. I mean, no one says anything sensitive on the telephone anymore! All the surveillance did was establish this guy's domestic pattern. Did he have a dog, or did he have a cat? If he had a dog, when did he walk it—and *where* did he walk it? Did he visit the dentist, did he go to a chiropractor? Did he have a mistress?"

"This is not a productive tangent, Mr. Dunphy." Rhinegold looked upset, but there was no stopping Dunphy, who was talking faster and faster.

"What did he do? Where did he do it? When did he do it? Because—let's face it—somewhere along the line, somebody found a way to pick this guy up in the middle of London, where they *operate*—surgically operate—until he's a fucking *torso*—which they *leave*—"

"Mr. Dunphy—"

"—outside a *church*, for Christ's sake—"

"Jack—"

"And *I'm* a fucking suspect?! Whattaya mean there wasn't any connection?!"

Dunphy looked wildly at his inquisitors. No one said anything. The seconds ticked by. Finally, Esterhazy cleared his throat, embarrassed.

"Actually," he said, "you're not."

"Not what?"

"A suspect."

"And how do you figure that?" Dunphy asked.

"Unless and until Mr. Davis is found, you aren't under suspicion yourself. You're more like a, uh, prospective *point of contact*."

"Which is why it's important that we locate Mr. Davis," Rhinegold explained.

"Exactly," Esterhazy said. "He may need our help."

The silence was huge. No one blinked.

Finally, Dunphy turned the palms of his hands toward the lights overhead and let them drop. "Sorry, man. I don't know where he is."

6

The debriefing was still under way at 7 P.M. when Rhinegold's watch made a high, twittering noise, reminding him that he had to be somewhere else.

The debriefers put their notes away, snapped their attaché cases closed, and got to their feet. "I think you ought to eat in your hotel," Rhinegold said.

"What a good idea!" Esterhazy interjected. "Room service! Talk about relaxing!"

"We'll get back to this at oh-eight-hundred," Rhinegold added.

"Do you think we could make it a little later?" Dunphy asked. "Noon would be good."

Esterhazy and Rhinegold looked at him with empty eyes.

"I need some clothes," he explained. "A change of socks. The stores don't open till ten."

Nothing. Not even a smile.

Dunphy sighed. "Okay. No problem. I'll wash 'em in the fuckin' bathtub."

And he did. He bought a bottle of Woolite at the 7-Eleven, went back to his hotel room, and filled the tub with water. Undressing, he knelt on the bathroom floor and, swearing, washed his sweats and socks and underwear. He wrung out the water with his hands and draped the clothes over a chair in front of the radiator. Then he sat down to watch a movie on TV, ordered a hamburger from room service, and fell asleep wearing a towel.

The debriefing resumed in the morning, with Dunphy in a

sweat suit that was still damp from the tub. It went on until dusk, when they broke for a second time, and continued again on Tuesday, covering the same ground.

It was exhausting, annoying, and in the end, it became perfunctory. With the exception of Tommy Davis's whereabouts, which Dunphy was determined not to give up, he didn't have any of the answers they wanted. On Tuesday afternoon, Esterhazy leaned back in his chair, raised his eyebrows, and said, "I think that's about as far as we can go."

Rhinegold nodded. "I agree. I'd say we're *finito*."

Together, they got to their feet, putting away their pens and pads, matches and cigarettes. Esterhazy picked up his watch from the table, and strapped it to his wrist.

Relieved that the ordeal was finally over, Dunphy pushed his chair back with a smile and got to his feet.

Rhinegold looked at him blankly as he snapped the locks shut on his attaché case. "Where are *you* going?" he asked.

Dunphy made a gesture, as if to say, *Out*.

"*You're* not done," Rhinegold said. "We are."

Nearly an hour dragged by before the door swung open, and a clubfooted man with oriented eyes walked in, carrying a pair of mismatched attaché cases. Nodding wordlessly to Dunphy, he laid the briefcases on the table, removed his sports jacket, and hung it carefully on the back of a chair. One of the attaché cases was slim, sleek, leather; the other was fat, indestructible, and slag-gray.

Almost ceremoniously, the visitor removed a pair of lurid objects from the American Tourister, placing them on the table in front of Dunphy. The first was a paperback with a primitive drawing on the cover. It showed a wet-looking blonde in shorts and a halter kneeling to scrub the kitchen floor while, a few feet away, a Great Dane leered. The book's title, Dunphy noticed, was *Man's Best Friend*.

The second artifact was a small, gilt-encrusted icon of Christ, eyes rolled toward Heaven from within a crown of blood and thorns. Dunphy looked from one to the other, cocked his head, and snorted at the cheap psychology.

The clubfooted man didn't blink. He opened the plastic attaché case and pulled a length of wire from the machine inside. Turning toward Dunphy, he leaned on the table with both hands, nodded toward the icon, and whispered, "I know what you did, and I know what you know—you lie to me, motherfucker, and you lie to Him. Now roll up your sleeve."

The rest of the day, and all of Wednesday, receded into a haze of questions that covered the entirety of Dunphy's career. It was a pointless exercise, of course. Like every career officer, Dunphy had been trained in ways, if not to beat the polygraph, then at least to muddle its results. If the test was a long one, as this one turned out to be, beating it was an exhausting process, requiring the subject to sustain a rather high level of concentration for hours at a time. Difficult, but not impossible. And quite worthwhile if there was something important to conceal.

The trick was to take advantage of the interval between the question and the answer, an interval that the polygraph examiner deliberately prolonged, the better to measure galvanic responses. To beat the machine, you had to establish a phony baseline for the truth. And the way to do this was to infuse every truthful answer with a measure of stress, making those answers indistinguishable from lies.

Generating stress wasn't difficult. All you had to do was a little math, something along the lines of fourteen times eleven before answering a question truthfully. And then, when the time came to lie, you lied without thinking, and the results came out more or less the same way. The polygraph examiner would conclude that you'd lied about everything, or else that you'd told the truth. And since the answers to some of the questions were known, the logical conclusion would be that the subject was truthful.

"Is today Wednesday?" the examiner asked, reading the question from a fanfolded computer printout.

Dunphy thought. Sixteen times nine is . . . ninety plus fifty-four: 144. "Yes," he said. His interrogator put a check next to the question.

"Have you ever been to London?"

Fourteen times twelve is, uhh . . . a hundred-and-forty plus twenty-eight: 168! "Yes." Another check.

And so it went.

"Are you familiar with the cryptonym MK-IMAGE?"

Twenty-seven times eight: 216. "No," Dunphy said, making a mental note. His arithmetic was getting better. (But what's *MK-IMAGE*?)

"Did Mr. Davis contact you on the day that he left London?"

Three hundred and forty-one divided by eight is . . . forty-two and—Dunphy's mind went blank. Forty-two and something. Forty-two and . . . *change*. "Yes," he said. Check.

"And did he tell you where he was going?"

Dunphy let his mind go blank. "No," he said. Just like that. Another little check.

And he was home free.

7

Dunphy's old passport, wallet, and clothes were waiting for him in a suitcase at his hotel that evening. So was a small plastic bag that held his toothbrush and razor, a fistful of old receipts, pocket change that had been on his dresser, a Mason Pearson hairbrush, and other miscellany. A black laundry marker had been used to label the bag *personal effects*, which gave Dunphy a weird sense of déjà vu. This is what it's like, he thought, this is what happens when you're dead. They put your toothbrush and pocket change in a Baggie and send it to the next of kin. Exhausted, he sat down on the bed, lay back for a moment, and . . . drifted off.

The telephone's insistent warble awakened him from a deep sleep, maybe ten hours later. The voice at the other end of the line told him to report immediately to the Central Cover Staff, and to "bring all your documentation with you."

Dunphy did as he was told. A black officer with graying hair and a checklist asked him to "surrender" the passport in Kerry Thornley's name, his Irish driver's license, and any "pocket litter" that he had. After each item was checked off the list, it was dropped into a red metal basket marked BURN.

For the first time, he knew for a certainty that he wasn't going back to England for the Agency.

In a daze, he took the elevator down to the Personnel Management Office, where he sat for an hour in a lime-green waiting room, leafing through a worn copy of *The Economist*. Finally, a small gray woman in a print dress appeared and told him that B-209 would be his office "for now."

Dunphy knew headquarters as well as anyone, but . . . "Where's that?"

"I'm not sure," she said, genuinely puzzled. "You'll have to ask security."

In fact, B-209 was in the basement of the North Building, on a wide corridor between two loading docks. The corridor doubled as a sort of storage area for new computer equipment, office supplies, and (as Dunphy soon realized) Agency fuckups and paramilitaries attached to the International Activities Division (IAD).

Forklifts rumbled down the corridor from one dock to another, slamming into each other and the walls. Because of the noise, people spoke louder here than elsewhere at headquarters, and there was a certain amount of "manly horseplay" (which is to say, juvenile clowning around) ongoing at all times. Indeed, it seemed to Dunphy as if a cloud of testosterone hung in the corridor like will-o'-the-wisp on a back road in Maine. It would have been impossible to think in such a place—if there had been anything to think about. But there was nothing. He was on hold.

His office was a buff-colored cubicle with tremulous partitions that served as sliding walls. It was furnished with a beige swivel chair, a hat rack, and an off-white bookcase. An empty filing cabinet sat in the corner next to a brand-new BURN basket. There was a telephone on the floor and a copy of *Roget's Thesaurus*, but there was no carpeting, and even more to the point: *there was no desk*.

Dunphy picked up the phone to call housekeeping, but it didn't have a dial tone. Furious, he stormed out of the cubicle (you couldn't call it a *room*, really) and headed toward personnel—only to lose himself in a maze of corridors. After suffering the humiliation of having to ask directions in his own headquarters, he arrived at personnel only to see his rage wilt before the sympathetic shrugs of the small gray lady in the print dress. "Be patient," she said. "They're sorting things out."

Dunphy commandeered a telephone and told the switchboard to connect him with his section chief, Fred Crisman, in the Directorate of Plans. If anyone could tell him what was going on, Fred could; Dunphy had been reporting to him through Jesse Curry for nearly a year.

"Sorry, guy," said a voice at the other end. "You missed him. Fred's been TDY in East Africa since last week."

Dunphy tried other numbers, but the people he wanted were all unavailable: in conference, away from their desks, traveling, in meetings all afternoon. Housekeeping said they'd "check into the problem," as if his job were a hotel, and promised to get back to him in a few minutes. "How ya gonna do that?" Dunphy asked. "I just told ya: the phone doesn't work!"

Adrift and smoldering, he embarked on what eventually became a routine, meandering from his "office" to personnel, from personnel to the cafeteria, from the cafeteria to the gym. He jumped rope, lifted weights, and boxed every other day. A week went by. Two. Three. He was getting into shape, but he felt like a technocrat's version of the Flying Dutchman, wandering anonymously through the broad halls of a clandestine bureaucracy. In the afternoons, he visited the Agency's library where newspapers from every country in the world were available. Settling into the same easy chair each day, Dunphy scanned the British press in vain for news of Professor Schidlof. After the first wave of headlines, reports of the investigation had disappeared, leading Dunphy to suspect that Her Majesty's government had issued a D-notice, killing the story. His stomach floated and churned, acid with anger and anxiety. Eventually, the other shoe *had* to drop. But when? And where? And on whose head?

Dunphy was tired of the hotel at Tysons Corner. He missed his apartment in Chelsea and the habits that, taken together, added up to a Life. He missed Clementine most of all, but there was nothing that he could say to her, really. Except, "I'm on the lam. I'll be in touch. G'bye." It wasn't much of a basis for a relationship. And the idea that he might never get back to England, much less to Clementine, appalled him.

As, in fact, did the postwar CIA. The Agency was adrift in

the aftermath of the Cold War, demoralized by the enemy's surrender, its mission obsolete, its raison d'être obscure. For years, it had gotten by without "a symmetrical enemy," making do with the likes of Noriega and Hussein, some cataract-encrusted terrorists, and Colombian *pistoleros* on the run. Now, Congress was stirring. There was talk about downsizing the intelligence community and "reallocating precious resources." Among the most expensive of those resources were agents under nonofficial cover, or NOCs, like Dunphy. Gradually, they were being withdrawn from the field and replaced by spooks from the Pentagon's Defense Human Intelligence Services. For the first time in its existence, the CIA's budget was seriously threatened—and Langley was an unhappy place to be.

If there was an inner sanctum to the malaise that permeated headquarters, it was the cafeteria. This was an elephant's graveyard of burnt-out cases, drunks, neurotics and loose cannons, whistle-blowers, and "damaged goods" that (for one reason or another) the Agency couldn't or wouldn't fire.

There were a score of such "disposal cases" hanging out at any given time. Most had no responsibilities at all, while a few, like Roscoe White, were simply underemployed.

White's case was a classic. A Princeton graduate with a master's degree in oriental languages (he was fluent in Mandarin Chinese and Korean), he'd joined the Agency in 1975. Posted to Seoul under military cover, he'd been grabbed inside the DMZ on what must have been his first mission. For nearly a year thereafter, he suffered a succession of brutal interrogations and mock executions until, in the end, his captors wearied of the routine. White was transferred to a prison farm in the far north, and seemingly forgotten. Finally, in 1991, as a sort of Cold War afterthought, he was taken to the DMZ and released without ceremony at the very spot where he'd been arrested more than fifteen years earlier. The gesture, or joke, or whatever it was, nearly unhinged him. He'd stood there, up to his ankles in mud, rooted to the place where his life had disappeared, spellbound with the thought (or the hope) that the past sixteen years had been a hallucination. Eventually, he was grabbed by an ROK soldier in camouflage fatigues and dragged to safety.

On returning to America, he found that he'd been declared legally dead ten years earlier.

White's own retirement was only three years away. Until then, he served as liaison officer between the Directorate of Operations and the Coordinator of Information and Privacy. In practice, this meant that it was his job to parcel out Freedom of Information requests to "reference analysts" in the Directorate of Operations—a task that seldom consumed more than an hour of his time each day, leaving him free to read in the cafeteria until it was time to go home.

It was a terrible waste of talent, but there was nothing to be done about it. After meticulous preparation at the best schools, White had missed almost the entirety of his working life. Now he sat in the cafeteria with a distracted smile, reading Marlowe's *Tragicall History of Dr. Faustus*.

Dunphy was fascinated by him.

"I tried to catch up on things," White explained one day, "but there was just too much missing. I mean—*Glasnost,* the Wall, AIDS, and the Internet. It was like that Billy Joel song except—none of it meant anything to me. All I'd heard were whispers. But Teflon and Saran Wrap, Krazy Glue and compact discs . . . Jesus H. Christ, now *that* stuff was something. Anyway, I realized after a while that reading the back issues of *Time* wasn't going to be enough. I could memorize every stat for every player who'd ever been with the Orioles, but I hadn't seen them play. I mean, who the hell is Cal Ripken, and whatever happened to Juan Pizarro? Anyway," White said, gesturing at the book that he was holding, "I find it less . . . stressful to read history, the classics—books that are *timeless*. You know what I mean?"

Dunphy nodded. Because there were so many lacunas in White's life, even the most casual conversations could turn into adventures. Dunphy liked him a lot, and so, when Roscoe

White asked him if he was "looking for a place," Dunphy didn't hesitate.

"Yeah. You know of one?"

"Well," Roscoe said, "if you don't mind sharing, I've got a farmhouse and five acres on Belleview Place. The rent's not bad. You interested?"

"Yeah," Dunphy replied, "but—I gotta tell ya, I may not be around too long."

"Why's that?"

"I've got a girlfriend in London, and—don't tell anyone— but I'm not all that crazy about my job. Also, I'm not the neatest person, y'know?"

Roscoe chuckled. "That's why I have a cleaning lady. Once a week—couldn't do it without her."

"In that case . . . you make wake-up calls?"

8

Dunphy's new assignment came down a few weeks after he'd moved in with Roscoe White, and it did not make him happy. While it was probably impossible for him to return to London, there was no obvious reason why the same operation couldn't be run from another city, and just as successfully. Geneva, for instance, or—better yet—Paris. He'd borrowed a typewriter and written memo after memo on the subject, but there was never any response. Finally, he received a terse directive ordering him to report to a three-day training course for information review officers, or IROs.

One look around, and Dunphy knew that his future was dim. With the exception of himself, all of the IROs were in their sixties and working part-time. They were "pensioned annuitants," retired case officers who welcomed the chance to supplement their monthly checks by putting in a couple of hours a day at headquarters. It didn't matter that the work was meaningless. It was, as they said (over and over again), "*great* to be back in the saddle."

For his part, Dunphy was ready to dismount. The only thing that kept him from doing so was the mystery of his own misfortune. For whatever reason, the Agency was trying to make him quit, and he didn't have a clue as to why. All he could be sure of was that, if he left the Agency now, he'd never know the truth.

And so he gritted his teeth, and stayed, and listened to the overweight IRO instructor explain the workings of the Freedom of Information Act as it applied to the CIA. The law was "a pain in the ass," the instructor said, because it gave the average guy in the street—"loyal or not"—the right to request government files on any subject that interested him. In practice, this meant that when a request was received (and the Agency got more than a dozen a day), a liaison officer (such as Roscoe White) would assign it to one of the IROs. The IRO would search the Central Registry in B building to locate the relevant files. These files would then be copied, and the IRO would begin to read them, using a felt-tipped pen to censor data that were statutorily exempted from release: information, for example, that might compromise intelligence sources or methods. Finally, the redacted copies would be sent to the Coordinator of Information's office, where a reference analyst would make a final review. Only then would anything be released to the requester.

Not that the Agency was interested in releasing much. As the instructor said, "What you have to remember is that this is the Central *Intelligence* Agency—and not the Central *Information* Agency." And, indeed, the distinction was manifest in the way FOIA requests were handled. While the law required the Agency to respond to each request within ten days of its receipt, there was no way to legislate how long it might take to locate, review, and release so much as a single file. *That* would depend upon how many resources the CIA allocated to its FOIA staff.

And here the instructor grinned. "Unfortunately," he said, "we don't *have* a lot of resources—so I guess you could say we're permanently swamped."

"How big is the backlog?" Dunphy asked.

"The last time I looked," the instructor said, "we had about twenty-four thousand requests on hold."

"So a new request—"

"—would begin to generate material in about nine years. As I said, it's the Central *Intelligence* Agency."

9

It was Roscoe who gave him the idea.

They were sitting at the bar in O'Toole's, a grungy Irish dive in the McLean Shopping Center not far from the CIA's headquarters (and therefore a gathering place for spooks), when Roscoe asked him—with a sly grin—about the FOIA request that he'd assigned to Dunphy that same afternoon.

"Which one?" Dunphy asked, not really paying attention. He was scrutinizing a photograph that hung on the wall with other memorabilia, all of it in need of a good dusting. There was a faded banner of the IRA's, a dartboard with Saddam Hussein's picture on it, some postcards from Havana (signed *Frank & Ruth*), and a Japanese ceremonial sword with what looked like dried blood on it. Some yellowing newspaper headlines (JFK SENDS ADVISERS TO VIETNAM) had been glued to the wall beside signed and framed photographs of George Bush, William Colby, and Richard Helms.

But the picture that held Dunphy's interest was a snapshot of three men standing in a jungle clearing, laughing. On the ground in front of them was the head of an Asian man who looked as if he'd been decapitated. In fact, he'd been buried standing, and though his eyes were glazed, you could see that he was still alive. A typed caption was stapled to the picture: *MAC/SOG,* it read. *12-25-66—Laos. Merry Xmas!*

"The one about root canals," Roscoe said.

Dunphy shook his head, still staring at the photo.

"You don't remember?" Roscoe asked.

Hearing his friend's incredulity, Dunphy turned to him. "What?"

"I was asking you about the FOIA request I sent—about the root-canal procedures on Naval cadets at Annapolis, 1979 to the present."

"Oh, yeah," Dunphy replied. "I got that this afternoon. Now, why the fuck would the Agency have anything like that?" he asked. "I mean, what's on this guy's mind?"

Roscoe shrugged. "Actually ... I can probably tell you exactly what's on his mind. He's one of our most frequent requesters."

"Okay," Dunphy said. "So hit me with it."

"Mind control. Mr. McWillie is obsessed with it. A lot of people are."

Dunphy cocked his head to the left and raised his eyebrows. "Maybe I missed something, but—I thought we were talking about dentistry."

"Well, yes—in a sense, we are. The guy's asking for dental records, but he doesn't have to tell us why. He doesn't have to tell us what he *suspects*. But after a while, when you've processed as many requests as I have, you get to know where people are coming from. And judging from the kinds of things that Mr. McWillie has asked for in the past, I'd say that he thinks that we're installing miniaturized radio receivers—"

Dunphy almost spewed his beer. "In people's molars?!"

"Yeah." Roscoe nodded.

"*Why,* fahchrissake?"

"I don't know. Subliminal messages. Stuff like that. Who *knows* what Lewis McWillie suspects? I mean, he's obviously a schizophrenic. Did you happen to catch the return address on his letter?"

"No," Dunphy said. "I didn't really look at it."

"Well, unless he's moved, the address is '86 Impala, Lot A, Fort Ward Park, Alexandria."

Dunphy rolled his eyes. "I gotta get out of this job. This is the stupidest fucking job I've ever had."

"Maybe," Roscoe said. "Then again, maybe not."

"Trust me. I'm pretty clear about this." He paused. "You know why I joined the Agency?"

Roscoe nodded. "Patriotism."

Dunphy chuckled. "No, Roscoe. It wasn't patriotism. 'Patriotism' didn't have anything to do with it."

"Then . . . what?"

"I joined the Agency because, until then, I'd wanted to be an historian. And what I found out was—what I learned in college was—it's no longer possible to *be* an historian."

Roscoe gave him a puzzled look. "Why do you say that?"

"Because historians collect facts and read documents. They do empirical research and analyze the information they've collected. Then they publish their findings. They call it the scientific method, and it's something you can't do in a university anymore."

"Why not?"

"Because the structuralists—or the *post*structuralists—or the post*colonialists*—or whatever they're calling themselves this week—take the position that reality is inaccessible, facts are fungible, and knowledge is impossible. Which reduces history to fiction and textual analysis. Which leaves us with . . . "

"What?" Roscoe asked.

"Gender studies. Cultural studies. What I think of as *the fuzzies.*"

Roscoe caught the bartender's eye and, with his forefinger, drew a circle in the air above their glasses. "So . . . you joined the CIA because you thought gender studies are *fuzzy?* That's what you're telling me?"

"Well, that was a big part of it. I realized I'd never get a job teaching, not at a good university anyway—the poststructuralists are running the show just about everywhere. And the other thing was—I was a modern-military-history guy—I went to grad school at Wisconsin—and one of the things that became apparent was the fact that a lot of the stuff that should have been available . . . wasn't."

"What are you talking about?" Roscoe asked.

"Information. The data weren't available."

"Why not?"

"Because they were classified. And as a baby historian, I didn't have a need to know. None of us did. And that pissed me off because . . . well, it's like we're living in a cryptocracy instead of a democracy."

Roscoe looked impressed. "Cryptocracy," he repeated. "That's good. I like that."

Dunphy laughed.

"So that's why you joined the Agency," Roscoe asked. "Poststructuralism and cryptocracy drove you to it."

"Right," Dunphy said. "And there was another reason, too."

Roscoe eyed him skeptically. "What?"

"A determination to live *large*."

Roscoe chuckled as the bartender brought them another round.

"This guy you mentioned," Dunphy said. "What's-his-face—"

"McWillie."

"Right. We were talking about McWillie and the implants. Which sounds like a rock group, when you think about it. Nutball and the Molars. But my point is, no matter how you slice it, I'm this guy's research assistant. That's what it amounts to. When you come right down to it, I'm like a P.A. for any schizophrenic—"

"What's a P.A.?"

"Personal assistant. I'm like a personal assistant for any schizophrenic who's got the money to buy a stamp. And you know what? It's no accident. Someone's fuckin' with me. Someone wants me out."

Roscoe nodded, and sipped his beer. "Probably one of the poststructuralists."

Dunphy frowned. "I'm serious."

Roscoe chuckled. "I know you are."

"And that reminds me," Dunphy added. "How'd I *get* that request, anyway?"

"What do you mean? You got it from me. That's what I do."

"I know that, but—"

"I'm the liaison officer. Assigning FOIA requests to IROs like you is my mission in life."

"That's not what I mean. What I'm wondering is, how come you processed it so quickly? I thought there was a nine-year wait. You got McWillie's letter on Tuesday and sent it down to me the same day. How come?"

Roscoe grunted. "Mr. McWillie always puts a line in his letters, asking to have his requests expedited. If the request is stupid enough, like the one you got today, I'm happy to expedite it, because it makes our stats look better when we can close out something that quickly."

"You can do that?"

"What?"

"Expedite requests."

"Sure, if I'm asked to, and if I think there's a good reason to approve it."

Dunphy sipped his beer thoughtfully. After a long while, a smile dawned, and he turned back to Roscoe. "Do me a favor," he said.

"What?"

"You get an FOIA request from a guy named . . . I dunno—what?—Eddie Piper! Any requests you get from someone named Eddie Piper, I want you to expedite them, okay?"

Roscoe thought about it. "Okay."

"And send them over to me. Anything Eddie Piper asks for, I wanta handle it."

Roscoe nodded, then cast a wary glance in Dunphy's direction. "Who's Eddie Piper?" he asked.

Dunphy shook his head. "I dunno," he said. "I just made him up. The point is, will you do it?"

"Yeah. Why not? It's not like I've got a whole lot left to lose, is it?"

10

Renting a mail-drop under a phony name was more difficult than Dunphy had expected, but it was essential to his scheme. Though he did not intend to release so much as a single document, correspondence between the Agency and Edward Piper could not be avoided. Every FOIA request had to be acknowledged in writing, and every denial required an explanation or a recitation of exemptions. These letters would have to be mailed. And if they were then to be returned with the notation *Addressee Unknown*, the Office of Privacy and Information would become curious. And they would begin to ask questions.

The difficulty with obtaining a mail drop, however, was that the post office insisted on a passport or a driver's license before it would rent a P.O. box to anyone. Even the commercial companies wanted some form of identification "to protect ourselves"—though against what was never said. It occurred to Dunphy that the requirements for establishing a Panamanian corporation or a bank account on the Isle of Man were fewer.

Still, it was hardly an unmanageable problem. He typed a phony address label in the name of Edward A. Piper and affixed it to the front of a used envelope, covering his own name and address. He then set off for Kinko's Copies in Georgetown, cruising down the G. W. Parkway toward the Key Bridge.

It was one of those rare, sparkling days in Washington, when the air blows in from the north, and a brisk wind kicks at the Potomac. The spires of Georgetown University rose at the edge of what he knew was a sea of louche boutiques, while eight-man crews rowed upriver in a regatta.

The sculls reminded Dunphy of his college days, rowing on Lake Mendota, and before he knew it, he was humming the maudlin "Varsity"—*Yooo raah raah WisCONNNsin*—and wondering where his letter jacket had gone. At Kinko's, he paid forty-five dollars for a set of five hundred business cards, picking an italicized Times Roman font for

E. A. Piper
Consultant

With the phony envelope and one of the business cards in hand, he drove back the way he'd come and, stopping at the Fairfax County Library, used the envelope to obtain a third piece of identification in the form of a library card.

By late afternoon, the fictitious Eddie Piper had a mail drop in Great Falls, a "suite" that (Dunphy knew) measured four inches by four inches by one foot.

Writing the actual FOIA request was even easier. Dunphy could by now recite from memory the boilerplate with which all such requests were girded. And while it would obviously not be prudent to request his own 201 file, there was nothing to stop him from seeking details about the late Professor Schidlof. In that way, he might find a clue to the situation in which he found himself. Accordingly, he wrote and mailed his first request that same afternoon. Three days later, it arrived on his own desk, routed there by his new roommate, the accommodating R. White in the Office of Privacy and Information.

Having managed in this way to assign himself to an investigation of what amounted to his own downward mobility, Dunphy was elated for the first time in months. With E. Piper's letter in hand, he took the elevator down to Central Registry. Though he neither whistled nor skipped, there was a smart-ass smile on his face that wouldn't go away.

Arriving at the registry, he signed the visitors log with a flourish and sat down at a computer terminal to obtain the necessary file-reference numbers. Though much of the Agency's day-to-day business relied upon data-processing equipment, most of the operational files continued to be stored on paper, as they had always been. While powerful arguments had been made to computerize all of the data in the Agency's system, the Office of Security vetoed the idea. The difficulty was that, while the Agency's computers could not be hacked from the *outside*, it simply wasn't possible to ensure their inviolability from *internal* attacks. And since the need-to-know doctrine was considered paramount, the operational files remained as and where they were: locked away in filing cabinets in kraft-colored folders of greater or lesser thickness, accordion style or not, in better or worse condition. Retrieving a file required that he obtain the relevant reference number from the computer, which he would then give to a data retrieval officer, or Drone, whose job was to locate files for IROs such as Dunphy. Though both positions were well removed from the fast track, IROs and Drones were virtually the only employees in the CIA with direct access to Central Registry computers and operational files in the Agency's underground vault.

As an information review officer, Dunphy's need to know was potentially boundless, with the result that his clearances were among the highest in the national security establishment. It was an irony of his situation that even as his career was crashing, his access to information was soaring. With the clearances he had, he could virtually *browse* through the Agency's files (once he'd obtained them from a Drone).

Seated in front of the terminal, Dunphy pressed his right thumb to the monitor's screen, initializing the program while, at the same time, the computer searched for his thumbprint in the Office of Security's data banks. A few seconds passed, and then the words:

WELCOME, JOHN DUNPHY, TO AEGIS.
PRESS SEND TO CONTINUE.

Dunphy hit the SEND key, and a menu shimmered onto the screen.

SUBJECT?

He thought about it. Whatever other mysteries might be involved, one thing was certain: his own world had begun to fall apart when Leo Schidlof had been murdered. That this was no coincidence was clear. Curry had screamed at him and sent him packing. So the solution to his problems, or at least an explanation for them, was somehow a function of a single question: *Who killed Schidlof, and why?*

Next to *Subject*, Dunphy typed:

/SCHIDLOF, LEO/+ALL X-REFS/

And the cursor began to blink.

11

To Dunphy's surprise, the file was a thin one, consisting almost entirely of documents in the public domain. There was an obituary from *The Observer*, a handful of clippings about the murder, and a worn copy of the first issue of an old magazine: *Archaeus: A Review of European Viticulture*.

Disappointed, Dunphy paged through the magazine. Though it was dedicated to the cultivation of grapes for wine, the magazine was filled with essays and articles on a variety of odd and disparate topics. Religious iconography ("John Paul II and the Black Madonna of Częstochowa"), public housing ("Redevelopment Options on Jerusalem's West Bank"), and chemistry ("A Form and Method of Perfecting Base Metals") were equal grist for *Archaeus*'s mill. So, also, was an essay on the early Middle Ages, the so-called Dark Ages, which asked the peculiar question "Who Turned Out the Lights?" By way of an answer, there was a photo of the pope and a cutline that read, "What was the Church trying to hide?"

Elsewhere, Dunphy found a page of weirdly illustrated horoscopes that led him to suspect that the editor must have been drunk when the magazine had been put together. Indeed, the only article having anything to do with viticulture, he saw, was an essay on "The Magdalene Cultivar: Old Wine from Palestine" by a man named Georges Watkin. Having only the most practical interest in wines, Dunphy set the magazine aside and turned to the last item in the file, a five-by-seven index card on which the following had been typed:

This is an Andromeda-sensitive, Special Access Program
(SAP) whose contents, in whole or part, have been transferred to the MK-IMAGE Registry at the Monarch Assurance Co. (15 Alpenstrasse, Zug, Switzerland). (See
cross-references on reverse.) Report all inquiries concerning this file to the Security Research Staff (SRS) in the
Office of the Director (Suite 404).

This gave Dunphy pause. The geeks who'd debriefed him—
Rhinegold and what's-his-name—had asked him about the
MK-IMAGE cryptonym. And he said he'd never heard of it.
Which was true. Until now.

Neither had he ever heard of the Security Research Staff.
But that didn't mean much. The CIA was probably the most
compartmented agency in government. Its components were
myriad, and their names were constantly changing. What
puzzled him more than the existence of the SRS was the fact
that the Agency would store sensitive files abroad, and that
inquiries about those files would have to be reported to a special staff. From a counterintelligence standpoint, the practice
was problematical. And even more importantly, from *Dunphy's*
standpoint (which is to say, from the standpoint of a thief in
the night), reports to a "Security Research Staff" could be
awkward indeed. What if, in pursuing some of the questions
that were troubling him, he requested a *series* of files marked
Andromeda-sensitive? What would happen? He thought
about it for a moment, then felt a shrug somewhere deep inside himself. He'd show them Eddie Piper's FOIA requests,
and they'd see that he was just doing his job. If they didn't like
it, they could send him back to London.

Having resolved what seemed, at first, to be a sticky issue,
he turned the card over in his hand.

SCHIDLOF, PROF. LEO (London)
X-refs—Zug

Gomelez (Family)   Davis, Thomas
Dagobert II   Curry, Jesse
Dulles, Allen   Optical Magick, Inc.
Dunphy, Jack   Pound, Ezra
Jung, Carl   Sigisbert IV

143rd Surgical Air Wing

Dunphy studied the card, more alarmed than flattered to find himself sandwiched between Allen Dulles and Carl Jung. Dulles was a legend, of course. He'd been a spy during the first world war, and a superspy in the second, operating out of Switzerland in both cases. When Hitler surrendered, Dulles had joined OSS chief Wild Bill Donovan in lobbying President Truman to create the Central Intelligence Agency— which Dulles had later gone on to lead.

But Dunphy knew less about Jung. A Swiss psychiatrist, or analyst. Wrote about the collective unconscious. (Whatever that was.) And archetypes. (Whatever they were.) And myths. And flying saucers. Or, wait a second: was that Carl Jung or Wilhelm Reich? Or Joseph Campbell? Dunphy couldn't remember. He'd had so many "brush contacts" with erudition while in college, it seemed at times as if he knew a little of everything—which is to say, next to nothing about anything. Well, he'd look up Jung when he had the chance.

Meanwhile, things were looking decidedly Swiss. According to its masthead, *Archaeus* was published in Zug, which was also home to the Special Registry. Availing himself of an atlas, Dunphy saw that the town was about twenty miles outside of Zürich.

Returning to the file, he scanned the other names on the list. Besides Davis and Curry, the only one that meant anything to him was Ezra Pound. Though he had not read Pound since his days as an undergraduate, Dunphy recalled that the poet had remained in Italy throughout the war, making propaganda broadcasts for Mussolini and the Fascists. When the war ended, he'd been captured and returned to the States, where it was expected that he'd stand trial for treason. But the trial never took place. Influential friends had intervened, psychiatrists were consulted, and the poet was declared insane. Instead of being hanged, he'd been committed, and so spent a good part of the Cold War across the river from where Dunphy now sat, receiving visitors in a private room at St. Elizabeth's Hospital.

Dunphy considered the other entries on the list. Sigisbert and Dagobert sounded like historical figures. Gomelez, he didn't know. That left Optical Magick, Inc., and the 143rd Surgical Air Wing. He'd never heard of either, but *Inc.* and *Air Wing* were subjects he could work with.

All in all, the file was a disappointment—but an interesting one, nevertheless. While its contents, a magazine and some newspaper clippings, were so apparently innocuous that no one could possibly object to their release, Dunphy's curiosity was piqued by the fact that the Agency had felt it necessary to stash his own personnel jacket in Switzerland, while at the same time placing him within the purview of the slightly mysterious Security Research Staff.

Dunphy called one of the Drones over, and tapped a forefinger on the five-by-seven card. "What do I do about this?" he asked.

The Drone glanced at the card and shrugged. "There's a form you fill out," he said. "I'll get you one in a second. But all of that MK-IMAGE crap is a no-brainer. There's nothing in the files except newspaper clips, so you can copy whatever you want and send it to the requester without redactions. The only thing you hold back is the note card with the cross-references. That's a B-7-C exemption."

Dunphy nodded. "This come up a lot?" he asked.

"What?"

"MK-IMAGE."

The Drone shook his head, crossed the room, and came back with a form. "I process about three hundred fifty file requests a week, and I haven't seen one of those cards in a couple of months. So you figure it out."

Dunphy looked at the form he'd been handed. There were only a few lines, and he filled them in.

Subject: <u>Schidlof, Leo</u>
Requester: <u>Piper, Edward</u>
IRO: <u>Dunphy, Jack</u>
Date: <u>February 23, 1999</u>
COI Liaison: <u>R. White</u>

Returning the form to the Drone, Dunphy crossed the room to a bank of Xerox machines and began copying. As he stood in the blinding wash of the strobe light, it occurred to him for the first time that what he was doing might be dangerous.

12

The eagles on Murray Fremaux's uniform lifted when he shrugged his shoulders, leaning forward in the bar at the Sheraton Premiere.

"There's no such thing," he said, "as the 143rd Surgical Air Wing. It doesn't exist. Never has."

Dunphy sipped his beer and sighed.

"Officially," the colonel added.

"Ahh," Dunphy said, and leaned forward. "Tell me about it."

"It's a black unit. Used to be headquartered in New Mexico."

"And now?"

"Middla nowhere."

Dunphy frowned. "Sounds kinda relative. I mean, if I was *driving*—"

"The closest *city* is Vegas—but that's about two hundred miles to the southwest. We're talking high desert. Smudge sticks and tumbleweed. *Jackalopes.*"

Dunphy thought about it. "Whatta they do?"

"Hoodoo!"

"The 143rd."

Murray laughed. "I wasn't asking a question—I was answering one. *That's* what they do. They do *hoodoo*—four ohs, no dubba-ewe."

"Murray—" Dunphy said.

"Okay! It's a helicopter unit. But that's as close I can get. I really can't tell you any more."

Dunphy took a deep breath and leaned forward. "We go back a long way, Murray."

"I know that."

Silence.

"We were *sophomores* together," Dunphy said.

"I know, I know."

"This is important to me. Why won't you tell me?"

"Because I can't—not won't, *can't*. I just don't know."

"Bullshit! You've got oversight of every black operation at the Pentagon."

"I'm an accountant—"

"You audit their books!"

"Not these books!"

"Why not?"

"Because they aren't ours. They're the Agency's."

Dunphy was nonplussed. "A surgical air wing?"

Murray shrugged. "Yeah. That's what I'm trying to tell you."

"Then . . . what does the Agency need with something like that? I mean . . . " Dunphy couldn't even formulate the question. "What *is* a surgical air wing?"

"I dunno," Murray said. "If you want, I could ask around, or maybe I should just shoot myself in the head. Same result, either way, but it might be a little quicker with a gun. Still . . . whatever's best for *you*. I mean, we go back a long way, right?"

The clock was ringing midnight when Dunphy got back to the house, letting the screen door to the kitchen slam behind him.

"You know," Roscoe called, "this is actually pretty interesting."

"What's that," Dunphy asked, looking in the refrigerator.

"*Archaeus*—however you pronounce it."

"Oh, yeah, right—the magazine." He opened a Budweiser, and kicked the refrigerator shut. "I thought you might be interested." Then he walked into the living room where Roscoe was sprawled in an overstuffed chair, a copy of the magazine in his lap. "You gettin' any tips?"

"About what?"

"Wine." Dunphy dropped to the couch and took a sip.

"No," Roscoe said. "There isn't anything in here about wine."

Dunphy looked at him. "It says on the cover it's about viticulture. Grapes. Vines. There's a story about . . . what?"

"The Magdalene Cultivar."

"Right!"

"Yeah, but that isn't about vines," Roscoe said. "It just sounds like it. It's actually about . . . "

"What?"

"Genealogy."

Dunphy's second FOIA request, mailed on Tuesday in E. Piper's name, was routed to his desk by Roscoe on Friday.

This is a Freedom of Information Act (FOIA) request (551 ASC, as amended) for any and all information you may have concerning the 143rd Surgical Air Wing. . . .

The Drone took the request to the files area, returning a few minutes later with a slim folder and the form reporting the fact that an "Andromeda-sensitive inquiry" had been made. As he had the other day, Dunphy answered the form's few questions:

Subject: <u>143rd Surgical Air Wing</u>
Requester: <u>Edward Piper</u>
IRO: <u>Jack Dunphy</u>
Date: <u>March 1, 1999</u>
COI Liaison: <u>R. White</u>

and returned it to the Drone.

The file contained a newspaper clipping and a five-by-seven index card. Dunphy looked at the card, and as he expected, it contained the same warning that he'd read in the Schidlof file:

> This is an Andromeda-sensitive, Special Access Program (SAP) whose contents, in whole or part, have been transferred to the MK-IMAGE Registry at the Monarch Assurance Co. (15 Alpenstrasse, Zug, Switzerland). (See cross-references on reverse.) Report all inquiries concerning this file to the Security Research Staff (SRS) in the Office of the Director (Suite 404).

On the opposite side of the card, Dunphy found the following cross-references:

Optical Magick, Inc.   Bovine Census (New Mexico)
Bovine Census (Colorado)   Allen Dulles
Carl Jung

There was nothing new, really, except the references to a Bovine Census. Dunphy wondered about that. Why would the Agency count cows? He put the card down and turned to the clipping.

It was a wedding photo, the kind of picture that you find in local newspapers. This one came from the *Roswell Daily Record*, dated June 17, 1987, and it showed a happy couple. There was nothing unusual about the pair except, perhaps, for the string tie that the groom was wearing. Dunphy examined the clipping more closely. The groom looked familiar. He began reading:

> Mr. and Mrs. Ulric Varange, of Los Alamos, have the pleasure of announcing the wedding of their daughter, Isolde, to Mr. Michael Rhinegold, of Knoxville, Tennessee.
>
> Ms. Varange is a 1985 graduate of Arizona State University's School of Nursing.
>
> Mr. Rhinegold was graduated cum laude from Bob Jones University in 1984.

Both the bride and the groom are civilian employees of the 143rd Surgical Air Wing.

A honeymoon is planned in Switzerland.

Dunphy's third FOIA request, seeking information about Optical Magick, Inc., generated the usual warning, along with a copy of the firm's articles of incorporation. In an apparent mistake, a sheaf of newspaper clippings about UFO sightings in different parts of the country was also included. Dunphy glanced at the clips, some of which were quite old, but there wasn't anything to be learned from them. They were mostly AP reports of incidents in New Mexico, Washington, Michigan, and Florida.

Turning to the articles of incorporation, he saw that Optical Magick was a Delaware corporation, formed in the spring of 1947. Jean DeMenil, of Bellingham, Washington, was listed as the company's president and registered agent. Everything else was boilerplate.

In the weeks that followed, "Edw. Piper" made FOIA requests on Carl Jung and the Bovine Censuses in New Mexico and Colorado. These requests were mixed in with legitimate inquiries from others: spouses seeking information about missing husbands (whom they suspected had been CIA agents); Kennedy-assassination researchers looking for a cultural Rosetta stone amid the events of Dealey Plaza; geologists wanting satellite photos of obscure regions; historians looking for evidence of treachery in high places; and a disturbing number of people who claimed to be victims of "mind control." Dunphy gave all of his requests to the Drone, who didn't seem to notice the statistically improbable number of Andromeda-sensitive inquiries, and made whatever copies Dunphy needed.

All in all, his little operation was working like a charm, but even so, the yield was slim. There was nothing in the Jung file except newspaper clippings and a five-by-seven warning— along with a handful of cross-references that Dunphy had already identified. The Bovine Census files were equally dismal. Each contained catalogs from a surgical supply house in

Chicago—another filing error, Dunphy thought—a five-by-seven notice, and nothing else. It was frustrating.

Dunphy's frustration turned to apprehension, however, when he returned to his office in the B corridor and found a note on his desk.

To: J. Dunphy, IRO
From: Security Research Staff

Message: Report to Suite 404.

Dunphy handed the note to a black-uniformed security guard who sat at a small table just inside the glass doors to suite 404. The guard entered Dunphy's name in a logbook, dropped the note in a BURN basket on the floor, and gestured to a heavy wooden door at the far end of the antechamber. "Mr. Matta is waiting for you."

As Dunphy approached it, the door sprung open with a metallic click, and he saw with surprise that what appeared to be oak was in fact steel, and nearly three inches thick. He stepped inside, and the door swung shut behind him.

It took a moment for his eyes to adjust to the light, and when they had, it seemed as if he'd walked into a Ralph Lauren catalog. The fluorescent lights that were everywhere at headquarters had been replaced by standing lamps with parchment shades and incandescent bulbs. The walls of the room were paneled in white pine and lined with books in leather bindings. Nearby, a fire guttered in the grate below a dentiled wooden mantel while, above, a darkened oil painting hung from the wall: two shepherds at a tomb, looking lost. At the far end of the room, a Remington manual typewriter, itself an antique, rested on a heavily carved oak desk. Persian and Azeri rugs were layered on the parquet floor, and the air was fragrant with wood smoke.

"Mr. Dunphy."

The voice made him jump. For the first time, he noticed a man standing at the window with his back toward him, looking out at the Virginia countryside. "Have a seat," the man said, and turning, crossed the room to his desk.

Dunphy settled into a leather wing chair and crossed his legs. The man in front of him was elderly, gray, and morose. Impeccable in what Dunphy guessed was a thousand-dollar suit and handmade shoes, he radiated courtesy, authority, and old money. For the first time, Dunphy noticed that the room was uncomfortably warm.

The man smiled wanly. "We have a really serious problem, Jack."

"I'm sorry to hear that, Mr. Matta."

"Call me Harold."

"Okay . . . Harold."

"As you've probably guessed, I'm in charge of the Security Research Staff."

Dunphy nodded.

"I was hoping we could have a chat about Mister Piper. Edward Piper. Ring a bell?"

Dunphy pursed his lips, wrinkled his brow, and finally shook his head. "Not really," he replied.

"Well, let me jog your memory. He's made a number of FOIA requests."

Dunphy nodded and tried to look blank—no easy feat, since his heart was tap-dancing on his ribs. "Right. I mean, if you say so."

"I do."

Dunphy wrinkled his brow and grunted. "I see. And, uhh . . . I guess I must have handled some of them."

"You did."

"And . . . what? Did I make a big release, or—"

"No. Not at all! Just some newspaper clippings. A magazine article or two. Nothing that wasn't in the public record."

Dunphy scratched his head and grinned. "Then . . . I don't see the problem."

"Well, the problem is—or, I should say, the problem *begins* with the fact that Mr. Piper probably doesn't exist."

"Oh." Dunphy began to hyperventilate as the silence grew between them. "So you think? . . ."

"He's a fiction."

"I see," Dunphy said. "Though, actually—I understand what you're saying, but I really *don't* see the problem. I mean, I guess what you're saying is that I've released next to nothing to . . . well, next to no one."

Matta watched Dunphy in silence as he filled a pipe with tobacco, tamping it down with his thumb. "Mr. Piper's address is a P.O. box—a Parcel Plus outlet in Great Falls."

"Hunh!" Dunphy said.

"But what's really interesting," Matta added, "and one of the things that really *bothers* us, is that he never picks up his mail."

Dunphy gulped. "No kidding."

"No kidding! It's as if he isn't interested in it. Which seems strange. I mean, after writing all those FOIA requests, you'd think—what *do* you think, Jack?"

"About what?" Dunphy asked.

"Mr. Piper's disinterest."

"I don't know," Dunphy said, waiting for an inspiration. "Maybe he's dead! And somebody's using his name!"

Matta puffed thoughtfully on his pipe. Finally, he said, "That's a really stupid hypothesis, Jack. It wouldn't explain anything. The question is, why would anyone make all these FOIA requests if they were uninterested in the information we release?"

"I don't know," Dunphy replied. "It's a conundrum." He was beginning to panic.

"At least! It is *at least* a conundrum. In fact, it's even more curious than that!"

"Oh?!" Dunphy asked, his voice a little too high, and a little too loud.

"Yes. Though you don't seem to recall, the fact is that Mr. Piper has made six requests to date, each of which might have been delegated to any of eleven IRO officers at headquarters. But—*incredibly*—every one of those requests has gone to you! Now, do you have any idea what the odds are on something like that?"

"No," Dunphy said.

"Neither do I," Matta replied, puffing. "But I should think they'd be quite high, wouldn't you?"

"I guess, but . . ."

"Astronomical, really," Matta said.

"I'm sure you're right, but . . . I don't know what to say. I don't have anything to say about the requests I get. They're handed down from—I don't know where they're from. They come from *on high*."

"Well, actually—not *so* high. They're 'handed down' by Mr. White."

"Okay. By Mr. White, then."

"With whom, as I understand it, in yet another remarkable coincidence, you're sharing a house."

For the first time, Dunphy noticed a clock ticking at the other end of the room. It was a very loud clock. Or so it seemed as the silence swelled, filling the room with the expectation of sound. Finally, Dunphy said, "Wait a second. You mean—Roscoe?!"

"Yes."

"So *that's* what he does!" Dunphy gave a strangled little laugh.

"Mmmm . . . that's what he does. I take it you've never discussed Mr. Piper with Mr. White?"

"No. Of course not. We don't talk about our work."

Matta grunted and leaned forward. "That's commendable, Jack. But you know what? I don't believe you."

Dunphy set his jaw. He didn't like to be called a liar, especially when he was being one. "I'm sorry to hear that," he said.

Matta reached into his desk drawer and pulled out a manila file. Wordlessly, he pushed it across the desk.

Dunphy took the folder and opened it. A handful of eight-by-ten glossies slid into his lap. He looked at them. Each of the pictures was stamped *MK-IMAGE*. Each was numbered, and they appeared to be the same: close-ups of a man's eyes with a small, vertical ruler superimposed upon the pupils. The ruler was demarcated in millimeters. Dunphy wrinkled his brows. "I don't get it."

"You passed your polygraph," Matta said.

"Good."

"Well . . . so did Aldrich Ames."

Dunphy grunted at the allusion. Ames was doing life without parole for spying on the CIA. Finally, he tapped the photos and asked, "So what are these?"

"You flunked your eye exam, Jack."

"What eye exam?" Dunphy looked more closely at the pictures. Slowly, it dawned on him that the eyes were his own, and the realization sent a chill down his spine.

"We don't rely on the polygraph that much. Not anymore. We've been burned too often. Retinal measurements are a lot harder to beat. A lot more reliable."

Dunphy was genuinely perplexed, and he looked like it. He shook his head and shrugged.

"You want to see a lie, Jack?"

Dunphy nodded. Ever so slightly.

"Look at number thirteen."

Dunphy did as he was told. The photo looked like the others. Except, he saw, that the eyes were bigger: the pupils were larger. Dilated.

"Turn it over," Matta said.

Dunphy did.

Subject's Statement:
"I'm sorry, I don't know where Davis is."

(To) Rhinegold, Esterhazy

Fuck. The word went off in his head like a gong, and for a moment, Dunphy feared that Matta must have heard it. But, no: the old man was sitting in his chair with his cheek pulled back in a kind of geriatric smirk, or rictus. Dunphy turned the photo over in his hand and looked into his own eyes. Where had the camera been? Instantly, the answer came to him: the turquoise bolo in Esterhazy's tie. "This is bullshit," Dunphy said. "I didn't lie to anyone."

Matta puffed thoughtfully on his pipe, then leaned forward with a confidential air. "I think a few days off would be a good idea, don't you, Jack? Give us some time to sort things out." As Dunphy started to protest, Matta shook him off. "Not to worry—it won't take long. I'll put my best people on it. And that's a promise."

13

Dunphy picked up the mail at the top of the driveway, parked, and went into the house. It was a stale joke, but he couldn't stop himself from calling out, "I'm home, honey!"

Roscoe was at the dining room table, reading *Archaeus*. He acknowledged the jest with a halfhearted smile and said, "They put me on administrative leave."

"Jesus." Dunphy said. "So that's what they're calling it? Me, too."

"You wanta know the truth?" Roscoe asked. "Matta scared the wits out of me. I'm thinking about taking early retirement."

"But, Roscoe—we hardly knew ye."

Roscoe chuckled.

"Look, man, I'm really sorry," Dunphy said. "I got you into this." There was a long pause. "I don't know what else to say. My bad, I guess."

Roscoe shrugged. "Don't worry about it. If you wanta know the truth, I'm not all that bullish on spying."

Dunphy shook his head.

"I'm serious! Redistributing FOIA requests to Agency fuckups—" Roscoe winced at Dunphy's look, caught his breath, and forged on. "Present company excepted— obviously! But this isn't what I signed on for. I mean, it's *depressing*. The Cold War's over. The enemy went away. We oughta be celebrating, but we aren't. And why not? Because the Russians' surrender was the ultimate betrayal. Now that we don't have an enemy—make that a 'symmetrical enemy'— one that's as strong as we are, or who can be packaged that way—how're we supposed to justify our budgets? Drugs? Terrorism? The medfly? Gimme a break. I'll be glad to be out." Roscoe paused, and nodded at the mail in Dunphy's hand. "Anything for me?"

Dunphy looked. There was a big envelope with Ed McMahon's picture on it and a huge headline—*WE'RE PROUD TO ANNOUNCE THAT ROSCOE WHITE IS A $10,000,000.00 WINNER!*—followed by the words, in small type, "if he fills out the enclosed entry form and holds the winning ticket." Dunphy tossed the letter to Roscoe. "Congratulations," he said, dropping into an armchair and glancing at the rest of the mail. Most of it was bills, but there was one envelope that, lacking a stamp, had been hand-delivered. It was addressed to Dunphy, and he opened it.

"Jack," it read, "You didn't get this from me, but . . .

I ran a computer check, and the long and the short of it is, Pentagon files show a single, open reference to the 143rd. The reference is to a disability pension for a Dodge City, Kansas, resident named Gene Brading, who contracted something called Creutzfeldt-Jakob Disease (?) while on assignment with the 143rd You-know-what. If you're still interested in the subject, you might want to contact him. I checked, and he's in the book.

The note, which was obviously from Murray, was signed *Omar the Tentmaker.*

"Jesus," Dunphy whispered.

Roscoe looked up from *Archaeus.* "What?"

"The guy's got Creutzfeldt-Jakob's Disease."

Roscoe frowned. "Who has? And what is it?"

Dunphy ignored the first question. "Mad cow disease," he said. "It's got another name in humans, but in England, where it's bad—I mean, they've lost a hundred thousand animals—that's what they call it. And kuru. In New Guinea, where the cannibals get it, they call it kuru."

"Hunh," Roscoe muttered. "Thinka that."

"You got any quarters?" Dunphy asked.

"Yeah ... I guess. On my bureau—where I keep my change. How many do you need?"

"I don't know—ten, twelve. How many you got?"

Roscoe shrugged. "Lots, but ... why do you want quarters?"

"I need to make a phone call."

Roscoe gave him a look. "That's why we have that thing in the hall—the one with all the buttons on it, and the curly plastic cord."

Dunphy shook his head. "I don't think I should call from here. I think I should use a pay phone. You need anything from the 7-Eleven?"

Brading wasn't inclined to help.

"I can't discuss any of that," he said. "All that's classified."

"Fine," Dunphy replied. "Then I'll put that in my report, and that'll be the end of that."

"Whattaya mean, the end of *that*? The end of *what*?"

Dunphy sighed audibly. "Well, hopefully—not your pension."

"My pension?!"

"Or the health care, but—"

"What?!"

"Look, Mr. Brading—Gene—you know what Washington's like: the GAO's looking for fraud. That's their job. They take a random sample of pensions and entitlements—not just from the Pentagon, but every agency—and check 'em out. Every year. So we're talking about maybe one person in two thousand who's audited, and the idea is to find out if the government's writing checks to someone who's dead. Anyway, your name was kicked out by the computer and—"

Brading groaned with exasperation.

"—you can see the problem. The way it looks to the accountant is, the army's paying a disability pension to someone whose military records don't exist, and who claims he was injured while serving with a unit that's nowhere on the books. So it looks like fraud—which is bad for you, and bad for us. 'Cause, as you know, we don't need the publicity."

"Oh, for cryin' out loud—can't you tell them—"

"We can't *tell* them anything. We can *talk* to them, but before I do that . . . I'm going to need some basic data about the circumstances of your illness, and—"

"Who'd you say you're with?"

"The Security Research Staff."

Brading grunted. "Well, you know as well as I do that we can't talk about any of this on an open phone. They'd cremate the both of us."

"Of course," Dunphy said. "I just wanted to touch base. Unless you're busy, I could fly out tomorrow and—"

"No, no, tomorrow's fine. Let's get it outa the way."

Dunphy flew to Kansas the next day, rented a car, and drove out to see Brading that same afternoon. He lived in an enclave of condominiums beside an eighteen-hole golf course, an oasis of bluegrass that surged toward a nearby shopping mall.

As it happened, Eugene Brading was a thin and sallow man in his sixties. He answered the door in a wheelchair, a blanket over his knees. His first words were, "Can I see your ID?"

Dunphy took a small black case from inside his jacket and flipped it open. Brading glanced at the laminated eagle, squinted at the name, and, apparently satisfied, gestured for his visitor to come into the living room.

"You want some lemonade?" he asked, rolling toward the kitchen.

"Sure," Dunphy said, glancing around the room. "Lemonade would be nice." His eyes fell on a gold-framed postcard that hung on the wall beside a small bookshelf. It was a picture of a religious statue, a golden-robed Madonna standing in a black marble chapel, gazing out at the camera. Surrounded by lightning bolts and clouds, and with armloads of carnations at her feet, the Madonna herself was inexplicably black. Coal black. And at her feet was a printed inscription:

La Vierge Noire
Protectrice de la ville

A handwritten note on white matting read *Einsiedeln, Switz., June 1987.*

Weird, Dunphy thought. But that was as far as it went. The postcard meant nothing to him, really, and so he let his eyes wander along the wall. There was a Keane painting of the usual doe-eyed waif, replete with a single tear, and farther along, something stranger: a square, black cloth hung like a curtain from the wall, concealing something that Dunphy very much wanted to see.

"I make it myself," Brading said, rolling into the room with a glass of lemonade. "All natural ingredients."

"No kidding." Dunphy took the glass and sipped. He paused for a second, savoring the taste. "Now that's what I call delicious."

"Me and some buddies," Brading said, nodding at a faded snapshot in a plain gold frame. The picture was of four men in black jumpsuits, standing together in a field of wheat. Their arms were around each other's shoulders, and they were smiling at the camera. Dunphy saw that one of the men was Brading, and another was Rhinegold. The photo was inscribed:

Men in Black!
Ha Ha Ha!!!

Brading gazed at the picture with a grin. "In-joke," he said.

Dunphy nodded, pretending to understand. "I see you and Mike were working together."

Brading chuckled, pleasantly surprised. "Yeah! You know Mike, huh?"

"Everyone knows Mike."

"I'll bet they do. Whatta guy!"

Dunphy and Brading gazed at the picture, grinning inanely, saying nothing. Finally, Brading broke the silence. "So what can I do for ya?"

"Well," Dunphy said, taking out a notebook and settling into a wing chair. "You can tell me about the 143rd."

Brading furrowed his brow. "Well, I guess . . . I mean, since you and Mike go back a ways . . . " Then he shook his head. "But . . . you don't mind me asking—just how high are you cleared, anyway?"

Dunphy coughed. "The usual. I've got Q-clearances through Cosmic—"

"A Q-clearance isn't gonna cut it. We're talking about some very heavy insulation."

"And, beyond that, I go up through Andromeda."

Brading grunted, suddenly satisfied. "Oh, well— *Andromeda*. I figured that. I mean, being with the SRS and all, you'd have to be. But, well—I had to ask. I'm sure you understand."

Dunphy nodded. "Of course."

"Anyway," Brading went on, "I was with the 143rd for, I don't know, maybe twenty-four years. Started out in Roswell—only then, it wasn't the 143rd. It was one of them no-name units that were part of the 509th."

"What's that?"

Brading frowned. "The 509th Composite Bomb Group. Ain't you read your history?"

"Of course," Dunphy said, placating the old guy with a smile.

"They dropped the A-bomb on the Japs," Brading explained, then added with a wink, "among *other* things."

A knowing smile seemed to be required, and Dunphy provided it. "Oh . . . right," he said, and let the smile flare.

"Anyway, I was with *them* for . . . what? Musta been twelve years."

"Starting when?"

" 'Sixty. Up through '71, '72, maybe. That's when we got our name. The 143rd."

Dunphy nodded.

"Aintcha gonna write that down?"

"Sure," Dunphy said, and made a note.

" 'Cause that's when the 143rd got started. Same year as Watergate. So it's easy to remember."

"Right."

"And, of course, you couldn't run something like the 143rd out of Roswell—I mean, it's a working town, for God's sake. People live there!"

Dunphy nodded in an understanding way. "So . . ."

"They set us up over in Dreamland."

Dunphy gave him a blank look.

"You don't know Dreamland?"

"No."

"Hunh! I thought everybody knew about Dreamland. I mean, it's been on *60 Minutes*!"

"Yeah, well . . . I don't watch a lot of television."

"By now, I expect there's books about it. Anyway, Dreamland's in the Nellis Range, a hundred and twenty miles northwest of Vegas. Emigrant Valley. They got about a hundred thousand acres up there—"

"They?"

"Uncle Sam. Three or four hangars, half a dozen runways."

"You lived there?"

"No one actually 'lives' there. All it is, really, is an antennae farm with rattlesnakes—and funny airplanes, of course. Most of us lived in Vegas and shuttled back and forth."

"There's a shuttle?"

"You had half a dozen flights a day out of McCarran Airport—still do, I guess. Takes about half an hour. The flights are run by a Lockheed subsidiary. I forget what it's called. Anyway, they fly 767s, painted black with a red line down the fuselage."

"So how many people were going up there every day?"

"Maybe a thousand. Back and forth."

"And they're all with the 143rd—"

"No, no, no. Nothing like it. When I was working, there were maybe ten of us—tops."

"And the others . . . "

Brading gave a dismissive shrug. "Testin', trainin' . . . there's an Aggressor Squadron, MiG-23s and Sukhoi Su-22s—they're outa Groom Lake. And I guess they've come up with a replacement for the Blackbird—"

"Really!"

"Oh, yeah! What I hear, it's a Tier III reconnaissance jet that'll do mach six with a radar profile the size of your hand."

"Wow," Dunphy said.

"Wow's right. It was all very impressive, and it was actually good cover for what we were doing. Though, if you wanta know the truth, the choppers *we* had were more advanced than the planes."

Dunphy blinked, uncertain that he'd heard correctly. He wanted to ask Brading to repeat what he'd said, the part about cover. Instead, he asked, "What kind of helicopters?"

Brading's eyes lighted up. "MJ-12 Micro Pave Lows! Best in the world. We're talking about a twin-turbo, tilt-rotor aircraft with the most advanced terrain-following/terrain-avoidance avionics anywhere. Totally Stealthed, low-light/no-light mission-capable with a twelve-hundred-mile range. I get all üggy inside, just thinkin' about it. I mean, this is a machine that's got four million lines of software in the computers, and an external cargo hook that can lift five thousand pounds. You could fly 'em low and slow, or tilt the rotors—wham, bam! you're in a turboprop. Absolutely revolutionary! We *cruised* at three hundred knots, and—here's the best part—here's the revolutionary part—the only sound we made was collateral! The wind kicked up, and sometimes things got blown around."

Dunphy must have looked skeptical because Brading became even more animated.

"I'm not exaggerating, y'know. That was *it*. Them things were dead silent."

"Jesus!"

"Hallelujah!"

The response took Dunphy by surprise, but he plunged on with the interview. "So you were in Dreamland until? . . ."

"'Seventy-nine."

"And then you retired."

"No," Brading corrected. "I didn't retire until '84. By then, Dreamland was lookin' a little iffy."

"What do you mean?"

"The handwritin' was on the wall. You couldn't have that many people flyin' in and outa Vegas all day without somebody blowin' the whistle."

"So they moved you."

"I'll say."

"Where to?"

"Vaca Base." When he saw that this meant nothing to Dunphy, he elaborated. "It's a hanging canyon in the Sawtooth Mountains. Over Idaho way. Only way in and out is with a chopper. It was *real* peaceful."

"I'll bet."

Brading cocked an eye at Dunphy. "I thought you were interested in my illness."

"I am," Dunphy said. "Tell me about it."

"I don't know what's to tell. I'm in remission, but . . . there isn't any cure, really. I got CJD—ever heard of it?"

"Yeah," Dunphy said. "It's, uhh . . . " He couldn't think of the technical name. Finally he said, "Mad cow disease."

Brading looked surprised.

"I lived in England," Dunphy explained.

"Oh, well, of course—it's bad there. I guess everybody's heard about it over there . . . but not here."

"How did you—"

"—get it?" Brading threw up his hands. "I got it on the Census—how else?"

"The Census . . . ," Dunphy said.

"The *Bovine* Census. Whattaya think we're talking about? Whattaya think I was doing?" Dunphy must have looked blank, because Brading wouldn't let it go. "You're Andromeda-cleared, and you ain't never heard of the Bovine Census?!"

Dunphy did his best to look impassive but, inside, he was wincing. He didn't say anything for a few moments, and then he leaned forward. "A mansion has many rooms, Mr. Brading." Saying it in the way that he did, in a voice no louder than a whisper, made the platitude seem like a warning.

Dunphy could hear the wheels turning behind Brading's forehead. *What does* that *mean? A mansion has . . . whut?* Finally, the older man grunted. "Well, anyway—what it was— maybe you know—we took off at night and—well, we went after the cows. On ranches."

"You went after the cows."

"Killed 'em. Not a lot on any one ranch—not a lot on any one night. But some."

Dunphy was stunned. He didn't know what to ask. " 'Some,' " he repeated. "How many would that be?"

"Well, let's see. Starting in '72 . . . I guess we slaughtered a couple thousand, all told. The newspapers said there were four or five times that many, but . . . after a while, you had copycats. Once these things get started, they sorta take on a life of their own. In fact, that was kinda the point—I mean, the way I understood it, that was the whole idea. Give it a life of its own."

"A couple thousand," Dunphy repeated.

"And some horses."

Dunphy nodded. Horses, too.

"In fact," Brading said, "one of the *first* animals we killed was a horse. Belonged to the King Ranch. Stripped the flesh from her neck up. Which was a big deal in the papers. Snippy the Horse. You probably saw the stories. It was front-page, ever'where. Poor thing."

Dunphy shook his head and thought, This is what they mean by *cognitive dissonance*. This is what they mean by *gob-smacked*.

"You can see her today," Brading added.

"Who?"

"Snippy! They got her skeleton in a museum. The Luther Bean Museum. Over in Alamosa."

Dunphy blinked. "But . . . "

"We tranquilized 'em first, of course."

Dunphy shook his head. "But . . . *why*?"

"*Why?!* Because it was painful!"

"No, that's not—"

"Oh, why'd we—well, for the organs. Supposedly, it was for the organs."

"*What* organs?"

Brading giggled. Nervously. "Genitals, mostly. And your tongues. Your rectum. We had one of the first portable lasers—portable, my ass, damn thing was about the size of a refrigerator—but, I'm telling you, it could core the rectum out of a cow in less than thirty seconds. Made a perfect circle. Now, I *admit*, it cooked the hemoglobin at the edge of the wound, but otherwise—just a perfect circle. Real *round*."

Dunphy's palms were suddenly quite damp, and the room seemed stuffier than before. He was thinking of Leo Schidlof's body and didn't know what to say. But that didn't matter: Brading was on a roll, and the information poured from him.

"The whole idea, of course, was the *effect*. Farmer walks into his field, and what's he see but ole Bossy, layin' on the ground with her hide turned inside out and folded next to her backbone. No rib bones, tissues, or internal organs—just the hide and the skull, laying in the snow, like a pile of laundry. No blood anywhere, *and no footprints*." Brading smiled at the recollection. "I can tell you this. It was a startling sight, if you weren't expecting it."

"How did you . . ." Dunphy's voice trailed off.

"Do it without footprints? Well, it depended on the time of year. If it was cold, and there was snow on the ground, we just landed and did what we had to do. And when we were done, we'd get back up in the air and *make* snow—just like the ski resorts do. We had a pretty big tank of water, pressure hoses, and ever'thing. So we covered our tracks that way. And if it was dry, we just lifted the cow with a hoist, did what we had to do, and dropped her half a mile from where we picked her up. So there weren't any tracks that way, either."

Dunphy's question came slowly. "And the farmers. They were supposed to think—what?"

Brading shrugged. "Oh, I dunno. Different things. There were stories about satanic cults . . . aliens . . . UFOs. Basically, they thought whatever Optical Magick wanted 'em to."

"Optical Magick?"

"Talk about ahead of the curve! Those boys were like a scaled-down version of the Skunk Works, only it wasn't airplanes, it was special effects. *Eff! Ecks!* Blow your mind!"

"Good, huh?"

"I kid you not! They had technology . . . special lights . . . projectors . . . holograms. . . . You couldn't tell the difference between what they was doin' and magic. In fact, I think some of it *was* magic!"

"No kiddin'. "

"I'm tellin' ya'! Those boys'd make you *believe*."

"*Would* they? In what? Give me an example."

Without hesitating, Brading said, "Paciparaná."

"What's a pocky? . . ."

"Paraná! It's a chickenshit little village in west Rondônia. Used to be, anyway."

"Where's Rondônia?"

"Brazil," Brading said. "They had a fungus there that Technical Services was interested in. Some kinda hallucinogen. Anyway, it don't grow anywhere else, and the Agency wanted it. Locals said no. Indian tribe. Sacred land. That kinda shit."

"So?"

"So we sent a Pentecostal preacher in, and he told 'em, '*Jeeeee*-sussss says ya gotta move.' "

"And did they?"

" 'Course not—they weren't Christians. They was savages."

"So what happened?"

"Optical Magick sets up shop down the road, and the next thing ya know, the Paciparaná Indians are lookin' at a forty-foot-high BVM—"

"BVM?"

"Blessed Virgin Mary. I'm talkin' about a hologram. Like I said, forty-foot-high, hangin' in the air right over the village—just like that, three nights running. And the moon over her shoulder! Beautiful sight—make ya weep! All blue light and—"

"So the Indians left."

"They walked away *on their knees*. They're probably still walkin'. "

"Optical Magick," Dunphy muttered.

"Right. They did Medjugorje, too. Roswell. Tremonton. Gulf Breeze. Hell, they did all the big ones."

Dunphy shook his head, as if to clear it.

"I know," Brading said. "It's wild. Not that they're perfect. No one's perfect." He hesitated a moment. "You want to see something?"

Dunphy shrugged, dazed. "Sure."

Brading chuckled. "Be right back," he said, and wheeled out of the room, obviously excited. A minute later, he rolled back in with a tape cassette in his lap. Crossing to the TV, he popped the cassette in the VCR and slapped a couple of buttons. "Watch this."

A test pattern flickered, snapped, and counted backward from ten to one. Suddenly, the pattern gave way to a grainy, black-and-white image of a man in a space suit. Or . . . no. Not a space suit. A surgeon, or someone like a surgeon, wearing a biohazard suit and leaning over an operating table.

"What's he doing?" Dunphy asked.

Brading shook his head. "Just watch," he said.

Dunphy could tell the film was old, probably an eight-millimeter transfer to video. The camera was shaky and obviously handheld. The image on the screen went in and out of focus as the cameraman moved around the room, searching for close-ups and a better angle. When it finally found one, Dunphy gasped.

"What the fuck is that?"

"Don't swear," Brading said, causing Dunphy to do a double take: he hadn't heard that since he was twelve.

Dunphy stared at the television screen. The . . . *object* . . . on the table was naked and not quite human. Or maybe it was *mostly* human, or just badly deformed. Whatever it was, it was dead. And a good thing, too: the guy in the biohazard suit was doing an autopsy.

Dunphy took a deep breath. The creature on the table was genderless, or so, at least, it seemed. It had two legs, one of which was badly mangled in the region of the right knee, and two arms. Dunphy saw that its left hand was missing, as if it had been torn off in an accident, and that the fingers on the right hand were one too many. Raising his eyes to the creature's face, he saw that the ears were much too small and that the eyes, black and bottomless, were impossibly large. The mouth, on the other hand, was about the size of a bullet hole and just as round. It did not have lips.

Slowly, the camera closed in on the surgeon's hands, the focus sharpening as he extracted a gray mass from the creature's chest, depositing it in a stainless steel tray. Dunphy didn't know what the mass was supposed to be—an organ of some kind, but what? No matter. There was something even more interesting to wonder about, something that was missing.

"Where's his navel?" Dunphy asked. Brading shook his head, impatient with the question. "He doesn't have a navel," Dunphy repeated. "Or breasts."

Brading nodded disinterestedly, then punched the air with his finger, gesturing toward the television set. "There," he said, suddenly excited, "you see it?" He pointed the remote control at the television and froze the frame.

Dunphy was in a fog. "See what?"

"What? *Hello!* What's *wrong* with this picture?"

Dunphy didn't know what he was talking about. "What's wrong with it? Everything's wrong with it! The guy doesn't have a navel. He doesn't have tits. He's got six fingers—"

Brading laughed. "No, no, no," he said. "I'm not talking about that! All that's well and good." He jabbed a finger at the TV. "I mean the telephone cord—in the background. Look at that."

Dunphy did. There was a wall phone in the background,

hanging above a tray of surgical instruments and . . . "So what?"

Brading giggled. "So AT&T didn't *make* coiled telephone cords until the early fifties—'51, '52. And this is supposed to have been shot in '47. Which is why the whole thing's just an outtake. Cost a million-five to make it, and then they had to throw it out. All because of a telephone cord! Can you believe it?" Brading laughed, and Dunphy heard himself chuckle in agreement.

"Where'd you get it?"

Brading shrugged. "Off the record?" Dunphy nodded. "One of the boys sent it to me."

"From Optical Magick?"

Brading nodded. "Talk about a blooper! There were some noses out of joint like you'd never believe. Important noses, too! Washington noses. And you can see why. I mean, do you have any idea how hard it is to come by Kodak film stock, *viable* film stock, that could have been used in '47?"

"No," Dunphy said.

"Well, it's hard. To say the least." Brading shut off the TV and looked up at Dunphy. "What were we talking about?"

It took Dunphy a moment to reply. Finally, he said, "Snippy. I mean, cattle."

"Right! I was about to say, the one thing *no one* believed was the official explanation."

Dunphy was momentarily nonplussed, having difficulty shifting from cattle mutilations to the autopsy hoax, and back again. "What explanation?" Dunphy asked. "Explanation for what?"

"For the *mutes*," Brading explained. "Because natural predators—which is what they tried to call it—just don't work that way. And besides that, a couple of people saw the helicopters, and that got reported in the papers."

Dunphy thought for a moment and asked, "What'd you do with the organs?"

"Took 'em. I mean, we had surgical technicians. Not doctors, actually—the boys we had were more like vets. Or medics, maybe. I guess animal medics would be the closest to what they were."

"But what happened to them?"

"To what?"

"To the *organs.*"

"I *told* you, the organs weren't the point. They were just a *by-product*—collateral damage, like the cows. But if you have to know, we incinerated 'em."

"So it wasn't like they were being studied, or anything."

"No," Brading replied. "Of course not. They weren't being studied. We just took the damn things and burned 'em." Brading paused. "Except . . . "

"Except?"

"A coupla times—we took the sweetbreads and cooked 'em."

"Sweetbreads."

"Brains. Thymus, actually. I'm a pretty good chef."

Dunphy nodded.

"And they figure that's how I got CJD—from the sweetbreads. Because brains're a vector."

Dunphy nodded, sitting there in silence, pen poised above his notebook. He wasn't sure what to write. Finally, he put the pen away, closed the notebook, and said, "I don't get it."

"You mean? . . ."

"What was the *point*?"

Brading raised his hands in mock surrender. "How do I know? As near as I could tell, the point was to create an *effect*. Get people thinking. Talking. Scare 'em, maybe. That's what happened, anyway, and I guess it was pretty successful or I wouldn't have been doing it for twenty years. I don't know if you followed it, but cattle mutilations were a big story for a long time."

Dunphy nodded. "And that was it? The whole assignment?"

"When I was with it, that's what we did. Later, near the end of my hitch, we started making these—I don't know what you'd call 'em—*designs*—in the wheat fields."

"What kind of designs?"

"Geometric. We did some circles, and then we made a few that were—I don't know—kind of artistic. The Agency called 'em agriglyphs. By then, I was gettin' pretty sick. Had to retire. But the principle was still the same. We never left any footprints there, either."

Dunphy sat in silence for a while, his mind turning like a compass at the South Pole. Finally, he got to his feet. "Well," he said, "that was very good lemonade."

"Thanks."

"I don't think there'll be any problem with the pension."

"Good. I was worried."

"It was all—"

"In the line of duty."

"Exactly. I'll call the GAO in the morning and straighten things out. I don't think they'll even contact you."

"Wonderful."

"But . . . "

"What?"

Dunphy nodded toward the black cloth. "Do you mind if I . . ."

Brading followed Dunphy's glance and started to object, but shrugged instead. "I don't see why not. Go ahead."

Dunphy walked over to the cloth and lifted it.

"It's all classified," Brading told him, rolling across the room to Dunphy's side. "The Purple Heart was for my illness—you can read the citation underneath. And the intelligence medal, that was a career award. And—"

"I'm sorry I had to see this."

Brading looked baffled. "Why? What's wrong?"

"You can't keep this," Dunphy said.

"The hell I can't!" Brading shot back. "They're *my* medals!"

"I don't mean the medals. You can keep those. I mean this!" Dunphy removed a small picture frame from the wall, letting the black cloth drop back across the medals. The frame contained a laminated security pass, about two and a half by four inches, replete with a beaded chain for wearing around the neck. In the upper left-hand corner of the pass was a smudgy hologram and, in the lower right, a thumbprint. A head shot of Brading was in the center of the pass and, under it, the words:

MK-IMAGE
Special Access Program
E. Brading
ANDROMEDA

"I'm sorry," Dunphy said, "but—"

"Oh, jeez—"

"I'm gonna have to take the ID back to Washington."

Brading looked stricken. "It's a souvenir!"

"I know," Dunphy sighed, his voice larded with sympathy and regret. "But . . . that's the point, isn't it? We can't have souvenirs like this hanging around. I mean, think about it. What if there were a burglary? What if it fell into the Wrong Hands?"

Brading snorted.

Dunphy put the ID in his attaché case, frame and all, and snapped it shut. "Well," he said, putting on a happy face, "thanks for the lemonade." He clapped Brading on the shoulder. "Now, I think it's time for *me* to get outa Dodge."

The two men chuckled for a moment, then Brading turned serious as Dunphy started toward the door.

"Shouldn't we pray first?"

Dunphy thought he'd misheard. "What?"

"I asked if you wanted to *pray* first."

Dunphy gazed at the older man for what seemed a long while, waiting for him to smile. Finally, he said, "No . . . thanks. I've got a plane to catch."

Brading looked disappointed—and not just disappointed. There was something else: puzzlement, maybe, or suspicion. Something like that.

14

Dunphy's mood followed the same trajectory as the 727 he was flying in. It rose precipitously on takeoff *(Optical Magick! Bim-bam-boom!)*, leveled off somewhere over Indiana *(Near the end of my hitch, we started making these designs . . .)*, and then began its descent into Washington. *(They did Medjugorje, too.)* By the time he landed, Dunphy was in a very black mood.

That was the biggest crock of shit I've ever heard, he thought. *(Tremonton. Gulf Breeze. All the big ones.)* And he'd fallen for it! Sitting there in the middle of Kansas, listening to Brading, Jack Dunphy had believed every word the man had spoken. And now, as he walked out of the terminal, he mocked his credulousness: a forty-foot Madonna, floating above the jungle canopy—well, why not? Sounds reasonable to me!

Dunphy walked toward the short-term parking lot, muttering to himself about how stupid he'd been. There wasn't anything left for him to do. The Brading business was dead in the water—a hoax. Obviously, the Security Research Staff had seen through his little scam, organized a surveillance, and fed him a barium meal to find out who was helping him. Somehow, they'd known that he and Murray had talked, and knowing that, they'd seeded the Pentagon's records with a single reference to the 143rd, guessing (correctly) that Fremaux would find it and tell Dunphy, and that Dunphy would then catch the first plane to Kansas. Where the SRS would have an actor waiting for him with a cock-and-bull story so crazy that, if Dunphy should ever try to check it out, he'd look like a lunatic. Chasing UFOs and cattle mutilations.

That was it, *of course,* Dunphy thought, taking the elevator to the top floor of the parking garage. Matta wanted to put him in a crazy suit so that, if he stumbled onto anything that actually had to do with Schidlof's murder, no one would listen to him. They'd think he was nuts. Well, Dunphy told himself, that's not going to happen. I'm *not* nuts. I'm—what?

Paranoid. Completely, and totally, paranoid.

He found his car in the space where he'd left it, got in and started the engine. You've gotta stop this shit, he told himself. This shit is trouble. And nothin' else.

Anyway, Dunphy thought, the whole thing was out of his hands. He and Roscoe were persona non grata at the Agency, and their access to classified information was nil. The whole scheme had blown up in their faces, and it was just a matter of time until each of them were fired—if, in fact, they had not already been.

So that was that. In effect, Dunphy's curiosity had been mooted by events. While he still wondered why his life had come unhinged, the reality was that it *had*, and there was nothing that he could do about it. Not anymore. It was time to get on with things. It was time to roll with it.

Still, he thought, maneuvering the car out of the parking garage and into the airport's traffic, it couldn't have been a barium meal—not really. Because the only people Dunphy could count on were Roscoe and Murray, and if the Agency already knew about them, why would it send him to Kansas?

And Brading was convincing. It wasn't as if he'd stumbled around, looking for answers. That stuff about the helicopters making snow—Brading hadn't made that up. Not on the spot, anyway. And what about the props? If Brading was put up to it, where'd they get the props? The picture of Rhinegold and Brading in the wheat field *(Ha Ha Ha!!!)*, and the MK-IMAGE ID. Harry Matta wouldn't have let him walk away with something like that—even if it *was* a phony. And it *had* to be a phony, because otherwise . . .

Otherwise, it was too weird.

Twenty minutes later, Dunphy turned off the G. W. Parkway onto Dolley Madison Boulevard. He cruised past the entrance to CIA headquarters and wound his way through McLean to Belleview Lane. That's when he saw the lights flickering in the trees, and his stomach tightened. Red lights, blue lights—*police lights*.

Trouble lights.

And then, as he drew closer to the house, he heard the crackle of radios, and something sank in his chest. There were a pair of squad cars in the driveway, and an ambulance near the back door. On the front lawn, a man sat in the front seat of a gray sedan, smoking, his features obscured by the night. Dunphy killed the engine at the top of the driveway, slammed the gear shift into Park, got out, and ran toward the house, ignoring a policeman's shout.

He nearly tore the screen door off its hinges as he burst into the living room, where an evidence technician was comparing notes with a police photographer. "Where's Roscoe? Where the fuck—"

A tall man in a cheap black suit came out of the kitchen, looking like Ichabod Crane. He looked about six foot four and 150, white shirt and string tie, with bags like bruises under his eyes. A laminated ID hung from his neck by a beaded chain. Dunphy stepped toward him, trying to read the ID.

"Who are you?" the Suit asked.

"I live here," Dunphy said. "Now where the fuck is Roscoe?" Dunphy saw the words *Special Access*, and then the Suit tucked the ID inside his jacket.

The police looked at each other, embarrassed. One of them coughed, and as Dunphy turned toward him, he saw the technician's eyes drift toward the coffee table. A half-dozen Polaroids were spread out to dry next to *Archaeus*. Dunphy walked over to the pictures, picked one up, and stared.

"The cleaning lady found him," said the cop.

The Suit nodded. "They took him out an hour ago," he said.

And then, with what sounded like genuine regret, he added, "You must be Dunphy."

Dunphy didn't say anything. He couldn't. Because the photo took his breath away. It showed a nude man in a pair of fishnet stockings, hanging by the neck from a set of exercise pulleys in what was definitely Roscoe's closet. The man's head—*Roscoe's* head—was covered with a clear plastic bag, fastened by what looked like a bungee cord. His eyes bulged. His tongue lolled. A thread of spittle hung from his chin. On the floor beneath his feet were an overturned stepstool, a paperback, and a scattering of magazines.

"What the fuck!" Dunphy whispered, and dropped the picture. He picked up another. It was a close-up of one of the magazines, a porno rag called *Blue Boy*, lying beneath Roscoe's dangling feet. Beside it was a paperback: *Man's Best Friend*.

"Autoerotic suicide." This, from the Suit.

Dunphy didn't know what to do. He put the snapshot back on the table and picked up *Archaeus*. He opened it. He closed it. He sat down. He got up. He took three steps this way, and three steps that. Finally, he said, "I don't believe it."

"What?"

"Roscoe didn't commit suicide. Not like that."

The Suit shrugged. "Well, maybe he just overdid things. I mean, the way I understand it, the closer you get to asphyxiation, the more you get your rocks off. But it's a fine line." He paused, and shrugged again. "That's what I'm told."

Dunphy shook his head. "He wouldn't have done this," he said. "He wouldn't have known how! I mean, it's not like he watched Oprah or something. This kinda thing was—*beyond his ken!*"

The evidence technician shook his head. "You never know," he said.

"I shared a house with this guy!" Dunphy replied, his voice rising. "After a while, you *do* know about people. And, anyway, someone who's into this kinda crap—he doesn't look for a roommate! Y'know what I mean?"

The Suit cleared his throat. "Maybe you could tell us where you've been—" At Dunphy's glare, the man took a step backward. "Just over the last day or so."

Dunphy ignored the question. "Who's the guy out front?" he asked.

"What guy?"

"The one on my fucking lawn! In the car."

"He means the crippled guy," the photographer suggested.

The Suit glowered at the photographer, then turned back to Dunphy. "I'll get back to you on that," he said. "Let's just say he's helping us find out what happened here." He paused for a moment, and then went on. "So," he said in a helpful voice, "you were traveling?"

"Fuck you," Dunphy said. "You're no cop."

The Suit bristled. "That's right," he shot back. "I'm with the same Agency you are."

"Not anymore." Turning on his heel, Dunphy stalked out of the house. The screen door slammed behind him.

"Hey!" the Suit shouted, "where you goin'? I'm not done with you. Hey! You *live* here!"

Not anymore, Dunphy thought. Jack Dunphy's gone. Jack Dunphy has *moved away*.

A cigarette glowed in the gray sedan as Dunphy strode toward his car at the top of the driveway. He tossed *Archaeus* onto the seat—he'd forgotten the magazine was still in his hand—and got in. Five minutes later, he was on the Beltway, and ten minutes after that, he left it.

And so it went: on again, off again, on again. For an hour and a half, he went through the tedium of countersurveillance, leaving the Beltway in search of lonely roads on which to reverse direction in the dark. He went south, then east, north again, south again, on again, off again—until, finally, at one in the morning, he was satisfied that no one was following him.

Heading north on I-95, he realized for the first time that, somewhere along the line, he'd started to hyperventilate. His palms were damp, and he felt light-headed, fogged-in one moment, focused the next. This was what it was like to be scared, like a fuse sizzling in your heart.

Meanwhile, he drove, going nowhere in particular, just getting away from the scene of the atrocity. Which was horrible, of course, and frightening, as well, because Dunphy was certain not only that Roscoe had been murdered, but that he, too, would have been killed if he hadn't been in Kansas.

Two hours later, he pulled into a truck stop near the Delaware Memorial Bridge and placed a call to Murray Fremaux. The phone rang six or seven times, and then Murray's voice came on the line, saturated with sleep and persecution. "Hulll-lo?"

"Murray—"

"Who *is* this?"

"Jack."

"Jack? Jesus Christ—what *time* is it?!"

"I think it's, like, three A.M."

"Well—"

"Don't talk. Don't say anything."

Dunphy could hear Murray catch his breath. He could hear him focusing.

"I have to go away," Dunphy said. He paused for a moment, and added, "Roscoe fell down."

"What?"

"I said, my roommate *fell down*."

"Ohhh . . . ohhh, shit."

"I just wanted to tell you to be careful. Really careful."

Murray's breath quivered on the line. The silence was perfect, digital, *pealing*.

"This is a really good line," Dunphy remarked, seemingly apropos of nothing.

"I know," Murray said. "It's like you're in the next room."

Fuck! Dunphy thought, they're already bugging him. He slammed the receiver down and jogged back to his car.

He couldn't erase the Polaroids from his mind. He didn't want to think about them, but there they were, pasted up on the back of his eyelids. And there was something about one of them, the one with the porno novel, that nagged at him. *Man's Best Friend*. Dunphy had seen the book before, but he couldn't remember where, and that was driving him crazy. It was right on the tip of his tongue, and it was important.

Crossing from Delaware into New Jersey, Dunphy tried not to think about the book. Sometimes, if you just let go, the memories would surface on their own. It was a kind of judo. So he pushed the Polaroid out of his mind and thought about something else that bothered him. What was it that the cop said?

Something about "the crippled guy." *He means the crippled guy.* That's what he'd said. And he'd meant the guy in the gray sedan, the one who'd been smoking.

Suddenly, Dunphy remembered where he'd seen the book before. It belonged to the polygraph examiner, the one with the clubfoot. That was the guy the cop was talking about. That was the guy in the gray sedan.

A couple of months before, the book had been used as a prop to heighten Dunphy's anxiety, increase the tension in the room. That was the way polygraph examiners worked. They didn't want a relaxed subject, because relaxation led to ambiguous results. Relaxed subjects made for mushy readouts, so the examiners did everything they could to jack up the tension, the better to highlight the lies.

And sex was always a reliable way to jack up the tension.

Fair enough, Dunphy thought. But now the book was being used for something else. It was being used as evidence of Roscoe's supposed perversion, and as such, it fed the lie that his death had been a kind of suicide. Or, if not a suicide, a shameful accident that Roscoe's friends and family would not be much inclined to investigate.

All of which suggested that his friend had been killed by the geeks with the bolos and string ties. Rhinegold and Esterhazy. The Suit. He held that thought for a hundred miles, turning it over and over in his mind, wondering what he was going to do about it. His eyes drifted to and from the rearview mirror, searching for a suspicious car, but there wasn't anyone. It was just Dunphy and the open road, the passing HoJos, and the occasional billboard that called to him. Like the one outside Metuchen, the one that read:

DON'T GET HIJACKED!
GET LO-JACK!
(WE KNOW WHERE YOU LIVE!)

Oh, fuck me, he thought. How stupid can you get?

15

No *wonder* there's no one behind me. They're sitting in the Communications Center, eating doughnuts and drinking coffee, with their feet on their desks and a map of the East Coast on the wall in front of them. They're having a great time, watching the transponder's signal slide north along the Jersey Turnpike, heading for New York. They must have been laughing like crazy a couple of hours ago when he'd tried to shake them, zigzagging on and off the Beltway, trying to lose a nonexistent tail.

Dunphy was furious with himself.

What the fuck was he thinking of? There wasn't anything exotic about transponders. The FBI used them all the time. And not just against the Russians. There were probably a hundred dips in the city who had transponders hardwired into the rocker panels or some other part of their cars. And not just the dips. Dunphy had been parking his car in G lot, less than a hundred yards from headquarters, for months. During that time, he'd become the centerpiece of an investigation that was obviously being run by psychopaths. How likely was it that his car was wired? About as likely as finding gravity in a mineshaft.

Seeing the sign for Newark Airport, he left the turnpike, thinking: *Once the signal becomes stationary—which it's about to do—they'll look for the car. And find it in the airport's parking lot. Then they'll canvas each of the airlines, checking the outbound passenger lists on the early morning flights. At some point or other, they'll start to follow my credit*

103

cards in real time, tracking me by the transactions that I make. Finally, whether this week or the next, everything will come together, and we'll converge. And that will be that.

And that will be the *end* of that.

Or so, Dunphy thought, Matta and his friends would like to think.

Dunphy pulled into the short-term parking lot and got out, leaving the doors unlocked, the windows down, and the keys in the ignition. It was unlikely that anyone would steal the car, but he had nothing to lose by leaving it there in that way. If he got lucky and someone did steal it, the Agency would continue to follow the transponder's signal—and Dunphy would have a few more hours, and maybe a few more days.

Grabbing his attaché case and the flight bag that he'd taken to Kansas, Dunphy walked to the bus stop outside the Arrivals terminal. There, he caught a bus into Manhattan, arriving at first light, and debarked at the Port Authority on Forty-second Street. Going inside, he bought a bus ticket for Montreal, paying cash, and then went into the men's room. There, he stood for a moment at the sink, splashed his face with cold water, and dried his hands with a paper towel. Then he walked outside, tossing his Visa and Mastercard on the tiled floor. Someone would make good use of the plastic— and that would confuse Harry Matta no end. *He's doing what?! He's buying a stereo?!*

There were three hours to kill before the bus left, and Dunphy murdered them one by one in a small café on West Fifty-seventh Street, drinking coffee and reading the *Times*. At 9 A.M., he walked across town to the American Express office and, flashing his Platinum card, cashed a check for five thousand dollars. It was all the cash he had—he wasn't much of a saver—and he was going to need every penny. Then he went back to the Port Authority and waited for the bus to Montreal.

For a moment, he didn't know where he was, or what time it was. He lay in the dark with his eyes open, a windowless monad in the deep space of his hotel room, suspended in blackness, seeing nothing. He was blind. He was dead. He was groggy with exhaustion or a surfeit of sleep—one or the other, he couldn't tell. Something like fear rose in his chest, and fighting against it, he sat up slowly, bringing his left wrist closer to his eyes.

The watch glowed. Eleven, Dunphy thought. It's eleven o'clock, and I'm in bed. Somewhere. But not at home.

Then he remembered—Brading, Roscoe, Newark, the bus. He was in Montreal, in a small hotel that didn't take credit cards. A few hours earlier, he'd closed the heavy drapes against the sunset, lay down on the bed, and . . .

Slowly, Dunphy got to his feet and, like Frankenstein, staggered through the dark with his arms in front of him, searching for the windows on the other side of the room. It was a small room, and it took him only three or four steps before he found the velvet curtains. Bunching them in his hands, he yawned and pulled them apart with a yank that, instantly, flooded his brain with sunlight. Reflexively, his eyes slammed shut and he recoiled, vampirelike, swearing at the sun.

It was eleven in the morning, not the night, and he had a lot to do.

With Roscoe's death, everything had changed. It was as if they'd been kids playing by a stream bank and, seeing a hole, poked it with a stick. The thing that crawled out had not been a garden snake, but something terrible and unexpected—mysterious, deadly, and misshapen. It had put an end to Roscoe, there and then, and now it was slithering toward Dunphy.

Who wanted to kill it. Who *had* to kill it. But how? Dunphy didn't know what it was—where it began, or where it ended. Neither did he know what it wanted (other than himself, dead).

What he did know was that there weren't any answers to be found in Montreal. The answers were in London and Zug, with Schidlof and the Special Registry. But getting to Europe required a passport—and that's where Canada came in.

His travel documents were in the top drawer of his dresser

in McLean. He'd have to replace them. What he wanted, of course, was "a genuine phony," a real passport with his own picture and someone else's name. But he didn't have the contacts for that—not in Canada, at least, and not in the States. The best that he could do on short notice was to get a new passport in his own name, use that document to reach Europe, and then ditch it for something specially made. This meant, of course, that he'd have to show up in person at the American consulate in Montreal, but Dunphy didn't think that would cause a problem. His name wasn't in the lookout books that State and Customs used, and it was unlikely that Matta had notified either agency of his sudden interest in a man named Dunphy. Matta would undoubtedly want to handle the situation on his own—in house—and would not involve other agencies unless, and until, the CIA's own efforts had failed. Which meant that, at the moment, Matta was probably going through passenger lists at Newark Airport and chasing Visa transactions all over New York.

So Dunphy would go to the consulate, where getting a new passport might be more easily accomplished than in the States themselves. In his experience, consular officials abroad tended to be more helpful than their counterparts at home. And why not? An American who'd lost his passport in a foreign country was at least marginally more sympathetic than the same idiot who'd lost his documents in Boston or New York. Even so, if he was going to get a passport that same day, he would have to demonstrate an urgent need to travel—and it wouldn't hurt if he could also show a certain amount of clout.

He satisfied the first requirement at a travel agency around the corner from his hotel. Paying cash, he bought a ticket to Prague on an Air France flight that left in six hours, connecting through Paris. This done, he crossed the street to Kinko's Copies, where he sat for passport photos while another part of the shop made up a set of business cards. The cards read:

Jack Dunphy, Producer
CBS News—60 Minutes
555 W. 57th St.
New York, N.Y. 10019

He kept three of the cards in his wallet and tossed the rest in a trash can outside. Then he walked to the American consulate and, going inside, strode up to the Information counter, looking friendly and frantic at the same time.

"Big problem!" he said, eyes wide and out of breath.

"Excuse me?" The clerk was an elegant black woman, all cornrows and polite skepticism.

"This is terrible! I mean, this is a goddamned disaster!"

"What is?"

"My passport!"

"What about it?"

"I lost it!"

The clerk smiled. "We can get you a new one," she said, pushing a form toward him. "Just fill this out, and—"

"I need it right away."

The clerk shrugged. "We can expedite it."

"Great," Dunphy said. "That's terrific."

"But there's a fifty-dollar fee."

Dunphy shrugged—"No problem"—and reached for his wallet.

"And if you pick it up yourself," she said, "you can have the new one in forty-eight hours."

Dunphy's smile faded to panic. His jaw sagged as he said, "You don't understand. I mean, I'm on a flight to Paris in a couple of hours." He pushed his ticket across the counter, but the clerk didn't look at it.

"There's no way," she said.

"Ohhh, jeez—don't do this," Dunphy replied, "I got two camera crews flying in—"

"I'm sorry . . ."

Dunphy pushed his new business card across the counter.

"Do you have a media liaison here? Someone I can talk to? Because, the truth is, I got Ed cooling his heels in a dump on Wenceslas Square, and if I don't get there by morning—this could be a big problem for me."

"Ed?"

"Ed Bradley."

The woman glanced at the business card for the first time. Picked it up. Put it down. Looked at him. And back to the card. Dunphy could see the question in her eyes: Is there a hidden camera? A hidden agenda?

"Let me see what I can do," she said, sliding off her stool with a crackle of static and a smile as bright as a searchlight.

An hour later, Dunphy had a passport, and enough time on his hands to satisfy his curiosity about something that was nagging at him. Taking a cab to the public library, he went inside and searched the periodicals' database for articles about the Jaciparaná Indians. It took him half an hour, but he found a reference to the tribe in a newsletter put out by the North American Congress on Latin America (NACLA). The article, which was actually about diamond smuggling in Rondônia, said that the Jaciparaná had left their homeland in 1987, after a sudden and mysterious conversion to Christianity. Most of the Indians were now living in the city of Pôrto Vehlo, where they survived by selling rosary beads carved from teak.

Brading had been telling the truth.

The flight to Paris was uneventful, the plane uncrowded. Dunphy sat on the aisle next to an unoccupied window seat, thinking about what had happened, and about what he was going to do.

He was lucky to be alive, and that wasn't good. Luck was a sailor who was here today and gone tomorrow. You could never be sure if it was coming or going, moving toward you or pulling away. In the end, it wasn't a good idea to be lucky, because in the long run, people who were lucky always *pressed their luck*. Then their *luck ran out*, like sand in an hourglass—and the next thing you knew, they were unlucky.

Still, it was luck that had saved him—not tradecraft. When the SRS had come banging on the door with their exercise pulleys and porno novels, Dunphy had been out. But Roscoe had been in, and now Roscoe was dead. That was *Roscoe's* luck. (To whom the adage unquestionably applied: If he didn't have *bad* luck, he wouldn't have *no* luck at all.)

Not so with Dunphy. If the cleaning lady had taken the day off, he'd be dead. But she hadn't. She'd come on time, as she always did, and finding Roscoe, she'd called the police. If it wasn't for her, Dunphy would have returned to a still and darkened house, a suburban mousetrap crawling with men in black suits and string ties. Instead, he'd come home to squad cars and flashing lights.

With the Fairfax County police in the living room, there was nothing (else) that the SRS could do, and no one to stop him from leaving. In all likelihood, Matta probably wasn't even told about Dunphy's escape until the next morning, by which time his car was sitting at the Newark Airport and Dunphy himself was on the Long Dog to Montreal.

So he was home free. But for how long? It could be a day, or a week, or—

That's it, Dunphy thought. A day or a week. Anything else was a fantasy. In either case, he was going to need money, and a lot of money at that. Being on the run was expensive, and the cash that he had would soon be gone.

He shifted in his seat, uncomfortable with the anger that he felt, and gazed out at the void beyond the wing. Darkness above, darkness below, and both of them stirred by his own black mood. There was nothing to be seen, but he knew that, somewhere out there, night and the ocean met to form an invisible horizon. And knew, also, that somewhere out there, men with string ties and dark suits were showing his picture to ticket agents and clerks in stores.

There was a third thing that he knew, as well, and that was where to get the money that he needed. There was an envelope in his attaché case, stamped with Her Majesty's likeness. It had been there for months, since the day he'd left England, and it represented quite a lot of money, none of which was his.

Dunphy sipped his Scotch and tore the envelope open. It was addressed to Roger Blémont in care of *poste restante*, Marbella. It contained the incorporation papers for Sirocco Services Ltd., a bank signature card, a handwritten deposit slip, and half a dozen counter checks issued by the Banque Privat de St. Helier on the isle of Jersey. The usual cover letter explained that printed checks would be sent to Blémont once the signature card was returned to the bank.

A sinewy Corsican with a preference for Armani suits and high-tech Breitling wristwatches, Blémont was a handsome sociopath with one foot in the Marseille underworld and the other in right-wing politics. A virulent anti-Semite, he was the publisher of a magazine called *Contre la boue (Against the Mud)*, which advocated, among other things, the forced deportation of the foreign poor. The magazine's name was taken from the snow-white banner of a defunct paramilitary group, whose members had been imprisoned for attacks on Turkish schoolchildren, a gay bar in Arles, and a synagogue in Lyon.

Dunphy despised him, and not only for his politics. The Corsican's arrogance was boundless, and it seemed to Dunphy that nothing pleased him more than other people's unhappiness. Simply put, he liked to fuck with people. As he had with Dunphy.

On a visit to London the year before, Blémont and Dunphy had concluded some business over a bottle of plonk—and then a second one—at El Vino in the City. Blémont had done most of the drinking, and when they were done, he'd put a hand on Dunphy's shoulder and confided, "I need a girl."

Dunphy had made a joke. "We all need a girl."

"But you'll get me one, okay? I'm at the Landmark. Have her there by three." Then he'd tossed some money on the table and pushed back in his chair, as if to leave.

Dunphy had raised his hands in mock surrender. "I think you've made a mistake," he told him. "I'm a consultant, not a pimp."

"Oh? Is that so?"

"Yeah. If you want a hooker, go to a phone booth. They've got their calling cards all over the windows."

Blémont had sat there for a moment, thinking it over. Finally he said, "You can call yourself whatever you want, my friend, but have the girl at the Landmark by three or I'll have a new consultant tomorrow."

And Dunphy had done as he'd been told. He'd found a whore and sent her to the Landmark because he couldn't afford to lose Blémont's business—not just then, anyway. The Corsican was involved in a complex money-laundering scheme being run by a crowd of black-metal fascists in Oslo. There was a lot of money involved, and at least some of it was coming from a militia group in the States. With the FBI, CIA, and DEA all interested, Dunphy's penetration of the scheme was the intelligence equivalent of hitting the trifecta. To blow the operation because his pride was hurt would have been inexcusable.

So Blémont deserved what he got or, more to the point, what he didn't get—which were the signature cards that Dunphy had never quite gotten around to mailing. It was a loose string that he might easily have tied up, simply by putting the envelope in the mail—but why should he? Blémont was a prick, and anyway, it wasn't as if he'd earned the money.

Usually, Dunphy opened his clients' accounts with token deposits: fifty pounds was typical. But Sirocco was different. Dunphy had already set up a dozen corporations for Blémont when, one wintry afternoon, the Corsican had come to his office with a proposition. Settling languidly into a leather wing chair, Blémont said that he wanted to open Sirocco's account with a line of credit, collateralized with stock. For his help with what he described as a "transaction that's a bit . . . difficult," Blémont promised Dunphy a three-percent commission on the amount of the loan.

"That's very generous," Dunphy said.

"I can afford to be generous," Blémont replied, his face cracking in a grin.

"How much collateral are we talking about?"

Blémont reached into his briefcase, withdrew a sheaf of stock certificates, and handed them to Dunphy. "There's a little more than ten thousand shares."

Dunphy riffed the certificates between his thumb and forefinger. "All IBM?"

Blémont nodded and leaned forward. *"Oui."*

"And what would the Big Blue be trading at, now? I'm thinkin' it's at one hundred ten—"

"One hundred twenty," Blémont replied. And then he added, "Dollars, of course."

Dunphy grunted. "Dollars, it is," Dunphy said. The certificates were in the name of a New York brokerage, and obviously they'd been stolen or Blémont would not be paying three points for placing them with a bank.

"How much—"

"I can probably get 40 percent of the street value," Dunphy said.

Blémont made a moue. "Fifty would be better."

"You could take it around the corner to the NatWest and get seventy-five or eighty. And you wouldn't have to pay me a commission. Of course, if you do that . . . " Dunphy didn't need to finish the sentence. If he did that, the National Westminster would fax New York to see if the stock had been stolen—big banks are funny that way.

Blémont held Dunphy's eyes for a moment and then he smiled. "I'm sure you'll do your best."

"Of course," Dunphy said. And with that, Blémont got up, shook hands, and left.

Blémont's scam was a Mafia favorite that amounted to minting money. The Costa del Sol had been built with it, and so had the Costa Brava. Stock certificates, stolen from couriers and brokerage vaults in America, were used as collateral for loans made in Europe. The loans were then used to finance real-estate developments, hotels, restaurants, golf courses—and, in Blémont's case, publications like *Contre la boue*. So long as the borrower did not default, which would have forced the bank to sell the stolen stock (and attempt to register a change of ownership), the scheme was foolproof. The hotels would prosper. The loans would be repaid, and the certificates might then be recycled as collateral for still other loans.

It had taken Dunphy a couple of weeks to find an accommodating bank, and in the end, it had been necessary to take the hydrofoil to St. Helier and present the certificates in person. Eventually, Sirocco's account was opened with a deposit of £290,000 and change. For his part in the felony, Dunphy took in a little less than $15,000—which he dutifully wire-transferred to one of the CIA's accounts at the Credit Suisse.

When the paperwork came back from the bank in St. Helier, Dunphy had put it in an envelope with Sirocco's incorporation papers and addressed it to Blémont. The package was sitting in his out box when Tommy Davis had called to say that Leo Schidlof was dead.

By keeping the envelope, rather than mailing it, Dunphy remained the only signatory on Blémont's new account. Looked at in a positive light, this meant that Dunphy had immediate access to rather a lot of money—the downside being that Blémont would tear his throat out if he ever found him. Not that there was anything that Dunphy could do about it. Even if he returned the money, the Corsican would not be forgiving: too much time had passed. He'd simply think that Dunphy had suffered a failure of nerve, and so Blémont would want to kill him twice—once for being a thief, and a second time for being a coward. Dunphy sipped his drink, rattled the ice in his glass, and gazed out at the stars over Iceland.

There was no doubt in his mind that Blémont was looking hard—but for whom? Not Dunphy. The man Blémont was after was an Irishman named "Kerry Thornley." Which is to say that Roger Blémont is the least of my problems, Dunphy thought.

A unique notion—that Blémont should be the least of

anyone's problems. And, in fact, when you thought about it, it seemed likely that this was a thought that had never occurred to anyone else in the world. Or, at least, no one who'd stayed in the world.

Dunphy would have bet on that.

16

Dunphy's plane got into Paris at 7 A.M., leaving him with two hours to kill before the flight to Prague. He spent a part of that time wandering through the duty-free shops, then stopped to have some passport pictures taken. Finally, he sat down in a small café with stone countertops and stools of poured concrete.

It was a horrid little place, a francophone purgatory for jet-lagged tourists who wandered in and out, looking worried and confused as they counted their unfamiliar change. In a corner of the room, an Algerian busboy rested his back against the wall, languidly smoking Turkish cigarettes as he watched the tables thicken with used cups and saucers. High on the wall, a single plastic speaker buzzed with the synthesized cadences of Europop—an upbeat disco howl that left Dunphy feeling woozy and depressed. Clearly, the idea was to maximize profits by accelerating customer turnover, which the café accomplished by making all who entered deeply unhappy—except *la propriétaire*, who understood the principle and approved. Impeccable in a double-breasted blazer and lightly tinted designer glasses, the man stood behind the cash register, sovereign with pride as he surveyed his own private circle of Hell. You could see it in his eyes: *C'est bon*, they said. *C'est* très *bon*.

Dunphy understood the game, and in less stressful circumstances, he might have sat in the café for an hour or more, just as a matter of principle. But in the end, he wasn't up to it. When the overhead speaker exploded with *Les BelleTones'*

version of "Le Spinning Wheel," he *ejected*, bursting through
the doors in the general direction of the duty-free shops. Even
without looking back, he knew that the proprietor was staring
after him, his lips curled in a triumphant moue.

Two hours later, he was in Prague. Though he'd have preferred to fly to London direct, it was essential to go to the
Czech Republic first. A plan was beginning to take shape in
his mind, and the shape that it took was the unmistakable silhouette of a garrulous hustler named Max Setyaev.

Max was a former science teacher, a Russian Jew who'd
come to Czechoslovakia from the Ukraine in 1986. A natural
pedant in the way that some people are natural athletes, he'd
found it impossible to reconcile his teacher's income of fifty-
six dollars per month with a taste for blondes, champagne,
and gravlax. With enormous regret, he'd left his job in the
classroom for employment as a documents man in Odessa,
forging identity cards and exit visas for the *Organizatsiya*. This
had been a profitable profession for many years, but the Cold
War's end had dampened the demand for phony documents—
even as laser printers and color copiers made Max's artistry increasingly less necessary. In the end, he'd forged his own visa
and headed west for what amounted to "retraining."

When Dunphy met him, two years later, the Russian was in
London, shopping for an intaglio press, special inks, and
hard-to-come-by papers. Claiming to represent the fledgling
(and very wobbly) republic of Chechnya, Max ensconced
himself at the Churchill Hotel, where he hosted a nonstop
party (later characterized in the press as an orgy) for the city's
bankers. To anyone who'd listen, whether call girl or stock-
broker, he claimed to represent the Chechen Ministry of
Finance—which, he explained, had commissioned his firm
(herewith, a gilded business card was produced) to mint the
new country's new currency (the *agrovar*, or some such thing).
As evidence of the claim, he brandished an impressively embossed letter that purported to come from the Ministry, urging
all concerned to facilitate "Prince Setyaev" on his sensitive and
sacred mission.

The letter was a forgery, of course. Max had no intention of printing Chechen currency. It was pounds he was after, as the *Mirror* discovered when a genuine Chechen delegation arrived in London, seeking humanitarian aid. Asked how the Chechens could reconcile their country's pleas for grain with Max's revelries at one of London's most expensive hotels, the Chechens replied that the man had nothing to do with them. He's *Russian*, they said. Why would we trust a Russian to print our currency? The next morning, Max was running through Heathrow with his shirttail on fire and the police not far behind.

Since then, Dunphy had formed a half-dozen companies for him, the most recent of which was a Prague-based import-export firm: Odessa Software, AG. According to the Russian, he'd seen the future, and its name was software piracy.

In the event, Max's address turned out to be a graceful, Art Deco building in the Holesovice neighborhood in northern Prague. Only a block from the vastness of Stromovka Park, 16 Ovenecka was a four-story mansion that housed more than a dozen small companies, including Max's.

Dunphy took the tiny elevator to Odessa's second-floor office, knocked, and entered. There was no secretary and no anteroom—just a large room with twelve-foot ceilings, velvet drapes, and an antique desk piled high with shrink-wrapped boxes of Microsoft Works, Myst, and Windows 98. For a moment, Dunphy thought he was alone, but then the desk beeped (or seemed to).

"Max?"

The Russian's bald pate, unruly brows, and beady eyes peered over the top of a nineteen-inch color monitor. "Kerry?" Max jumped to his feet. "I was playing SimCity," he said, striding across the room with his arms wide. "*2000,* of course! How are you? And what are you doing here?"

"Well," Dunphy replied, extricating himself from Max's bear hug and moving to a chair beside the window. "It's funny you should ask. There's been a bit of trouble."

Max nodded. "I know," he said, producing a half bottle of Becherovka and two small glasses.

Dunphy looked at him, surprised. "You do?"

"Of course! I called your office—months ago—and guess what?" Max poured each of them a drink and sat down.

"No phone."

The Russian shook his head. *"Prozit,"* he said, clinking his glass with Dunphy's. A little sip. A big smile. And back to business. "No—phone is fine. Man answers: 'Mr. Thornley is away from desk,' he says. 'May I have him call you?' Well, why not? Am I in hiding? Of course not! So I give him number. Two hours later, I have prick from British embassy banging on door—and Czech detectives."

"Jesus, Max, I'm sorry. What did they want?"

"You."

Dunphy grunted. "And what did you tell them?"

The Russian shrugged. "Nothing. I said I got your number from *Herald Tribune*. Old copy."

"And they believed you?"

"No! Of course not." He paused and, without quite changing the subject, brought the conversation into focus. "So, my friend, *what*?"

Dunphy looked puzzled. "What what?"

"What can I do for you? You're a long way from home."

Dunphy grinned. He liked the man's directness. "Well, for openers," he said, tossing a small envelope on the desk, "I need a passport . . . a couple of credit cards. Some pocket litter." He gestured at the envelope. "I had some pictures taken at the airport."

The Russian nodded to himself. "Good. What nationality?"

Dunphy smiled. "As long as it isn't Nigerian or Japanese—"

"Canadian. I get blanks. Any name you want. Totally legit."

"That would be grand."

"Not cheap—but clean. Credit cards, too—this is no problem."

"Great."

"But, first, I need deposit. Cash—not for me—for Visa! Okay?"

"Yeah," Dunphy said, "that's fine." He took a sip of the Becherovka and felt his eyebrows bounce. "What is this stuff?"

"No one knows. Is secret. Czechs say it takes twenty herbs to make it. They don't say which ones."

"I like it."

"So do I. Now, about passport, you didn't ask how much."

Dunphy shrugged.

"Which means trouble! Or, maybe . . . you didn't just come for passport."

"Right."

Max smiled. "Which?"

"Both."

"Ah." Max sipped the liqueur, inhaled mightily through his nose, and asked, "So what are we talking about?"

"This," Dunphy said, removing Gene Brading's Andromeda pass from his briefcase and handing it to the Russian.

Max settled a pair of reading glasses on the bridge of his nose and turned the ID over in his hands, studying it. He didn't say anything for nearly a minute, and then he looked at Dunphy. "You know what this is?"

"Of course. It's a hologram—like the ones on your desk. That's why I'm here. I figure, if anyone can make one of these things, you can."

Max shook his head. "It's not *just* hologram. Is *rainbow* hologram—"

"Which is what?"

"You can see in ordinary light, white light—like now."

"Hard to copy?"

"Last year? Very hard. Today? Not so hard. But expensive." Max rotated the ID in his hands, squinting at it. "You know how these things are put together?"

"No," Dunphy said.

"Well, don't try at home. You need lasers. Mine, I get made

at institute in Kiev. They have best scientists. And fast—prototypes in two, three days."

"Just so it works," Dunphy replied, uninterested in the details.

Max looked at him with disapproval. "This is going to cost big money, my friend. If it was me, I'd want to know why."

"Sorry," Dunphy answered, sounding like a kid who'd been caught talking in class.

"You know lasers, right? You know what laser is!"

"Of course."

Max shook his head. "No, you don't. You only think you do. In *fact*, is beam of light with single frequency. One color. Very intense. When they make hologram, they split beam."

Dunphy nodded.

"So now they have two beams with single source. And first one is like *flashbulb*. Bang! It hits object and . . . what happens to light?"

Dunphy shrugged. "I don't know," he said. "It goes away. It goes into outer space or something."

"Please," Max said, rebuking him with his patience. "When light meets object—any object, any light—what happens?"

"It's reflected."

"And reflected light? . . ."

"I don't know. It shoots off somewhere."

"No. It exposes film to make hologram," Max corrected him.

Stupidly, Dunphy tried to defend himself. "You didn't say there was any film involved."

A dismissive puff of air flew from the Russian's lips. "What do you think? Hologram lives in space? Is image on film!"

"Okay, so . . ."

"So, with hologram—have *two* rays of light. Because you've split beam. And second ray doesn't shine on object—is focused directly on film—instead. So two beams converge on surface, and make interference pattern—which is map, *encoded* map of object. All whorls and stripes—and depth cues. Is visual mess. But when laser shines through at certain angle, image is reconstructed. In three dimensions! A miracle! As if object is in front of you. In space!"

"Spooky," Dunphy muttered, shifting uncomfortably. "What'll they think of next?"

"Mr. Sarcasm! You laugh, but it's even spookier," Max replied. "Put film through blender, and chop it up, image is still intact. You didn't know that, did you?"

Dunphy shook his head.

"Is because image is *distributed* throughout film. So every fragment contains whole—like memory and brain cells." Max sat back with a smile. "Cosmic, no?"

Dunphy was quiet for a moment, contemplating Max's didactic glow. Finally, he said, "I'm in a lot of trouble, Max. I mean, really a lot. And time is—"

Max nodded vigorously. "I understand," he said, leaning forward with a confidential air. "But this is conventional hologram—you look at in dark, or with special lights. To make one like this—to make *rainbow* hologram—we have to increase brightness of image."

"And you're gonna tell me how we do that, aren't you?"

"Yes, of course, I hold nothing back." He took a deep breath. "So, what happens?" he asked. "We photograph object through slit—*horizontal* slit. This concentrates light even more, so image is brighter. Is rainbow hologram because slit is like prism. Move head—or credit card, or Microsoft box— whatever hologram is *on*—light breaks up in spectrum."

"Colors."

"Exactly. Is rainbow."

"Well, thanks for the science lesson, but—maybe I don't need to get a hologram made. All I really need is an ID, just like that one, but with my own thumbprint. So why don't we just forget about Kiev—take this guy's fingerprint out, and put mine in?"

Max shook his head. "Is not possible. If I open laminate, hologram is ruined."

"But you could copy it, right?"

"Yes, yes, of course, but . . . this is big deal. I'll have to re-make whole thing—"

"I can pay."

"You can pay. It's expensive! I'll need copy of Virgin—*this* Virgin—which means trip to Switzerland."

"What are you talking about?" Dunphy asked.

"Einsiedeln." He nodded at the hologram. "Her."

Dunphy frowned with puzzlement. "She's a virgin?"

Max threw his hands in the air. "You're a Christian? And you ask this? What do you think we're talking about? I say, 'Madonna,' you're thinking rock 'n' roll?"

Dunphy picked up the ID. "I never really looked at it. It seemed smudged. I mean—for Christ's sake, she's black!"

"Of course she's black. That's why she's famous: *La Vierge Noire*. Everyone knows about this."

The postcard at Brading's house flashed through Dunphy's mind. What did it say? *Protectrice de la ville.* (Protector of the city—but *which* city?) Dunphy knocked back the Becherovka and poured himself another. Finally, he asked, "So, why is she black?"

Max snorted. "Who knows? Maybe is from smoke. Five hundred years, candles and incense."

Dunphy thought about that for a moment and shook his head. "I don't think so. I mean . . . if you look, it's just her hands and face. If it was smoke, why aren't her robes black, too?"

Max sighed. "You're asking Jew about Christian mysticism? How should I know? Are we talking about security passes—or mystery cults?"

Dunphy shook his head, as if to clear it. "Okay. So you go to this place . . . "

"Einsiedeln. Is in mountains."

"And you go there, and . . . then what?"

"I go there and make replica of statue, or buy one. Once I have that, I can duplicate hologram. But even then, you still have problem."

"What." Dunphy said the word without inflection, as if it were an answer, as if it were a demand.

"Fingerprint."

"Why is that a problem? If you're gonna remake the thing, all you have to do is put one of mine on the pass. I mean, that's the point, isn't it?"

"Of course, but . . . maybe it doesn't work."

"Why not?"

"Because . . . " Max was silent for a long while.

"Because what?" Dunphy insisted.

The Russian shifted uncomfortably in his chair. "I am thinking, why is fingerprint on pass?"

"For identification," Dunphy answered. "Obviously."

Max nodded his head impatiently, as if Dunphy had missed the point. "Of course, but . . . how does it work?"

Dunphy thought about it. "They compare the fingerprint on the pass to . . . "

"What?"

Dunphy frowned. "My thumbprint," he said, and rubbed his forefinger against his thumb. "They probably have a scanner at the door—where you go in. So if the fingerprint on the pass matches the fingerprint on the thumb, everything's jake."

"Yes," Max replied. "Good. I hope so."

For a moment, each of the men sunk into their own thoughts. Finally, Dunphy asked, "What do you mean, you *hope* so?"

The Russian nodded. "Yes, because . . . is possible— maybe this is more complicated."

"How could it be more complicated?"

"Maybe they have prints on file."

"Yea-ah? Then what?"

"If they have prints on file, maybe they don't compare *two* prints. Maybe they compare *three*—one on finger, one on pass, one on file."

Dunphy thought about it. "Well, if they do that," he said, "I'm fucked."

"Yes, totally, I agree."

A long silence ensued.

Finally, Dunphy asked, "So what do we do?"

The Russian's shoulders rose and fell. "Maybe, you take chance?"

Dunphy shook his head. "I don't think so. There's like a big downside."

"Okay! So I make new pass—and special fingerprint."

"What do you mean?"

Max ignored the question. "You know, fingerprints are interesting business."

Dunphy's eyes narrowed, but Max paid no attention.

"Like treads on tire. Give fingers traction—so don't slip." Max sipped his Becherovka. "Buenos Aires police were maybe first to use," he continued. "Hundred years ago. And no false positives—ever! These fingerprints are more reliable than DNA, irises—anything! Absolutely best biometric."

"Well, that's great," Dunphy said, "but what's it got to do with me and the guy on the pass?"

Max glanced at the pass and said, "I could copy Mr. Brading's fingerprint to new ID. That would give us match with file copy. And then, I make little *glove*—"

"A *glove*?" Dunphy said.

"A *little* glove. Just for thumb. I could digitize this man's fingerprint, and use laser to etch it onto . . . I don't know what. Latex . . . lambskin—"

"I'm not shopping for a condom, Max."

"Or soft plastic—like for contact lenses. We could glue it to your thumb! And you know what?" The Russian beamed. "It would probably work!"

"Probably?"

"Absolutely! It would absolutely probably work."

Dunphy thought about it. Finally he said, "These are unforgiving people, Max. Don't you give a guarantee, or something?"

Max laughed. "Of course! Whatever guarantee you want! Just like washing machine!"

"I'm serious."

"So am I," he said, suddenly sober. "But, this is complicated. Is like printing money—and not just American money. I mean hard kind. Francs, marks, guilders . . . " He picked up the pass and brought it closer to his eyes. "Look—is thread! *There!*"

"So what?"

"So . . . it could be imperfection. Or, maybe, security thread. I need to look at it with microscope. If it's security thread, there could be microprinting on it. A few words, over and over."

"Like what?"

Max chuckled. " 'Shoot this man.' "

"Very funny," Dunphy said, and paused. Then he shook his head. "Look: just do what you have to. But, for Christ's sake, get it right the first time."

"Naturally. But . . . we have to talk money. Otherwise . . . I don't know what else to say about it."

"I thought we might. How much will you need?"

"Believe me, it would be easier to counterfeit guilders for the blind—"

"How *much*, Max?"

The Russian opened his mouth, gulped, and shrugged. "Twenty-five thousand."

Dunphy stared at him.

The Russian cleared his throat. "Is difficult!"

Dunphy thought about it. On the one hand, it was a rip-off. On the other hand, the money wasn't his. "It has to be perfect," he warned.

"Of course! And passport? This, I do for cost!"

"And how much would that be?"

"Five thousand."

"That's very generous, Max."

"Thank you. Of course . . . "

Dunphy's eyes narrowed. "What?"

"There is deposit for credit cards. How much you want? Five thousand? Two thousand?"

"Ten would be grand," Dunphy told him. "And what does that bring us to? Forty thousand?"

Max made a face. "Is cost of doing business," he explained.

"Oh, I realize that," Dunphy said. "But there's a wee something else."

Max raised his eyebrows in an unasked question.

"I need you to front the money, Max. And then I need you to bring the whole nine yards to Zürich when it's done. I can't come back here."

Max winced. "Please—Kerry, I'm not Tele Pizza," he said.

Dunphy finished his second Becherovka, put the glass down, and got to his feet. "I'll pay you fifty-thousand dollars— that's ten grand more than you asked for, and what you asked for was extortion. But it has to be perfect. It has to be quick. You have to front the costs—and you have to bring it to Zürich."

You could almost hear the wheels turning in the Russian's head: *ka-ching! ka-ching! ka-ching!* "Okay," he said. "For you—"

"I'll call you in a few days."

Max looked doubtful. "Maybe telephone is not so good. Prick from embassy—"

"The telephone is fine. I'll ask for a woman—Genevieve. You say it's a wrong number and hang up, like you're pissed off. Then you get on a plane to Zürich—right away— okay?"

Max nodded.

"You know the Zum Storchen?" Dunphy asked.

"Sure. In Old Town—by river."

"Get a room there, and I'll meet you."

Max stood up and shook hands. Then he frowned.

"What's the matter?" Dunphy asked.

"I worry."

"About what?"

"About you."

Dunphy was touched. "Oh, Max, for Christ's sake—"

"Is big problem. Holograms are expensive. You get killed, how do I get paid?"

"I don't know," Dunphy said. "It's a conundrum. But thanks for your concern."

17

Threads of rain. The screech of tires. A smattering of applause. And then, the flight attendant, welcoming them to "London's Heathrow Airport."

An hour later, Dunphy was rattling through the West End on the Piccadilly Line, thinking about the last time he'd taken the Underground. In one way, almost nothing had changed. He'd been on the run from murder then, and he was on the run from murder now. Not that anything was actually the same: four months ago, he'd been fleeing someone else's murder; and now, as the train rocked through the same watery landscape, he was escaping his own. And that made all the difference.

Or it should have. In fact, he was having difficulty concentrating. His mind was everywhere at once. No matter what he thought about, or tried to think about, the murder scene in McLean flashed through his mind like the cheap snapshot that it was.

Clementine.

Roscoe

What would she do when he appeared on her doorstep? Out of nowhere. Unannounced.

Strangled

Dunphy hoped that she'd be overjoyed, but he suspected that her happiness at seeing him would be tempered by a wish to kill him. After all, he'd run out on her. Or so it seemed.

Hanging there

And then there was "the situation"—Dunphy and the world, Dunphy versus the world. This was the subject that had his mind racing like a digital stopwatch, the hundredths turning over in a liquid-crystal blur.

He was traveling on a legitimate passport—which was both good and bad. It was good because the British had zero interest in an American named Dunphy. Their concern (admittedly intense) rested with a notional Irish national named Kerry Thornley—who'd disappeared some months before. Thornley was a suspect character, all right, but his connection to Dunphy was unknown to them. All of which was fine.

The bad part was that the Agency would soon find out that he'd obtained a new passport in his own name. And knowing that, they'd begin to look for him abroad and, in particular, in England. This was, indeed, the bad part, Dunphy mused, as the train disgorged a flood of passengers at Earl's Court. And another bad bit about the name was that Clementine would want an explanation.

Eyes, tongue, and the plastic bag over his head

A startled look flashed upon the face of the woman across from him, and Dunphy realized that he'd actually moaned aloud. So he smiled ruefully and muttered, "Tooth." The woman looked relieved.

Maybe he should have gone to the Canaries, *directly* to the Canaries. Looked up Tommy Davis. Gone on a bender. Gotten laid. After a while, the whole business might have blown over.

Right, Dunphy thought. As if . . . In his considerable experience, things almost never blew over. If they blew in any direction, they tended to blow things *away*. (Usually people.) And besides, it wasn't just a matter of being on the run. He was on a mission: *when I find the guy who whacked Roscoe, I'll . . .*

What? What would he do? What would he actually *do*? Would he kill the guy? Dunphy thought about it and decided that he would. Definitely. In *cold blood*? Yeah. He would. He could do that. But that wasn't the point. Not really. It wasn't a question of "a guy." Roscoe's killer was a soldier ant in someone else's army, and it was the "someone else" that Dunphy wanted. Or to be exact: him, the army, *and* the guy.

When I find him, I'll kill him with my hands. And then I'll bury him. That was the important part—the burial. Because without it, he wouldn't be able to piss on the man's grave.

Twenty minutes later, Dunphy was standing in the rain outside Clementine's flat, looking up at the second-floor window, wondering if she was watching *him*. And then he was at her door, knocking. A couple of soft taps. Harder.

"Clem?" His voice was a whisper. "Clem?" No answer.

Ah well, he thought, she's not here, and turned to leave, at once disappointed and relieved. He was thinking that he'd come back tomorrow, when, suddenly, he heard the latch turn and the door swing open.

"Kerry?"

He turned to her, suitcase in hand, and it was as if his eyes inhaled her—a straight shot to the brain. She'd been sleeping, and an aura of warmth and softness clung to her.

"Jack," he answered, shuffling his feet. "Actually, it's Jack Dunphy." He paused and added, "No more lies."

He was grinning like a dunce as he stepped toward her, reaching out to take her in his arms—and so was unprepared for the palm of her hand, whistling out of nowhere to land onto his cheek.

"Ow—Jesus!"

"You *prick*," she said.

She went after him again, this time leading with her right, but he caught it just in time and pulled her to him. "Don't do that," he said. "It hurts." He shook his head to clear it. Then the fierceness left her as suddenly as it had come. Tears welled in her eyes as she subsided into his arms. "I missed you *so* much," she said. "You made me so unhappy."

Together, they went inside, passing directly from the living room to bed. Falling into each other's arms, they made love with the urgency of desperadoes. And again. Then the light began to fade, and him, too—until, quite suddenly, it was night, and Clementine was shaking him awake.

They went to a Greek restaurant in Charlotte Street, all

wood smoke and candles. At a table in the corner, Dunphy tried to explain, in the most circumspect and inarticulate way, why he'd had to leave England. "It was one of those things that . . . well, you know, it was something that . . . well, to tell you the truth, there wasn't anything I could do about it. I mean . . . the people I work for—or *worked* for—"

"Exactly, and who *was* that? You haven't really said."

"Well . . . that was . . . actually, that was a government agency."

"So you're a spy."

Dunphy shook his head. "No. I *was* a spy. Now, I'm . . . " He didn't know quite how to finish.

"What?"

"Well, *now,* I guess you'd have to say I'm unemployed."

"You're redundant, then?"

"Yes. That's exactly it. I'm redundant. I am absolutely fucking redundant."

She cocked her head to the side and looked at him. "And just what does that mean . . . in the spy business?"

"Pretty much what it means anywhere else." Suddenly, he leaned toward her with a confidential smile. "The waiter's in love with you," he whispered.

She gave him a look. "You're changing the subject."

"I can't help it," he said.

"Why not?"

"There's a thing called 'need to know.' "

"So?"

"You don't have one."

Clementine frowned. "We'll see about that," she said.

A silence fell between them. Finally, and seemingly out of the blue—and seemingly apropos of nothing—Dunphy asked, "So . . . still taking classes at King's?"

Clementine nodded. "Mmmm," she said.

"Y'know, I was wondering, about the professor. The one who died—old what's-his-name . . . Schidlof. Do you think I could talk with one of his students?"

"Dunno!" Clem replied, savoring an olive. "Maybe. Do you know who they are?"

"No. I haven't a clue," Dunphy said. "How would I know that?"

Clem shrugged. "You're the bloody spy, not me. I thought the CIA knew everything."

"Yeah, well, maybe, but . . . at the moment, I'm not in a position to ask the Agency a lot of questions. Still . . . maybe there's a list of some kind. I mean, the school has to keep track of who took what!"

"Of course it does. But I don't know anyone in the registrar's office, and even if I did, there's a privacy issue. They'd never give it to me." She paused. "Why are you smiling?"

"The way you said *privacy*. With a soft *i*."

"That makes you *happy*?"

"Yeah."

Clementine rolled her eyes. "Well! *You're* quite the cheap date, then, aren't you?"

The waiter delivered plates of moussaka, dolmades, and hummus to their table, and filled Dunphy's glass with a pale yellow wine that tasted remarkably like shellac. They fell into a comfortable silence, quietly enjoying one another's company. Suddenly, Clem looked up from her plate, leaned forward, and exclaimed, "Simon!"

"What?"

"Simon!"

Dunphy looked around. "What am I supposed to do? Close my eyes? Spin around? What?"

"Simon was taking psychology courses. It's a big department, but . . . he *might* have had a class with Schidlof."

"Can you call him?"

She shook her head. "I don't think he has a phone. And I don't know his last name."

Dunphy's shoulders sank. "That's gonna make it harder."

"But we could see him."

"Where?"

"At the market in Camden Lock. His parents have a sort of kiosk. Plumbing fixtures, old uniforms. Usual hodgepodge."

"You'll introduce me?" he asked.

"If you'll buy me a Sgt. Pepper's jacket—absolutely."

Sunday was cold, and the wind chill out of the Underground was ferocious. Riding the long escalator up to the street, Dunphy and Clementine leaned into one another, bracing against the vacuum-driven gale.

"Fuckin' 'ell," Clem said. "I'm freezin', and I'm not even outside!" She held his right arm tightly, with both hands, as if he might try to escape, and jittered on her feet to keep her toes from freezing.

She was effortlessly beautiful, in the way that models sometimes are when they pass through airports in New York, Paris, and Milan. Her clothes were just a happenstance, the first things she'd found to wear that morning: a ratty cotton sweater (black); a pair of jeans (also black, and frayed at the knees). Soft leather boots, turned down at the tops, and a thin leather jacket that did nothing to keep her warm. The wind fanned her hair this way and that, covering her face and then revealing it. She hadn't bothered with makeup—but, then, she never needed any. And, anyway, her clear, pale skin was rouged by the cold. Standing beside her on the escalator, rattling toward the surface at a forty-five-degree angle, Dunphy could feel the peripheral gaze of half a dozen men.

The wind ceased the moment they stepped outside, plunging into the tumult and crowds on Camden High Street. The sidewalks were thronged with the young and the stoned, edgy-looking kids in leather jackets, African vendors, drug addicts, headbangers, yuppies, punks, drunks, schizophrenics, tourists—and a mime. The air was a casserole of sweet and sour smells, of roasting chestnuts and stale beer, sausages, onions, and sweat. And all of it stirred by the contending rhythms of reggae, rap, and zouk, Yellowman, Bill Haley, and Pearl Jam. Clem held his hand tightly, her face alight as they let the crowds carry them along the street past rickety stands heaped with sweaters, racks of clothes, and trays of bootlegged tapes.

"It's like the summer of love," she said. "Except it's winter and freezing. And I guess the people look different."

Dunphy grunted. "I'm sure you're right, but what do *you* know about the summer of love? You weren't even protein."

"I saw a documentary."

They found Simon at his parents' shop, which turned out to be an open storefront amid a warren of alleys, alcoves, and rooms that, long ago, had been a part of the city's stables. Rail thin and twenty something, Simon braved the cold in a Pink Floyd T-shirt, blue jeans, and Doc Martens. A Betty Boop tattoo was embedded in the flesh where a bicep should have been. Nearby, an electric heater glowed the bright orange that hunters wear in deer season.

Seeing Clem, Simon went off like a flare. "Hal-lo," he cried, and staggered toward her with his arms wide. Embracing, they rocked from side to side for what Dunphy thought was a bit too long. Finally, Simon noticed him and, somewhat sheepishly, stepped back. "Cuppa tea? For you and your friend?"

"No—"

" 'Course ya will!" he said, and disappeared behind a tassled curtain.

Dunphy looked at her. "I thought you said you didn't know him very well."

Clementine shook her head. "What I actually *said* was, I didn't know his last name."

Moments later, Simon reemerged from behind the curtain, carrying a pair of chipped and steaming cups. "Tetley. Best I can do. But it *is* hot." He handed the cups to Dunphy and Clementine and plopped into one of the many easy chairs that were scattered around the room. "So," he said, rubbing his hands together with an avaricious look, "what's it to be? Good-as-new showerhead? Slightly used vibrator? Look no further!"

Clem shook her head. "Not today, thanks. Jack's interested in that professor—the one that was done."

"Schidlof?"

"Right," Clem said. "I told Jack you'd taken one of his classes—or I thought you had."

Simon looked at Dunphy more closely. "You a cop, then?"

"No," Dunphy said.

"Friend of the family?"

Dunphy shook his head. "Uh-uh . . . just a friend of Clem's."

Simon nodded. "Right, well, she's got more friends than Bill, doesn't she?"

Dunphy smiled. "I suspect she does, but . . . you *did* take his class, right?"

"Yeah. So what?"

"I was hoping you might have saved your notes."

"Wha'? From Schidlof's class?"

"Yeah."

"Not likely. And if I did, the police would have 'em by now, wouldn't they?"

"I don't know. Why would they?"

"Because they came 'round. You took the class, you got a visit."

"And they confiscated the students' notes?"

"Said they were collecting evidence. 'Evidence of what?' I asked. 'Never you mind!' they said. Real exercise in academic freedom, that was."

"Well," Dunphy asked, "can you tell me about the class?"

"Yeah?"

"What was it about?"

Simon looked at Clementine as if to ask, Who *is* this guy? Clem shrugged, as if to say, *Humor him*.

"Welllll," Simon said, "it was a bit complicated, wasn't it?"

"I don't know. I wasn't there."

"*I* was. And it was *very* complicated."

"Perhaps you could be a bit more specific, Simon," Clementine suggested.

The kid took a deep breath and sighed. "Right," he said, and turned to Dunphy. "Know much about Jung?"

Dunphy shook his head. "Not really."

"Well, that makes it harder, then, doesn't it? I mean—this wasn't a basic course. It was a seminar."

"In Jung?"

"It was called Mapping the Archetypal Field, and what it was about was . . . " Simon glanced helplessly at Clem, who reassured him with a twinkle. With a smile, he took a deep breath, cleared his throat, and turned to Dunphy. "Right!" he repeated. "What it was about was: Jung. Founder of analytic psychology. Colleague of Freud. Now regarded with a measure of suspicion for what critics say was an inordinate interest in *volkish* matters. Which is to say, he's suspected of taking a few too many phone calls from the bunker. Not to mention that he's said to have fabricated patient histories. I could mention the Solar Phallus Man."

"The who?"

"The Solar Phallus Man."

"And who was he?"

Simon shrugged. "A nutter," he said. "But not a relevant one, at least not to us. Because we didn't study the case. I'm just giving you a bit of background. Because it's a big subject. I mean, old Jung had lots of ideas—about religion. Myth. Alchemy. *Synchronicity.*"

"What's that?" Clem asked.

Simon frowned, and his eyes asked, *How to put it?*

"It's the idea that coincidences are something other than coincidental," Dunphy told her.

"Very good!" Simon exclaimed. "That's exactly right. Synchronicity is . . . just what you said: it's the idea of meaningful coincidence."

"Is that what the seminar was about?" Dunphy asked.

"No," Simon replied. "It was supposed to be an exploration of the collective unconscious—which is . . . " The kid fell into thought, his breath hanging in the cold like cumulus clouds. Dunphy was about to break the silence when the younger man put a finger in the air, looked up, and began to quote from memory: "Which *is* . . . a 'matrix . . . of images and dreams, embodying'—I hope you're listening, because every word's a jewel—'*embodying* the phylogenetic experience of all mankind, connecting and affecting everyone, everywhere.' " Simon shut his trap and smiled.

Dunphy nodded, but Clem was unimpressed. "What's that, then?" she asked.

Simon sighed, the wind gone from his sails. Finally, he said, "It's like the Internet—except without the advertising. Or you could say it's a cloud of ideas and images, but *big* ideas and *powerful* images—the kind that can fuck you up—and they're everywhere and nowhere, all at once. And the modem, the modem's hardwired into the back of your head. The main difference being, you don't jack into the collective unconscious. It jacks into *you.*"

Clem smiled. "That's what I thought," she said. "I've always believed that." Dunphy did a double take. She was seated beside him in a tattered easy chair with her legs crossed, leaning forward and hugging herself against the cold. Her right foot tapped the air, impatient or freezing or both. "Now, give it up," she said, turning to Dunphy.

"Give what up?"

"The wallet. You promised me a coat. So let's have it."

Dunphy grimaced, reached into his back pocket, and handed his wallet to her.

"I'll only be a minute," she told them. "I know just where I'm going." And with that, she got to her feet, turned on her heel, and sauntered off. Dunphy and Simon looked after her until she turned a corner, and then they returned to the subject at hand.

"Where were we?" Simon asked.

" 'It jacks into you,' " Dunphy answered.

"And so it does."

Dunphy thought for a moment. His feet were frozen, toes numb. Finally, he said, "The thing is, I don't see how any of that could get anyone killed."

"Well, you had to be there. Schidlof could be pretty lethal at eight in the morning. I mean, some of us *were* bored to death."

Dunphy acknowledged the pun with a thin smile and asked, "But what was his take on it all? You said it was a seminar, a seminar in . . . what? Mapping—"

"—the archetypal field. Right! As I said. But what you have to understand is Schidlof was a believer. To him, this wasn't just a theory. The unconscious—the collective unconscious—was as real as you or me. Which meant that it could be described—or mapped—or enumerated—at least in terms of its contents."

"What contents?"

"The archetypes. When Schidlof talked about the collective unconscious, he was talking about a field of *archetypes*—primordial images, pictures, and pictograms that go back to the beginning of time. Which is mind-blowing when you think of it."

"And the point of all this was . . . what?" Dunphy asked.

Simon thought for a moment and said, "I think Schidlof was trying to prove a theory."

"A theory of what?" Dunphy asked.

"It's just a guess."

"I'm listening."

"He was working on a biography of Jung, and apparently, he found some papers—in Switzerland. He was always going to Zürich for research. To interview people and—"

"What papers?"

"Letters. Something no one had ever seen before. He said it would make a splash when his book came out."

Dunphy thought about it. Finally he asked, "So what do you think he was trying to prove?"

Simon pursed his lips and grimaced. "He didn't talk about it much, but once or twice, he let on."

"Yeah?"

"Well, he thought someone—or something—he never said

what—but he thought . . . well, he thought . . . someone was manipulating things."

"What things?"

"The collective unconscious."

"What?"

"He thought someone was reprogramming the collective unconscious—introducing *new* archetypes, revitalizing old ones."

"And just how would you *do* that?" Dunphy asked, his voice thick with skepticism.

Simon shrugged. "Dunno. But if you did . . . well, you'd rewire the human race, wouldn't you? I mean, you'd be sitting right at the switchboard. You'd have your hands on the back brain of the whole planet! So what Schidlof was up to with the seminar—and this is just *my* idea, you understand—I think he wanted to make an inventory, a sort of *catalog*, of the archetypes—to see if we could identify any of the new ones. Or any that we felt had been . . . revitalized."

"And did you?"

Simon surprised him. "Yeah," he said. "I think we did."

"Like what?"

"Well, UFOs, obviously—"

"Obviously?"

"Yeah. Obviously, because Jung wrote a book about them, back in the fifties, and . . . well, he said it then. He called them 'an emerging new archetype.' And the 'forerunner of the Messiah.' That's a quote. And he said they signaled the birth of a new age." Simon paused and, with a twinkle, added, "So that was a pretty good clue."

"What else?"

Simon tilted his head from one side to another. "We talked about crop circles, cattle mutilations, lots of—*What?*"

Dunphy shook his head, which seemed to be spinning. "Nothing," he replied.

"Well, anyway, the next thing you know, the professor was popped, the cops took our notes—and that was that. End of seminar."

Dunphy was quiet for a moment. Finally he asked, "Why cattle mutilations?"

Simon snorted. "Well, it's an animal sacrifice, i'nit? Old as the hills. Schidlof said someone was stirring the pot. 'Revitalizing a dormant archetype.' "

"But *why*?"

Simon shook his head. "Dunno. But if you believe Jung—and in Schidlof's class, you'd *better* believe Jung—it's all tied up with religion. Second Coming. New age. That sort of thing." The kid looked around for a moment and started to get up. "Look," he said, "I'm losing customers . . . "

"There's fifty quid in it for you."

He sat back down. "Anyway," Simon went on, "if you ask me, it's bollocks."

Dunphy nodded, eyes on the floor, trying hard to connect the dots. Finally he shook his head.

"If you want to know what I think . . . ," Simon said.

"About what?" Dunphy asked.

"Schidlof's death. If it was me and I was interested, I'd call traffic control out at bloody Heathrow. Ask *them* what *they* saw."

"What do you mean?"

"I mean, the fucking helicopter."

"What helicopter?"

"Quiet. The papers didn't report it, but it was *seen*. I read about it on the Internet: alt.rec.mutes. The kid what found old Schidlof said the papers were wrong: he didn't *trip* over the professor. Kid said this great, bloody chopper was sittin' in the air over the Inner Temple—but so quiet, it was more like an *animated* helicopter than a real one. And the next thing he knew, the guv'ner falls out the door and drops with a plop on the lawn. Said he fell about fifty feet."

"Fuck," Dunphy said.

"I'm serious!"

"I know you are, but—"

Simon grinned, saw Clementine, and waved to her as she walked back into the store. A long blue jacket with gold epaulets hung from her shoulders to midthigh. Above her left breast, an ormolu hammer-and-sickle was pinned next to an AIDS ribbon.

"You two still at it?" she asked, handing Dunphy his wallet.

Dunphy shook his head. "No, I think we're probably done. How much did that set me back?" he asked, nodding at the coat.

"Sixty quid," Clem replied.

Dunphy grunted, took a fifty-pound note from his wallet, and handed it to Simon. "Ta," he said.

"That's it, then?" The kid slid the money into his pocket.

"Yeah," Dunphy replied, getting to his feet. "That's it. My head's spinning."

Simon's grin grew ever wider. "Did I help?"

"Yeah," Dunphy said. "You were a big help. Now I'm *totally* confused."

18

He couldn't sleep.

He lay in the bed beside Clementine and watched the lights of cars climb the walls and slide across the ceiling. Music seeped through the windowpanes from somewhere down the street—an old Leonard Cohen song, played over and over. And then, quite suddenly, nothing—the silence hitting him like a ship's engine cutting out at sea.

He rolled toward her and, with his left arm, pulled her to him. He buried his face in the warmth of her hair, lay still for a bit—and rolled away. His mind was at the races.

Sitting up, he swung his feet from the bed and looked around. A shaft of watery light, cast by the street lamp outside, poured through the windows, pooling on the surface of a battered red dhurrie. On the bedside table, books.

Dunphy squinted: *The Genesis Code. Time's Arrow. The Van.* He hadn't realized that she read so much.

Getting to his feet, he dressed slowly and quietly, standing in the pale darkness of the room. He wanted to go for a long run, but that was out. He hadn't any running shoes, shorts, or socks. But he could walk. And that would be better than sitting in the dark.

The apartment was too small, really, for him to stay awake while she slept. It was a single room with a high ceiling and a bank of double-glazed windows that looked out on Bolton Gardens. Just around the corner from the hip and busy Old Brompton Road, it had been a pied-à-terre for Clem's actress aunt, an older woman who'd moved to Los Angeles the year before. It cost nothing and came with a season's pass to the football matches at Stamford Bridge.

He could hear Clementine's soft breathing as he closed the door behind him and followed the stairs down to the street. Though it wasn't yet five in the morning, he was more than wide awake. *Matta. Blémont. Roscoe. Schidlof.* Their faces came and went like flash cards.

Walking along Cromwell Road in the direction of Thurloe Square, he passed the Victoria and Albert Museum, then turned up Brompton Road in the direction of Harrod's. It was the same road, really, but its name changed every few blocks, as if the street was on the run. It amused him to think that, in this, he and Cromwell Road held something in common.

It was a night meant for lovers. A warm front was rolling in from the west, riding a tide of fog that caught the starlight and smudged it. The air was fresh and effervescent. Passing Harrod's, he crossed the street to the Scotch House and stood for a while beneath its awning, looking at the window. There was no reason to think that he might have been followed, but under the circumstances, paranoia died hard. So he studied the world behind his back in the reflection before him. And was relieved to see only himself. Turning away from the Scotch House, he crossed the street in the direction of the old Hyde Park Hotel, then kept on walking until he was in the park itself.

I should call Max, he thought. From a pay phone. But, no. There was no point calling Max, or seeing him, either—not until he'd gone to the bank. Not until he'd gotten the money.

In a way, and very much in spite of the circumstances, he was looking forward to it. He and Clem could spend a day or two in St. Helier enjoying one another—until it was time for him to go to Zürich.

He walked for a while along Rotten Row, then crossed the grass to the banks of the Serpentine.

The first time he'd seen the lake had been at a track meet. He had been twenty years old at the time, and it had been the only time in anyone's memory that the Bates College track team had actually gone abroad. He'd run the mile, finishing a respectable fourth against a dozen other schools. Oxford, Haverford, Morehouse, Harvard. He forgot who else was there, but he'd never forget his time: 4:12 and change, his best ever.

Fog rose from the lake like steam. That was twelve years ago, Dunphy thought. And I'm still running.

The air was brighter now, as if the night had begun to anticipate the sun. Dunphy wandered along a path that took him out of the park, and then returned the way he'd come, retracing his steps along Brompton Road and Cromwell Gardens. At the Gloucester Road Underground, he stopped at a workmen's café for a cup of tea and a scone. The place was just beginning to fill with men in steel-toed boots and dirty jeans, and the air was thick with the smoke of cheap cigarettes. It was a warm and secret sort of place, sequestered from the street by a clouded window that ran with steam. The tea was hot, sweet, and delicious, and he took his time drinking it, reading an abandoned copy of the *Sun*. Manchester United was on top again, and Fergie . . . well, Fergie was stooging for Weight Watchers.

When he was done, he left the café and continued walking down Cromwell Road in the direction of Bolton Gardens. The sun was just below the horizon now, and the street had begun to brighten and stir. A man in a three-piece suit and a bowler hurried toward the Underground. With the *Times* under one arm and a furled umbrella lashed to his attaché case, he seemed an apparition—the Ghost of Business Past, or something like it.

Trash cans tumbled and crashed in a nearby alley as the dustmen went about their work. And then he heard another sound, one that he couldn't quite place: a faraway whine that grew louder and lower until, turning, he suddenly realized what it was—the growl of pure acceleration. The source was a black Jaguar and, no sooner had Dunphy identified it, than the car dopplered past so quickly that, seeing it, he gasped. Jesus, he thought, where the fuck are *they* going—and where are the cops when you need them? He watched as the car decelerated sharply in the vicinity of Collingham Road. There was a popping sound, like distant gunfire, and the Jag swung left, fishtailed, and disappeared.

Collingham Road was Dunphy's turn, as well. Trudging along in the Jaguar's wake, he saw the first rays of morning strike the third-story windows of the mansion blocks on his right. It was a five-minute walk to Clem's flat, and when he got there, he knew immediately that something was very wrong. The Jag was outside her apartment, nearly three feet from the curb, so illegally parked as to seem abandoned. Dunphy stood for a moment, listening to its engine cool, ticking, then turned on his heel and walked back in the direction from which he'd come. There was no doubt in his mind that the car's occupants were there for him. How many, then? Two? Three? Two. And given the way they'd driven, and the way they'd abandoned their car, it was obvious they didn't just want to *talk* to him.

They wanted to get *at* him. And feeling that way, when they found him gone from the apartment, what would they do? Would they wait for him to return? Of course. And while they waited, would they take it out on Clem? Maybe—they weren't bobbies, after all. That much was obvious. Cops—bobbies—didn't drive XJ12s. So what would they do? Would they hurt her? Would they *fuck* her? Dunphy didn't have a clue. All he knew was that he had to do something and do it right away—but what? The apartment was a trap, and no matter how much he thought about it, that wouldn't change. In the end, he'd have to take the bait. He'd have to go in. But when? And how?

When he got back to Cromwell Road, he stood in the doorway of the newsagent's, thinking hard. They'd ask Clementine where he was, and when she said she didn't know—and she didn't—they'd smack her around. They'd do this because they *could*, and because there wasn't any downside to it. Maybe she'd change her mind, and if she didn't, so what?

It occurred to Dunphy that he might be able to affect this

with a telephone call. He bought a Fonecard from the news-agent's and crossed the street to a pay phone outside the Cat & Bells. There, he slotted the card into the box, punched in her number, and listened to the telephone ring in her flat.

If she was alone, he'd know it. He'd hear it in her voice, no matter what it was that she actually *said*. And if she wasn't alone, he'd know that, too, because they'd never let her answer. They couldn't, because they had no way of knowing what she'd say or do. And it would take only a word to warn him, an inflection, or a long silence. If they were any good, they'd know that, and if they worked for the Agency, as Dunphy suspected, they were probably very good, indeed.

"Hullo—Clem here!" Dunphy jumped, and the tension slid from his shoulders. She was fine. She was happy. And she wasn't faking it. He could tell from her tone.

"Oh, babe," he began, "I was—"

"I'm out of the flat or on the other line just now, but if you'll leave your name and number, I'll ring you up as soon as I return."

Fuck. It was an answering machine. His shoulders tightened and bunched as he waited for the beep. When it finally came, he did his best to sound nonchalant. "Yeah, Clem! It's Jack. Sorry I had to go out. Listen—I won't be back for a couple of hours—I'm all the way across town—but stay where you are and I'll treat you to breakfast."

He hung up the phone and looked around. That should hold them for a while, and a while was just what he needed. Time to think—about how to get them out of the flat, how to make them come to *him*. And not just *come* to him, but come to him in a *panic*. Dunphy groaned. This could take some time, he thought, because I haven't got a clue.

Turning into the alley behind the Cat & Bells, he passed an abandoned sofa, moldering in the stink from a nearby Dumpster. The sofa reminded him how tired he was, but it didn't tempt him to sit. Its cushions were covered with a paisley bedspread so leprous with grime that Dunphy couldn't guess its color. They ought to burn that thing, Dunphy thought. And that made him think again.

Twenty minutes later, and fifty quid lighter, Jack Dunphy was walking up Collingham Road with a long strip of paisley in one hand and a can of gas in the other. Turning the corner into Bolton Gardens, he crossed the street to the Jag and, using the can as a battering ram, smashed the window on the driver's side. Brushing the webs of shattered glass aside, he leaned through the window and, reaching down to the floor, popped the latch on the gas tank. Then he went around to the back of the car.

He was in plain view of the flat, but there wasn't anything he could do about that. If the car's owners were watching the street, they'd see him—but that was unlikely. He wasn't expected for a couple of hours. Still . . .

He shoved a length of the rag into the gas tank and let the rest hang down to the street. Pulling open the doors to the car, he shook the gas onto the seats and tossed the jerry can inside. His heart was pounding, jump-started by the stench of gasoline. Patting his pockets, he found the three-penny box of Swans and, taking one out, was about to strike it—when he heard a sound and turned.

He expected to be shot in the face. He expected a man with a string tie and a gun—but it was a woman in a nightdress, standing on the porch behind him, holding a bottle of milk, staring at him.

"Is this your car, madam?"

The woman shook her head slowly.

"Then it might be best if you went back inside."

She nodded and took a step backward, feeling for the doorknob. Finding it, she let herself into the house, closed the door quietly behind her, and yelped—a terse little cry that was all vowels and went nowhere. Dunphy turned his back on the noise, struck a match, and, stooping, touched it to the bottom of the rag. Then he started running, sprinting toward Clementine's, wondering how long it would take before—

Whuuuummmppp! The noise was like a carpet being struck, a single blow with a flat broom—and then a sound like cellophane crackling, and a shout from somewhere up the street. The air was suddenly very warm.

Clem's flat was on the second floor of a Victorian duplex with a small porch and white columns. A galvanized iron trash can stood by the curb, and seeing it, Dunphy grabbed its cover on the run. Taking the steps three at a time, he ran to the front door, pushed it open, and, stepping back, waited. By now, the car was ablaze, fulminating with smoke and fire, and the postman was running up and down the street, yelling insanely, shouting at the houses in a cockney accent. *Oiii! Oiiii!*

Still, Dunphy waited, wired, his shirt damp with sweat and adrenaline. Any second, the men in the flat would hear the commotion, and when they did, they'd walk to the window and—

"*FUCK! FUCK!* He's torched the fuckin' car!" The words burst in the air like a Roman candle shot from the windows of Clem's apartment. Three seconds later, a door crashed open on the second floor, and Dunphy heard the *thump-thump-thump* of a man coming down the stairs in a hurry. And then the noise was in the vestibule, and Dunphy, proud of his timing, was pivoting on the balls of his feet, swinging the trash-can cover through 180 degrees, slamming it full tilt into the face of a running man who never saw it coming. What looked like a Walther flew from his hand as his feet left the ground, bicycling toward the roof. There was a moment in which he seemed to be suspended in the air, his head level with his toes, about three feet off the ground—as if he were part of a magician's trick. And then he dropped to the porch, flat and hard, and lay there, twitching soundlessly. Well, Dunphy thought, *that* worked. Stooping, he picked up the gun (it *was* a Walther) and glanced at the man on the ground. His nose was broken and there was a lot of blood, but he was still breathing—and Dunphy recognized him. It was Everyboy, the kid with the tattooed wrists, the sarcastic courier who'd carried a sign at the airport, waiting for Mr. Torbitt. (What was the last thing he'd said? *Have a nice day?!*)

Dunphy picked a tooth—an incisor—out of the sole of his shoe and edged into the doorway.

"Freddy? Freddy?" Jesse Curry's plaintive voice drifted down from the second floor.

"Down 'ere!" Dunphy whispered, his voice urgent, clipped, and unconvincingly cockney.

"Is that you, Freddy? Where are you, then?"

Dunphy didn't answer. He was afraid that if he said more than a word or two, Curry would recognize his voice. Stepping into the vestibule, he ducked behind the stairs and held his breath. If Curry was smart, Dunphy thought, he'd stay where he was.

But he wasn't, and he didn't. There was a brief scuffle on the stairs above, and Clem's voice—"Owww! You prick!"

"Shut up!" Curry muttered.

"Owww!"

"Freddy? C'mon, guy—talk to me."

Dunphy could hear the fire department klaxoning toward Collingham Road and, under the noise, Curry's footsteps as he moved slowly down the stairs, pushing Clementine in front of him. A moment later, Dunphy could see them: Curry held her close to him by the hair at the back of her head, bunching it tightly in his left hand and pulling it back, keeping her off balance and compliant at the same time. His right hand waved a gun in the general direction of the front door.

Which, Dunphy knew, was not the way you did this sort of thing. If you had a hostage, you put the barrel to her head and kept it there. Otherwise, someone like Dunphy could step up from behind (as, in fact, Dunphy did at that very moment), and smack you in the back of the head—which Dunphy also did, slamming the butt of the Walther into the mastoid bone just behind Curry's ear.

Clem yelped with surprise as Curry staggered, swayed, and fell against the wall, dropping his gun. Holding the back of his head with his right hand, he was doubled over and moaning, a soft, sad sound.

Dunphy turned to Clementine. "You okay?" She nodded,

and he could see that it was a lie. Her left eye was swollen, and the side of her face was bruised. "Oh, jeez," Dunphy muttered.

Curry looked up, wincing through the pain. "That wasn't me," he said. "That was Freddy. Ask her—"

"I don't give a fuck about Freddy," Dunphy said. "I wanta know how you found me."

Curry gritted his teeth against the pain and straightened up, wincing. "We had your credit cards tagged."

"Bullshit."

"I'm gonna lie about that? Why the fuck would I lie about that?"

"I don't know."

"I think I've got a concussion."

"I don't care. Now, tell me how you found me."

"I already told you. We traced your credit cards. Talk about stupid. Talk about fucking up . . . "

"I didn't use my cards, Jesse!"

"*She* did. She bought a coat."

"What?"

Curry glanced at Clementine and sneered. "She bought a *coat*. At Camden Lock. Oh-Muh-Darlin' bought a—"

Clem lunged at him, but Dunphy caught her by the arm. "C'mon," he said. "We gotta go."

"What about him?" Clem asked. "He'll just come after us."

Dunphy thought about it. Finally he said, "No, he won't."

"Why not?"

"Because I'm going to shoot him."

Clem's eyes widened, and Curry turned pale. "Heyyyy," he said, backing into the wall.

Dunphy shrugged. "Can't help it. No choice."

"Tie me up!"

"No rope."

"Use a *belt*, for Christ's sake!"

Dunphy shook his head. "Wouldn't work. You'd just get away."

"You can't just shoot him," Clem said.

"Why don't you go outside?" Dunphy suggested.

"No! You'll shoot him."

"I won't."

"He will!" Curry shouted. "Don't leave!"

Dunphy kept his eyes on Curry, but his words were meant for Clem. "Just go out, and make sure the coast is clear. I won't hurt him."

Clementine looked him in the eyes. "You promise?"

"Scout's honor."

Reluctantly, Clem slipped out the front door to the porch. As the door closed behind her, Dunphy took a step toward Curry, and then another. Suddenly, they were toe to toe, the Walther in Dunphy's hand, his arm hanging down by his side.

Curry's back was pressed against the wall, and Dunphy saw that his shirt collar was soaked with blood from where he'd been smacked with the gun. "This is a joke," Curry said. "Right?"

Dunphy shook his head.

"We go back a ways," Curry pleaded. "A long ways."

A soft, derisive puff fell from Dunphy's lips.

"I know what you're lookin' for," Curry insisted. "I could tell you stuff you want to know."

"Yeah, but you'd lie," Dunphy replied. "And, anyway, there's gonna be a lotta cops here, so—well, it's just not a good time."

"But—" Curry's eyes grew round as the muzzle of the Walther pressed against his kneecap.

"Hang on," Dunphy said, "this is only gonna take a second."

"For God's sake, Jack—"

"Stop whining—it's not gonna kill ya." And he fired.

19

They ran hand in hand along the Old Brompton Road, looking over their shoulders, desperate for a taxi. Police cars careened down the street at ferocious speeds, klaxons shrieking. Finally, they found a cab in front of a Pakistani shop that seemed to specialize in plastic luggage.

"Victoria Station," Dunphy said, and yanked the door open. A second later, the two of them fell into the cab's cracked leather seats, lay back, and listened to their hearts slam against their chests. Hot air rattled from a heater on the back of the driver's seat, toasting their ankles.

It was a full minute before Clem looked at him. "Where are we going?" she asked, her voice dull with shock.

Dunphy shook his head. A little nod in the direction of the driver.

"I don't have my passport," Clem said.

"Don't worry about it."

Lost to the world in the thickening rush hour, they rode in silence, with Dunphy doing his best to ignore the tears on his girlfriend's cheeks. After a while, he couldn't take it any longer. "Look," he said, "I didn't have any choice."

She kept her eyes on the street beyond the window.

"And, anyway," he went on, "it's not like—" The driver's eyes loomed in the rearview mirror. Dunphy lowered his voice to a whisper. "It's not like he's gonna croak, for Christ's sake. He's a *tough* guy."

Clem turned to him in disbelief, then looked away.

Dunphy grinned. "A little spackle, a cane—he'll be fine."

She burst into tears.

Dunphy rolled his eyes. "It's the truth. Not that I give a shit, but the son of a bitch'll be hunky-dory in no time."

Clementine looked at him as if he were insane. "And the other man? What about him? Will he be fine, too?"

"A little dental work—he'll be right as rain, doing what he does best."

"And what's that?"

"Hurting people."

Nothing else was said between them until they arrived at the train station. Dunphy gave the driver ten quid, and with Clementine in tow, led her through the crowds to the building's far side, where he hailed a second cab to a second train station—this time, King's Cross. The traffic was even thicker than before, the ride slower, and the conversation nonexistent.

Which was fine with Dunphy, who had a lot of thinking to do—not to mention the explaining that would come later. But first, he had to get cash—and lots of it. Which meant a visit to Jersey.

He looked out the window. The cab was crawling along Victoria Street past New Scotland Yard, heading toward Westminster Abbey and Whitehall. Rivers of businessmen, shop girls, cops, pols, and tourists thronged the sidewalks, moving at a surprising clip.

The thing is, Dunphy thought, there's no way Blémont hasn't been in touch with the bank. He would have called them months ago. He'd have explained about the money, about how it was actually his, and—then what? Then, nothing. A hapless shrug from the banker—what's-his-name?—old man Picard. Who'd have expressed his regrets and shown Blémont to the door. "Sorry, old man, nothing to be done, I'm afraid. We'll just have to pray your chap turns up!"

And that's exactly what Blémont would do—wait for Thornley to show up. He'd have searched everywhere, of course, but he'd have known there was one place that Thornley was certain to come: the Banque Privat de St. Helier on Jersey.

Because that's where the money was, and that's what this was all about, right?

The cab went around a little square whose name Dunphy didn't catch, and swung left, heading up Whitehall past the Admiralty and Old War Office. Clem made a sniffling sound, but shrank away when Dunphy tried to comfort her.

Ah, well, he thought. One thing at a time.

Jersey . . . Blémont . . . the Frenchman wouldn't have sat around for months, watching the bank. He'd have paid someone to tell him if and when Kerry Thornley showed up. But who would that someone have been? Someone who worked in the bank. Which meant old man Picard, a secretary, or clerk. But probably not Picard himself: discretion was his business.

The taxi swung past Charing Cross, heading up the Strand in the direction of the Inner Temple. For a fleeting moment, Dunphy was tempted to have the cab stop, so that he could check out the site where everything had started. The place where Schidlof—or at least the *middle* part of Schidlof—had been dropped. But the cab turned before it got to the temple, moving north on Kingsway in the direction of Bloomsbury and the British Museum.

If it was a clerk who'd been bribed, Dunphy thought, he'd have been given the name of someone else to call—someone on the island. Whoever that was would notify Blémont of Thornley's whereabouts and follow him wherever he went. Eventually, Blémont himself would show up, and that's when things would get ugly.

But what if it was Picard? What if Blémont had actually gotten to the old man himself? What then?

Dunphy thought about it. Well, then, he thought, in that case, he'd try to keep me there. Perhaps until Blémont himself could arrive. Dunphy grunted softly, as if he were on a bicycle and was suddenly pedaling uphill.

"What?"

He turned to her. "I was just thinking," he said. "When we get to King's Cross, I have to make a phone call." She looked away. They were passing a row of chic furniture stores on Tottenham Court Road.

If Picard tried to stall him, he'd probably make up an excuse about not having enough cash on hand to close out the account. And, in fact, that wouldn't be such a stretch: the Banque Privat was, as its name implied, a private bank and not a commercial one. It did not have tellers or ATMs, and it did not cash checks for workmen. Even more to the point, it *was* a lot of cash that Dunphy was seeking: nearly three hundred thousand pounds—about half a million dollars—the entire take from Blémont's scam with the stolen IBM stock. The idea, then, was to make sure that the money (and not Blémont) would be waiting for him when he got to the bank.

When the cab pulled into the turnaround at King's Cross, Dunphy gave Clem a fistful of cash and told her to buy two tickets to Southend-on-Sea.

"Where will *you* be?" she asked suspiciously.

"Right there," Dunphy said, gesturing. "On the phone."

It took a while to get the number for the Banque Privat, but when he did, the call went straight through.

The woman who answered was crisply efficient. She said that Mr. Picard was in a meeting and would not be available until the afternoon. Perhaps she could be of help?

"Well, ah certainly hope so," Dunphy said, affecting a southern accent. "This is Taylor Brooks—from Crozet, Vuhginya?"

"Yes?"

"And how're yew, ma'am?"

"I'm very well, thank you."

"Ah sure am glad to hear that, on accounta ah'll be stoppin' by tomorrah—fo' a visit? The man I work for said I should call ahead, give y'all a little notice."

"I see. And who might that be?"

Dunphy chuckled. "Well, ma'am, that's not something we discuss much on the telephone—bein' as how he's real discreet. But we do have several accounts with yew. Ah believe they were set up by a Mr. Thawnly."

Silence.

"Well, I haven't seen hide nor hair of that jokah for *quite* some time, but—what it is—ah'll be making a withdrawal. And the Big Fellah—that's my boss—thought I should call aheada time—on account of the *amount* involved."

"Well, that was very thoughtful of him."

"Thank you, ma'am, ah'll tell him you said that. Truth is, we're about as busy as a dawg with two dicks—"

"Pardon me?"

"I *said* we're about as busy as a *dawg* with two dicks. Which is a saying we have—means we're *real* busy. Anyway, like y'all said, ah'm gonna need three hundred thousand pounds—"

"Oh, dear . . ."

"—and I'd appreciate it if you'd have it on hand when ah get there. Hunnuds, if you got 'em. Fifties, if you don't."

"Yes, well . . . you said you're a Mr. . . . . Taylor?"

"No, ma'am. Ah said ah'm a Mr. Brooks. Taylor's my fus' name."

"Excuse me."

"No need to apologize, ma'am. Happens all the time."

"And the account—"

"Well, now, that's not something we should go into just now, but if you'll tell Mr. Picard that I called, and that these are his Crozet, Vuhginia, accounts, he'll know exactly where ah'm comin' from."

"I see."

"Well, praise Jesus! That's all I had to say. Just a little heads-up. Ah'll look fo'wut, then, to seein' ya—fust thing."

And with that, Dunphy rang off.

"Who was *that*?" Clem asked, startling him as he turned away from the phone.

"My bank," he said, taking one of the tickets from her hand. "Jesus, Clem, I swear I'm gonna get you a bell."

"I don't mean *that*—I mean who were *you* supposed to be? You sounded like that old television show. *Dukes of Hazzard!*"

"Thanks," Dunphy said dryly. "I do the best I can. So where's the train?"

"Track seventeen. We've got about four minutes." She was looking at him strangely, as if she'd just begun to realize that Dunphy was a lot more than she'd bargained for.

They walked double-time through the crowded station, hurrying without ever quite running. At Track 17, they broke into a jog on the platform, making their way toward the front of the train, where the last of the first-class cars was waiting. With the exception of an impeccably dressed elderly couple wrestling with shopping bags, and a young man talking boisterously into a cell phone, they were alone.

Dunphy dropped into a seat near the back of the car and closed his eyes. He was thinking about the Banque Privat. The secretary, or whoever she was, would tell old man Picard about the phone call she'd just had. Picard would recognize the reference to Crozet immediately.

These were accounts that Dunphy had set up for the Reverend James MacLeod, a burly evangelist with a radio and television ministry that netted his Second Baptist Primitive Church about fifty thousand dollars a week in cash and checks, sent through the mail by enraptured admirers. The checks, and about 10 percent of the cash, were properly declared and publicly accounted for. The remaining 90 percent of the cash was smuggled abroad into MacLeod's accounts at the Banque Privat.

Dunphy had no intention (or, indeed, any way) of touching that money. He was no longer a signatory to any of the accounts, and his reference to them was simply a way of making sure that Picard had the necessary cash on hand—without tipping him to Merry Kerry's arrival.

The train lurched. He opened his eyes. "You okay?" he asked.

Clem shook her head. "No, I'm not okay. I don't know what's happening—or who you really are—or what any of this is all about. And it's not fair. Because I'm the one who's probably going to get killed."

Dunphy shifted uncomfortably in his seat. "No, you're not," he said. "But . . . it's kind of complicated."

She made a low, growling sound and looked away.

"All right! I'm sorry. It's just . . . " He lowered his voice. "Just don't go off the deep end on me." He thought about it for a moment and then plunged in. "Remember, the other day? I mentioned a thing called need to know. And I said you didn't have it, but—it turns out—you did. I was thinking, the less you knew, the safer you'd be, but—" He paused, then added, "My bad," and paused again, uncertain how this would play. Finally, he plunged on. "So the point is, I fucked up. There's no way to get around that, and now—well, now, we're in a lot of trouble. Both of us." He sighed. "Got a cigarette?"

Clem blinked. "You don't smoke."

"I was thinking of taking it up again. I mean, why not?" When she didn't laugh, he hurried on. "Anyway, it's like this. When I told you I'd left the Agency, when I said that I was—"

"Redundant."

"Right—when I said that I was redundant—well, that was kind of an understatement."

A quizzical look from this beautiful girl. "What does *that* mean?"

"Well, it means that, while it's true that I don't work for the Agency anymore, there's more to it."

"Like what?"

"Like what you saw. They're looking for me. And they're pissed."

"Who is?"

"The people I used to work for. And, you see, what happened was . . . they were tracking my credit cards, trying to see where I've gone. Which, of course, I knew they'd do, so, naturally, I didn't use them. Only then, when you went out to buy the coat—I kind of forgot about it. Because I was listening to Simon, and—"

She shook her head impatiently. "What did you *do*?" she asked, enunciating each word as if he were deaf and had to read lips. "What did you do to *them* that made them so angry at *you*?"

Dunphy waved the question away. "What's that got to do with anything? The point is—"

"You didn't embezzle funds?!" she asked, more thrilled than scared. "You aren't an *embezzler*?!"

Her excitement made him smile. "It wasn't money," he said. "It was more like . . . information. Like I was embezzling information." Clem frowned, not understanding. "I got *curious*," Dunphy went on. "About Schidlof. And now . . ." He couldn't bring himself to finish the sentence. It sounded so melodramatic.

But Clem wouldn't let it go. "Now, *what*?" she asked.

The train lurched a second time and began to move.

"Well," he went on, "*now* they want to kill me. I mean, any idiot could see *that*."

She fell silent for a long while, and then, "How did they find us?"

"Like I said, they traced the charge. I kept one of my cards to get cash from an ATM, and then I forgot to throw it away. Then I gave you the wallet in Camden Lock, and you used the card to buy a coat. And when you did that, the credit-card people got on the phone to Langley. And they told them there was activity in one of the accounts they'd been told to watch."

She shook her head. "They wouldn't do that," she said firmly.

"Who wouldn't?"

"Visa. American Express."

"Why not?"

"Because it's an invasion of privacy!"

Dunphy stared at her. Finally he said, "You're right. Cynical me. God knows what I was thinking."

"And, anyway—who's Langley?"

"It's a place—not a person. Outside Washington. And if you can suspend your sense of disbelief, just for a minute, I'll finish telling you what happened. When the credit-card people called Langley, Langley called the embassy in London—"

"But how do you *know* all this? You're just making it up!"

"I'm not making it up. It's the way things are done."

"How do you know?"

"Because I've done it!"

"*Killed* people?" She was aghast.

Dunphy shook his head. "No! *Located* them."

"But why would you do that?"

"I don't know. There are lots of reasons! What's the difference? The point is, maybe ten minutes after they called the embassy, a couple of guys—"

"What guys?"

"The ones back there. They got in their car—"

"The Jaguar."

"Right. They got into the *Jag*-yew-are and drove it to Camden Lock. Where they looked for the shop. And when they found it, they went through the day's receipts until they found a sixty-quid Amex transaction. And when they found the transaction, they asked the guy who ran the shop if he could remember the sale." Dunphy paused. "Which he apparently did. Not that I'm surprised. You're kind of memorable."

Clementine looked glum. "That was Jeffrey. He's a friend of Simon's."

"So he's someone you know."

She shrugged. "Just to say hello. We shared a taxi once. And he told me he had these coats." She fell silent for a moment, and then turned back to him. "Why are they after *you*? You must have done something to them."

Dunphy made a gesture with his hands. "Not really. I mean, I asked a lot of questions, and . . . obviously, they were the wrong questions, or maybe they were the right questions, but . . . I don't know what to tell you. It's not entirely clear."

"Someone's trying to kill you, and you don't know why?"

Her sarcasm angered him. "Well, I'm trying to find out, *aren't* I? I mean . . . it's not as if I haven't thought about it! You can understand my *curiosity*."

She flinched at the hard edge in his voice. Finally, and in a dull voice, she asked, "Where are we going?"

Dunphy gazed out the window at the wintry landscape. "I don't know," he said, "but—this train?—it's beginning to look a lot like a handbasket."

The airport at Southend-on-Sea was sufficiently obscure that Dunphy felt certain that no one would be looking for them there. It would take a few hours, at least, for the Agency to sort out Curry's misfortune and to invent a reason for MI5 to put Dunphy in its lookout books. By then, he and Clem would be on a British Midland flight to St. Helier.

This was the capital of Jersey, largest of the Anglo-Normandes, or Channel Islands. A British dependency only twelve miles off the coast of France, the islands were a feudal anachronism—a bilingual tax haven with more registered corporations than actual people. Famous for its soft climate, Jersey was one of the favorite banking venues of (the unfortunately defunct) Anglo-Erin Business Services, PLC.—and its proprietor, K. Thornley.

Which was why Dunphy decided not to stay at his usual bolt-hole, where he was known to the management by his pseudonym, but to take a suite at the rather more posh Longueville Manor. (Or, as it was formally known, *The* Longueville Manor.)

An Edwardian pile of ivy-clad granite and tiles, the Manor was situated in a private wood, a few miles outside the capital. As their taxi entered the hotel's circular drive, Clem remarked how spooky it looked, opaque in the winter mist.

But once inside the hotel, the Channel's damp surrendered to ancient tapestries, candlelight, and a roaring fireplace.

"Will you need help with your luggage, Mr.? . . ." The clerk squinted at the registration card.

"Dunphy. Jack Dunphy. And no, we won't—the fucking airline lost it on our way in from the States."

The clerk winced. "Oh, dear . . . well, I'm sure it will turn up. It always does." Bright smile.

Dunphy grunted. "Yeah, only now it's beginning to look like this could turn into a major shopping opportunity." Clem rocked back and forth on her heels, mugging her glee, as if a director had called out *Eyes and teeth, dahling!* "You do have *stores* here," Dunphy asked, "or is it just banks?"

The clerk grinned. "No, sir, I'm afraid we do indeed have shops, as well." The two men exchanged rueful chuckles as Dunphy accepted a plastic room key. "Just down the hall, sir," the clerk said, and folding his hands with a smug smile, watched the American couple wander off in the direction of their suite.

Which was large, and more Ralph Lauren than Laura Ashley, with birch logs crackling in the hearth. Hunting scenes hung from the walls in dark wooden frames, and a bowl of fresh flowers bloomed beside the bed. "Have you been here before, then?" Clem asked, falling backward onto a velvet couch and staring up at the ceiling.

"Not here," Dunphy said, fixing each of them a drink from the minibar. "But Jersey—yeah."

"It's very nice."

"Uh-huh." He swirled the Laphroaig in her glass and gave it to her. Then he sat down on the floor beside the couch, facing the fireplace, and sipped. "Only we can't stay here for long." He could feel her frown on his shoulder blades. "It wouldn't be safe. They'll be looking for us."

"On Jersey?"

"Everywhere."

"Then why don't we just go to the police?"

Dunphy sighed. "Because the police think I had something to do with . . . what happened to Schidlof. And maybe I did, indirectly. I mean, I *was* bugging the guy."

"You were *what*?"

"Recording his telephone calls. And then he got killed."

She was quiet for a moment, and then, "Why were you listening—"

"I wasn't listening. I was having the calls recorded."

"Why?"

"I don't know," Dunphy replied. "I wasn't told."

"You weren't *told*?"

"It was my *job*. I did what they said."

She was quiet again, and then spoke up. "I still think the police . . ."

Dunphy dismissed the idea with a flick of his hand. "No. If we go to the police, the embassy will get into it, and the next thing you know, they'll be telling the Brits it's a 'national security matter.' And that wouldn't be good."

"Why not?"

"Because as soon as that happens, I'm on the next flight out, wrapped in a rug." He took another sip of whiskey, relishing its heat on his palate. "And that's just *me*. I don't know *what* happens to you. You fall between the cracks or something."

"I *what*?"

"You fall between the cracks. Which I suppose could be good or bad, depending—"

"On what?"

"The cracks—and how *deep* they are."

A long silence ensued. Finally Clem asked, "So what do we do?"

Dunphy turned to her. "We have to get you a passport—"

"I've already got one. I mean, at home. I could say I lost it, and—"

He shook his head. "No. We need something in a different name."

"Which name?" she asked.

"I don't know. Any name you like."

The idea seemed to please her, and she thought about it. "Could it be Veroushka?"

Dunphy did a double take. "I guess, but . . . what the fuck is a Veroushka?"

Clem's shoulders rose and fell in a little shrug. "It's just a name I like."

"Okay . . . Veroushka it is."

"And I'll need a last name, too."

"No problem. There's a million of them. Windsong is taken, but how about Stankovic? Or Zipwitz?"

"I don't think so."

"Why not? Veroushka Zipwitz! It's got a ring to it."

She smiled. "Bell will do. One *e*, two *l*s."

"Got it."

"It was my grandmother's name."

"No problem. Veroushka Bell. I *like* it." She smacked him on the shoulder. "No, I mean it," he said. "It's great."

"Okay, so now that I have a name—how are you going to get a passport made?"

"No problem. I can do it in Zürich."

"I'm sure you can. But we aren't *in* Zürich."

"Riii-ight," he replied, and got to his feet. "That's the bad part."

"What is?" she asked.

He didn't answer her at first, but fetched another miniature from the minibar. "Refill?"

"What's the bad part?" she demanded.

"The part about your going home—but not to your flat." Suddenly, she looked frightened, and he hurried on. "Can you get a room for a few days? Until I can get you a passport?"

"No!"

"Clem—"

"I can't!"

"You can. You have to. C'mon, babe . . . it's the only way."

She looked at him in a way that was almost as surly as it was sad—as if she were a child who'd been cheated by an adult. Her lower lip trembled, and her forehead plunged. It would have been comical if it weren't so heartrending.

Finally, she nodded.

"We'll get pictures taken for your passport," Dunphy said, "and have a really good dinner. In the morning, I'll take you down to the docks. You can get the hydrofoil to Southend—ever been in one?" She shook her head, tears flying. "You'll like it. It's very exciting. Like sitting inside a vacuum cleaner."

She giggled in spite of herself. "And what about you?"

"I'll be at the bank. And then on a boat to France, and then a train to Zürich. There's a hotel there, the Zum Storchen. It's right in the middle of town, so you won't have any trouble finding it. But I'm going to need an address *for you*—so I can send the passport."

"I guess I could stay at my girlfriend's," Clem said. "She has a cottage near Oxford." She wrote the address on a scrap of paper and handed it to him.

"Look for a FedEx truck, okay?"

She nodded. "You won't just leave me there?" she asked.

Dunphy shook his head. "No," he said. "I'm not gonna do that again."

The morning was bright and blustery, with soft, lenticular clouds floating over a meringue of whitecaps in St. Helier's harbor. He bought a ticket for the hydrofoil and waited with Clementine until it was time to leave.

"I'll call you from Switzerland," he said, and held her in his arms.

"You won't lose the number?"

"No."

"Because if you do, she's ex-Directory—"

"I've memorized it," he said, feeling her jump as a bell rang to signal the boat's departure. "And remember—"

"I know, pay cash for everything. Don't use the phone. And don't talk to strangers."

He kissed her gently. "What else?"

She thought about it, then shook her head. "I don't remember."

"Look both ways . . ."

The Banque Privat de St. Helier was in a three-story town-house on Poonah Road, about a block from the Parade Garden. In a niche beside the front door, a gleaming brass plaque announced the building's identity, and that of its tenant, J. Picard. Climbing out of his taxi, Dunphy was assailed by the smell of hops from the brewery around the corner.

It was his second visit to the bank in as many years. The nature of his work, or what had been his work, dictated that he should establish as many contacts as possible in the worlds of offshore banking and "creative accountancy." Accordingly, he had made it a point to spread his business around, so that, on Jersey alone, he'd opened nearly fifty accounts in as many as six or seven banks.

But he'd met Jules Picard only once. This was two years earlier, when he'd introduced himself as a new customer, establishing his bona fides with a large cash deposit and a letter of introduction from a solicitor in the Outer Hebrides.

Mounting the steps to the bank's impressive oak door, Dunphy remembered Picard as a wheezing old man who'd climbed the steps to his office with so much effort that he, Dunphy, had feared the banker would have a heart attack, there and then.

"May I help you?"

The words crackled out of the speaker phone beside the door. Dunphy leaned closer to it and, speaking in a soft brogue, replied, "Mr. Thornley for Mr. Picard."

There was no response for what seemed like a long time. Beginning to feel the cold, Dunphy took a step back and glanced around. Helluva way to run a bank, he thought, noticing for the first time the closed-circuit cameras in the eaves. "I'll just wait out here, then," he said, smiling at the nearest camera. "No rush a-tall."

Soon afterward, the door swung open noiselessly, revealing an older woman whose elegant demeanor was at odds with her improbable size. By Dunphy's guess, she was half an inch this way or that of six feet tall and built like a rower—not what one expected of a woman in her sixties.

"Was Mr. Picard expecting you?"

It was the woman he'd spoken to on the phone the day before. "Not unless the man's gone clairvoyant on us," Dunphy replied.

A thin smile from his hostess, who led him down a narrow corridor hung with a brace of Orientalist paintings. Elegant in a black pantsuit, she wore her battleship-gray hair compressed at the back in a no-nonsense bun.

"If you'll have a seat," she suggested, ushering Dunphy

into a brightly lighted room that looked out upon a winter-withered garden. "I'll let him know you're here."

Dunphy did as she suggested, and took a seat on the leather couch, crossing his legs. Soon, a brisk knock rattled the door, and a tall man strode in wearing a houndstooth jacket and slacks so sharply creased as to be dangerous. "Mr. Thornley!" he declared.

"The very one," Dunphy acknowledged, getting to his feet and shaking hands. "But I was expecting Mr. Picard."

"Then you won't be disappointed. I *am* Mr. Picard. And it's a pleasure to meet you—I've heard so much."

Dunphy shot him a questioning look.

"Lewis Picard," the banker announced. "With a *w*." Bright smile.

Dunphy thought about it for a moment and said, "Well, it's grand to meet you, but—"

"You were expecting Jules. My father!"

"Exactly."

The man gave him a pained look. "Well, I'm afraid he's *dead*—so that's not on. But *perhaps* I can be of help?"

The young man's brisk demeanor was unsettling, and it was only with an effort that Dunphy remembered his brogue. "Well, I expect so," he said. "I mean, of course ya can, but . . . Jay-sus, man, how did it happen?"

"You mean, old Jules?"

"Yes!"

"No great surprise, really. Heart attack on the stairs. Tumble tumble! Dead before he hit the ground."

Dunphy winced. "Poor man!"

"Mmmm. Pity. So much to give."

"And when did it happen?"

"About a year ago."

"Oh. I see."

A silence fell between them, which Lewis Picard finally broke. "I take it you weren't *close* to Dad?"

"No," Dunphy replied. "Not close, not really."

"Well, then, no need to grieve at this late date! What can I do for you?"

Dunphy cleared his throat. "I'm havin' to make a small withdrawal."

Picard *fils* removed an elasticated policeman's notebook from the inner pocket of his jacket. A fountain pen was conjured from the same site, uncapped, and pointed at the page. "Very well. That's what we're here for. And which account would that be?"

"Sirocco Services."

Picard began to write the name in his book, then hesitated—as if something had suddenly occurred to him. Something unpleasant. Slowly, he looked up and smiled. "Sirocco?"

"Exactly."

"I see. And, umm, how much will you be withdrawing?"

"The entire amount."

Picard nodded thoughtfully. "As I recall, that's rather a lot of currency."

"About three hundred thousand quid—a little less." Dunphy patted the attaché case that he'd stopped to buy on the way to the bank. "But I think it will fit."

"Mmmm," Picard mused, rapidly tapping his expensive pen on the little notebook in his hand.

"Is there a problem, then?" Dunphy asked.

"No," Picard answered, regarding Dunphy with a dubious eye. "It's just that . . . we seem to be having a bit of a run this morning."

Dunphy leaned toward him and, as he did, dropped his voice almost to a whisper. "Now, about that, Mr. Picard. I wouldn't be too upset, if I were you, because I have a small confession to make."

"Oh?"

"Indeed. I should have told you, right off. I was on the phone with your assistant yesterday and—Now, that reminds me, I've been meaning to ask, is she the only one who works with you here?"

"She is, and quite competently."

"Oh, there's no doubt about that—the woman has a demeanor of great efficiency," Dunphy agreed, thinking, The bitch is probably on the blower even now, ratting me out to Blémont's man, telling him where I am. "But as I was sayin', I got on the phone to her yesterday morning, having just gotten in from the night before, if you get my meaning . . ."

"You were drunk."

"As a lord. And, no malice intended, of course, but I will admit to having played a role—for the laugh that was in it."

"I see," Picard said, nodding to himself as if he'd just confirmed a dark suspicion. "Not that I'm surprised. She told me she'd spoken to someone who'd pretended to be an American. I take it that was you?"

Dunphy shrugged, slightly hurt by the characterization. "It may well have been."

"And that leaves us . . . precisely where?" The banker looked expectantly at Dunphy, who handed him a letter written on stationery from The Longueville Manor.

"The letter's self-explanatory," he said. "If you'll lend me your pen, I'll give you my signature. There's only one on the account. And the number's right there at the top of the page, where it says *in re*. Once I've had my money, I won't bother you any further."

Picard gave him the pen and watched as Dunphy signed the letter, requesting the bank close out the Sirocco account. "You know," Picard remarked, returning the pen to his pocket and taking the letter that Dunphy had signed, "we had some unpleasantness here."

"Oh?"

"Yes. About this very account."

"Did you now?" Dunphy asked, his voice thick with incredulity.

"Ye-esss . . . chap named Blémont stopped in. This was several months ago. Said the money was his."

"Jay-sus, Mary, and Joseph—they're gettin' nervier every day!" Dunphy exclaimed.

"Mmmm."

"And what did you tell the man?"

"Well, you can imagine," Picard replied. "No one here knew him from a bale of hay. No signature on record. No references. Though, mind you, he did mention *your* name!"

"*My* name?!"

"In fact, and repeatedly."

"The nerve! And what did you do?"

"Showed him the door. Told him I'd ring the police. What else could I do?"

"Quite right."

"More than my job's worth! Though I *will* say, he seemed quite determined. Outraged, even."

"A great actor, no doubt!"

"Precisely. And I must say, not terribly happy in the presence of noes."

"Jay-sus. Was he threatening, then?"

"Indeed. Well," the banker said, clapping his hands together, "just a little heads-up for you. Mustn't grumble."

Dunphy blushed.

"Now, if you'll just follow me, we'll get your money," Picard said, smiling widely. "Whomever it belongs to."

20

The voyage from St. Helier to Saint-Malo was rough, the Channel a froth of whitecaps. Sitting at a table in the first-class restaurant, drinking coffee, Dunphy surveyed his fellow passengers and wondered which, if any, of them was following him.

On leaving the bank, he had almost expected to find Blémont waiting for him on the corner, but, of course, the Frenchman was nowhere around. Just to be sure, Dunphy had taken taxis from one end of the island to the other, directing the drivers down roads that were more like country lanes. And while the drivers thought he was odd, it was apparent, from all the doubling back that they did, that no one was on their tail.

On the other hand, Dunphy thought, why should they be? Jersey was an island, which meant that there were only two ways to leave—by boat and by plane. So there was no need, really, to follow him on Jersey itself. All Blémont had to do was to watch the airport and the docks. If he did that, he'd know exactly where Dunphy was going and when he'd get there.

And that would make the surveillance hard to spot. There might be someone on the ferry with him—or there might not. If they preferred, they could pick him up when he debarked at Saint-Malo. In either case, he wouldn't be alone. Dunphy was sure of that.

So when the ferry arrived at Saint-Malo, Dunphy made it a point to be the last man off. Standing beside the gangplank, he scanned the docks for what he thought would be a two-man team. But it was impossible to sort the people out. There were customs officials and tourists, businessmen and house-wives, shop girls and workmen. Any one of them might have been working for Blémont—or none of them.

Leaning against the deck rail of the Emeraude Lines ferry, it occurred to Dunphy that Blémont's reaction time might not be all that good. The Frenchman traveled a lot, and he might easily have been abroad when the call came from Jersey, re-porting Thornley's arrival at the Banque Privat. In that case, Blémont would have arranged for Dunphy to be tailed until he himself could get to the scene. Blémont was, if anything, a hands-on guy and, no doubt, would want to handle the inter-rogation personally.

Still, there wasn't any choice. If Dunphy remained where he was, standing on deck, he'd soon find himself on his way back to Jersey. After six or seven trips like that, they'd slap him in the bin, and that would be the end of that. Accordingly, he took a deep breath, stood up, and straightened his shoul-ders. Then he sauntered down the gangplank with his bag full of money, shook off a choir of taxi drivers, and wandered into the port.

The air was cold and damp, but the port was lively, its restaurants brightly lighted, packed with people, and fragrant with garlic and olive oil. Hungry, he bought some francs at a *bureau de change*, then stopped at a kiosk for something to read. Though the *Herald Tribune* was available, he settled for *Le Point*, not wanting to seem conspicuously American. Finally, he picked a restaurant and found a table that was agreeable—one where he could sit with his back to the wall and his eyes on the door.

No one.

Beginning to think that perhaps he had not been followed after all, he ordered a bowl of *cotriade*—a sort of chowder— and a tall glass of Belgian beer. Then he leafed through *Le Point*. Although his spoken French was clumsy, at best, he could read it well enough, and soon found a story that interested him.

It was a think piece about the Middle East peace talks, highlighting the CIA's role in negotiations between the Palestinians and the Israelis. According to the article, a key sticking point had been the question of Jewish access to the Temple Mount. This was said to be "the spiritual epicenter of Israel," a Jerusalem hill on which the First and Second Temples had been built. It was purported to be the last resting place of the Ark of the Covenant, and the predestined spot where the Third, and last, Temple would one day be constructed.

But only, as it happened, over the dead bodies of a great many Arabs, who'd worshipped for centuries at the Dome of the Rock and Al-Aqsa Mosque—each of which stood upon the same hill (and, in fact, upon the ruins of the earlier Temples), and were themselves among the most sacred sites in Islam. Israeli officials, fearful that pious Jews would spark unending riots if they tried to worship on the Temple Mount, had made it unlawful for Jews to pray there. Now, Israeli negotiators and their CIA helpmates were seeking Arafat's assistance in getting equal time for Jewish prayer on the Mount.

It was an interesting story, and somehow tied up with Biblical prophecies about the end of the world—which Scripture declared would occur when the Third Temple was finally built. Funny to think, Dunphy thought, that the CIA should be involved in eschatology. But, then again, why not? If Brading had been telling the truth, the Agency was into a lot of strange things.

Once again, Dunphy glanced up from his magazine and scanned the room. There was a man at the bar who'd been on the boat. He was maybe thirty-five or forty years old, with platinum hair, a medium build, and acne scars. Loden coat with staghorn buttons. Smoking. Dunphy couldn't quite see his face, but his hair was unforgettable. No mistake.

And the young couple at the table by the door. Dunphy had seen them on the dock in St. Helier, buying their tickets. They must have come into the restaurant while he was reading.

But so what? Everyone had to eat somewhere—even Blondie. That didn't mean they were following him.

Still, he wished he had a gun. After kneecapping Curry and ripping off Blémont, getting strapped would not be an over-reaction. Especially since he was walking around with nearly half a million dollars in cash—motive enough for a lot of people to take him out, including a great many who didn't even know him, much less hold a grudge against him.

But first things first. The *cotriade* was terrific. He wiped the bowl with a crust of bread and washed it down with a second glass of Corsendonk, a supernaturally expensive Belgian ale made by monks for millionaires. Finally, he had an espresso and smoked a cigarette as he tried to decide whether or not he could risk renting a hotel room. He'd checked the SNCF schedules on Jersey, and there was a bullet train leaving Saint-Malo for Paris in about an hour. Once he got to Paris, it would be easy to get to Zürich—a place he knew well. There, he could rent a safe-deposit box and stash the money he was carrying.

Or . . .

He could defer the trip and get a good night's sleep—find a hotel, wedge a chair against the door, and . . . chill. The idea was tempting. He'd picked up a cold on the way to Saint-Malo, and it was beginning to get to him. A night in the Hotel de Ville, with the prospect of a hot bath and cool sheets, would be just the thing.

But hotels were a problem and would continue to be until he could get a new passport. Wherever he stayed, they'd want an imprint of his credit card—to guarantee phone calls and other charges to the room. And while the hotel would promise to destroy the invoice without processing it, they sometimes made mistakes—which, in this case, could be fatal rather than merely inconvenient. Moreover, if he got a hotel room, he'd have to fill out a registration card, which the police would pick up later that night. Usually, the cards were sorted in the early morning hours, with the cops checking the names of guests against whichever lookout lists were then current. And while it was true that the police were sometimes lax, it was always a mistake to depend on the other side's incompetence. After all, even a stopped clock was right twice a day.

Wiser, then, to catch the train and spend the night on the rails, rocking his way toward Switzerland.

Reluctantly, Dunphy pushed back his chair. Getting to his feet, he left some francs on the table with the check and, asking the way, walked to the train station in a cold drizzle. An hour later, he was sneezing in a first-class seat on the TGV *Atlantique*, speeding through Normandy at two hundred klicks an hour.

As fast as the train went, it still took all night to get to Zürich. Stuck with a two-hour layover in the gritty Gare de l'Est, Dunphy bought a phone card in a late-night kiosk and telephoned Max Setyaev in Prague. The phone rang five or six times before a sleep-drenched voice came on the line.

"Hallo?"

"Genevieve, s'il vous plait."

"Hoo?"

"Genevieve," Dunphy repeated, suddenly apprehensive that Max might have forgotten their arrangement or, worse, that he would try to ham it up by engaging him in conversation.

But to Dunphy's relief, the Russian muttered an imprecation in a language that Dunphy didn't understand, then slammed the phone down in its cradle—just as he was supposed to do. If anyone was listening, the conversation would not have been worth reporting.

Replacing the phone on its hook, Dunphy turned—and there he was again, the blond guy who'd been on the ferry (maybe), and in the restaurant at Saint-Malo (definitely). He was seated on a wooden bench, maybe twenty yards away, smoking.

What are the odds? Dunphy asked himself. What are the odds that it's a coincidence? That two people who don't know each other would take the same ferry from Jersey on the same day, and then catch the same train to Paris that evening? What are the odds?

Well, actually, he thought, they're pretty good. I think they call it 'public transportation.'

Still . . .

Mechanical difficulties kept them on a siding outside Dijon for nearly two hours. Dunphy slept fitfully through the repairs, but as soon as the train got going again, he sank into a sleep so deep it might have been confused with a coma. When they neared the Swiss border, a Customs official appeared and asked to see his passport, then waved it aside when he realized that Dunphy was an American.

By then, his cold was worse. Somewhere in the night, between Paris and the border, it had taken hold in his chest, raising his temperature just enough to make him feel uncomfortable. Neither sick nor well, but somewhere in between, he felt played out—as if he hadn't slept for days. (Which, now that he thought of it, he hadn't.)

Debarking from the train at Zürich, he headed for the exit closest to the Bahnhofstrasse.

It was familiar turf. He'd been to Zürich a dozen times before, and the station was just as he remembered it—a huge volume of dimly lighted air, more outside than in, suffused with winter. Woozy from the cold that he had, and shivering from the cold all around him, he was tempted to take a seat in one of the station's brightly lighted cafés, where the windows ran with steam and the air was spiked with the aromas of pastry and espresso.

But sitting down would not be a good idea. Though Blondie was nowhere to be seen, Zürich's *Bahnhof* was itself a rumpus room for German junkies and Dutch drunks, African grifters and the ever-present Legions of the Lost— hippies, hikers, headbangers, and Goths. Better to move on with his briefcase full of cash.

Outside, a light snow swirled in gusts of wind. It was a lot colder here than on Jersey or in Saint-Malo, and he could feel it in his hands and feet. Leaning into the weather, he pulled the collar of his topcoat close to his neck and made his way along Switzerland's most glamorous street. Soon, he found a branch of the Credit Suisse and, ten minutes later, was standing by himself in a locked room, stacking bundles of pounds in a dark steel box that rented for thirty-five Swiss francs a month.

When he'd finished with the money, he left the bank and headed for the Zum Storchen, feeling considerably lighter—though hardly weightless. He still had fifty thousand pounds in the attaché case, enough to pay Max and keep going for as long as he had to. And that could be a while. Despite all that had happened, and all that he'd learned, he still didn't know why Schidlof had been killed, or why his own life had suffered so much collateral damage on the periphery of that murder. When you thought about it, all he'd done was ruin his life and put everyone he knew in danger.

Well, not really. It wasn't all that bad. He was being too modest. He had also managed to rip off Blémont and kneecap Curry—which was, if nothing else, a *beginning*.

Old Zürich was a cluster of narrow, cobbled streets and stone buildings on a hill above the ice-cold, dead-black, and utterly transparent Limmat River. The snow was a little heavier now as Dunphy made his way down the hill toward the Zum Storchen. It sifted from the sky like flour, stuck to his eyelashes, and blanketed the hair on his head. Melting, it ran under the collar of his topcoat and down the nape of his neck, chilling him to the marrow. Arriving at the river, he stood for a moment on the embankment and watched the swans float past, oblivious to both the cold and falling snow.

Unlike Dunphy himself who, coughing, stopped in a men's store to buy a pair of leather gloves and a scarf, only to be given a bill that seemed to have an extra *0*. Not that it mattered. Money was the least of his problems. Returning to the quay, he walked the last two blocks to the Zum Storchen, crossed the hotel's frozen terrace, and went inside.

Hard by the river in the shadow of an ancient and enormous clock tower, the Zum Storchen had been in continuous operation for more than six hundred years. Passing a roaring fire as he crossed the lobby to the reception desk, Dunphy asked if a Mr. Setyaev had arrived.

"Not yet, sir."

"When he gets in, would you tell him that his friend is in the restaurant?"

"Of course."

He'd been ready to sit for hours, watching the river and drinking coffee, but the Russian was on the scene before Dunphy could finish his second croissant.

"You look like shit," Max said by way of greeting.

"Thanks, Max. You're looking well yourself. Have a seat."

The Russian dropped into the chair across from him. "What I have done for you," he whispered, "could not have been done by any other man."

"Then I guess I went to the right guy."

"You bet," he said. And with that, Max nudged a manila envelope across the table and reached for the check. "I'll get this," he said, scrutinizing the bill.

"Really?" Dunphy exclaimed. "The coffee *and* the croissants?"

The Russian nodded, mostly to himself, and muttered, "Mr. Smart-ass." Then he took a pen from his pocket and scrawled a room number on the check. "Let's go," he said, getting to his feet. "We can do business upstairs."

Dunphy rode with him in the elevator to the hotel's fifth, and uppermost, floor. The suite was at the end of the corridor, with windows overlooking both the river and the lake. Inside, Max's overnight bag rested on the carpet below the window, unopened.

"I'm whacked," Dunphy said, as he fell into a wing chair.

"What's wrong?" Max asked.

"I've got a cold."

"So, we finish business . . . I go home . . . you keep room. Get sleep."

"I think I will," Dunphy replied. "I'm really out of it."

The Russian removed a manila envelope from his overnight

bag, tore it open, and dumped its contents on the coffee table between them. There were a couple of credit cards, a driver's license, and a passport. Dunphy opened the passport, checked the picture, and glanced at the name. "Very nice," he said, then did a double take. "Harrison Pitt!?"

Max beamed. "Is good name, huh?"

"Good name? What kind of fucking name—"

"Is American name! True blue!"

"Are you kidding? I don't know anyone named Harrison."

"No, of course not. In Ireland, this is not popular name. In Canada—America—there are many, many Harrisons."

"Name one."

Instantly, the Russian replied, "Ford."

It took a moment for the suspicion to dawn. "And Pitt?"

"There is also Brad Pitt," Max replied. "And this is just movie stars. Many average Americans have these names."

Dunphy sighed. "Right. So what about the other stuff?"

Max removed a letter-sized envelope from his jacket and handed it to Dunphy, who ripped it open.

A laminated Andromeda pass fell into his lap. In the upper left-hand corner was the hologram, a rainbow image of the black Virgin of Einsiedeln; and at the bottom, on the right side, a thumbprint. Dunphy's own picture was in the middle of the pass, under the words:

MK-IMAGE
Special Access Program
E. Brading
ANDROMEDA

"Well done, man! It's very, very good."

The Russian looked insulted. "No! Is perfect."

"My words exactly! And the thumbprint? What have we done about that?"

Max unzipped the outside compartment of his overnight bag and removed a hardbound copy of Nabokov's *Ada, or Ardor*. *"Voilà,"* he said, and handed the book to Dunphy.

"What do I do with it?"

"Hold it," the Russian said. Then, returning to his overnight bag, he worked the main zipper and removed a small leather case from the bag's central compartment. Inside the case were a jumble of toiletries—toothpaste, toothbrush, disposable razors, pill bottles . . . and a tube of something called bio-glue.

"What's that?" Dunphy asked, as the Russian removed the tube from the ditty bag.

"Bio-glue."

"I know what it *says*—"

"Is protein polymer for doctors. Stronger than stitches. No pain. So, is progress."

"And what are you gonna do with it?"

"Give book, please."

Dunphy gave him the book, and the Russian opened it. Inside was a glassine envelope. Max pressed the sides of the envelope together, blew into it, and shook out what looked like a translucent piece of skin.

"Fingerprint," Max said.

Dunphy stared at the object, which rested on Max's palm like a surrealist joke. "What's it made of?" he asked.

"Hydrogel. Same as contact lens—soft kind. Is biomimetic."

"And what's that supposed to mean?"

"It means human-compatible plastic. Ultrathin. Now, please, wash hands, then dry."

Dunphy got up and did as he was told, then returned to his seat beside the window.

Max took Dunphy's right hand in his own and dabbed the bio-glue on the American's thumb, using a Q-Tip. Then he laid the fingerprint on the glue and smoothed it down. "Four minutes," he said.

Dunphy studied the appliqué, which appeared to be seamless. "How do I get it off?" he asked.

The Russian frowned. Finally he said, "Sandpaper, maybe."

"Sandpaper?!"

"Sure."

"Okay . . . sandpaper it is. Now, tell me how you made it."

Max smiled. "Photoengraving. When glue dries, you'll see—finger will be smooth."

"And that'll get the job done? You don't have to emboss it, or something?"

"*Emboss?* Why emboss? Is building pass! They check with scanner."

Dunphy gave him a skeptical look.

"Don't worry!" Max said. "Be happy."

And, in fact, he didn't have much choice. Max was the best. If the pass didn't work, it didn't work, and that would be the end of it (and me, too, Dunphy thought). There wasn't anything he could do about it except go with the flow and see what happened. Getting to his feet, Dunphy crossed the room to his attaché case. Placing it on the bed, he snapped open the locks and removed six bundles of cash, each of which contained fifty one-hundred-pound notes—altogether, the equivalent of about fifty thousand dollars. As he handed the currency to Max, bundle by bundle, he said, "Tell me something."

"What?" Max asked, eyes on the money.

"In Russia, when you were living there—did you ever read about any . . . I don't know . . . "

"Ask!"

"Cattle mutilations."

The Russian gave him a puzzled look. "You mean . . . dead cows?"

"Yeah. Cows getting cut up . . . in the pastures."

Max chuckled. "No. I never heard of this. Not while I was there. Why?"

"I was just wondering," Dunphy replied, and handed him the last of the bundles.

"But after *glasnost*," Max said, "there are many of these reports."

Dunphy looked at him. "About cattle mutilations?"

The Russian nodded as he shoved the money into his

overnight bag. "UFOs, too. All kinds of craziness. But this is new—with communists, we never have this."

Dunphy sat down on the bed. "There's one other thing," he said.

Max smiled and rezipped his overnight bag. "Always, there is one other thing."

"I need a second passport—for a friend." Removing another bundle of notes from the attaché case, Dunphy counted out thirty-five hundred-pound notes, and handed them to Max. Then he gave him an envelope with Clementine's pictures inside. "Her address is on the back. It's kind of an emergency."

"I'll do it tonight," Max promised, and glanced at the pictures. "Attractive girl."

"Thanks."

"What name you want?"

"Veroushka Bell."

He smiled and wrote the name on the back of the envelope containing the pictures. "She's Russian?"

"No. Just romantic."

"Even better." He looked up, suddenly serious. "Veroushka's passport—it's like yours, okay?"

Dunphy nodded.

"Is blank—from embassy. I don't say which one. But never issued—so no bad history. Go anywhere, except—maybe not to Canada. Okay?"

"We aren't going to Canada."

"Then you don't have problem."

"Do me a favor," Dunphy asked, walking Max to the door.

"Ask."

Dunphy went over to a desk in the corner of the room and, taking out a sheet of hotel stationery, wrote down the number of the room he was in. Finally, he sealed the page in an envelope, addressed it to Veroushka, and handed it to Max. "Make sure she gets this when she gets the passport."

He went out only once over the next three days, buying magazines at a small store on Fraumünsterstrasse. The rest of the time, he rode out his cold in the comfort of Max's hotel room, sitting by the window above the river, listening to the hard little pellets of snow tick against the glass. The only people he saw were the ones who turned down the bed, changed the towels, or delivered room service. There were no phone calls, or only a couple, and both of those were hang-ups. All in all, it would have been an excellent time to be sick, if it weren't for the weakness that he felt, the fever that he had, and the cough that he couldn't seem to shake.

Of the three, it was the fever that bothered him the most— because it invaded his dreams, imposing a kind of boredom on his sleep. Ordinarily, Dunphy didn't pay much attention to his dreams, but fever dreams were different, as repetitive and monotonous as a test pattern. Waking from them in a sweat, he felt more tired than when he'd first gone to sleep.

By the afternoon of the fourth day, impatient with his body and for Clementine, as well, he decided to go out. Getting dressed, he rode the elevator down to the lobby and walked out into the little street behind the hotel. He needed a couple of things. In fact, he needed everything—and something to carry it in besides. Once Clementine arrived—and once they got to Zug—the world would shift into overdrive. He just knew it would. And when it did, it would be nice to have a change of underwear.

So he went out and bought clothes. For two and a half hours, he wandered through the Old Town's cobblestone streets, weaving in and out of some of the planet's most expensive men's furnishings stores. He bought an overnight bag that had more pockets than a pool hall, and which the salesman swore was stronger than the nose cone of a Saturn rocket (nine hundred Swiss francs). There were shirts from France at four hundred francs apiece, a couple of pairs of German slacks for about the same price, Armani T-shirts at one hundred thirty francs a pop, and socks at twenty francs a foot. He found a houndstooth sports jacket that made him want to shoot grouse (whatever they were, and whatever they'd done to deserve it), and the basic necessities for running: shoes-shorts-and-socks.

And when he was done, it was four o'clock in the afternoon, and he'd learned two things. One: Zürich was a very expensive city in which to buy clothes. And, two: he was definitely being followed.

There was a pair of them, just as he'd always known there would be. The blond guy in the loden coat was one, and there was a second guy, a thug on a red Vespa. And they weren't being secretive. Though they kept their distance, they did nothing to conceal the fact that they were following him. Which meant they owned him, or thought they did.

The guy on the scooter looked like a jock. He had the bull neck and bunchy shoulders of a boxer, piggy little eyes, and a flattop shaved around the sides. Lightly dressed in jeans and a sweatshirt, he seemed impervious to the weather—or wanted others to think that he was. His pal huffed along the street about fifty yards behind, hands jammed in his pockets, sucking on a cigarette.

They've been waiting outside the Zum Storchen for three days, Dunphy thought. Which means they're persistent little fucks, and what I oughta do is call 'em out.

Yo! Fuckhead!

But, no. That would not be a good idea. For one thing, he had too many packages in his hands. For another, he wasn't feeling all that good, or all that brave. On the contrary, he felt a lot like a novice swimmer standing at the end of the high diving board, looking down at the deep and rock-hard water. It wasn't vertigo, exactly, but he did notice a tightening of the scrotum, as if it had just been taken in an inch.

Which surprised him because he was supposed to be a pro at this. When he'd joined the Agency, he'd gone through the usual surveillance and countersurveillance exercises in Williamsburg and Washington. It was standard procedure, and he'd been pretty good at it. So the situation was not entirely unfamiliar— but neither was it the same. Unlike the instructors that he'd had at the Farm, these people did not mean him well.

Still, they hadn't tried to kill him yet, either. Which suggested that their brief was limited to baby-sitting. And, in fact, while making no effort to conceal their interest, they seemed content just to keep him in view. And while they didn't encourage eye contact, neither did they avoid it. It was, in other words, a very passive surveillance. Similar, perhaps, to the one he'd run on Schidlof.

Slowly, Dunphy's adrenaline dwindled to a trickle. His breathing slowed and, with it, his pulse. Studying his adversaries in the reflection of the window at Jil Sander, it occurred to him that being followed was in some ways like being on stage, however involuntarily. Suddenly, the world was screaming *lights! camera! action!* Your heart began to race, your lungs seemed to collapse, and then . . . well, then, if you weren't snatched or blown away, *you got on with it.* Because, in the end, there wasn't anything else you could do. People were watching. So what?

They must be Blémont's people, Dunphy thought. They can't be the Agency's. He'd lost the Agency in London—left its finest bleeding in the foyer of Clementine's apartment. Curry and his goons didn't know where he'd gone. They'd been in too much pain. So these guys were Blémont's.

Which wasn't good, but it wasn't the worst case, either. Unless he was badly mistaken, the Agency didn't want to question him. It simply wanted him dead—because that was the most efficient way to end the inquiry that he'd begun. Blémont, on the other hand, had lots of questions to ask—beginning with where his money was, and how he could get it back. There was nothing to fear from the Frenchman, really, except kidnapping and torture.

On reflection, Dunphy thought, it might be better to be dead—though not, perhaps, under the present circumstances. To be found in a pool of blood, surrounded by shopping bags with designer labels, was not his idea of a good way to go. He could imagine the headlines in the *Post*: CIA MAN SHOPS TILL HE'S DROPPED.

Up ahead, the Zum Storchen's flags fluttered from the

hotel's rooftop, and Dunphy quickened his pace. The thing about it was, Blondie and the Jock were not going to follow him forever. It wasn't a *study*, after all. It was a *hunt*. And they'd reached the point where the fox was treed, and there was nothing left for the dogs to do but wait for the shooter to arrive. Which meant that Dunphy was in the crosshairs of an interregnum, and that, if he hoped to survive, he had better figure out a way to lose the surveillance.

Entering the Zum Storchen, Dunphy took the lift to the fifth floor and let himself into his room. The walk seemed to have done him some good. His cough had abated, and he was breathing more easily than he had for days. Tossing the overnight bag on the bed, he began to pack the clothes that he'd bought—when a soft knock came at the door.

I have to get a gun, he told himself. Or a baseball bat—or something. Glancing wildly around the room, his eyes settled on a stand of andirons beside the fireplace. Grabbing a poker, he crossed the floor as quietly as he could, and put his eye against the peephole in the door.

"Jack?" Clem's voice, soft as fog.

He pulled open the door, drew her into the room, then into his arms. "I thought you'd never get here," he told her.

"Are you making a fire?" she asked, nodding at the poker in his hand.

For a moment, he didn't know what she meant. And then he felt foolish. "Oh, this," he said. "This is . . . well, I was just . . . *yes*. A fire." He returned the poker to its stand as Clem went to the window and looked out.

"Verrry nice," she declared. "Much nicer than Val's."

"Who's Val?"

"My girlfriend. And I see we've been shopping," she added, gesturing to the empty bags at the bottom of the bed. "What fun you've been having! And here I was, worried about you!"

"Well—"

"Is there anything for? . . ."

"Who?"

"Moi?" A demure smile.

And Dunphy thought, She's winding me up. But that wasn't what he said. What he said was, "Oh! Yeah, but . . . they had to have it *reset*."

"Reset?!" A suspicious look from the Clemster as she perched on the arm of an easy chair beside the windows.

"Yeah, it was too big, but—otherwise, I just got a couple of things for myself. Necessities."

She was silent for a moment. Then, "Jack."

"What?"

"Gucci doesn't make necessities."

He decided to change the subject. "You'd be surprised," he said, "and, anyway, we've got a bigger problem than what you obviously think is my shopping jones."

"And what would that be?"

"I was followed from Jersey."

She didn't say anything for a long while, as he made each of them a drink from the minibar. Finally she asked, "By who? What do they want?"

He rattled the ice in her drink and handed it to her. Then he sat down on the side of the bed and told her about Blémont.

"So you *are* an embezzler!" Once again, the round-eyed, exclamatory look.

"It wasn't his money," Dunphy said. "It's not like he earned it."

"Maybe not, but—"

"And since he didn't earn it, how could I *steal* it from him?" He used his forefingers to enclose the verb in quotation marks.

Clementine gave him a sort of look-*sans*-look. "Good point," she said (rather dryly, he thought). "*Now* what do we do?"

Dunphy fell back on the bed, so that he found himself gazing at the pixilated ceiling tiles. The pillow cases gave off a whiff of laundry detergent. "They don't know you," he replied, as much to himself as to Clementine. "So they don't know you're here." He raised his head and cocked an eye at her. "*Do* they?"

Clementine shook her head. "I don't think so."

His head fell back on the pillows. "You didn't ask for me at the desk?"

"No. I came straight up."

They must have changed the sheets when he was out, because they were nice and crisp. "I was thinking," Dunphy said, "maybe you could get a room—across the hall, or something. And I could check out of this one and move in with you." He gave her an expectant look.

"Ye-esss . . . we could do that . . . and then what?"

"I don't know—maybe they'd think I'd left."

For a moment, Clementine didn't say anything. Finally she cleared her throat and asked, "That's your plan?" There was a tone in her voice, and when she said the word *plan*, she made a face and gave her head a funny little shake. Suggesting, perhaps, incredulity. Or dumbfoundment. Or worse—incredulous dumbfoundment. Soon, perhaps, to turn to anger.

Dunphy rose to the occasion, propping himself up on his elbow. "It's not a *plan*," he explained. "It's just an idea." Taste of whiskey (very nice, and good for the cold, too).

"But there is a plan, right? I mean, you do have one?" Clem asked.

"Of course I have a plan," Dunphy answered. "Do I look like a man who doesn't have a plan?" Was it Lemon-Fresh— or what? Some sweet perfume, acquired in the wash. There must be a laundry, Dunphy thought, where they wash the linens and towels of all the big hotels.

"Uhhh, Jack?"

The chambermaids collect the sheets in the morning, and take them somewhere—probably to the basement. Is there a basement in the Zum Storchen?

"Earth to Jack?"

There must be. And a truck would pick them up—

"Hel-*lo*?"

Dunphy looked up. "What?"

"The plan. You were going to tell me what the plan is."

"Oh," he said, "yeah, I was."

"Go on."

"Well . . . the plan is . . . what I was thinking was, you get a room in the hotel—"

"What's the matter with *this* room?"

"Nothing, except . . . I want to check out—you can do it on the TV. So, when I move over to your room, and they don't see me for a while, they'll call *this* room and get someone else. And when they ask the front desk where I am, they'll say I took off. And maybe they'll believe that."

"And then what?" Clementine asked.

"Then I want you to get another room—in Zug—for tomorrow night."

"What's Zug?"

"It's just outside of Zürich—about twenty miles. So we'll need a car, too. Ask the concierge."

"So I get a room, and a car."

Dunphy swung his legs over the side of the bed, sat up, and reached into his pocket. Removing a small key, he tossed it to her.

"And this is what? The key to your heart?"

"Better," Dunphy said. "It fits a safe-deposit box at the Credit Suisse. On the Bahnhofstrasse. Number two-three-zero-nine. Can you remember that?" She nodded. "Ask to see the manager and give him the key. He'll want to see your passport—"

"Which one?"

"Veroushka's. I put both our names on the box, so there won't be any hassle."

"Then what?"

"There's a lot of money in the box. Take some. In fact, take about fifty grand."

"Fifty *what*?"

"Thousand."

She hesitated a moment. "Francs?"

Dunphy shook his head. "Pounds."

Her jaw dropped.

"Just take the money," Dunphy told her, "and meet me in

the parking lot at the train station in Zug. I'll get there as soon after six as I can."

"But—"

"It's just a commuter stop. You'll see me as soon as I come out."

"That's not what I mean. What I mean is, how are you going to get out of the hotel? Without those people seeing you?"

Dunphy picked up one of the pillows and fluffed it. "Don't worry about it," he said. "Now, come here."

21

From the basement of the Zum Storchen to the steps of the train station was barely a mile, but it cost Dunphy one hundred pounds to get there. The Turk who drove the laundry truck was surprised, at first, to find an American businessman in the basement of the hotel. But, once he saw the money, he was more than happy to help his fellow man flee what Dunphy claimed was an angry husband.

The trains to Zug ran all day long, and it would have been a simple matter for Dunphy to get there in time for lunch. But then he'd have hours to kill before Clem arrived, and Zug didn't seem like a good place to do that. The only thing he knew about the town was that it was home to the most secret archive in the world, a font of data so important—or so dangerous—that it could not be kept in America. And since this archive was at once the focal point of his investigation and the reason that he was being hunted, screwing around in Zug did not look like a good idea.

Better to get in and get out.

So a day trip was in order, and he knew exactly where he wanted to go: to Einsiedeln. To see the lady in the hologram—*la protectrice.*

There were trains every thirty minutes, which was about as long as it took to get there. The tracks followed the shoreline of the *Zürichsee*, wending their way through the suburbs. In a perverse way, the trip seemed a neatly scrubbed and altitudinous version of the ride out to Bridgeport. A montage of half-seen vignettes, glimpsed along the route, revealed the Swiss

in the most ordinary of ways: it showed them in their backyards and daily lives, which, as it happened, were not so very
different from other people's backyards and daily lives. The
men and women he saw were leaning out their windows,
smoking cigarettes, hanging laundry, riding bikes, sweeping stairs, chatting, arguing, and generally going about their
business.

When the train turned inland and began its climb into the
mountains, the suburbs—Thalwil, Horgen, and Wädenswil—
gave way to a series of pleasant little towns, each of which was
snowier than its predecessor.

Biberbrugg.

Bennau.

Einsiedeln.

Leaving the station, Dunphy picked up a tourist brochure
and, following the map on its cover, began walking uphill
along the diminutive main street, past ski shops and restaurants, heading in the direction of the Benedictine Abbey con-
secrated to Our Lady of Einsiedeln. The word, he saw, meant
hermits—which made her (in postmodern terms, at least)
Our Lady of the Homeless. In any case, the black Madonna.

The town itself was a ski resort or, if not quite a resort, a
place where *some* people came to ski—though not, it seemed,
all that many. Dunphy passed two or three small hotels on his
way to the abbey, but there were only a few cars on the street
and not that many passersby. The impression he got was of a
quietly prosperous village whose only claim to fame was the
peculiar statue in its midst.

About six blocks from the train station, this impression
gave way to astonishment, as he emerged from the high street
into a square of vast proportions. In the center of the square,
maybe fifty yards away, was a fountain, its waters frozen. Beyond the fountain, hunkering atop a broad expanse of steps,
was the abbey itself. Flanked by a string of souvenir shops
selling trinkets and postcards, the building was as graceful as
it was massive. Seeing it for the first time, Dunphy was as-
tounded by its size and, also, by the building's simplicity and

lack of ornamentation. At once beautiful and immensely plain, it made Dunphy think of a Mona Lisa carved in stone.

Mounting the steps one by one, he turned at the top to look out over the square, the town, and the surrounding mountains. A soft breeze filled his lungs with the wet scent of melting snow—and hay, and manure. Glancing at the brochure, he saw that the abbey had been a working farm for more than five hundred years. The monks were said to be famous for the horses and cattle that they bred.

Turning, he entered the church through a towering doorway and stood, blinking, in the voluminous gloom. Larger than some cathedrals, the church was a hive of flickering candles, redolent of beeswax and the lingering fragrance of incense. As his eyes adjusted to the building's eternal twilight, he realized that he was standing in an architectural oxymoron, the spectacular interior of the church revoking the simplicity of the walls that contained it. Simply put, the interior of the church was a bedlam of flowers and ornament, tapestries, paintings, frescoes, and gold. Cherubim peeked from every crevice. Candelabra blazed. Angels leaped and spread their wings across pillars and walls. It was as if a medieval Disney had been given free rein and a palette of three colors: ebony, ivory, and gold.

This isn't the church I went to as a child, Dunphy mused. This is something else . . . but what?

Moving deeper into the building, which seemed to brighten as his eyes adjusted and it drew him in, he found himself standing at the entrance to the Lady Chapel. This was a free-standing inner sanctum fashioned entirely of black marble, with alabaster saints standing on the roof and bas-reliefs etched in gold. About the size of a large gazebo, the chapel was banked with armloads of flowers, so that the air was pregnant with the scent of wet ferns and roses. Nearby, a strange assortment of people—pilgrims from every country, he supposed—knelt on the unforgiving floor, praying with an intensity that Dunphy could not imagine.

The focal point of their adoration was a statue, about four

feet tall, of what seemed to be—what *had* to be—the Virgin Mary. Dressed in robes of gold wrought with images of fruit and grain, she wore a crown while cradling a child in her left arm.

And the thing about it was: she was black—and so was the child. Not brown, but black. Black as pitch. Black as anthracite. Black as space.

The improbability of the image was so startling that it took Dunphy's breath away and forced the sacrilegious question: What the fuck . . . is this doing . . . in Switzerland? And, immediately, the answer came back: What's it doing . . . anywhere?

Taking a few steps back from the shrine, Dunphy pulled out the tourist brochure from the pocket of his coat and, standing behind the prayerful, began to read:

> For seven years, a Hohenzollern count (Meinrad) lived as a hermit in the Dark Forest above the site where the abbey church now stands. In the winter of 861, Meinrad was beaten to death by robbers, who were then followed to Zürich by Meinrad's only friends—magical ravens whom the hermit had befriended during his long years of solitude. In Zürich, the ravens attacked the old monk's murderers, causing such a stir that the brigands were quickly brought to justice.
>
> The abbey and church were built on the site above Meinrad's cave in 934. In the centuries that followed, the abbey suffered a series of fires until it was rebuilt in its present form in the eighteenth century.
>
> In 1799, agents of Napoléon were sent to Einsiedeln to capture the black Madonna, but the abbey's monks learned of the foray in advance and smuggled Our Lady over the mountains to Austria. There, she was painted white in an effort to conceal her identity. After three years in exile, the statue was restored to its original color and returned to Einsiedeln.
>
> Today, Saint Meinrad's skull is preserved in a golden

casket beneath the feet of the Madonna. Each year, the skull is taken out and blessed at a special mass.

"Sie ist verblüfft, nicht ist sie?"

The question came at Dunphy in an awed whisper, so close that it knocked him back on his heels, an involuntary little jump that he couldn't conceal. Thinking he'd been followed, he turned toward the voice, expecting the worst. But it wasn't Blondie, and it wasn't the Jock. It was a pale American in a black trench coat. Vandyke beard.

"Excuse me?" Dunphy asked.

It was the man's turn to look surprised. "Oh!" he said. "You're American! I was just saying . . . " His voice returned to a whisper. "I was just saying, she's really something, isn't she?"

Dunphy nodded. "Yeah, she is."

The man looked embarrassed. "I thought you were German," he confided. "I can usually tell."

Dunphy frowned in a thoughtful way and cocked his head to the side, as if to say, It happens.

"I go by the shoes," the man added, nodding toward the floor. "The shoes are the giveaway, every time."

Dunphy cocked his head the same way as before, as if to say, No shit, when, over the man's shoulder, he saw a very unlikely tour group shuffling toward them. It consisted of eight or nine pallid-faced men in their late thirties, wearing identical black trench coats.

"My fan club," the man next to him explained.

For a moment, Dunphy thought they were there for *him*. But, no, it really *was* a tour group, albeit one that seemed to consist entirely of middle-aged vampires. Then Dunphy noticed, with a frisson of anxiety, that at least two of the men in the group were wearing string ties and bolos—accoutrements that somehow made him nervous.

Suddenly, one of the tourists turned on his heel and, with his back to the shrine, addressed the group in an accent straight out of *Deliverance*. "The question ah asked earlier—

about Meinrad's life befo' he came heah? Who knows the ansuh?" No one moved, which made the man smile in a self-satisfied way. "It's a stumpah, ah'll admit, but the ansuh is: Paracelsus!" He looked from face to face, nodding at their amazement. "That's raht. Ole Paracelsus—probably the greatest alchemist of all time—bawn raht up there on Etzel peak, same place Meinrad was livin'. Now, you tell me! How 'bout *them* blue apples?"

With little nods, and chuckles, and looks of bemused astonishment, the men in the group exchanged glances with one another. To Dunphy, it was apparent that they shared a secret, or imagined that they did.

"Well, I gotta get back," Dunphy said. "Nice talkin' to you." And with a little salute, he backed away from the shrine, turned, and left.

Outside, snowflakes curled through the air in such small numbers that it seemed to Dunphy he could count them. Jamming his hands into the pockets of his topcoat, he descended the steps to the plaza, walking double-time. He was thinking about the man in the trench coat and the people he was with, wondering who they were and if they were whom he thought they were—when his suspicion was confirmed. At the edge of the square, a black minivan sat in the cold, its engine running, wisps of smoke curling from its tailpipes. On its side, a peculiar crest—a crown with a halo, flanked by angels, and the words:

MONARCH ASSURANCE
ZUG

He met Clementine (or Veroushka, as she now preferred to be called), in the parking lot at the commuter rail station in Zug. She was driving a rented VW Golf and told him excitedly that she'd already checked into the Ochsen Hotel—which was "fab"—and had been "on a jaunt" around the town.

"There are more corporations registered in Zug than there are people!" she gushed. "Did you know that?"

"Uh-uh," Dunphy replied, looking over his shoulder. "And where's the hotel?"

"It's just down Baarstrasse—which means Bear Street—that's what we're on. And the waterfront's only a hop, skip, and a jump."

Dunphy adjusted the side mirror to see if she'd been followed, but he couldn't tell. Baarstrasse was a busy street, and there were lots of cars behind them. "Why would we want to go to the waterfront?"

"Because it's beautiful," she said, "and because I'm hungry. And that's where the nicest restaurants are."

Might as well, Dunphy thought. We're going to be busy in the morning.

The town surprised him. It was tastefully modern and obviously high-tech, an attractive collection of modern office buildings that stood shoulder to shoulder with more traditional structures—including some that were very old. This might have been an architectural disaster, but it was not because what was new was built to human scale. There were no skyscrapers that Dunphy could see, and lots of trees.

And in the center of it all, only five minutes from the train station, was the medieval quarter, a warren of cobblestone lanes whose antique city walls housed an array of exquisite little shops selling jewelry and art, ancient maps and fine wine. Leaving their car in the courtyard of the Ochsen Hotel, Dunphy let Clem lead him across the street and into the Old Town.

Entering through a passage in the wall outside the Rathaus, they wandered along a gaslit lane until they reached a small park at the edge of the Zuger See. The twilight was fading now, and a full moon was rising over the Alps. Putting his arm around Clem's waist, he pulled her close to him. "What are you thinking about?" he whispered.

"Food," she said.

They settled on a bistro with mullioned windows and lace curtains, overlooking the water. As early as it was, they had the restaurant almost to themselves. Seated at a wooden table with their backs to a softly hissing fireplace, they ordered lake fish and *longeole* with a plate of rosti and a chilled bottle of Château Carbonnieux. Then they got down to business.

"We have to get up early," Dunphy said. "It's critical."

"What time?" she asked.

"I don't know. Five-thirty or six. The thing is, I've only got from seven to one—and that's cutting it close. Seven to noon would be safer."

She took a sip of wine, smacked her lips, and smiled. "Foxy," she said.

"Just like Clem."

She smiled. "You should call me Veroushka."

"Clem . . ."

"Anyway—what is this place you're going to?"

"It's called Monarch Assurance—on Alpenstrasse."

"So it's an insurance company."

"No."

"Then what?"

Dunphy shook his head. "I'm not sure," he replied. "Some kind of special archive."

"For who?"

"The Company," Dunphy said.

"You mean . . ."

"The company I used to work for."

"And they keep this archive over here? In bloody Zug?"

Dunphy nodded.

"But why?" she asked. "Why would anyone keep *anything* over here?"

"I don't know," Dunphy answered. "But it's the most sensitive information they have."

"Then I should think they'd want to keep it close to home."

"Right. That's exactly what you'd think. But you'd be wrong."

Clem frowned. "How do you know about this place?" she asked.

Dunphy poured himself a second glass of wine, swirled it in the firelight, and told her what he'd done as a reference analyst on the FOIA desk.

"No wonder they're angry with you," she exclaimed.

"Yeah," Dunphy muttered, "no wonder . . ."

"So how are we going to get out of this? Because if that Frenchman doesn't kill you for stealing his money—"

"It wasn't his money."

"—the CIA will." She looked at him expectantly, but he didn't say anything. *"Well?"*

"Well, *what*?"

"What are you going to *do* about it?"

"Which?" he asked. "The Frenchman or the Agency?"

She just looked at him.

"Because they're two different problems," he said, "though I don't think we'll have to worry about Blémont—unless you were followed. And I don't know why you *would* have been followed. They don't know you. Anyway, I didn't see anybody, so . . . that leaves the Agency. And I don't know what to say about the Agency, because I don't even know what the question is."

"Then it's hopeless," Clem opined.

Dunphy shook his head. "No, it's not hopeless. Because even if I don't know what the question is, I know where the answers are. They're in that archive, just up the street. And you're going to help me get at them, because otherwise . . ."

"What?"

He looked at her for a long moment. Then he leaned forward in a confidential way and whispered, "Yikes."

They awoke the next morning at five-thirty, and breakfasted on toast and coffee in a café on the Alpenstrasse, a couple of blocks from the Monarch Assurance Company. The idea was for Dunphy to talk his way into the Special Registry while Clementine made reservations for a flight to Tenerife that same afternoon.

"Go to the airport," Dunphy said. "Buy the tickets and then come back for me."

Clem nodded. "At one."

"You have to be *waiting* at one—right here, with the car running. Or I'm fucked. Because timing's everything. There's a six-hour difference between Washington and Zug—and that's the window. Max's pass will get me in the building, but getting into the archive . . . they're gonna want to check with Langley. And not just Langley, they're gonna want to talk to a guy named Matta."

"And he'll say it's okay?" Clem asked.

"No. He'll tell 'em to kill me. But that's where the time difference comes in. They won't call him in the middle of the night because there's no real emergency. Or no obvious one, anyway. And it's not like I'm going anywhere. I mean, not as far as *they're* concerned. So they'll wait until it's morning in the States, and then they'll call. I figure my pull date's about one o'clock in the afternoon. After that, it all goes bad."

Clementine thought about it for a moment. Finally, she asked, "What if they don't mind waking him up?"

Dunphy hesitated, and then he shrugged. "Well, *Veroushka,* if I'm not sitting in the car with you by five after one? Just take the money and run."

Leaving Clem with her coffee, Dunphy walked up Alpenstrasse in search of Monarch Assurance. He didn't bother looking at the numbers. He could see the building ahead, about three blocks away. It was an ultramodern, blue-glass cube, six stories high and completely opaque. It had CIA written all over it—only, as it turned out, he'd come too far. The cube was the headquarters of a commodities trading firm. Monarch was back the other way.

Retracing his steps, he would have walked past the building a second time if he hadn't overheard American voices. Turning, he found himself outside 15 Alpenstrasse. Nearby, a dull brass plaque clung to the wall of a cross-timbered old pile with leaded-glass windows.

MONARCH ASSURANCE, AG

The building needed renovation, but it was busy nonetheless, with people streaming into work even at this early hour. Most of them, Dunphy saw, were men, and almost all of them were wearing dark topcoats over dark suits—a circumstance that made him want to keep his coat on. Who knew what they'd make of his houndstooth sports jacket?

Taking a deep breath, Dunphy joined the stream, passing through a towering doorway whose antique wooden doors were thrown open to the winter.

Inside, a bank of male receptionists sat behind a polished mahogany counter, fielding phone calls and visitors. Dunphy did his best to ignore them, joining a queue of office workers waiting to pass through a high-tech turnstile. Thronged and buzzing, the place reminded Dunphy of a hive.

Observing the people in front of him, Dunphy saw how each of them inserted his building pass in a slot on the left side of the turnstile, while at the same time pressing his right thumb on an illuminated glass panel to the right. Barely a second went by before the turnstile went *chnnnk!*—as if it were a time clock being punched—and the worker passed through to a hallway on the other side.

When Dunphy's turn came, he was beginning to hyperventilate. Inserting his building pass in the slot, he pressed his right thumb to the glass and waited . . . counting the seconds as they passed. *Three. Four. Five.* A low murmur, more impatient than threatening, washed up against his back.

"I don't get it," he said, muttering to no one in particular. "It's always worked before." He could see one of the receptionists getting to his feet, eyes on Dunphy. The man looked worried.

I'm gonna kill that fuckin' Russian, Dunphy thought, and tried the pass again. Once again, nothing happened. The receptionist was on his feet now, and Dunphy was about to bolt. With a little luck, he could hit the door at a run and lose himself—

"You're upside down."

The voice made him jump, so that when he turned to its source, Dunphy's heart was slamming against his ribs. Black trench coat. String tie. Bifocals.

"What?"

"Your pass—it's upside down." The guy nodded toward the turnstile.

Dunphy looked. "Oh, yeah," he said, and fumbling, reinserted the pass so that the hologram went into the slot. *Chnnnk!* "Thanks." He was sweating.

The hallway ran in a straight line for about thirty feet, then doglegged to the right before emptying into a mezzanine that seemed to have been lifted from a Batman film. Black marble floors and travertine walls glittered against a backdrop of stainless steel elevators. And in the center of the room, its only ornament, stood a transparent cylinder on a golden pillar, surrounded by flowers. Inside the jar, a replica of *la protectrice*. Blacker, even, than the marble on the floor. And a most unusual installation for a government building—if that's what this was.

Dunphy watched the elevator indicators sweep from one to five, and realized, a little belatedly, that he was in the presence of a major contradiction: a one-story building with five floors. Which meant that most of the place was underground.

"Heyyy, stranger!" A clap on the back made Dunphy start. Turning, he saw the man with the Vandyke beard, the one from the abbey, the guy with the posse.

"Heyyy," Dunphy replied, forcing a smile. "You're up bright and early."

The man shrugged. "That's nothing new. But what about you? This your first time here?"

Dunphy shook his head. "It's been a while, but—yeah, when I saw you, I'd just gotten into town."

"And you *couldn't! wait!* to see Her!" The man laughed and shook his head in mock amazement.

For a moment, Dunphy didn't know what he meant. But

then he understood, and treated the guy to what he was looking for: a sheepish smile. "I guess," he said.

The elevator arrived, and the two of them got in. Classical music played softly on the intercom. The *Messiah*, Dunphy thought, but, then, that's what he always thought when he heard classical music. His own tastes ran to Cesaria Evora or, if he'd been drinking, the Cowboy Junkies.

"Where you headed?" the man asked, punching a button.

For the second time in the same minute, Dunphy didn't know what to say. The guy with the beard stood there with an expectant look, his forefinger pointing at the control panel. Finally Dunphy replied, "Chief's office."

The man made a moue, to show just how impressed he was, then stabbed at the panel with his finger. A couple of other people got on, the doors closed, and the elevator began what seemed like a motionless descent. A few seconds later, the doors opened, and when no one moved, Dunphy stepped out.

"It's on your left," the guy said. "All the way down the hall."

The corridor was broad and softly lighted, with plum-colored carpeting, mauve walls, and Art Deco sconces. Paintings and drawings hung from the walls in elaborately hand-carved and gilded frames. An ancient woodcut, limning *The Tombe of Jacques de Molay*. An architectural drawing, rendering the floor plan of an unidentified castle—cathedral—both. An oil painting in which a recumbent knight is shorn of his hair by a beautiful maid. A second painting that Dunphy thought of as an alas-poor-Yorick number, depicting a shepherd in what can only have been Acadia, contemplating the skull of . . . Yorick. Meinrad. Someone.

Finally, Dunphy arrived at a smoked-glass door at the end of the corridor. On the glass, a single word: DIREKTOR.

His heart was banging against his chest, so that it took all the courage he had to rap smartly on the door and then, without waiting for an answer, to barge in. A birdlike woman with salt-and-pepper hair looked up from behind a wafer-thin computer screen. She was wearing tortoiseshell reading glasses and seemed more irritated than startled.

"Kann ich Ihnen helfen?"

"Not unless you speak English," Dunphy told her, and glanced around the room. "I'm here to see the *Direktor*."

She gave him a skeptical look. "That's impossible," she said, speaking in a clipped German accent. "For one thing, you must have an appointment. And I don't think you have one."

"No," Dunphy replied, "I don't. But I've got something better."

"Oh?"

"Yeah. I've got an assignment." He nodded toward a door in the corner of the room and began to move toward it. "Is this his office?"

He thought she was going to levitate. As it was, she half rose out of her chair. "No! I mean, yes, of course it is—but that has nothing to do with you. He isn't here. And who *are* you, anyway?" She had her hand on the telephone.

With a show of irritation, he pulled out his building pass and held it out to her. She squinted at it for a moment, then copied his name into a little book on her desk.

"You've been here before," she said, looking unsure.

Dunphy nodded uncomfortably. "Once or twice, but that was a long time ago."

"Because I remember your name, but . . . " She peered at him over her reading glasses, then shook her head.

"You must've seen it in a file or something, because I haven't been here in years."

She looked doubtful. "Perhaps."

"Anyway, when does the *Direktor* get in?" Dunphy asked, eager to change the subject.

"Usually, not until eight. Today, not at all."

The reply caught Dunphy by surprise, and for a moment, he was off balance. He'd been counting on the guy being at work. "Not at all?" he asked.

"No."

"Well, why not? Where is he?"

"In Washington—there's been a flap. Now, if you don't mind—"

Dunphy made a guess. "You mean, the Schidlof business."

The woman's demeanor softened with surprise. "Yes," she said, settling back in her seat. "There was a shooting—"

Dunphy nodded impatiently, as if he'd heard it all before. "In London," he said. Run with it, he told himself. This could be good.

She gave a little nod, but was obviously impressed by how much he knew.

"That's why I'm here," Dunphy told her. "Poor Jesse."

"They say he'll be all right."

"All right, maybe. Good as new, I doubt." He gave her a thoughtful look. "I'm going to need some office space," he said, "for a couple of days—maybe a week. And an open line to Harry Matta's office in Langley."

Her eyes rounded at the mention of Matta's name. "Well," she said, looking uncertain.

"Well what?"

"Well, I don't know."

"About what?"

"This!"

"You're the *Direktor*'s secretary, aren't you?"

"Actually," she corrected, "I'm his executive assistant."

"Even better." He peered at the nameplate on her desk. "It's Hilda, right?"

She gave him the tiniest of nods, suspicious of his familiarity.

"Okay, Hilda, so what I'm suggesting is—we ought to get started."

"But I can't give you an office. For this, I would need permission. Perhaps the deputy *Direktor* . . . " She reached for the phone.

Dunphy rolled his eyes, then cocked his head, and asked, "Do I look like the town crier? Do I look like someone's advance man?"

The questions confused her for a moment. Then she shook her head. "No."

"Good. Because if it comes down to it, let's just call the Man."

"Who?"

"The *Direktor*. You know where he's staying, right?"

"Of course, but—"

"What's the number?" He reached for the phone, but she covered the receiver with her hand.

"We can't call him now. It's one-thirty there."

"Well, if you don't want to wake up your boss, call Langley," Dunphy insisted. "Tell them to patch you through to Matta. Let's get *him* outa bed!"

"But what would I say?" she asked, her eyes widening with panic.

"Tell him you want to know if I can have an office. At two in the morning, I'm sure he'll be very impressed."

She looked puzzled. "With what?"

"Your sense of initiative."

"Oh," she said, "*now* we have sarcasm."

Dunphy smiled apologetically. "Sorry . . . I'm under a lot of pressure." He paused and leaned toward her with a sympathetic and confidential air. "Look," he said, "if you'll hook me up with an office, we can talk to them this afternoon—first thing. Your boss, my boss, whoever you want. And they'll confirm what I've said. You've seen my pass. I wouldn't be here if I didn't belong." He could see the wheels turning in her mind. Matta . . . Curry . . . the pass.

"Okay!" she said, raising her hand to shut him up. "There's a room on the fourth floor—"

"The fourth floor will be fine."

"I'll call the *Direktor* at one o'clock—he's an early riser. Then, if he thinks it is necessary, we can contact *Herr* Matta."

"Fine," Dunphy said. "If you'll just point the way, I'll get started."

She picked up the phone. "Security will show you where to go."

"One other thing."

"Yes?"

"I'm gonna need someone to hump files for me."

She looked blank. "Files? *Hump?*"

"Absolutely. Why do you think I need the office?"

"I don't know. Why *do* you?"

"For damage control."

"What?"

"Damage control." He peered at her closely. "You know what happened to Curry, right?"

"Of course. There was a cable."

"I know," he said. "I wrote it. Anyway, the guy who shot him—"

"Dunphy."

He looked impressed. He *was* impressed. "Right. *Jack* Dunphy—who, incidentally, is one mean son of a bitch. Pardon my French."

She shrugged. "I live among men," she said. "I'm used to it."

"Understood. Anyway, Dunphy worked for the Agency—you knew that, right?"

"Of course."

"And you know what he did—what his job was?"

"No."

Dunphy frowned. "I thought I put it in the cable . . ."

"I don't think so."

"Well, anyway, he was an FOIA guy." Seeing her puzzled look, he elaborated. "Part of the Freedom of Information staff."

"Oh, yes?" She looked bemused—and relieved. "Is *that* all?"

"Yes. That's all. And that's why I'm doing damage control."

She looked at him in a way that told him she didn't understand.

"Harry thinks there's been a breach," he explained.

"A breach?"

"In the Andromeda files. The son of a bitch went through 'em like he was surfin' the Net."

The information didn't seem to register. And then, after a moment or two, she swayed, ever so slightly in her chair. For a second, Dunphy thought she was about to lose her balance. But she didn't. She just sat there, getting whiter and whiter until, in the end, she lurched to her feet and said, "Let's get you set up right away, shall we?"

22

The first of the files didn't arrive for almost an hour, by which time Dunphy was nearly paralyzed with paranoia. Though he knew they wouldn't call Matta at two in the morning, it occurred to him for the first time that the Special Registry might have a copy of Brading's personnel file. After all, it was they who'd issued the pass. If they did, then the woman he'd spoken to, Hilda, might be suspicious enough to pull it—in which case, she'd see in an instant that Dunphy was impersonating a much older man. And then they'd come for him.

The room he'd been given resembled a cell without windows. It measured three strides by three and was barely large enough to contain the desk and chair in which Dunphy now sat. His overcoat hung from a coatrack next to the door—and that was that. There was a telephone, but no books, so that he had nothing to do until his "assistant"—a bull-necked security guard named Dieter—barged in with half a dozen kraft-colored folders marked *Schidlof*. Dunphy checked his watch. It was 8:25 A.M.

"You must sign for them," Dieter said, handing Dunphy a clipboard.

"While I'm reading these," Dunphy said, scrawling Braden's name on the Document Control List, "I'd like you to pull whatever you've got on a guy named Dunphy—D-U-N-P-H-Y—first name, Jack. Got it?"

"Sure."

"And I'll want to see the Optical Magick files, too, and anything you can get me on the . . . uhhh . . . Bovine Census."

Dieter frowned.

"What's wrong?" Dunphy asked.

"We have pushcarts," Dieter said, "but the Census—this is impossible. I'd need a truck."

Dunphy tried to conceal his mistake. "Just the last two months. New Mexico and Arizona."

This seemed to satisfy his new assistant. When the door closed, Dunphy sat back with a sigh of relief, then turned to the files with the relish and alarm of a twelve-year-old boy who's just stumbled upon his parents' pornography stash.

His first impression was that the file was atypical of other dossiers that he'd seen at the Agency. Usually, if a person was of "operational interest" to the CIA, a 201 file would be opened and interviews laid on. But there were no interviews in Schidlof's dossier—just data. His telephone records and credit-card receipts were in separate folders, as were copies of the pages in his passport, showing most of the places he'd traveled during the past ten years. There were some black-and-white contact sheets whose images seemed to have been taken from a car with the help of a telephoto lens. Looking at the pictures, Dunphy recognized the professor's house (he'd helped Tommy Davis case the place) and Schidlof, too. There were pictures of the professor—leaving for work, getting his mail, coming home, and so on. Looks healthy enough, Dunphy thought, for someone who's about to become a torso.

And that was the point, really. The Schidlof dossier was not an investigative file. Whoever put it together hadn't been interested in Schidlof, the man, as much as they were in Schidlof, the Problem. So it didn't matter, really, who the professor's friends were, or what his neighbors thought of him. All that was needed was the old boy's address and a good likeness.

So that, when the time came, they'd whack the right guy.

Which meant that Schidlof had pissed somebody off (Curry or Matta). Or worse—he'd scared them. And when he'd done that, the question had gone out, "Who *is* this son of a bitch?" And bang! the answer came back in the form of the dossier at hand: He's this guy, it said. This is what he looks like. This is where he lives.

Most of the information seemed to have been collected in a single sweep. And while Dunphy couldn't be sure when the sweep had been initiated, it looked as if it was last September. Riffling through a folder that bulged with copies of credit-card receipts, and a second folder that held Schidlof's telephone toll records, Dunphy could see that there were no entries after September 9. Which meant that Schidlof had come to Matta's attention at about that time, some six or seven months ago. And this is what Dunphy learned:

Leon Aaron Schidlof, (M.A., Oxon.; Dip. Anal. Psy., Zürich) was a British citizen, born October 14, 1942, in the city of Hull. He was a graduate of Oxford's New College (1963), and trained as an analyst at the C. G. Jung Institute in Zürich (1964–7). A contributor to numerous anthologies and professional journals, Schidlof was the author of two books: *A Dictionary of Symbols* (New York, 1979), and a book on Jungian psychology, *Die Weiblichen in der Jungian Psychologie* (Heidelberg, 1986). After twenty years as an analyst in London, he had taken on the responsibility of teaching a seminar at King's College in the Strand. Never married, his nearest relative was an older sister, a resident of Tunbridge Wells. Schidlof's own address (which Dunphy knew by heart) followed.

Pretty innocuous, Dunphy thought. You wouldn't think a guy like him would hit the fan.

The second folder held Schidlof's credit-card receipts and telephone records. Dunphy didn't know what to make of them, really, and wondered if Matta really cared. In all likelihood, the data were collected because it was easy to get them, and doing so made the gumshoes look as if they knew what they were doing. Still, a couple of things stood out. Like the fact that there were rather a lot of trips on Swissair. Two in June, then one each in July, August, and September. What was *that* all about?

The Swissair charges didn't say where he'd flown to, but

they didn't have to: the credit-card receipts included hotel charges for the same months. And the charges were always the same: Hotel Florida, Seefeldstrasse 63, Zürich.

Dunphy knew the place. It was a clean, midrange hotel, a few blocks east of Bellevueplatz, which was a mixing bowl for the city's trams. It was a decent enough place, if you were on a budget, and exactly the kind of hotel where you'd expect an academic to stay while doing research in a country as expensive as Switzerland.

But Swissair wasn't the only airline Schidlof flew. His Visa bill listed a £371 expenditure with British Airways, incurred September 5. Other charges documented Schidlof's visit to New York on the sixth and seventh of that same month. He'd stayed at the Washington Square Hotel and eaten at a couple of Indian joints on Third Avenue.

So what?

Dunphy reexamined the earlier charges. The professor's last visit to Zürich had occurred on September 3. The New York trip followed about three days later—and soon after that, the old boy was put under telephone surveillance. Which suggested (but certainly didn't prove) that the three events were related: the trip to Zürich, the visit to New York, and the bugged phones.

What was he doing in New York? Dunphy asked himself. And the reply came back: What was he doing in Zürich? And then, in frustration: What was he doing anywhere?

The third folder contained Schidlof's bank statements, canceled checks, and . . . pay dirt. On September 4, while in Zürich, the professor had written a check for two thousand pounds to someone named Margaritha Vogelei. Three days later, while visiting New York, he'd written a smaller check to an enterprise known as Gil Beckley Associates.

The name was familiar. Dunphy had seen it before, or heard it somewhere—on television, or in the movies. Beckley was an actor, or something. No. Not an actor. But . . .

Dunphy looked at the check. It was in the amount of five hundred pounds and had taken almost two months to clear from Schidlof's account at the National Westminster, in London, to Beckley's account at Citibank, New York. At the bottom of the check, on a line labeled *Memo*, was a notation in Schidlof's handwriting: *Retainer,* it said—but not for what.

Then Dunphy remembered.

Handwriting. Beckley wasn't an actor, but he'd been on television a lot. The guy was a graphologist—or as he liked to say, a "documents examiner." He'd put in his time at the FBI, retired, and gone into private practice. He was an expert witness, and as Dunphy recalled, he had a keen sense of his own importance. Dunphy had seen him on an A&E show— *Investigative Reports.* He'd been hired to authenticate love letters purportedly written by J. Edgar Hoover to an agent named Purvis. As Dunphy recalled, Beckley had trashed the letters, calling them "clumsy forgeries."

It was beginning to get interesting. Schidlof goes to Zürich and pays this Vogelei woman a couple of grand—*for something.* Then he flies to New York and shells out another five hundred pounds to retain a graphologist. After that, his phones are bugged—and then he's dead. So what happened? Dunphy asked himself.

Well, duh . . . he found some *documents* in Zürich.

Okay . . . but why authenticate them in the States? Why not in London?

Because they're American documents, Dunphy supposed, or the writer was. But who?

Dunphy sat back in his chair and looked up at the ceiling. He was trying to remember when Curry had called, saying he needed a favor. Sometime in the fall. September. October. Something like that. He didn't remember, really. But around the time that Schidlof had come back from New York.

There was a folder with copies of Schidlof's *Who's Who* entries, his lease and medical records—none of which were of interest to Dunphy. Finally, there was a slim folder that contained two cables. The first read:

FLASH

TEXT OF TELEGRAM 98LANGLEY 009100

PAGE 01

FROM SECURITY RESEARCH STAFF

    OFFICE OF DIRECTOR/LANGLEY HQS

TO CIA/COS/LONDON

    AMERICAN EMBASSY IMMEDIATE 1130

PRIORITY

TAGS: NONE

SUBJ: SCHIDLOF

REF: ANDROMEDA

1. TOP SECRET/ULTRA ENTIRE TEXT
2. UNILATERALLY CONTROLLED SOURCE REPORTS TELE-
   PHONE CONTACT WITH UKCIT/SCHIDLOF LEO/SEPT 5.
   SUBSEQUENT F-2-F CONTACT NEW YORK SEPT 7–8.
3. SCHIDLOF CLAIMS TO BE RESIDENT OF LONDON.
4. SCHIDLOF IN POSSESSION OF ANDROMEDA-SENSITIVE
   MATERIALS.
5. WHO'S SCHIDLOF?

The reply came back from Jesse Curry the following afternoon. Stripped of its headers, it read:

VISA APPLICATION (AND WHO'S WHO ENTRIES) INDICATE
LEON SCHIDLOF IS A JUNGIAN ANALYST AND KING'S COL-
LEGE DON. NO CRIMINAL RECORD. WHAT AM I LOOKING FOR?

There were no other cables, though there must have been
other communications. If Matta hadn't told him to do it,
Curry wouldn't have collected the information that he had,
and he wouldn't have tasked Dunphy to organize coverage of
the professor's phones. Which meant . . . what? Just that
Matta was minimizing the paper trail—which was prudent.

And so was the decision to use someone like Dunphy, working under nonofficial cover, as a cutout to someone like Tommy Davis. Matta *could* have requested coverage from MI5, but this way, deniability was absolute. In the event of unwanted publicity, it would appear that Schidlof had been bugged by an Irish criminal, who was in turn working for a man who didn't exist.

The next-to-last folder sent a surge through his heart. It contained a small manila envelope with a circular tab on the flap. A length of very thin string was stapled to the envelope itself and wrapped around the tab, keeping the contents locked inside. Unwinding the string, Dunphy upended the envelope and a dozen microcassettes spilled out on the desk. *Hel-lo!*

He recognized the tapes. Each of them was numbered and dated in his own handwriting. Number one bore the notation, *9/14–9/19*—which answered his earlier question: when was the coverage initiated? About a week after Schidlof returned to England from New York. In other words, almost immediately after Matta's cable to Curry, asking *Who's Schidlof?*

Which was nice to know, but now he had a decision to make: he could ask the security guard to find him a tape recorder so that he could listen to the tapes, or he could continue to read from the files. The tapes were tempting. If nothing else, it would be interesting to hear Schidlof's voice again. On the other hand, he didn't have a lot of time to spend in the Special Registry, and he could cover more ground going through files than he could listening to tapes. Better, then, to read.

The last folder contained a packet of letters, folded in thirds and bundled together by a length of jute twine. Dunphy undid the knot and unfolded the first page. It was, he saw, a congratulatory note addressed to C. G. Jung, Küsnacht, Switzerland. Dated February 23, 1931, the page was written by hand in green ink on the letterhead of a New York law firm, Sullivan & Cromwell:

Dear Dr. Jung,

Please accept my profound thanks for your unrelenting efforts on behalf of my election to the Magdalene Society. From this moment forward, it will always be the beacon that guides my life. In our mutual pursuit of the New Jerusalem, I want you to know that I will always be your ally. (My brother, John, writes separately, but I have spoken with him, and his feelings are a mirror of my own.) With *deep* respect, and all my gratitude,

Allen

A postscript followed:

P. S. Clove sends her love (and, thanks to you, is thriving).

Allen? Allen who? Dunphy wondered. And then he remembered the cross-references in Schidlof's file—not the one on the desk in front of him, but the one he'd seen in Langley. Dulles . . . Dunphy . . . Jung. And then what? Dunphy tried to recall. Optical Magick . . . or the 143rd. But Dulles, in any case. John's brother. Allen.

Dunphy riffled the letters in his hands. This is what Schidlof bought from the Vogelei woman. It had to be. But who was she? he wondered, and immediately the answer came back: an antiquarian, a relative—someone who worked for Jung. It didn't matter, really. The point was: these were the papers that Schidlof had tried to authenticate. These were the papers that had gotten him killed.

Feeling for the first time that he was beginning to get somewhere, Dunphy unfolded the second letter and continued to read. Like its predecessor, this letter was also on Sullivan & Cromwell stationery. Written almost two years after the first, it pretended to be a thank-you note for the hospitality that Jung had shown to Dulles and his wife the previous summer. Once the thank-you had been fulsomely expressed, however, Dulles got down to a more delicate business—expressing his worries about "our new Helmsman."

His genius is, of course, deeply engraved on the literary record. Few men have written so well, and fewer still have had so profound an influence upon their contemporaries. Surely, the vision and courage that are everywhere apparent in his writing will serve him well as he exercises the terrible responsibilities of his new position.

And yet, while our Helmsmen have often been artists or men of letters (Bacon, Hugo, Debussy—no roll call could be more illustrious), I fear that we are on the brink of what the Chinese call "interesting times." And in such times, an order such as our own might best be served by a quiet diplomat, someone capable of navigating safe passage amid the clashing ships of state. My feeling is that Ezra may be too outspoken—indeed, that he may be too flamboyant—to steer our small band safely toward the millennium.

Allen

Makes you wonder, Dunphy thought. Bacon, Hugo, and Debussy? Ezra? Were they talking about the man he thought they were talking about? There wasn't any doubt, really. How many outspoken and "flamboyant" Ezras were writing in the 1930s—and how many of those were cross-references in the Andromeda file? Just one. E. Pound.

Which made Pound the Helmsman. But, of what? The Magdalene Society. But what's that? And this business of the New Jerusalem . . .

Arranging the letters in chronological order, Dunphy saw that Dulles wrote to Jung on four or five occasions each year. For the most part, these letters were transparent in meaning, as when Dulles sought advice about his wife's "nervous condition." But there were mysteries, too, and not the least of them was the identity of someone whom Dulles repeatedly referred to as "our young man." Of this person, few details could be gleaned beyond his youth and gender. But one such detail concerned a birthmark. In a letter from Biarritz, dated July 9, 1936, Dulles wrote of the great privilege I had in spending the afternoon with our young man. Down from Paris for the weekend, he joined us at our cabana on the beach. There, I saw the mark upon his chest—the "blazon" that you spoke of. The figure is so precise that Clove mistook it, at first, for a common tattoo—much to our young man's delight.

Still other letters showed remarkable prescience on geopolitical matters, as in a missive dated July 12, 1937:
"I suspect it will prove easier, in the end," Dulles wrote,

to restore Jerusalem to the Jews than to unite the fractious continent on which our hopes so much depend. And yet, both must be done, and shall be—if not in this century's middle age, then by its end. There will be an Israel soon enough (though I sometimes wonder if any Jews will be left to people it), and a united Europe, too. And have no doubt about my meaning. By "a united Europe," I mean a Europe that speaks with one voice, spends with one currency, and prays to one king. A continent with no internal borders.

How these events shall be brought to bear is another issue, and frankly, I fear that our Helmsman may have put his faith in a broken bowl. (What good has ever come from Rome—or from Berlin, for that matter?)

My feeling is that Europe's borders must someday be dissolved by men with pens, rather than by soldiers riding tanks. So, too, with the Holy Land and its restoration to the Jews. But whichever way these ends are reached, rest assured, my friend, we *will* prevail.

He's right, of course, Dunphy thought. Their "Helmsman" 's faith was indeed misplaced. Embracing Mussolini at the expense of Roosevelt, Pound scored an own-goal against himself *and* the Society he headed.

Or maybe not. If you looked at it in a different way, you could make the case that, however unintentionally, Hitler's genocidal war had paved the way for both Israel and the Common Market—since each was, to some extent, a reaction to the carnage that had gone before.

Dunphy glanced at the letter a second time and noticed something he'd glossed over on first reading. "Prays to one king . . . " Dunphy frowned. You don't pray to kings. It was a thought that Dunphy felt sure was worth taking up, but the idea was soon forgotten as he came upon the shortest and most cryptic of the letters in the packet. Dated November 22, 1937, it read:

For God's sake—*now what?*

Dunphy would have given a lot to know what *that* was all about, but in the absence of Jung's reply, there was no way to make sense of it. The next letter, however, suggested that powerful events had been set in motion.

My dear Carl,
Your letter was a great consolation. I knew nothing of the institute in Küsnacht, nor of the donation that he'd made. Thank God it's been preserved! Science may one day find a way to accomplish that which he no longer can.

And perhaps it was meant to be. After learning of the disaster in Spain, I turned to the *Apocryphon* for solace, and for the first time understood those fateful and mysterious lines:

His kingdom comes and goes,
Then comes again when,
wounded to the root,
He is the last, yet not the last,
emblazoned and alone.
These many lands will then be one
and he their king till, past,
he sires sons down all the days,
while deathly still and celibate.

That His kingdom "comes and goes" is a circumstance we have been living with for centuries. That it must come again, when he is "wounded to the root," is cause for joy. Because, dear Carl, this is precisely what has happened to our young man, whose terrible injuries could not be more aptly described. Nor is this all. Wounded thus, and without siblings, it is as apparent as the blazon on his chest that he must be "the last" of his line.

But there my scrying ends. That he should be "the last, yet not the last" is a conundrum whose solution may not be known until, perhaps, the day when "these many lands (are) one."

Nor is this the only conundrum. What are we to make of the promise that "he (shall be) their king till, past, he sires sons down all the days, while deathly still and celibate"? I can only hope that the meaning of this passage may one day be explained by the gift that he has made to the institute in Küsnacht. If so, then Science will prove to be the savior of Salvation—and our young man will indeed have been "the last, yet not the last."

Reading the *Apocryphon* in this way, as a kind of Christian kabbalah, is a speculative exercise, of course. But if my reading of these lines is correct, then the young man in our care is himself the fulfillment of a prophecy and, as such, *the last portent*. Accordingly, he is the sine qua non of all our hopes. For that reason, then, no effort or expense should be spared to keep him safe until such a time as every other sign and omen has been manifested and evinced.

Then, and only then, can our young man, however old, be king. And if his kingdom lasts for but the smallest part of a minute, that will not matter. He will be "past," as prophesied, and Science willing, father to an eternity of sons.

Dunphy rubbed his head, but he might as well have scratched it. What's the *Apocryphon*, he wondered, and what did any of it actually mean? There was no way to know. The correspondence was filled with mysteries large and small, important and not. Reading them was like listening to one end of a telephone conversation. Some things were obvious. Some things were revealed. But everything else was left to surmise:

July 12, 1941

My dear Carl,
I am delighted to read that you have persuaded Mr. Pound that our young man may not be safe in Paris. None of us can predict what may happen in the next year, but prudence dictates that he, at least, should be placed at a safe remove from all hostilities. He is, after all, our raison d'être, and without him, we have nothing—neither hope nor purpose any longer.

As you suggest, Switzerland should be quite safe—and not only for our Gomelez. The Society's assets will prove essential to our mission in the postwar environment, whatever else may come, and they, too, must be safeguarded. Given the magnitude of these assets, care needs to be taken that their removal from the combatant countries should not cause unnecessary dislocations or publicity. I would suggest, therefore, that these transfers should be placed in the hands of our contacts at the Bank for International Settlements in Basel. They will know how to liquidate the various equities, which can then be reinvested through Zürich and Vaduz. (I feel our goal should be preservation of capital, rather than growth.)

So "our young man" has a name, Dunphy thought. Gomelez. Who is he? Dunphy wondered, and then turned the thought aside. There was no way of knowing.

But one thing that *was* becoming clear was that Dulles and Jung were acceding to more and more important responsibilities in the secret society to which they belonged. Viz.,

May 19, 1942

My dear Carl,

By the time you read this letter, I will have taken up my confidential duties in Bern. I appreciate your offer to act as liaison between our Helmsman and myself, but fear that travel to and from Italy is out of the question for both of us.

I will, however, embrace your offer of a clandestine démarche to Herr Speer. Am I to understand that he is one of us? I am amazed. How is it that I've never met him?

Speer aside, I have the names of several good fellows whom I think we would do well to have aboard. Neither of these gentlemen will come as a surprise. We've discussed their bona fides on several occasions, and you have met both of them socially. I mean Dr. Vannevar Bush and young Angleton. Please consider this letter a formal submission of their names to membership in our society.

Dunphy sat back in his chair. It was one of those moments when a cigarette would have been more than a pleasure. Vannevar Bush and "young Angleton." Could it be? he wondered. How many Angletons would Dulles have known? Probably one: James Jesus Angleton, who in the years after the war, headed the CIA's counterintelligence staff. He was a legendary spook, up to his ears in everything from Israeli politics to the Warren Commission. Where was—*what* was—Angleton in '42? Dunphy thought about it. Just a college kid, albeit a supremely well connected one . . . in, or on his way into, the OSS.

Dunphy was less familiar with Bush, but as he recalled, he'd been in charge of scientific research and weapons development for the United States throughout the Second World War.

Useful men to have on your side, Dunphy supposed, especially if you're running a secret society. But . . . Speer? *Albert* Speer? Who was . . . what? Hitler's architect, and . . . Minister of Armaments. A nice contact for someone like Dulles, running intel operations for the Allies out of Switzerland.

But . . . was it possible that a Nazi like Speer would have any-thing in common—and, in particular, something *secret* in common—with the likes of Dulles and Jung?

Dunphy muttered to himself. Why not? In fact, how could he not? The Magdalene Society had its own agenda, clearly, and there was no reason to assume that its agenda was pecu-liarly American—or liberal. On the contrary, the guy who was running the show, or who was supposed to be running the show—the "Helmsman"—was a loony, pro-Fascist poet making propaganda broadcasts from Italy and hailing Mus-solini as a savior. Dunphy knew that much from History 101. So why *not* Speer? If anything, Speer was probably less ec-centric than Pound. Moreover, it was becoming increasingly clear to Dunphy that the Magdalene Society (at least the or-ganization had a name) was a kind of secret church.

But, which kind? There was nothing to glean from the name: Mary Magdalene was a prostitute who'd gotten reli-gion. She manifested the idea that even the most serious sin-ners could be forgiven. But so what? What did *that* have to do with anything?

Maybe everything, maybe nothing. But what was certain was that if the Society was indeed a kind of church, then its adherents might come from every corner of the globe, re-gardless of political boundaries—even boundaries between countries at war.

Which only went to prove that while politics made strange bedfellows, religion made even stranger ones.

He checked his watch. It was nine fifty-five. Three hours to go. And then he'd turn into a pumpkin (if he was lucky)—or a torso (if he wasn't).

There was a soft knock on the door, and Dieter entered, carrying an armload of files. Stacking them on the desk, he gestured inanely and said, "The Dumpy file is not available."

"You mean *Dun*phy."

"Yes—that one. But . . . as I said, it is not available."

"Why not?"

"Someone uses it."

Dunphy tried not to look too disappointed—or too interested. "Do you know who?"

Dieter nodded. "The *Direktor*."

A weak smile from Dunphy. And a shiver. "It's cold in here," Dunphy complained.

"You get used to it," Dieter replied.

When the big guy had gone, Dunphy returned to the Schidlof file. Having moved to Bern, Dulles saw Jung more often, but wrote to him less frequently—perhaps because the war made communications chancy. Even so, there were gems to be found among the few missives written between '42 and '44. "I am particularly grateful," Dulles wrote after a 1943 visit to Jung in Küsnacht,

> to your Miss Vogelei, who was kind enough to take Mrs. Dulles on a delightful sail to Rapperswill and back. You are very lucky to have a secretary as talented and gracious as she.

So that's who she is, Dunphy thought, happy to see another loose string tied into a bow. He glanced at his watch. Ten-fifteen.

The next letter wasn't a letter at all, but a postcard. It had been sent by Dulles on April 12, 1943. On its face was a picture of an exquisite mountain wilderness, where all the trees were flocked with snow. A cutline on the opposite side identified the image as a part of the Swiss National Park (est. 1914) in the canton of Graubünden, near the Italian border.

"I have been to see our young man," Dulles wrote.

> He is unhappy, as you know, with his confinement and shows no interest whatsoever in our plans. Nevertheless, he is in reasonable health and gets about as much as his wounds will allow.

There's "Our young man" again, Dunphy thought. Gomelez.

The next letter was written *after* the war. Dated May 29, 1945, it had been sent from Rome.

Dear Carl,

I have just been to the Disciplinary Training Center in Pisa, where Ezra is being held until the paperwork is completed for his return to the United States.

As you may imagine, the Center is a rough place—a holding pen for American soldiers charged with serious crimes (murder and rape, desertion and drug addiction). To find our Helmsman there nearly broke my heart.

Still, it could be worse. His "capture" was arranged by Major Angleton, who made certain that no interrogation took place. (According to Ez, I was the first American "to spit two words" at him since the arrest.)

Even so, the conditions under which he is being held are predictably appalling. So, also, is the evidence against him: scores, if not hundreds, of radio broadcasts attacking the Jews, the bankers, and all things American, while celebrating the courage and vision of *Il Duce*.

I don't know what to say. I think there is a possibility that he might be hanged.

A half-dozen communiqués followed over the next six months. Some were long, others short, but all revolved around the same theme: how to save the Helmsman? American sentiment was running strongly toward a lynching, and Dulles thought a trial would be a catastrophe. Accordingly, a strategy was decided upon by which Pound would plead guilty to insanity, but not to treason. And, in this, Jung proved the most valuable of allies. As the founder of analytic psychology, he was an icon of the psychiatric community. It was an easy matter, then, for him to assist Dulles and "young Angleton" in marshaling a tidal wave of expertise in behalf of the otherwise dubious proposition that the politically incorrect Pound was in fact raving mad.

October 12, 1946

And so we have prevailed.

Ezra is committed to the federal asylum in Washington, D.C. There, at St. Elizabeth's, he will remain under the care of Dr. Winfred Overholser—who is one of our own. While I have not yet had the opportunity to visit the great man in his psychiatric haven, I am reliably informed that Ezra has been given a sort of suite in which he holds court for admirers from every corner of the globe.

Winnie assures me that no privileges have been (or will be) withheld from him—save the freedom to move about outside the grounds. His dinners are prepared by caterers, and a stream of visitors moves constantly through his rooms—so much so that he has begun to complain that he does not have time to write, so busy is his schedule.

This much, at least, is well and good....

Two months later, Dulles wished Jung the merriest of Christmases and reported "a fascinating tête-à-tête with Dr. Overholser's patient."

With Pisa behind him, and the trial, too, he seems to have regained much of the vitality he'd lost—and all of the acuity. Indeed, on the basis of the afternoon that I spent with him, I can assure you that his long incarceration was anything but unproductive. Indeed, it would appear to have focused his attention to an amazing degree.

From his rooms in the asylum, our Helmsman suggests a strategy that just might work. "What is needed," he told me, "is for our little band to take a proactive stance toward the *Apocryphon*, [There's that word again, Dunphy thought.] whose prophecies will be no less fulfilled for having endured a midwife."

You see the point. Rather than standing passively by, our *Nautonnier* would have us intervene, reifying the portents enumerated in the *Apocryphon*, while making its prophecies come true—in effect, acting as midwives to the millennium. In that way, Ez suggests, it may be possible to achieve our ends while our young man is still among the quick.

Dunphy wasn't entirely sure what Dulles was talking about. For one thing, he didn't know what *reifying* meant, and for another, he'd never heard of the *Apocryphon*. Even so, he understood the part about making prophecies come true—though what that had to do with achieving their ends "while our young man is still among the quick" was a mystery.

"To accomplish this," the letter went on, a political and psychological strategy will, of course, be required. And, in particular, a mechanism will be needed to protect the Magdalene Society from the scrutiny of the mob. Happily, such a mechanism is at hand.

The next letter, dated February 19, 1947, went a long way toward answering that question.

In our meeting last week, Ezra remarked that the secret services provide an ideal refuge for a brotherhood such as our own. This is so because the day-to-day activities of the intelligence services are, by their very nature, clandestine. It is, indeed, the hallmark of their ordinary business. Accordingly, a secret society within a secret service would be about as visible as a pane of glass at the bottom of the sea. (The metaphor was his.)

As you can imagine, this is an insight from which our Society might easily benefit.

Unfortunately, the British and French services are essentially unavailable to us at this time. While members of our order have served both organizations at the very highest levels (Vincent Walsingham was for nine years our *Nautonnier*, after all), we do not currently have the same degree of influence among them as we once did. (I blame Nesta Webster.)

Dunphy got to his feet and stretched. He didn't know who
Walsingham was, but Nesta Webster was notorious as an author of books about secret societies.

He rolled his head in a circle, trying to get the kinks out. It
had been a long time since he'd gone for a run, and he missed
it. Maybe tomorrow, Dunphy thought, and heard himself
reply, If there *is* a tomorrow. And so he sat back down and resumed reading.

Still, an opportunity has arisen over the past year. In January,
President Truman signed the secret charter of a new
American intelligence service—one that will build upon the
work of the OSS. Called the Central Intelligence Group, the
new agency has the Red Menace as its brief, with Moscow
as its focal point. I think you will not be surprised to learn
that I have been given a central role in getting the CIG up
and running—prior to the appointment of the organization's
first director.

In this capacity, it has been a relatively simple matter to
create a sort of inner sanctum *within the CIG*, enabling us to
act without fear of scrutiny or unintended consequences.
The enterprise to which I refer is the Security Research
Staff, a component of the counterintelligence apparatus
that will soon be headed by young Angleton. With his help,
the Society's activities will be concealed within a sea of
muzzy invisibilities, the day-to-day spookery that both
press and government must soon take for granted.

If the metaphor of an inner sanctum seems obscure,
think of us instead as the political equivalent of *Dracunculus medinensis*. (I invite you to look it up.)

Dunphy let the letter drop from his hand. Falling back in
his chair, he looked at the ceiling and heaved a sigh of weary
astonishment. It's like the CIA is just a cover, he thought, for
something more important. And the Cold War: an excuse for
something else. This Magdalene thing . . .

"Excuse? . . ."

Dunphy looked up. Dieter was standing in the doorway. "What?" Dunphy asked, pronouncing the word as if he were asking a blackjack dealer to hit him.

"I thought—I heard you. I thought you asked . . . " Dieter looked confused, but it was Dunphy who was embarrassed: he'd been talking to himself.

"I need an encyclopedia," Dunphy said.

Dieter blinked. "A *whole* encyclopedia? In English?"

Dunphy shook his head and tried to get a grip. "No," he said. "Just the *D*s. But definitely in English."

When the door closed, Dunphy glanced at his watch. It was eleven-fifteen—just after five in the morning in the States. Which meant that he had about an hour and a half before he'd have to leave.

Time sure flies when you're having fun, he thought, flattening the next letter on the desk in front of him.

April 23, 1947

Dear Carl,

I am now back at my desk after eight days in the West, visiting the Jet Propulsion Laboratory in California and certain facilities that we have in Nevada. Doctor Bush accompanied me on the last leg of the trip, and I can report that our time was put to especially good purpose.

The first archetype will be introduced within the next few weeks. The event will take place in the vicinity of Roswell, New Mexico (a small town not far from Sandia Laboratories). Members of the Security Research Staff, on temporary assignment to the 509th Composite Bomb Group, will be responsible for the object's "recovery," and all subsequent relations with the public and the press.

As agreed, the existence of the recovered artifact (in actuality, a weather balloon) will be acknowledged and then denied, turning the event into what you have so aptly described as "a symbolic rumor."

Reinforcement of that rumor will take place from time to time, until such a time as the archetype is found to be self-generating. Toward that end, the CIG is establishing a reinforcement facility under Air Force cover at Wright Field (in Dayton, Ohio). Convenient to U.S. and foreign news media, the facility will legitimize the phenomenon by denying its reality, whatever evidence may be put forward in its behalf.

A knock at the door interrupted his reading. He looked up. Dieter was standing in the doorway, holding a couple of books. "Here," he said, crossing the room in a single step. "It's '93, okay?"

Dunphy accepted the books with an impatient nod, then watched his baby-sitter turn on his heel. A moment later, the door closed behind him.

There were two thick volumes, bound in Moroccan leather. For a moment, Dunphy didn't remember why he'd asked for the encyclopedias. Something in one of Dulles's letters, something Latin, but . . . what? His mind was spinning—and not like a compact disc. It was more like a top at the end of its rotation, leaning to one side and another as it begins to wobble, soon to spin out.

He went back to Dulles's earlier letters, scanning the pages until he found the one he was looking for—February 19— and the words "the political counterpart of *Dracunculus medinensus*. (I invite you to look it up.)" Dunphy did.

GUINEA WORM. A waterborne nematode that causes an appalling disease. The females are larviparous, and grow to a length of one meter or more, working their way through the duodenum to the subcutaneous tissue, where the parasite discharges millions of eggs into the definitive host (*Homo sapiens*). The intermediate host is the copepod, *Cyclops*. The appearance of an inflamed papule on a person's skin betrays the worm, which can be removed in a painful procedure of gradual extraction, using a short stick around which the worm is slowly wound over a period of several weeks. The procedure is thought to have inspired the medical symbol of the serpent entwined upon a caduceus.

It was eleven fifty-five.

He'd been reading the Dulles correspondence for nearly four hours, and he felt like he was going to lose it. The paranoia that he'd felt a few hours earlier was making a comeback. Every so often, it hit him that he was four stories underground, and the realization triggered a twinge of claustrophobia that he hadn't known that he'd had. And a question had arisen—one of those hostile questions whose origin seems to be in the spleen, rather than in the brain: what made him think he could walk in and out of the Special Registry, just because he had a building pass? What if Hilda and her friends wouldn't let him leave until they'd talked to Harry Matta?

Well, that's easy, Dunphy told himself. If they do that, you're a torso.

Suddenly, he needed a breath of fresh air—at least, that's what he told himself. But the lie didn't take. He knew what he really wanted: to see if Dieter would let him out of the room. Getting up from the desk, he went to the door and opened it. As he suspected, Dieter was outside, sitting in a straight-back chair, reading *Maus*.

"Is there any coffee around here?" Dunphy asked.

"Sure," Dieter said, nodding toward the elevators. "In the canteen on the second floor."

Dunphy pulled the door shut behind him and, walking backward, told the security guard not to let anyone in the room.

"Of course not," Dieter replied, and turned the page.

Finding the cafeteria wasn't hard. It was noon, and it seemed like half the building was heading in its direction. By following the crowd, Dunphy soon found himself in the most wonderful—indeed, the only wonderful—cafeteria he'd ever been in. There were frescoes on every wall—pastoral scenes with modern faces—including those of Dulles and Jung, Pound and Harry Matta. There were no cash registers.

Everyone just helped themselves. And Dunphy was tempted:
there were heaps of seeded rolls and crusty breads, and plat-
ters of thinly sliced roast beef, duck, and venison. There were
plates of raclette, spaetzle, and rosti, charred bratwurst and
smoldering fondues flanked by icy beers and little bottles of
wine. There were plates of cheese, towers of fruit, and bas-
kets of salad.

He helped himself to a cup of decaf and returned the way
he'd come.

"Here," Dieter said, holding out a folded piece of paper.

"What's that?" Dunphy asked, his apprehension returning.

"A note—"

"For me?"

"Yes, take it! It's from your friend—Mike."

Mike?

Dunphy took the note and went into the office, shutting the
door behind him.

Gene!

What are *you* doing here? I thought you were sick! I saw
Hilda this morning, and your name on her desk, and she
mentioned you're doing some kind of damage control—
what's all *that* about? Since when did you know anything
about "damage control"? You're just a cowboy! (Ha ha!)
Anyway, let's do lunch—I'll be back in ten minutes.

The signature was a practiced scrawl: *R something something something G-O-L-D.* R-gold. Mike R-gold. Rhinegold! Fuck!

Though it no longer mattered what time it was, Dunphy
looked at his watch: twelve twenty-two. He had to get outa here
because . . . because Dunphy knows Rhinegold, and Rhinegold knows Brading—and that ain't good. Rhinegold was the
psycho nerd who'd debriefed him in the anechoic chamber at
Langley, and *if he sees me here—in Zug—at the Registry . . .
gotta go gotta go gotta go.*

And leave my nice topcoat. The one that cost a thousand

pounds in the little square past the Zum Storchen. Because I don't think Dieter's gonna let me out of here with my coat on.

With a rueful look, Dunphy cast his eyes toward the files on the desk. There were half a dozen unread letters from Dulles to Jung, and a stack of files marked *Bovine Census— N.M.*, and *Bovine Census, CO.* He'd never get to read them now. Unless . . .

He slipped one of the Census files inside his shirt and stuffed the last of the Dulles letters into one of his pockets. He was reaching for the Schidlof tapes when the door flew open, and Mike Rhinegold waltzed in with a glad hand and a dopey grin that dwindled in an instant to incomprehension— then swelled at the memory. Finally, a deep frown.

"Heyyy . . ."

Dunphy was about as red-handed as a man could be, but his reflexes were excellent. Before Rhinegold could react, he had one hand at the scruff of the smaller man's neck and the other in the roots of his pompadour. Kicking the door shut, Dunphy jerked the geek into the room and slammed the bridge of his nose into the edge of the desk. A spritz of blood flew in an arc as the tapes jumped, and Rhinegold sagged.

Holding him up by the arms, Dunphy gave him a little shake, as if he were a piggy bank. Nothing there. Out cold.

And then a knock at the door. "Hallo?"

"It's okay," Dunphy said. "Mike and I are just—"

Rhinegold's heel came down on Dunphy's instep, twisting and grinding, pulling an agonized yelp from Dunphy's mouth.

"Dieter!" Rhinegold screamed as Dunphy lifted him off his feet and, pivoting, slammed him into the wall. Again. And again, until the door burst open, and Dieter stepped in, startled to see Dunphy's pal drop to the floor like a sack of mulch. And the wall behind Dunphy dappled with little loops of Michael Rhinegold's blood.

"Was der Fuck?!" The big man took a step toward Dunphy, and another, backing the American into a corner of the little

room. His eyes were bright with excitement as he feinted to the left, then jabbed with his right, hitting Dunphy twice in the same second. The American's head smacked against the wall as his upper lip split and started to bleed. He's a boxer, Dunphy thought with a sinking feeling, as Dieter's heavy left hand piled into the pit of his stomach, folding Dunphy in half.

Then the German made a mistake. He grabbed Dunphy by the tie and straightened him up with a single jerk. "So!" he demanded in his corny accent, "you want rough games, hey?" And, with a smile, he smacked Dunphy in the face with his open hand. Dunphy was on his way out, consciousness fading, when it happened—and he just couldn't believe it. This meatball had bitch-slapped him!

And again! *The motherfucker had done it again!*

Dunphy's hand came up fast and flat, the knuckles curled into a wedge that slammed into Dieter's throat like the edge of a board, crushing the cartilage around his larynx. In an instant, Dieter was doubled over, holding his throat as if it were trying to get away.

The noise he made was awful, a gargling gasp that went on and on. Dunphy glanced wildly around the room, looking for something to shut him up, but the only thing he could find was the metal stapler on the desk. It wasn't much, but he picked it up, turned it around, and ejecting a staple—*ping!*—used it as a blackjack, slamming it into the back of the security guard's head. Then again, and again, staggering the man until his skin softened to a kind of pudding. Finally, the big guy sagged to his knees, fell forward, and sprawled. The gargle became a gurgle, now.

Dunphy's heart was beating like a conga drum as he wiped the blood from his hands and dried them on Rhinegold's coattails. Adjusting his tie, he ran his tongue over his upper lip, wincing as it caught on the place where it was split. Then he pulled on his topcoat, patted down his hair, and—

The telephone warbled, a weird electronic trill.

Dunphy stared at it, uncertain what to do. It rang again, and then a third time. Finally, he picked it up.

"Hello?"

"This is Hilda."

"Hello, Hilda."

"Eugene?"

"Yes."

"I think your friend Michael has been to see you."

"Yeah," Dunphy said. "We were just talking."

"Well, I think perhaps we should call the *Direktor* now. So, if you will come up to my office . . ."

"I'll be right up."

"And perhaps I could have a word with Dieter?"

"Uhh . . . lemme see if he's outside." Dunphy paused, took a deep breath, and then another. Finally, he said, "I think he stepped away from his chair."

"Excuse?"

"He's getting me a file. Do you want me to wait for him, or just come up by myself?"

"Oh, well . . . I think . . . just come up."

"I'm on the way." Dunphy hung up the phone, reached down, and jerked the cord out of the wall. Then he went over to Dieter and patted him down. Finding the key in the fallen man's pocket, he went to the door and, pulling it open a crack, peered out.

A slow but steady stream of people moved through the hallway, going about their business. Dunphy stepped outside the room, pulled the door shut, and locked it. Summoning an inane smile to his broken lips, he walked toward the elevator as slowly as he could, fighting the urge to break into a run. A woman caught his eye, and as he looked away, he saw a frown flash across her face, as if she were thinking, There's something wrong with that guy.

He could tell it wasn't just the blood on his lip, or the disarray that he must have been in: it was the vibe he was giving off. She could see it in his eyes, and *she* knew that *he* knew she could see it. But then he was past her, strolling and smiling, and there was nothing for her to do, really: it had only been a moment, a moment in passing, and now that moment was gone. She must have been mistaken.

Or so, he hoped, she thought.

Arriving at the elevator's doors, he pressed the button that would summon it, then waited for what seemed an age, waiting for an outcry at his back. But there was nothing, and then the doors opened and it was as if he were onstage: half a dozen people looked him up and down—it took only a second—and then he was among them, and the doors closed. Slowly, the elevator began to ascend in a silence so deafening, so pointed, and, somehow, so incriminating that it occurred to him to whistle. A happy tune.

Then the elevator opened, and he was in the lobby, moving quickly toward the revolving doors that stood between him and the street. One—three—five strides. Now, he was through the doors and trotting down the steps, setting off toward his rendezvous—

When a hand fell on his shoulder, and a man's voice said, *"Entschuldigen Sie mich?"*

Dunphy turned with his right hand low, down at his side, but fully cocked and ready to tee off.

"Ich denke, daß Sie dieses fallenließen." Dunphy didn't understand the words, and what was worse, he must have looked like it because the man's smile turned to a scowl. He was holding a piece of paper, and at a glance, Dunphy saw what it was: one of the Dulles letters must have fallen out of his pocket in the lobby. As Dunphy reached for it, the man's eyes dropped to the page he was holding. There was a frown of incomprehension, followed by a look of startled recognition. For an instant, they were holding the letter at the same time. Then the man let go and, backing away, turned and started to run.

Dunphy took a few steps backward, shoving the letter into his pocket. Then he turned and, slowly at first, started jogging toward the little café where Clementine was supposed to be waiting. As he moved, he glanced at his watch, and it was as he'd expected: the big hand was on *Torso*, and the little hand on *Run!*

23

She was a minute late.

Or he was a minute early. In either case, he found himself standing in front of the café on Alpenstrasse, looking left and right, like a deer getting ready to bolt across a busy highway. Any second now, Hilda would wonder what had happened to him. Dieter and Rhinegold would begin to stir. The guy who'd found the letter would report what he'd seen. And then a posse would come boiling out of the Special Registry, moving north, south, east, and west until they found him.

So where is she? he wondered. Getting the money.

Right. The money. It occurred to Dunphy, not for the first time, that there really *was* quite a bit of money in the safe-deposit box on the Bahnhofstrasse. And after the way he'd treated Clementine, disappearing for months without a word, who could blame her if she just kept going? Fly to Rio, work on her tan for a couple of years, fall in love with someone who wasn't on the run.

Veroushka

Paulinho

Then again, he asked himself, where's she gonna find someone who's so much fun?

Looking back the way he'd come, Dunphy sensed, rather than saw, a commotion on the sidewalk outside the Special Registry. Half a dozen guys in black suits, looking like the

Blues Brothers, turning their heads this way and that. I'm dead, he thought. They'll see me any second. Oh, Clem, I can't believe you fucked me like this. And with that his eyes swung left and right, looking for a car to jack.

Then he saw her, coming up Alpenstrasse in the rented Golf, beeping and waving as if she were a soccer mom delivering the kids to the field seconds before the big game. Very un-Swiss, Dunphy decided as he covered the ground between them in a dozen strides, yanked open the door, and dived in.

"Do you want to drive?" she asked.

"No," Dunphy replied, jackknifing into the seat so that his head couldn't be seen above the dashboard.

"Because I don't mind, really."

"No, it's okay."

"If you'd like—"

"Will you fucking *go*?!"

She looked at him for a deliberately long moment, then threw the car in gear. "No need to be snappish," she said, as the car began to move.

"I'm *sorry*," he replied, gritting his teeth. "It's just that—there are people who want to kill me. So, if you'd just tell me what you see? That would be good. *Please*."

"People. Rather a lot of people, actually. Coming out of a building—in a hurry."

"*Which* building?"

"I don't know. It's an old one. Number 15."

"Jesus!"

"Is that where *you* were?"

"Yes."

"Well, it looks as if they're having a sort of . . . fire drill. Except, it's gone all wrong."

"Don't look at them."

"Why not?"

"Just drive."

"It's rather hard not to look at them," she said. "They're all over the place."

He felt the car brake, and then they were idling, going nowhere. "Now what?"

"We're stopped."

"I can tell that we're stopped—but why?"

"Because there's a red light. Would you like me to go through it?"

"No!"

"Good, because I don't fancy backseat drivers—especially when they're sitting next to me with their heads under the glove box."

Son of a bitch, he thought. It's like we're married. "Just . . . tell me when we're out of town, okay?"

"Ab-zoob-ally."

The car lurched, and once again they were moving. Doubled over in the seat, Dunphy held his peace until Clem confirmed that they were in the country. Straightening, he sat up and looked around. They were winding their way through the mountains, heading for the airport.

"You get the tickets?" he asked.

"Business class. Cost a bloody fortune."

"And the money?"

She nodded.

Dunphy heaved a sigh of relief, then went into her handbag, looking for the cigarettes that he knew would be there. Finding a pack of Marlboros, he lighted one. Sat back and exhaled. His mind was at the races, ricocheting from Dulles to Jung to Brading and his cows.

After a while, Clem turned to him and, with a raised eyebrow, said, "So?"

Dunphy looked at her. "What?"

"Did you find what you were looking for?"

He thought about it. "I don't know," he said. "I think so—but it's complicated. I have to sort things out."

She gave him a skeptical look and kept driving.

Kloten Airport was a risk, but not as much of a risk as Heathrow would have been a few days earlier. While the

Agency was not without influence in Switzerland, it did not have anything like the clout that it did in England. The Swiss were protective of their independence and neutrality and kept their distance from the special services of other countries—including those of the United States. This meant that things tended to be done by the book, and slowly, so that if the Agency wanted the airport watched, it would almost certainly have to do so itself.

But they couldn't have moved that fast. It was less than an hour from Zug to the airport, and once there, Dunphy and Clem had checked in for their flight within minutes of returning the rental car. For the next half hour, they sat in the Swissair lounge, chain-drinking cups of coffee as they waited for their flight to be called. At any minute, Dunphy expected Rhinegold to show up with half a dozen knuckle-draggers at his side, but nothing happened. Their flight was called at two fifty-five. Half an hour later, they were soaring above the Bernese Oberland on their way to Madrid. Dunphy sipped from a flute of nonvintage Mumm.

Once again, he'd gotten out of Dodge.

"Tell me," Clem said.

"What?"

"What it's all about."

Dunphy thought about it. She certainly had a right to know—they were in this together, and she was in as much danger as he. On the other hand, he didn't really *know* what it was all about. "I just know some of it," he told her. "Bits and pieces. A couple of names. I don't even know who some of them are, or what they mean."

"Just tell me."

He looked over his shoulder. The seat behind them was empty, and there was only the pilot's cabin in front of them. Across the aisle, a young African man was slumped in his seat, eyes closed, listening to his Walkman. Dunphy could hear it, a tinny buzz that was just loud enough to be familiar: Cesaria Evora.

"You'll think I'm crazy," he said.

"No, I won't."

"Yeah, you will."

"Why?"

"Because," Dunphy said, "it's, like, a secret society."

Clem gave him a look, thinking he was kidding. "Is it now?"

Dunphy smiled ruefully. "Uh-huh."

She held his gaze until she saw that he was serious. "You're not kidding, are you?"

"No," he said, "I'm not."

She thought about it for a moment. "So, it's like the Freemasons?"

Dunphy shook his head. "No. Not like them."

"Then what?"

He sipped his champagne. "I don't know," he said. "I'm not sure *what* they're like. But it's called the Magdalene Society. And it's very old."

"*How* old?"

Dunphy shrugged. "According to them—Francis Bacon was a member."

Clementine scoffed. "You're having me on."

"I'm not."

She looked uncertain. "Well, that would make it four hundred years old."

Dunphy shook his head. "They said he was a member. They didn't say he was the first member. It could be older than that. Maybe a lot older." He looked out the window at what might have been a Swissair postcard: cerulean skies and umber mountains, plastered with snow. It was a beautiful world at thirty-five thousand feet.

But it was a dangerous one on the ground.

Adjusting the pitch to his seat, he sat back and closed his eyes. It's too big, he thought. Whatever it is, it's just too big. We'll never get out of it. He opened his eyes and looked out the window once again, thinking, It doesn't matter how much I find out. What do I do with it—go to the police? Go to the press? They'd have me committed.

"A penny for your thoughts," Clem suggested.

In fact, he was thinking, *These guys are gonna kill us.* But what he said was, "You'd be overpaying."

Clem raised her glass and sipped, then put it down on the little tray that covered her lap. "You haven't told me why we're going to Tenerife," she said.

"I've got a friend there."

Another skeptical look. "No one has friends on Tenerife," she said. "It's the middle of nowhere."

Dunphy grinned. "Tommy's special."

"Why?"

"Because he's caught up in the same thing we are."

They didn't say anything for what seemed like a long time. Dunphy watched the clouds wrap themselves around the Alps, while Clem leafed through a copy of *Mein schöner Garten*. Finally, she stuffed the magazine into the seat pocket in front of her.

"Is it a religious society?" she asked.

Dunphy nodded.

"I thought so," she said.

"Why?"

"Because of the Magdalene part." She gave him a sly look. "You know," she said, "I always wondered if there wasn't something between them, didn't you?"

He didn't know what she meant. "Who?" he asked.

"*You* know—Him! And her. Mary Magdalene!"

Dunphy winced. "Clem—I had nuns as a kid, so . . . "

"What?"

"Well, you talk like that, and next thing you know, the plane crashes. Hit by lightning. Happens all the time."

"I'm serious, Jack!"

"Clem . . . "

"Washed his feet, she did!"

"So?"

"Nothing. I just wonder if there wasn't something *there*, that's all!"

Dunphy shook his head as if to clear it. "I don't get it."

"I'm just saying, she washed his *feet*, Jack. I've never washed yours."

"Noted." Once again, the two of them retreated into their own thoughts, with Dunphy trying to make sense of what he'd read that morning, and Clem—well, Clem—who knew what Clem was thinking? After a while, he leaned closer to her and began to muse aloud. "There's this statue in Einsiedeln."

"That place you went? In the mountains?"

"Yeah. And they have a statue—like the Virgin Mary, except—she's black. And Jesus, too. *He's* black. And the place I went in Zug? The Special Registry? They have the same image on their security passes. It's a hologram. And there's a shrine on the first floor, right where you go in."

"Is that what you call the place? The Special Registry?"

"Uh-huh."

"How boring."

"They're bureaucrats."

"Still . . . What was it like?" she asked.

Dunphy thought about it. "Shakespeare on the outside, Arthur C. Clarke when you got in."

"And they have files there?"

"They do."

Clem made an exasperated sound. *"Well?"*

"Well, what?"

"Did you *read* any?"

"A couple."

"And?!"

Dunphy shifted uncomfortably in his seat. "There were letters," he said. "And some other files that I didn't get to read—but it doesn't matter. I know what they're about."

"How?"

"Because I interviewed a guy who figures in them."

"Interviewed? When?"

"A few weeks ago. He lives in Kansas."

"And what did he say?"

"He said he'd spent his entire military career—twenty years—mutilating cattle."

Clem gave him a droll look.

"And that was only part of it. It gets stranger. UFOs and crop circles—it's the craziest shit you ever heard."

Clementine giggled. Nervously.

"But the thing is, none of that's important," Dunphy said. "Not really. All of that's just . . . "

"What?"

He tried to find the right word. "A light show."

Her puzzled look told him that she didn't know what he meant.

"It's smoke and mirrors," he explained. "They do it for an effect."

"Who does?"

"The Magdalene Society."

"But, I thought you said the man you interviewed—"

"Was in the military. He was. But that was just a cover."

"And this effect?" she began. "What sort of an effect was it?"

"A psychological one."

"The cattle—and all that?"

"Yeah."

She thought about it. "So what you're saying is, it's a bit like the Wizard of Oz."

Dunphy nodded. "Yeah—like him—but working for Ted Bundy."

Clementine frowned. "I don't know who he is."

Dunphy shook his head. "Bad joke. The point is, your pal Simon was right: Schidlof found some letters that were written to Jung. About the Magdalene Society, and the, uhhh, collective unconscious."

"What about it?" she asked.

"They were planning to rewire it."

"What do you mean?"

"Just what I said. They were planning to rewire the collective unconscious." When Clementine didn't say anything, he added, "It's really quite magnificent when you think about it."

"That's just it—I don't want to think about it," she said. "It's crazy."

"It sounds crazy, but it's not. It explains a lot."

"Like what?"

"The fact that people see things in the sky that don't make sense; and that hundreds of cattle are mutilated every year by someone or something that no one ever sees; and that all these geometric designs are turning up in wheat fields all over the world. Now we know why."

"No, we don't," she said. "Even if you're right, we don't know why. We just know who—and how."

She was right, of course. "Anyway," Dunphy continued, "the important thing is, the letters I read were the ones that got Schidlof killed. And you'll never guess who they're from."

She gave him a look: *Tell me.*

"Allen Dulles."

"Oh!" she said. And then she frowned. "I don't know who he is, either."

Dunphy smiled. "He was an American diplomat. And a spy. Back in the forties. Earlier even."

"So?"

"So he and Jung were major players in this thing. And one of the things they did was set up the CIA so it could be used as a cover."

"For what?" Clem asked.

"The Magdalene Society. Dulles practically invented the Agency, and it was perfect for what they wanted to do. Because everything the Agency does is secret, it's like a black hole: anything that comes within its orbit, disappears."

"But what were they doing?"

"Psy-ops," Dunphy said. "The light show we were talking about."

She thought about it for a moment, then asked, "But what's the point? What are they after?"

Dunphy shook his head as if to say, Who knows? "The letters I saw talked about Jerusalem for the Jews. And a European union."

"That's not so bad," Clem asked. "We already *have* that!"

"I know we do. And there's a good chance they had a lot to do with it, too. But that's not the point. The political stuff is secondary."

"To what?"

Dunphy shrugged. "I don't know. But these guys have been around forever. The Inquisition was page one for them. And the War of the Roses. And . . . a lot more that I've forgotten."

"So . . . what are they after?" Clem asked.

"I don't know," Dunphy said. "I had to leave in a hurry."

They arrived at Madrid in the early evening and headed directly for La Venta Quemada, a small hotel or inn on the Plaza Zubeida. Dunphy had stayed there two or three years earlier, when he'd done business with the very crooked manager of a stable of bullfighters. It was a hangout for the death-in-the-afternoon trade and had been so for the better part of the century. It had been a home away from home for both Manolete and Dominguin, and a great many lesser lights, picadors, and aficionados. Dunphy liked the place, and in particular, he liked the guy at the desk—an avowed anarchist who, for a small surcharge, would let rooms without actually registering the guests.

Having checked in, Dunphy and Clem went out almost immediately, taking a cab to the Gran Via. One of the great European boulevards, now down-at-the-heels (but glitzy in a faded way), the street was chockablock with jazz-age theaters, music halls, and the palatial cinemas of another era. Gigantic, hand-painted posters covered the walls of buildings, advertising Stallone's muscles and Basinger's lips. In the middle of the street, a performance artist stood stock-still, apparently oblivious to the traffic jam around him, his clothes and skin tinted the color of brushed aluminum. The Tin Man, Dunphy supposed, or maybe just a tin can.

Whatever. Middle-aged shoeshine boys pointed accusingly at Dunphy's feet. Gypsy kids circled like coyotes. Beautiful, curious, wide-eyed, and paranoid, Clementine clung to his right arm with both hands, as if the chaos around them was trying to tear them apart. Somewhere along the avenue an Art Deco sign flashed *Bis* in luminous neon letters. Nearby, a lighted menu promised seafood and steak. With a glance at Clem and a shrug, Dunphy led the way up a flight of stairs to a softly lighted, second-story restaurant. With its tuxedoed waiters, white tablecloths, and old oak wainscotting, the place had the feel of a men's club—and a good one at that. It was early for dinner in Madrid—barely 10 P.M.—so they wiled away an hour with a *mezze* of *tapas* and a bottle of Spanish red.

Seated by themselves beside a bank of huge, double-glazed windows overlooking the Gran Via, Dunphy told her everything *else* that he knew about the fix they were in. He told her how Dulles and the CIA had protected Ezra Pound—the Society's "Helmsman"—by arranging for his commitment to St. Elizabeth's Hospital. He told her about the importance of a mystery man named Gomelez, and how Dulles and Jung had conspired "to stir the pot" by launching new archetypes and revitalizing old ones. When she asked what the hell he was talking about, he told her what Simon had said about Schidlof's theories on the archetypal field, and about the hoax at Roswell. Then he asked her a question. "What's *reify* mean?"

She stabbed a *pinchito* with a toothpick and smiled as she transferred it to her mouth.

"What's so funny?" he asked.

"I had a boyfriend who was a Trot," she replied.

"A what?"

"A Trotskyite. Long time ago. And *reify* was practically his favorite word."

"Jesus Christ! Were you a communist?"

"No. I was sixteen. *He* was a communist."

"So what does it mean?"

"What does what mean?"

"Reify!"

"Oh, that," she said. "It's when you make something real that's otherwise just an abstraction."

"Like what?" Dunphy asked.

Clem thought about it. "Oh, I don't know . . . *time*. Time is an abstraction. And clocks 'reify' it. But what's that got to do with anything?"

"In one of the letters Dulles wrote, he talks about 'reifying portents.' He tells Jung they have to take—I'm quoting now, okay?—they have to take 'a proactive stance toward prophecies and portents' in this book of theirs."

"Which book?" Clem asked.

"I can't believe I'm talking about portents," Dunphy complained, and signaled for the waiter to take their order.

"Which *book*?" Clem repeated.

Dunphy sighed. "I forget what it was called. *The Apocryphal* or something. Some quack-quack piece of—"

"I don't think so."

"Why not?"

"Well, I think you mean the *Apocryphon*—and it's really quite old."

Dunphy looked at her in surprise. "You astound me."

"I've seen it," she said, "in Skoob. It's a paperback. There's a Dover edition, and it's not really a book. It's just a poem, but they call it a booke—with an *e* at the end. Dover put it out as part of an anthology about the end of the world: I think they called it . . . *Millenarian Yearnings*."

In the morning, they went looking for English-language bookstores and found several, but none of them carried any of Dover's publications. With a couple of hours to kill before their flight, they took a taxi to the Puerto del Sol, where they found an Internet café that featured

450-MHZ PCS & IMACS
+
LOS CHURROS MEJORES EN MADRID!

It was fifty degrees outside, but it was warm in the café, where the air was fat with the smell of *churros* baking.

Dunphy ordered a plate of the Spanish doughnuts for himself and Clementine, then ruined both their breakfasts when he opened the file he'd stolen from the Special Registry. Bovine Census.

Clem saw one photo and gasped.

"That's horrid," she cried. "Why would anyone do such a thing?"

Dunphy thought about it. "According to Schidlof, according to Simon? They're 'stirring the pot.' 'Revitalizing an archetype.' "

"That's crap," Clem said, her eyes suddenly wet.

"I'm just telling you what he said. You weren't there. He said animal sacrifice was as old as the hills—and he was right."

"Well, I don't have to look at it," she replied. "I'm going to get a newspaper." And with that, she got to her feet.

"There's a newsagent just up the street," Dunphy told her. "I saw the racks."

As she left, Dunphy's eyes followed her. She had the kind of lacquered walk that you sometimes see in Rio and Milan. Nearby, a bearded young man sat motionless in front of a twenty-one-inch monitor, gazing after her with a look that might have been mistaken for malnutrition.

Moments later, the *churros* arrived and, with them, two steaming cups of *café con leche*. The little doughnuts lay on the plate like a handful of very thick pickup sticks, golden and warm. Dunphy sprinkled a spoonful of sugar on the mound, extracted one from the pile, and dunked it in his coffee. Then he turned to the file in front of him and began reading.

It took only a minute or two to realize that there wasn't much there. The file had evidentiary value as a way of documenting the mutilations, but Dunphy was already a believer. He didn't need the details. And realizing that made him nervous. It made him think about the fact that he didn't really have a plan, or a strategy, for getting out from under. There wasn't a police force in the world that could stand up to the Magdalene Society. Not that he'd be taken seriously, in any case. Black Virgins and cattle mutilations, secret societies and the CIA? He could imagine sitting down with a homicide detective—or Mike Wallace, for that matter. He'd start to talk, and about the time he got to Snippy the Horse or Our Lady of Einsiedeln, the little red light on the camera would wink out, and Wallace would be looking around for a cab. The "story" was too big, the players too powerful, the conspiracy too grand and bizarre. No matter how much evidence Dunphy might assemble, it wouldn't really matter. This wasn't "news you can use." It was news that could get you killed.

Which meant that there were only a few ways out for Dunphy and Clem. One: they could be *carried* out in body bags. (Unacceptable.) Two: they could find a place to hide, and spend the rest of their lives walking back-to-back. (Also unacceptable, and probably ineffective, as well.) Three: they could destroy the Magdalene Society before it destroyed them. *(Good idea, Jack, but? . . .)* In the last analysis, going to ground was the only reasonable course of action. It was, after all, a big planet—just as it was a big CIA—and there was at least a chance that they'd survive.

Turning back to the reports, he saw that they were all of a piece. They gave the date of each flight, with the times of departure and return. Crew members' names were listed, and meteorological conditions noted. Finally, there was a brief account of each mission.

> 03-03-99 Dep. 0510Z Ret. 1121Z
> 143rd Surgical Air Wing
> J. Nesbitt (pilot)
> R. Kerr   E. Pagan
> P. Guidry   T. Conway
> J. Sozio   J. MacLeod
> Dr. S. Amirpashaie (operating)
>
> Temp. 23° Winds SW, 4–10 knots
> Visibility 18 kilometers
> Baro. press. 30.11 and ↑

Black Angus specimen secured on ranchland belonging to one Jimmy Re, Platte 66, Lot 49, 16.3 kilometers north-northwest of Silverton. Anesthetic administered by Capt. Brown. Extraction of ocular tissue, eyes, tongue, internal and external auditory organs. 6.5-cm. incisions made in lower axillary regions, and digestive organs removed. Anal orifice extracted, cavity suctioned with vacuum gun. Reproductive organs excised. 2.5-cm. perforations made in thorax and chest. Spinal column severed in three places using laser saw. Animal drained, and returned to pasture. No citizen contact.

There were dozens of such reports that, when read alongside the photographs, became an adventure in nausea. When Clem returned with a copy of *The Independent*, Dunphy closed the file and pushed it aside.

"Happy reading?" she asked.

"No," Dunphy said. "It's pretty awful."

Reaching across the table, she picked up the file and began to page through it, lingering over the photographs. "What are you going to do with it?" she asked.

"I don't know," Dunphy said. "Probably nothing."

"In that case . . . may I have it?"

He thought about it. "Why not?" he said.

She smiled and got to her feet. Turning on her heel, she walked over to the counter and told a waiting clerk that she'd like to use one of the computers. He gave her a membership card, which she filled out in the name of Veroushka Bell. Then he collected a fifteen-hundred-peseta fee, and escorted her to one of the computers. Seating herself, she logged on to the Internet and, using the Alta Vista search engine, hunted for an address in London.

It took only a minute to find what she was looking for, and when she had it, she withdrew a packing envelope from her handbag. Slapping what looked like too many stamps on its face, she printed the address she'd found on its cover. Then she returned to the table where Dunphy was sitting, mystified, and put the file inside the envelope. Finally, she sealed the envelope and, with a satisfied smile, said, "Shouldn't we be going?"

Dunphy looked at what she'd written:

> People for the Ethical
> Treatment of Animals
> 10 Parkgate House
> Broomhill Rd.
> London SW 18 4JQ
> England

"You sure that's a good idea?" he asked.

She smiled. "Yup."

24

Europe and Africa dwindled behind them as the plane headed out over the open Atlantic, with Dunphy gazing through the window at a blue-on-blue world. There were places you could lose yourself, he thought. It happens all the time. You settled in a place where the people hunting you hadn't any influence. Places like . . . Kabul. Pyŏngyang. Baghdad.

The problem being that places like Kabul tended to be a little short on the kinds of amenities that Dunphy and Clem took for granted. Things like . . . the twentieth century. Honey-roasted peanuts. Decent plumbing. Better, then, to take one's chances in a venue like Tenerife which, while remote, had honey-roasted peanuts in abundance.

Located about a hundred miles off the southernmost tip of Morocco, Tenerife was the largest island in the Canarian archipelago. Famous for its spectacular and varied scenery (which ranged from sun-pounded beaches to the highest mountain "in Spain"), the island was infamous for its sprawling tourist resorts and decadent nightlife—which tended to get started shortly after breakfast. Having been to the island twice before, Dunphy both loved and hated the place.

They'd been flying over the ocean for almost an hour when the flight attendant arrived at their seats and, reaching past Clem, pulled Dunphy's tray from its armrest. Covering the tray with a white linen tablecloth, she handed Dunphy a menu and asked if he'd like a glass of champagne. He declined, and she repeated the sequence with Clem—who asked for a Perrier.

"Do you know where we'll stay?" she asked.

Dunphy shrugged. "We'll find a place."

"And then what?"

"Then? Well, then, I guess we'll just . . . play it as it lays." When he saw her frown, he elaborated. "After I talk to Tommy, I'll have a better idea about what to do."

"Why don't we just go to the newspapers?" Clem asked.

The idea made him smile. "You mean, like in *Three Days of the Condor*?"

"It was just an idea," she said. "You don't have to make fun of me."

"I'm not making fun of you," he told her. "But the papers wouldn't do anything."

"How do you know?"

"Trust me."

"Then, why not just put it on the Internet?" Clem asked. "No one could stop you, and everyone in the world would be able to read it."

Dunphy thought about it. For a second. Then he shook his head and said, "There's already a million crazy sites on the Internet. Flying saucers, chupa cabras, Satanic sexual abuse— everyone from the Abominable Snowman to Zorro has got a home page. So who's gonna notice our little complaint—or care that we've got evidence? Files. *Everyone's* got files."

The flight attendant brought Clementine her water and asked if they'd prefer veal or linguine for dinner. Clem chose the pasta, and Dunphy opted for the veal. When the attendant left, Clem turned to him with an accusing look and asked, "How can you *do* that?"

Dunphy didn't get it. "What?" he asked.

She looked away.

"How could I do *what*?" Dunphy repeated.

She reached into the seat pocket in front of her and pulled out a tattered in-flight magazine. "Eat veal!" she said. Turning away from him, she opened the magazine and began to read, ignoring Dunphy as she twirled a tendril of hair around her forefinger.

Baby cows?

"I'm gonna stretch my legs," Dunphy said, and getting to his feet, walked slowly aft, feeling the plane tremble beneath him. Stopping at the galley, he caught the flight attendant's attention and changed his order. "I think I'll have the linguine," he said. She smiled her okay.

Passing from business class to economy, he caught a whiff of cigarette smoke emanating from the back of the plane, where a knot of people were lounging in front of the lavatories. Looking around, he saw that the plane wasn't as crowded as he'd thought it would be. Still, it was a diverse lot. There were mothers with little children, businessmen and college kids, backpackers and Arabs. A tour group of sixty-something Brits was having a grand time, drinking with enormous enthusiasm, and playing cards. About a third of them were wearing identical red cardigans with a sort of coat of arms emblazoned on the breast. Edging past them in the aisle, Dunphy saw that he was sharing the plane with the Sacred Order of the Gorse. Sensing his perplexity, one of the men looked up from his cards and smiled. "Golfers," he explained.

Continuing down the aisle, Dunphy paused beside an emergency exit, crouched, and looked out through the little window. Far below, the ocean glittered in every direction, its azure surface flecked with whitecaps and crisscrossed by freighters. He watched the panorama for a minute or so, half wondering if Clem was still upset with him.

Then he straightened up and, turning from the window, headed back the way he'd come. He'd almost reached the little curtain that separates business class from coach when he felt something on the back of his neck—the weight and tingle of another person's stare. Turning, his eyes met those of a middle-aged man with platinum hair and bad skin.

Blondie.

And, over there, by the bulkhead, asleep in his seat: *the Jock.*

Fuck all, Dunphy thought. I've had it. He could feel the adrenaline surging through his heart like a spring tide, then draining away, then surging again.

He wasn't sure what to do. Or how they'd found him. Or what might be waiting for him when the plane touched down at the airport on Tenerife. And then, to his surprise, he found himself walking toward the older man.

"Is this seat taken?" Without waiting for an answer, Dunphy stepped over his surveillant's legs and dropped into the seat next to him.

"You speak English?" Dunphy asked, raising the armrest that separated them.

The man nodded. Gulped.

"Good," Dunphy said, "because it's important you get this right. If you don't tell me the truth, I'm going to break your fucking neck—right here. You understand *neck*, right? *Le cou?*"

The man looked wildly around, as if searching for help, then reached for his seat belt, fumbling to unfasten the buckle. "No trouble, please," he warned, speaking in a thick, Alsatian accent. "Or I call *la hôtesse*." Abandoning the seat belt, he reached overhead for the flight attendant's call button, then froze and fell back as Dunphy's left hand seized him by the balls. And squeezed. Hard.

The man's eyes bulged, then threatened to explode as Dunphy's grip tightened.

"Please!"

And tightened some more.

In the seat across the aisle, a little boy began tugging at his mother's sleeve and pointing at them. Dunphy smiled at him, as if it were all a big joke. Finally, he opened his hand, and the Alsatian gasped with relief.

"How'd you find me?" Dunphy asked.

The other man squeezed his eyes shut, blinked, and shook his head, as if to clear it. Then he took a deep breath and said, "The girl."

"What girl?"

"English. When she comes to Zürich, I recognize her from Jersey."

"So you were on me—"

"From St. Helier to Zurich. Then you lose us at the hotel. But . . . *she* comes there, so we follow *her*." The way he said it made it sound like a rebuke, as if he were criticizing Dunphy's tradecraft.

"I didn't know you'd seen her on Jersey," Dunphy explained.

"Yes. We see her. And hard to forget."

"So . . ."

"We follow her to bank. Then to airport. Then Zug."

"And Madrid."

"Yes, of course," the man replied, unbuttoning the collar of his shirt. "Madrid."

"Now what?" Dunphy asked.

The Alsatian shrugged. "I think, maybe you speak with Roger. Because, now . . . he kills you."

"Does he?" Dunphy asked rhetorically. "And is he waiting for me on Tenerife?"

When the man didn't answer, Dunphy turned toward him, but the Alsatian raised his hands in a calming gesture. "I cannot say. You understand, he has legal problems—in Kraków. When you are in St. Helier, the Poles are holding his passport. If not, you would have seen him in Zürich, I promise you."

"And now?"

A little moue. "I think, maybe he gets his passport back."

Dunphy rested his hand on the man's forearm. "You *think*?"

A wary look crossed the Alsatian's face. "Yes, I think now he has it."

Dunphy nodded, then spoke in a low voice. "So you're gonna see him real soon—which is good. Because I want you to tell him something. Tell him I can get him half the money right away—and the rest . . . a little later. But *not* if I see him on Tenerife. If I see him on Tenerife . . ." He left the sentence hanging, hoping his uncertainty would seem like a threat.

The Alsatian turned to him, all po'-faced innocence,

bemusement dancing past the fear in his eyes. "Yes?" he asked. "If you see him on Tenerife? What should I tell him?"

Are you fucking with me? Dunphy wondered. Because if you are . . . there is absolutely nothing that I can do about it. Not on the plane. Finally he said, "Tell him it will be a surprise." Then he got up and walked back to his seat.

The ride from Reina Sofía Airport to Playa de las Americas was like passing through a diorama built by road warriors in collusion with an angry volcano god. The setting was an ocher barren of cactus, rock, and hardpan cleft in two by a seemingly permanent traffic jam. After forty-five minutes of stop-and-go traffic, this desert wasteland gave way to its urban counterpart—las Americas. This was a sprawling tourist enclave overrun by packaged tours, kitschy pubs, throbbing discotheques and shops selling T-shirts and souvenirs. A sign outside the Banco Santander recorded the temperature as ninety-seven degrees.

"Welcome to hell," Dunphy said.

The taxi came to a stop outside an ALL ADULT! nightclub in the Veronicas neighborhood. *"Abajo alli,"* the driver said, pointing toward a pedestrian byway that meandered along a gentle hillside past palm trees and flower gardens, switching back and forth on its way down to the sea.

Dunphy gave him a thousand pesetas. "We have to walk the rest of the way," he explained to Clem.

It took them half an hour to find the Broken Tiller, which Dunphy hadn't visited for nearly three years. During that time, buildings had gone up on either side and in the back, so that Frank Boylan's watering hole now sat in the lee of a whitewashed, six-story "apart-hotel" called the Miramar. On either side: a German *bierstube* and a discotheque (Studio 666). Otherwise, nothing much had changed.

Bolted into the side of a green and well-watered hill, the Tiller was a simple, almost elegant, seafood restaurant-cumbar that looked out to sea over a nude beach. The sunsets,

Dunphy remembered, were often spectacular, especially in the rainy season. And this evening was no exception.

A plump red sun lolled on the horizon at the bottom of a mackerel sky, oscillating with peach and butter colors. Setting their carry-on bags next to a pale blue couch, Dunphy and Clem sat down at a small table with white wicker chairs. A handsome, young Tenerifeño came out from behind the bar with a smile.

"What can I get for you?" he asked.

"Beer for me," Dunphy replied, "and . . . what?" He looked at Clem.

"I'll have a gin and tonic, please."

Before the bartender had a chance to leave, Dunphy told him, "I'm looking for a friend of mine."

"Oh? Yes?"

"Yeah. His name's Tommy Davis. I thought, maybe you'd seen him."

The kid—he couldn't have been more than eighteen years old—blinked, then made a show of thinking about it. Finally, he shook his head and shrugged. *"Lo siento."*

Dumb question, Dunphy thought. Tommy didn't want to be found, so the answer would have been the same whether he'd seen him or not. "And Frank Boylan? What about him? Does he still own the place?"

Big smile. "Oh, sure. He'll never sell. You know Mr. Boylan?"

Dunphy nodded. "We're old friends. Can you get him on the phone for me?"

"Yes, I think so," the kid said. "If he's not drinking. Sometimes, when he drinks—"

"I know."

"—he turns off his cell phone. Says he doesn't want to be bothered."

"Yeah, well—see if you can reach him. Tell him Merry Kerry's at the bar."

"Mary Kelly?"

"Merry . . . Kerry," Dunphy corrected. "Like *Happy*

Kerry, except with different letters. And while you're at it—check behind the bar. I think there's a package for me."

It was half past eight when Tommy sailed in with the diminutive, but burly, Francis Boylan at his side. "If it isn't himself!" Tommy cried, his brogue even thicker for all the months he'd been in Spain. "I tried to reach ya time and again," he crowed, "but all I got for my trouble was a lot of funny noises on the phone. I thought you were tits up, f'sure!"

Big *abrazo*, then Dunphy disengaged to shake hands with Boylan. "The night's still young," he replied. "I could go at any second." Finally, he introduced Clementine.

"Pleased to meet ya," Tommy said, embracing her with a bit more enthusiasm than was strictly necessary.

"And this is our host," Dunphy announced, taking Clem by the elbow and introducing her to "the great Francis Boylan."

The Irishman shook hands and turned to Dunphy with a look of approval. "Good job."

Soon, they were seated around a platter of *tapas*, drinking, with Tommy complaining about the "hard life" on Tenerife.

"It's killin' the two of us," he claimed. "Francis, here, is a ghost of the man he was. Just look at him, wastin' away, with the bags under his eyes—"

"He looks rather fit to me," Clem said.

"Thank you," Boylan remarked.

"It's the sex and the sun and the booze," Tommy insisted. "I mean, when you think of it, there's a thousand women a day flyin' in, and every one of them's charged up for a good time. So, if you're livin' here full-time and know your way around—well, it's a wonder there isn't a medical study bein' done."

In the hours that followed, they tested the kitchen at the Broken Tiller and found the chef in good form. Between mouthfuls of swordfish and new potatoes, french beans and Riesling, Dunphy told his companions about Blémont, and his encounter on the flight from Madrid.

"So you nobbled the man's money," Boylan said. "And now he's after gettin' it back."

"He is," Dunphy replied.

"Well, who can blame him?" Tommy asked. "I'd do the same."

"Of course you would," Dunphy explained, "anyone would. But let's keep it in perspective. This is a very bad man. It's not like I robbed the Poor Clares."

"Still . . . "

"He's an anti-Semite!" Dunphy insisted. "And it wasn't even his money in the first place."

"Then let the Jews rob him!" Tommy suggested.

Before Dunphy could reply, Boylan offered a suggestion. "I could have a word with him, if you'd like. Send a couple of lads around. Ask for a bit of patience."

Dunphy thought about it, then shook his head. "It's my problem. I'll handle it."

"In that case . . . " Boylan reached around to the small of his back and came up with a sleek little handgun. Sliding it into the pages of a folded copy of the local newspaper, *Canarias7,* he pushed it across the table to Dunphy. "It's a P7," Boylan said. "Heckler & Koch. Eight rounds in the clip."

Clem rolled her eyes, sat back, and looked away.

"*Thank* you, Jesus!" Dunphy exclaimed, jamming the gun into the space between his belt and his shirt. "I'll get it back to you before we leave."

Boylan nodded. "I'd be grateful. It cost a grand."

"So where are you staying?" Tommy asked.

"I don't know," Dunphy said. "We just got in a couple of hours ago."

"Then you may as well stay at Nicky Slade's," Boylan suggested. "You remember Nicky, don't you?"

"The merc," Dunphy said.

"The very one," Tommy agreed.

"It's a nice place," Boylan remarked, "and Nicky won't be needin' it for a while."

"Why not?" Dunphy asked.

Boylan glanced at Tommy, then back to Dunphy. "Well, he's traveling, isn't he?"

"I don't know. Is he?" Dunphy asked.

"He is," Tommy replied. "In fact, he's traveling for the foreseeable future."

"So it's an extended trip," Dunphy suggested.

"It is."

"And why is that?" Dunphy inquired.

"Well," Boylan explained, "because the man's in bad odor, isn't he?"

"With who?"

"Certain parties."

"Which parties?"

"NATO," Tommy replied. "You're very insistent—y'know that, don't ya?"

Clem giggled, and Dunphy frowned. "How do you get in 'bad odor' with NATO, for Christ's sake?"

"In fact, there was a small typo on one of his end-user certificates," Boylan said.

"*Was* there?" Dunphy asked.

"Indeed, there was," Tommy replied. "And wouldn't ya know, the bureaucrats are makin' a federal case of it."

"What was the typo?" Dunphy asked.

"From what I've been told, he typed *chardonnay* in one of the tiny spaces on the form when, strictly speaking, the appropriate answer would have been closer to *grenades*."

They got to Nicky Slade's place a little after midnight. It was one of a dozen small condos on a quiet street in Las Galletas, just down the coast from las Americas, and not far from the beach. A trio of flight attendants were renting the house on the left, Tommy said, while an elderly Scotswoman occupied the one on the right. "You'll be fine here," Tommy told them.

A musty smell greeted them as they entered. "Must be NATO," Tommy joked. The place had apparently been unoccupied for weeks. But that was easy to fix. With the windows opened and the drapes pulled back, a fresh breeze soon cleared the air. Dunphy switched on the lights in the living room.

"I'll bring the Pearlcorder with me in the morning," Tommy said. "So you can listen to the tape." He meant the tape recording that Dunphy had sent to himself in care of the Broken Tiller.

"Just give me a call before you come over," Dunphy replied. "I don't want to shoot you through the door."

"I'll make a point of it," Tommy promised, backing out with a little wave. "Cheers."

Dunphy locked the door behind him and went into the kitchen. Opening the refrigerator, he found half a case of Budweiser, two kinds of mustard, and not much else. Reflecting that a case of Bud must have cost a fortune in the Canaries, Dunphy snapped one open and returned to the living room.

"I think your friends are nice," Clem said, looking through a pile of CDs. "Though . . . "

"What?"

"A bit rough."

Dunphy nodded. "Well, yeah," he said. "It's what they do." Removing the handgun from his waistband, he laid it on the coffee table next to a vase of dusty silk carnations. Then he walked over to the windows and took in a lungful of warm sea air.

"Do you think they'll find us?" Clem asked.

"I don't know," Dunphy said, wondering which pursuers she had in mind—Blémont or the Agency. "I don't think we were followed from the airport, but then, I didn't think we were followed from Jersey, either. So what do I know?"

She put a CD in the tray, and soon, a soulful voice filled the room with the complaint that *"Easy's gettin' harder every day."* "Iris Dement," Clem said, swaying to it.

Dunphy leaned against the windowsill and sipped his beer. He was looking out across a little garden (who would have guessed that someone like Slade would be a gardener?), gazing at a string of lights on the dark horizon. Freighters and passenger liners, sailboats and tankers. It was a beautiful, even romantic, scene, but he couldn't get into it. He was thinking about the men on the plane—Blondie and the Jock. And how they'd disappeared, once they'd landed on Tenerife.

Which should have been comforting.

With no bags to fetch, Dunphy and Clem had soared through Customs and then through the airport, taking the first cab they'd found into town. If his pursuers had been anywhere near, Dunphy would have seen them. But they weren't. Which made him wonder if . . .

Nah.

For a moment, Dunphy had entertained the possibility that he had somehow scared them off. But how likely was that? Blondie hadn't seemed frightened, really—more inconvenienced than anything else. So . . .

They must have called ahead from Madrid. Had someone waiting at the airport. Which meant . . .

With a grimace, Dunphy pulled the curtains shut and checked the locks on the French doors leading out to the garden. The locks weren't much. A good kick would send them flying open.

Returning to the living room, he retrieved the nine-millimeter that Boylan had given him, and slipped it in his pocket. Clem was still moving to the music.

"Jack?" she asked.

"Yeah."

"We're going to be all right, aren't we?"

Tommy came by in the morning, a little after ten. Since there wasn't anything to eat in Slade's apartment, they went out for crescent rolls at the local market, then drove into las Americas.

"We might as well go to the Tiller," Tommy suggested. "Boylan's coffee is as good as any—and it's twice as strong."

They left Tommy's red Deux Chevaux at a car park near the Cinema Dumas and walked down the hill to the Broken

Tiller. The same kid who'd been there the night before was standing behind the bar, drying glasses.

Otherwise, the place was deserted. Dark and cool.

"Espressos, Miguel!"

"None for me, thanks," Clem said. "I'm going for a swim."

Dunphy looked skeptical. "Aren't you forgetting something?"

She gave him a puzzled look. "What?"

"A swimsuit," Dunphy replied, sitting down at a table in a corner of the bar.

Clem kissed him on the top of the head. "You're so cute," she said, and turning on her heel, walked out into the sunlight with a bath towel under her arm.

"This I've gotta see!" Tommy exclaimed.

"No, you don't," Dunphy told him, and taking him by the elbow, pulled him into the seat beside himself. "You bring the Pearlcorder?" he asked.

"I did," Tommy replied, retrieving it from the pocket of his shirt and handing it to Dunphy. "Is it the professor you've got on tape?"

Dunphy nodded, pressing the microcassette onto the tape recorder's reels. "It's the last tape we made before he was chopped."

"Well, if you don't mind," Tommy said, "seein' as how only one of us can listen to it at a time, I'll take my coffee down to the beach."

Dunphy plugged the earphones into the Pearlcorder, and slipped them on over his head. "You aren't going to ogle my girlfriend, are you?"

"Come on!" Tommy protested. "What do you take me for?"

"A pervert."

Whatever Tommy said in response was lost to Dunphy as he pressed the Play button, and the little reels began to turn.

—Meadow gold.
Meadow gold?

Yes.

Well, if you say so, but . . . don't you think it's a little . . .

What?

Yellow?

I knew you'd say that! But, no, I don't think it is. It will look great with the Kirman.

Oh, that's right! You have the Kirman!

It took Dunphy a little while to sort out the voices, and another minute to guess what they were talking about—in this case, a chair that Schidlof was having covered.

The second conversation was relatively transparent—Schidlof making a doctor's appointment for what he suspected was bursitis. Then Dunphy's coffee appeared, suddenly and out of nowhere. Hunched over the Pearlcorder, listening intently through the earphones, he hadn't heard Miguel's approach.

"Thanks," he said, a bit too loud. And took a sip. *Yowzah!*

The third and fourth calls were from students, asking Schidlof if they could rearrange their meetings with him. The fifth call was placed by Schidlof, and it was international—Dunphy counted fifteen distinct tones before the phone began to ring at the other end. And then an American voice came on the line.

Gibeglisociates.

Hallo! Schidlof here!

Yeah—

Dunphy stopped the tape and rewound it.

Gibegli Associates.

And again.

Gil Beckley Associates.

Schidlof here!

Yeah, Dr. Schidlof. Good to hear from you.

I was calling about the check that I sent.

Right—well, I want to thank you for that.

It was meant to be a retainer.

So I understand.

*And I was wondering if you'd had a chance to look at the
letter.*

I have.

And? Were you able to form an opinion?

Oh, it's authentic. No question.

The tape turned silently for five or ten seconds.

Professor?

Yes.

I thought I'd lost you for a second.

No, it's just that—

*If you'd like, I can put you in touch with someone who, uh,
works for Sotheby's. Top-notch.*

No—

*He could probably get you a thousand for it—maybe more.
So you wouldn't be out of pocket.*

Beckley's voice reminded Dunphy of where he'd seen
him—on one of Diane Sawyer's shows, talking about the
Hitler diaries that weren't.

*Well, I appreciate that, but . . . at the moment, I just want to
authenticate the letters.*

It was Beckley's turn to be quiet. Then, *Oh! I didn't realize
there was—*

Yes. It's a correspondence. I thought I'd made that clear.

No.

Well . . .

And these are . . . you say they're all from Allen Dulles?

*Yes. They begin in the early thirties. Jung died in 1961. So
that was the end of it.*

I see. Beckley went quiet again. *Y'know, this could be a
little sensitive.*

Oh? And how is that?

*Well . . . Allen Dulles was a very big guy. Had his fingers in
a lot of pies.*

I realize that, of course, but . . .

*If you'd like, I could take a look at the rest of the
correspondence.*

That's kind of you, but—

No charge.

There's no point, really.

The conversation went on for perhaps another minute, with Beckley wheedling to see the other letters, and Schidlof politely declining. Finally, the professor rang off, saying he had a tutorial.

Dunphy recalled the flash cable that he'd seen in the Special Registry—the one from Matta to Curry. "Unilaterally controlled source ... Andromeda-sensitive materials ... Who's Schidlof?"

Well, Dunphy thought, at least now we know who the source was—not that there was ever much doubt. Poor Schidlof had gone to absolutely the wrong man. Beckley was one of those Washington types who never quite get over losing their security clearances. Retiring, *perforce,* at fifty, they would do anything to demonstrate their continued usefulness to the intelligence community, anything to "keep their hand in," anything to remain "a player."

And so Beckley had shopped his client to the Agency's Office of Security in exchange for a pat on the back. I wonder if he got one, Dunphy thought. Or if, like Schidlof, he's sleeping with the fishes. Dunphy hoped it was the latter.

Looking up from the tape recorder, he signaled Miguel for another espresso, and glanced around. To his surprise, he saw that he was no longer the bar's only customer. A young couple were sitting at a table on the veranda, talking animatedly about something or other. And there was a man at the bar with his back turned, quietly drinking a beer. Nice work shirt, Dunphy thought, admiring its color, which was a sort of cobalt blue.

Then he looked out over the beach, searching for Clem, but he couldn't find her. There were dozens of swimmers, wading in and out of the water, and at least a hundred sunbathers, about half of them nude—sleeping, reading, baking in the heat.

Unlike himself. The bar was cool. Damp, even.

Dunphy readjusted the headphones over his ears, pressed the Play button, and began to listen.

Schidlof reserving tickets to a Spurs match. Schidlof canceling a dental appointment. Schidlof commiserating with another teacher about their intolerable course loads. Schidlof listening compliantly to a telemarketing pitch. And then— Schidlof dialing out—and a chirpy voice:

Hallo 'allo?!

Dr. Van Worden?

Just Al, thank you very much!

Oh! Well, this is Leo Schidlof—King's College?

Yes?

I was hoping I might see you.

Oh?

Mmmm. In fact, I was hoping that, if you're free, we might have lunch. A pause, which Schidlof rushes to fill. *I've become quite interested in the Magdalene Society.*

A chuckle from Van Worden. *Really?!*

Yes. And, uhhh, from what I understand, you're one of the few people who can tell me about it.

Welll, yes . . . . I suppose I am, but—you're a historian?

Miguel arrived with Dunphy's espresso, silently setting it on the table.

A psychologist, actually.

Oh . . . I see. Long pause. *Though, I don't, really. Why would a psychologist be interested in something like that? I mean, they died out two hundred years ago!* Silence from Schidlof. *Professor?*

Yes?

I was wondering why a psychologist—

Because I'm not sure they did.

Did what?

Died out.

This time, it was Van Worden's turn to be quiet. Finally, he said, *Well! By all means, then. Let's have lunch.*

Dunphy wondered who Van Worden was. A professor of some sort—probably history. Someone, in any case, who knew enough about the Magdalene Society that Schidlof would seek him out.

He rewound the tape to a point just before the beginning of the conversation. There were seven dialing tones, and then Van Worden's cheerful voice. *Hallo 'allo?!* Which meant that it was a local call from Schidlof's house. Which put Van Worden somewhere in central London.

Dunphy was thinking that Van Worden was probably in the London telephone book when he heard a muffled shout. As he looked up, something loomed in the corner of his left eye, but even as he turned toward it, he froze with shock as the man at the bar hit Miguel with a bottle. Then a bat or a brick or *something* hit him behind the ear, and the world flashed, a blaze of white that faded fast as Dunphy went over and down, hitting the tiled floor, hard. The earphones were gone now, and the scream was louder, a ululating shriek as Dunphy clawed at his waist for the handgun that Boylan had given him. He had it halfway out of his waistband when the toe of a boot slammed into his kidney, and into his shoulder, and into his kidney again. Now there were two people shouting or screaming, and dimly, he realized the second person was himself. Someone's instep smashed into his ribs, rolling him over, and then the gun was going off, wild and fast. He didn't know who or what or how many he was shooting at, but somehow he'd started firing, flailing and firing, crabbing across the floor on his back, trying to keep away from the boot. People were shouting—*he* was shouting—

Then something happened in the back of his head, and the world snapped off with a soft *click* and a shower of little bright lights.

25

He was sick to his stomach. Sick to his head. Sick to everything. His lower back felt as if it was broken, and his rib cage was in splinters.

He was sitting somewhere, eyes on his knees, afraid to look up. Afraid, almost, to breathe. And then a wave of dizziness and nausea came over him, and made him retch, a dry heave. The world swam into view.

He was in a workshop of some kind. Fluorescent lights flickered and buzzed, and a sharp, unpleasant smell filled the air. Wood stain. His head was pounding as if it were being squeezed and released, squeezed and released. Almost against his will, he looked up and saw—

Furniture. Lots of it. And bolts of fabric. Wires and springs. An upholstery shop. And then—slowly, and from what at first seemed far away—a clapping sound filled the room. Dunphy turned toward it.

Roger Blémont was sitting in an overstuffed green wing chair, applauding so slowly that each clap began to fade before its successor split the air. He was smiling and, as always, impeccably dressed. The Breitling watch and Cole-Haans, the razor-creased trousers and . . . work shirt.

He'd been sitting at the bar while Dunphy listened to the Schidlof tape. Dunphy had seen him, but only from the back, and now . . .

"You look like shit," Blémont remarked.

A soft groan fell from Dunphy's lips.

"Un vrai merdiers."

272

Dunphy heard a little laugh and turned his head to see who it was: the Jock, with his boots and leather jacket, lounging against the back of a couch, watching Dunphy with undisguised curiosity. And in a chair nearby, the Alsatian, looking blank.

Why here? Dunphy wondered, looking around. Then he saw it—the white flag, like the pin Blémont sometimes wore, hanging above a cluttered workbench. And on it, a blue-and-gold banner with the words: *Contre la boue.* Blémont, it seemed, had friends even in the Canaries.

Get out, Dunphy told himself. Instinctively, he struggled to stand, gritting his teeth against the pain—but, no. His wrists were tied behind his back.

"You know, Kerry—" Blémont began in a soft voice.

"My name's not Kerry," Dunphy muttered.

Blémont chuckled. "I don't give a shit what your name is."

"You ought to," Dunphy shot back. "You're going to need it to get your money back."

"Ahhhh," the Corsican said, as if he'd just remembered something. "The money. I told Marcel, I said, 'We'll talk about the money, Kerry and I.' " He glanced at the Jock. "Didn't I?"

The big man nodded, lighting a small cigar.

Still smiling, Blémont crossed the room, then sank to his haunches in front of Dunphy, and looked him in the eyes. "Why did you take my money?" he asked.

"I needed it," Dunphy said. "I was in a lot of trouble."

"Was?"

Dunphy looked away. He hurt all over, and he knew it was just the beginning. Blémont was going to fuck him up. He could see it in his eyes.

"You know, it really is quite a lot of money," the Corsican remarked. "And not just the money from the stock. There is the interest, as well. *N'est-ce-pas?*"

Dunphy sighed.

"And, after the interest, there is also the . . . " Blémont frowned. "How do you say—*le dessous de table?*"

"The bribe," the Jock said.

"Exactly."

"What bribe?" Dunphy asked.

"For the secretary," Blémont replied. "In St. Helier. How do you think we found you?"

So he'd been right. Great.

"And there are expenses, too. Marcel and Luc. They have their fees, as you can imagine. Their costs. Quite a *lot* of costs. Ships. Planes. Hotels. Restaurants. Well, they have to eat."

Dunphy's eyes went from Blémont to the Jock, and then to the Alsatian.

"Hey," Blémont said in a softly chiding voice. "I'm over here."

But Dunphy couldn't turn away. His eyes were locked with the Alsatian's, who sat slumped in an overstuffed armchair, glaring at him. For a moment, it seemed to Dunphy that this was meant to be a hard stare, the kind of stare that enemies exchange when they see each other across a crowded room. But then he saw the red sash around the man's waist and knew it wasn't a cumberbund. The Alsatian was bleeding to death— right there, right in the chair. And the look on his face was that of a guy who was doing everything he could *not to lose it*. To stay in control. Hold it in. Hold it *all* in.

Fuck all, Dunphy thought. I've *had* it.

Blémont followed his gaze, and once again, the realization siren went off. "Aaaaaaah, I see your point," the Corsican exclaimed. "You're thinking, if Luc is *passé*, there is no need to pay him." He pushed his lips together in a little moue. "Good point. But Luc will be okay, won't you, Luc?"

A doubtful murmur from the Alsatian.

"What happened?" Dunphy asked.

Blémont made a comical expression. "You shot him."

Dunphy's surprise was obvious.

"You were falling," the Jock explained. "You got off a couple of shots. It was luck."

"He's dying," Dunphy told them.

Blémont dismissed the idea. "He'll be all right."

"He's bleeding to death."

"No, no. He's *fine*." Blémont put his mouth next to Dunphy's right ear and whispered, "You're going to frighten him."

It was the funniest thing Dunphy had heard all day, but he didn't laugh. "Look," he said, "I can get you your money back."

Blémont nodded indifferently. "I know."

The Jock muttered to himself, then tossed the cheroot that he'd been smoking to the floor. Grinding it out with the toe of his boot, he turned to Blémont. *"Pourquoi juste ne le détruisons? . . ."*

Dunphy didn't get it all. His own French was mediocre, at best. "Why don't we . . ." something . . . something.

"Soyez patient," Blémont said. Then he turned to Dunphy, and explained, "He wants to kill you."

Dunphy glanced in the Jock's direction. "Why? I don't even know him."

Once again, Blémont leaned in close and whispered. "Because he thinks you've killed his boyfriend—and, you know? Just between us? I think he may be right." Then he laughed.

It took Dunphy a moment to understand. Blondie and the Jock weren't just a team. They were an item. "Look," he said, trying to keep the conversation businesslike, "I can get you the money. Not just what's in the bank. The rest, too."

"The rest? How much have you spent?" Blémont asked.

Dunphy hesitated for a moment and lied. "Twenty thousand," he said. "Maybe twenty-two."

"Pounds?"

"Dollars."

Blémont rolled his head from side to side, thinking about it. Then he said, "Tell me something."

"What?"

"What took you so long?"

Dunphy didn't know what he meant. "To do what?" he asked.

"Go after the money. You'd been gone for months."

Dunphy thought about it, unsure what to say or how much. Finally, he shrugged. "I was in the States. I couldn't get away."

Blémont wagged his forefinger at him. "Don't bullshit me."

"I'm not."

"You're running from something," Blémont told him. "And not just me."

Dunphy didn't say anything.

"We went to your office," Blémont continued. "*Nothing.* And your flat—it's the same thing. So I think, my old friend, Kerry— he's taken *everyone's* money. But, no. I go to Kroll. You know Kroll?"

Dunphy nodded. "The investigators."

"Right. I go to them—it's two hundred bucks an hour, and—guess what? They say it's just me. No one else is complaining. No one else got burned. Now, why is that?"

"I only took what I needed," Dunphy answered.

"You needed half a million *bucks*?"

"Yeah. I did."

Blémont held his eyes for a moment, then shook his head, as if to clear it. "Okay, so you needed a lot of dough. Why *me*?"

"Because . . . " You're a pig, Dunphy thought. "The money was there," he said. "It was in the account. It was easy, that's all."

"You mean it *looked* easy," Blémont said, and Dunphy nodded. "And now—who are you running from, when you're not running from me?"

Dunphy shook his head.

"Not the police," Blémont mused. "Not in London, anyway. So who?"

"What's the difference? This isn't about me. It's about the money I took."

"No. It's not just about the money," Blémont replied.

Dunphy gave him a skeptical look.

"It's about friendship," the Corsican insisted, his voice larded with enough phony sincerity to launch a telemarketing campaign for Hizbollah.

Dunphy almost laughed. "You're so fucked up—" he began.

Blémont hit him as hard as Dunphy had ever been hit in his life, a looping roundhouse that broke his nose with a sharp crack and sent a spray of blood across the front of his shirt. Dunphy gasped and reeled as his eyes flew shut, and his brain swam with stars. After a moment, Blémont raised his chin with the palm of his hand. *"Pardon?"*

The blood was running into his throat from his sinuses, and it took him a moment to spit it out. Finally he said, "I misspoke."

Blémont smiled.

Dunphy tilted his head back in a vain effort to staunch the bleeding.

"Eh, bien," Blémont remarked, removing a packet of cigarettes from his shirt pocket. Lighting one with the flame from a silver-plated Zippo, he inhaled mightily, then blew a stream of smoke in the American's direction. "These things happen," he said. "But, really, all those lunches we had—my God, Kerry, how we laughed, eh?"

"Coupla lunches," Dunphy said. "We weren't that close."

"What *happened*?" Blémont asked in a plaintive voice, as if he were talking to a lover who'd jilted him.

Dunphy shook his head. Slowly, slightly. Took a deep breath. "It's complicated," he replied.

The Corsican dismissed the idea with a little puff of air. "There's time. We have all day. Tell me about it."

A sigh from Dunphy, who knew that Blémont was playing with him. Still, the longer they talked, the better it was for him. Tommy and Boylan would be looking for him. There'd been a shooting in the bar. There was blood on the floor.

"My name's Jack Dunphy," he said in a voice thick with blood and pain. "Not Thornley. Not Irish. American." Am I going to tell him everything? Dunphy wondered. And the answer came back: Yeah. Why not? What's the difference?

Blémont cocked his head in mild curiosity, listening

distractedly as he refilled his lighter with the liquid from a small can of Ronson lighter fluid.

"The job in London—the company I had . . . " His broken nose was making it hard to breathe.

Blémont squirted a thin stream of gas into the cotton wadding at the bottom of the lighter. "Yes?"

"It was a cover."

Blémont was momentarily perplexed. "A cover? You mean—"

"A front."

"For who?"

"The CIA."

The Jock laughed out loud—a single, sharp burst of incredulity.

Blémont continued to fill his lighter. Finally, he put the Zippo back together, flicked it on and off, on and off—and looked Dunphy in the eye. "Do you think I'm stupid?"

Dunphy shook his head.

"Do you think I'm here to amuse you?"

"No!"

"Because if I do—"

"You *don't*."

"We can *end* this. Right now! Okay? Is that what you want?" The Corsican's voice rose louder and louder, his rage mounting with the volume. *"Is it? Okay!"*

"Look," Dunphy said—but got no further as Blémont began to spray his chest with lighter fluid, swirling it over his shirt as if he, Blémont, were Jackson Pollock and Dunphy was his canvas. "Ohhh, Christ, Roger—"

It happened in an instant. Blémont leaned in with his Zippo. There was a sharp click, a flash of light, and a curtain of blue and yellow flames exploded with a *whoooof* in Dunphy's face. Blinded by the light, too shocked to cry out, it was all he could do to gasp. *The heat . . .* And then, as suddenly as they'd appeared, the flames fluttered out.

Blémont and the Jock were laughing. "Look at the smoke!" the Corsican said, patting Dunphy's shirt with his fingertips.

"He's smoking!" He sniffed the air, glanced at the Jock, and chuckled. *"Peux-tu sentir les cheveux?"*

A giggle came in reply.

"Jesus Christ!" Dunphy said through gritted teeth. "What do you *want*?"

Blémont adopted a serious mien, clearing his throat and frowning in an effort to repress his laughter. Then he spoke in a low voice that was a parody of sincerity and confidentiality. "Well, obviously—Jack—I want to *torture* you." Whereupon, Blémont and the Jock burst into laughter yet again.

Dunphy's heart was thumping away like an oompah band. He didn't know if Blémont was going to kick him, punch him, set him on fire—or what. A heart attack would be fine, Dunphy thought. And I could die, here and now. But that wasn't going to happen, he knew. So he wrenched at the bonds that held his wrists, and to his surprise, they seemed to give—just a bit.

"That was just a ..." Blémont snapped his fingers, searching for the idiom, then chuckled dryly. "Just a warm-up." Then he laughed uproariously.

He's insane, Dunphy thought.

"And look at this!" Blémont picked up an electric drill, or something like it. A long, orange wire ran from its base to a machine on the floor, which was itself plugged into the wall. Stooping, the Corsican snapped on a switch at the side of the machine, and instantly, the shop was filled with the vibrating din of an air compressor. *"My grandfather was a carpenter!"* Blémont yelled. *"In Ajaccio!"*

Dunphy wriggled his hands and looked away. He didn't want to know what Blémont was going to do, because whatever it was, it was going to be done to him.

"I've seen his work! It's not—" The compressor cut off, as quickly as it had come on. "It's not bad." Suddenly, the room was dead silent. "Of course, they didn't have nail guns then. Everything was done by hand. But with this ... " Blémont pointed the tool in Dunphy's direction and, with a sadistic grin, squeezed the trigger.

Szzzunkk!

It made a sound like a time clock being punched, and in that instant, a nail smacked into the plaster wall behind him. To Dunphy's horror, there was no ricochet.

"With *this*, I could pound nails all day long, and never get tired. Every nail—*powww!* like a sledgehammer. A hundred pounds an inch." He paused for a moment and frowned. "Of course, there are so many kinds of nails. Long nails, short nails, framing nails, roofing nails." He held up what looked like a foot-long bandolier of two-inch nails. "These are finishing nails," he explained, slotting them into the gun. "A hundred of them."

Dunphy was sitting stock-still, even as his fingers clawed at the knots behind his back. He could feel the blood draining from his face as Blémont raised the nail gun yet again, this time aiming lower. Dunphy's right thumb and forefinger wrenched at the knot behind his back.

And Blémont raved. "The ones with the big heads are framing nails. But these—they have almost no head at all. Look." And, with that, he squeezed the trigger.

Dunphy jackknifed involuntarily as the nail slammed into his lower leg, punching through the flesh past the shinbone to the calf muscle underneath. The pain was astounding and, somehow, high pitched, an agonizing rip, as if the full length of a hypodermic needle had been driven into *and through* his leg. A bellow of pain and shock reverberated through the room. It came from him.

"Owww," Blémont remarked in a coy voice.

Dunphy shivered, suddenly cold and faint. Pitching forward, he saw a neat little hole in his pants leg. A spot of blood. Behind his back, his fingers fumbled frantically with the cord that bound him.

And there was hope. Whoever had tied his wrists had not been a sailor. In place of a single, useful knot, the cord had been wrapped repeatedly around his hands and wrists, over and under, and tied in a series of what seemed to be square knots. One of these had come undone from repeated tugging, and the bonds now felt a little looser. For what it was worth, he could at least imagine getting free.

Blémont raised the nail gun with both hands, holding it like a homicide cop on late-night TV, then brought it down slowly, sighting along its barrel. *"Les bijoux de famille . . .* it's a tough shot."

Szzunnnk! A nail tore into his thigh, just below the hip, dragging a choked cry from his throat as Blémont whooped with delight and the Jock smiled broadly.

"Roger—laissez-moi essayer," the Jock said.

"Why not?" Blémont replied, and tossed him the gun. Then he turned to search among the tools on the upholsterer's workbench, looking for other toys.

The Jock sauntered over to Dunphy with a little smile in the corner of his mouth. "How do you want it?" he asked.

Dunphy took a deep breath and looked away. Whatever he said, they were going to crucify him. There was no point in pleading, and nothing to be gained by telling the Frog to go fuck himself. Whatever he said, he was going to hurt. So he kept his peace, even as his hands worked frantically behind his back, tearing at the knots.

The Jock studied the gun in his hands, then turned to Blémont. "What if I nail his *couilles* to the chair?" he asked.

Blémont snickered. "As long as you don't kill him," he replied, "you can nail him to the ceiling, for all I care."

"Eh, bien," the Jock replied, and turned back to Dunphy.

Just then, the air compressor went off with the suddenness of a fire alarm, its pneumatic engine rattling the air. Startled, the Jock turned, and as he did, Dunphy's leg lashed out, slashing at the man's knee.

Dunphy was as surprised as the Jock. He hadn't planned to kick him. It was a reflex, or something like it—a suicidal gesture, perhaps. In the event, the Jock buckled, yelped, and staggered backward, then came up firing the nail gun.

Szzunnnk! Szzunnnk! Szzunnnk!

The first three nails slammed into the wall behind him, but the fourth caught Dunphy in the right side, the pain so sudden and intense that it wrenched him around in the chair and sent him crashing to the floor. The next nail blew past his face, while the two after that tore into the ball of his foot and his elbow. By then, Blémont was shouting at the Jock to stop— which he did, just as the air compressor switched off.

The Frenchman rubbed his knee and cursed, while Blémont righted Dunphy in his chair. "You could have killed him," the Corsican complained.

For his part, Dunphy was fighting against his body's wish for sweet surrender. He could sense his nervous system shutting down, his hands and feet growing colder, his pain becoming increasingly remote. It occurred to him, in a distracted way, that he was going into shock—and that, if he did, he'd die without knowing it.

With a low growl, he sought out the pain, retrieving it one nail at a time—finding it first in his foot, then in his elbow, side, and leg. In the end, he wondered if there was any part of him that didn't hurt, and shuddered to think that if there was, that part was certain to be next.

Blémont crouched in front of him. "Let's do business," he said.

Dunphy looked away.

"There is a banker in Santa Cruz," the Corsican continued. "A man I know. He can arrange to have the money transferred. We do that—and you can go."

Right, Dunphy thought. Just like that. He shook his head.

Blémont's smile disappeared. "It's *my* money, Jack."

"I know," Dunphy said. "But you can't get it that way. They won't give it to you."

The Corsican stared at him. "Why not?" he asked.

"Because it's in a safe-deposit box," Dunphy explained.

"Then you'll give us the key," Blémont said.

Once again, Dunphy shook his head. "I'll give you the key, but it won't do any good. If you aren't on the box-holder's list, it doesn't matter if you've got the key. You'd have to show them a court order."

"How do they know—"

"They look at your passport."

Blémont thought about it.

"We could go together," Dunphy suggested.

Blémont shook his head. "I think you'd be hard to handle in public."

"It's the only way," Dunphy told him.

"Is it? What about the girl?" Blémont asked.

Dunphy pretended that he hadn't heard. "I won't give you any trouble," he said.

"What about the *girl*?" the Corsican repeated.

"What girl?"

This time, he saw it coming and backed off enough that the punch caught him a glancing blow on the side of his head.

"Don't fuck with me!" Blémont warned, his eyes bulging. "I'm talking about that bitch of yours—Veroushka."

"Oh," Dunphy said, shaking his head to clear it. *"Her."*

Blémont flexed the fingers on his right hand and composed himself. "She went to the bank for you in Zürich," he said calmly, "when you lost my friends at the hotel."

"On the Bahnhofstrasse," the Jock said. "La Credit Suisse."

"So her name's on the box," Blémont stated.

Dunphy nodded. "Yeah," he said. "You're right. I forgot."

"Then she can get the money."

"I could call her," Dunphy suggested. "She'll be at the Tiller—waiting to hear."

Blémont smiled thinly. "I don't think so."

"If you're worried about the police—" Dunphy began.

Blémont shook his head. "It's always better to do business in person."

In the course of the next hour, three things happened: the Jock went out to buy a tape recorder. Dunphy loosened the last of the knots that bound his wrists. And Luc expired.

This last event was entirely without fanfare. Seated in his overstuffed chair, Blémont's henchman gave a sort of myoclonic jerk, then sank back with a quiet rattle in his throat. Hearing the whispered gargle, Dunphy turned toward the noise in time to see the dying man's face go slack and his eyes roll back in his head.

Blémont remained at the workbench with his back to the room.

Dunphy cleared his throat.

"I heard it," the Corsican said, without turning. *"C'est triste."*

The Jock came back about ten minutes later, carrying an inexpensive Sony with a built-in microphone. On seeing the Alsatian in his chair, he went over to the dead man and carefully closed his eyes. Then he turned with a growl and lunged at Dunphy—only to have Blémont seize him by the arm and pull him away, whispering in French. Eventually, the Jock nodded, took a deep breath, and exhaled mightily. *"Eh, bien,"* he said, and leaned back against the workbench.

Blémont came over to Dunphy with the tape recorder in his hand. "Okay," he said, "here's how it goes. You tell your girlfriend to go to Zürich with Marcel. When they get the money, I let you go. Until then, you're here with me."

Dunphy turned the proposal upside down and inside out. "What if Marcel keeps going?"

Blémont dismissed the idea with a forceful shake of his head. "He won't," the Corsican said. "I know where he lives. And he knows I know—don't you, Marcel?"

A grunt from the workbench.

"And after I make the tape," Dunphy said, "the reason you don't kill me is . . . what? I forget that part."

Blémont made an impatient gesture with his hands, as if the answer was obvious. When Dunphy didn't react, the Corsican said, "The money!"

"Which money?" Dunphy asked, confused.

"The *rest* of the money—the money you owe me. You said it yourself—you spent twenty grand. I'm betting twenty-two. And I told you: that's just the beginning. There's interest on top of that—and expenses. When we find out how much is in Zürich, we'll know how much more you've got to pay."

He's right, Dunphy thought. If Blémont was ever going to

get all of his money back, it would have to come from Dunphy—not that it ever would. He didn't have it. Still, Blémont didn't know that.

"All right," he said. "I'll do it. What do you want me to say?"

"That you're okay. That she shouldn't look for you. Tell her she's going to Zürich with Marcel. Once she gives him the money—that's that." Blémont looked expectantly at Dunphy. "Okay?"

Dunphy thought about it. Finally he nodded, and Blémont put the little tape recorder next to his mouth. Then he pressed the Record button and said, "Tell her."

It was Dunphy's turn to clear his throat. Finally, he said, "*Veroushka*—it's Jack. I'm okay, but I want you to do something for me. . . ."

When the recording was done, Blémont rewound the tape and set it aside. Then he turned to the Jock and snapped his fingers. "Now we can get down to business," he said. The change in Blémont's mood caught Dunphy by surprise, but its meaning was soon evident.

"You haven't got any money, Jack—if you had, Kroll would have found it. And I'll bet there's a lot more than twenty grand missing. Am I right?"

Dunphy's fingers ripped at the loops of cord behind his back.

"So we'll have to take it out of you," Blémont went on, "and since it's more than you're worth, I suppose we'll have to take it *all* out of you. What do you say, Marcel?"

The Jock grinned.

Blémont sauntered over to the workbench, where a length of electrical cord was waiting. "A hanging would be interesting," he said, then paused and dropped the cord. "Then again . . . " The Corsican picked up a piece of one-inch pipe that looked to be about three feet long. Dunphy figured they'd beat him to death with it—until he saw that the pipe was fitted with a pair of movable clamps, each of which was about a foot from the other. It took him a moment to grasp the tool's significance. Then he understood. The pipe was a portable vise, the kind that carpenters use to hold sections of wood together while the glue sets.

Blémont was looking at him in a curious way, as if he was sizing him up—which, Dunphy soon realized, was precisely the case.

"I could crack your skull with this," Blémont told him, adjusting the clamps to fit the size of his head. "What are you—about a six and a half?"

The cord that held his wrists was virtually untied, but tangled in such a way that Dunphy couldn't quite free his hands. Frantically, but with as much economy of movement as he could manage, he picked and tugged at the cord's loops and lengths, sweat rolling down his cheeks and sides.

With a grimace, Blémont tossed the pipe back on the workbench and picked up the nail gun. "Too much work," he said. "But, hey—with this, we could turn you into a real *pelote d'épingles*. What do you think?" The Corsican waved the nail gun at him, and in spite of himself, Dunphy flinched.

He'd never heard the phrase before, but under the circumstances, it wasn't hard to guess what a *pelote d'épingles* was.

"A hundred shots," Blémont continued, "more or less. Well, definitely less." He tapped the nail gun against the palm of his left hand. "How long do you think it would take before you bled to death—like Luc over there?"

Dunphy's fingers coiled around the cord behind his back. It was loose enough now that he could slip the fingers of his right hand into the cord's nested loops—which he did. It took a moment, but with a tug, he was free, holding the cord behind his back, his face as impassive as he could make it.

Now what? he wondered, as the elation seeped away. Even if Dunphy were at his best, Blémont would be a handful. And Dunphy was far from his best. His nose was broken, and he'd lost some blood. Where he'd been kicked, his ribs were cracked, and his back was sore enough to make him think that he was bleeding from the kidneys. And then there were the nails. Like slivers of glass, they made even the slightest movement painful. So Blémont would be a problem, if and when it came to that (and it would).

As for the Jock, well . . . Jesus, he was a steamer trunk of muscle and testosterone. He'd need an elephant gun to take him down.

Blémont turned to his accomplice. *"Dites-moi,"* he said. *"Que pensez-vous? Le pistolet ou la corde?"*

The Jock smiled and replied softly in the same language. Dunphy didn't catch what he said, but Blémont was quick to explain. "He says we shouldn't kill you." With a shrug, Blémont laid the nail gun on the cushions of a pumpkin-colored couch, then folded his arms to watch.

Blémont's bemusement worried Dunphy even more than the nail gun, and his worry turned to fear as the Jock picked up a sawhorse and carried it across the room to where Dunphy sat. Still smiling, he spoke to Blémont in French, then set the sawhorse down a few feet away.

"Your English is as good as mine," Blémont told the Jock. "Tell him what you're telling me."

The Jock smiled and shook his head.

Blémont rolled his eyes. "What he said was, he can break your back across the sawhorse."

Dunphy felt his jaw drop.

"What do you think?" Blémont asked.

Dunphy's stomach turned over. "I think you're a sick son of a bitch," he answered, trying to find the courage to move. If he was fast enough, he might get to the door—and, if he was lucky, through it.

"I've done it before," the Jock explained. "In Cyprus, on a bet. Left the bastard flopping—like a fish." He made a little flapping motion with his hand.

Blémont winced.

"When it happens, it's like a shot! Pow!" The Jock clapped his hands together, by way of illustration. The air compressor came on again, and Blémont raised his voice so he could be heard.

"A thousand francs," the Corsican shouted, "if you can do

it in one try." He looked at Dunphy. "Are you a betting man?" Dunphy returned his gaze with a glassy stare. "No? Well, I don't blame you," Blémont muttered.

"You'll see," the Jock yelled, taking a step toward Dunphy. "Basically, it's *la clean-and-jerk*." He looked his prisoner up and down. "How much do you weigh?" The compressor cut off.

"Fuck you," Dunphy replied, more quietly than he'd intended.

"I think, maybe . . . eighty kilos." The Jock turned to Blémont. "No problem! I can do one hundred, easy. It's all in the grip." He looked Dunphy squarely in the eye and lowered his voice to a whisper. "You're not going to like this," he confided, "but you'll have a long time to think about it." Then he reached for Dunphy's belt and seized it in his right hand. With his left, he grabbed him by the collar, took three quick and shallow breaths, flexed his knees, and leaned in.

If Dunphy had waited another second, he'd have been too late: the Jock would have had him in the air above his head. From there, it would have been a slow turn—and then the body slam across the sawhorse. His spine would have snapped like a pencil.

But he didn't wait. With a sharp nod, he drove his forehead into the bridge of the Jock's nose, smashing the septum, then swept the big man's legs with a slashing kick and a backhand to the side of his face. Blémont gaped as the Jock crashed to the floor, sprawling, even as Dunphy sprang from his chair with a snarl of pain, swinging wildly.

So wildly, in fact, that none of the punches landed, though the Corsican was driven backward, as much by surprise as by the fury of Dunphy's attack. With a crash, the two men piled into the workbench. For a moment, Dunphy had the best of him, but the moment didn't last. The nails were tearing him up inside, while the Corsican was fresh and strong. Dunphy could feel his own strength ebbing, even as the Jock scrabbled, growling, to get up from the floor.

I can't do it, Dunphy thought. I haven't got enough.

He had Blémont by the throat, but the Corsican was

throwing punches, and some of them were landing—hitting Dunphy in the mouth, the ears, and, once, on the soft pulp of his nose. Then the Corsican brought his knee up, hard and fast, slamming Dunphy in the groin. With a cry of pain, he rolled away, and Blémont hit him again, sending him flying toward the end of the workbench. Breaking his fall with his left arm, Dunphy saw Blémont coming at him, and reached, reflexively, for the first tool his hand could find. Coming up with a hammer, he swung it in an arc and, to his amazement, buried the claw in the Corsican's temple.

With a look of mild surprise, Blémont came to a stop and straightened up, the hammer hanging from the side of his head. Like a bull who doesn't yet know that he's dead, but stands in the ring with a sword through his heart, the Corsican swayed. Then his legs went out from under him, and he crashed to the floor. A seizure rippled though his body, sending a tremor from his head to his feet, and then he was still.

The Jock came at him like a nose tackle, charging hard and low, looking to take the American down by the knees. Dunphy rolled to the right, and around the workbench, his hands searching for a weapon—any weapon—but there was nothing. The Jock crashed into the bench with his shoulder, driving it into Dunphy as if it were a tackling dummy. Clambering to his feet with a snarl, the Jock turned the corner with far more speed than Dunphy himself could muster. For a moment, their eyes locked as the Jock considered the distance between them and the number of steps it would take to cross it—three—while Dunphy came to grips with his own mortality.

Then he turned for the door—but the Jock was on him before his foot could leave the ground. And the Frenchman's anger was so great that, instead of taking Dunphy by the throat and breaking his neck—which in Dunphy's weakened state the Jock might easily have done—he began throwing punches. And the punches landed hard, bouncing Dunphy off the wall and the workbench. Then he was caught and shoved across the room like a shopping cart, crashing into and over the pumpkin-colored couch. The air exploded from his lungs as his shoulders crashed against the wooden floor. And then the Jock came across the top of the couch in a racing dive, flattening the airless Dunphy.

I'm gone, he thought, hands flailing. Brushing something, something heavy and hard, knocking it away. *Nail gun.* But where?

The Jock's thumbs were pressing hard on Dunphy's windpipe, and it seemed as if the slowly spinning room was growing darker. Dunphy's eyes bulged until he thought they would explode. Then his hand found the nail gun for the second time, and bringing it up in an arc, he pressed its muzzle against the broken bridge of the Jock's nose, and—

Szzzunkk! Szzzunkk! Szzzunkk!

26

He wanted to stay there, there on the floor, until he healed or died. It seemed to Dunphy that he was broken inside and out, and that the only thing that he could safely do was lie there. But after a bit, his eyes fell upon the *Contre la boue* banner over the workbench, and he remembered that he was in enemy territory.

Behind the lines.

Pushing the Jock's lifeless body off his own, he dragged himself to his hands and knees, and stood, swaying in the twilight.

He must have been out cold for hours. It was nearly dark now, so that his shadow stretched across the floor and halfway up the wall. Using the furniture to steady himself, he made his way past Blémont's corpse to a telephone that sat upon a rolltop desk in a corner of the room. Lifting the receiver, he dialed the number for the Broken Tiller.

"Boylan." The voice was low and matter-of-fact, almost a whisper, as if its owner was expecting bad news.

"It's me," Dunphy said.

There were a few seconds of silence, and then, "Where are ya?"

Dunphy thought about it. Looked around.

"Where are ya?" Boylan repeated.

"I don't know," Dunphy replied. And glanced around the room. "Upholstery shop."

"Where?"

"Hang on." One by one, Dunphy pulled open the drawers

of the desk until he found a stack of invoices, each of which bore the same name and address. "I think it's . . . something called Casa Tapizada. Saragossa Street. In Candelaria."

"You *think*?"

"Yeah. I can't be sure."

"Well, *ask* someone!"

"I can't."

"Why not?"

"Because they're *dead*. And I'm not feelin' that good myself."

It took Boylan, Davis, and Clem half an hour to get there, and when they did, Clem buckled at the scene. The Alsatian, with his scarlet girdle. Blémont with the hammer buried in his head. The Jock.

And Dunphy himself, the last man standing, looking for all the world as if he'd taken a swan dive into a dry pool.

"Jay-sus Christ!" Tommy cried, blanching even as he rushed to his friend's side. "What happened?"

"I fell down," Dunphy told him.

They took him to a village in the mountains, where Boylan knew a retired gynecologist, a Scot, who supplemented his income by performing an occasional abortion. The man gave Dunphy a healthy shot of recreational codeine and extracted the nails from his body, one by one.

There wasn't anything to be done, really, about the broken nose or ribs. "The nose will heal," the doctor told them, "and as for the ribs, well . . . they don't seem to have punctured anything of great interest—or we wouldn't be talking about it. So, all in all, I'd say that while it sucks to be you, it isn't fatal. Anyway, that's my prognosis, and I'm sticking to it."

The real concern was infection. To guard against it, the doctor put Dunphy on a regime of powerful antibiotics and placed him under Clementine's care in a suite of rooms on the second floor of the villa.

None of this came cheap. In return for his professional

services, hospitality, and silence, the good physician asked for and got five thousand pounds. Clem would have much preferred to have taken Dunphy to the hospital in Santa Cruz, but that was out of the question. "The massacre in Candelaria" was front-page news, and every paper in the Canaries was obsessed with the fact that one French gangster had been "stapled to death," while a second had been killed with a hammer. For Dunphy to show up at an emergency room looking like a pincushion would not have been a good idea.

So they stayed at the doctor's house in Masca, where they wiled away the hours on the terrace, reading and playing chess. Dunphy's wounds healed nicely, and without infection, though his nose was more beaklike than it had been before. And there was progress, too, in their shared quest to fathom Leo Schidlof's murder.

One evening, as they sat amid the bougainvillea on the terrace, sipping sangrias, Dunphy complained to Clem that "after all the shit we've been through, we're still on the run. We aren't any closer to the truth than we were a month ago."

"That's not true," Clem said. "You told me you learned a lot in Zug, about Dulles and Jung—"

"And Pound," Dunphy added. "And that there's something called the Magdalene Society. But that doesn't get us anywhere. All I've really done is double the number of questions I had to begin with: like, who's Gomelez—or *was*? He'd be ninety or one hundred now. And the *Apocryphon*—what's that got to do with anything, let alone Schidlof? It's like I'm asking the wrong questions, because if you want to know the truth, all I really want to do is get back to where I was six months ago."

"No, you don't," Clem told him.

"I don't?"

"No. Because you can't go back—you never can."

"Why not?"

"Well, to begin with, what about your friend—Roscoe?"

She was right, of course. You couldn't step in the same river twice, especially after someone you cared about had been strangled upstream. Dunphy sighed. "So what's the point?"

Clem shook her head. "There isn't any point. You just . . . don't have any choice. Neither of us do."

The day before they left Masca for London, where Dunphy hoped he'd find Van Worden, Clem brought him a letter that she'd found while packing. "This was in your slacks," she said, handing it to him. "I think you must have taken it from Zug."

Dunphy glanced at the handwriting and nodded. He'd almost forgotten about it. The letter was dated April 19, 1946. "My dear Carl," it began.

I apologize for my delay in replying to your most recent communiqué. My brother and I have been working almost nonstop in an effort to establish the postwar infrastructure to implement the geopolitical goals that have become our destiny. Returning Jerusalem to the Jews is, I think, a legitimate and easily defended foreign-policy objective of the United States—however much it may destabilize the region in the near term. Still, we appear to hold the moral high ground, and that, of course, is always a great convenience.

The unification of Europe is a horse of a different color. The Soviets will do everything to oppose it, and so the stage is set for what must certainly be the next great confrontation. That we will emerge triumphant, I have no doubt. It is a matter, only, of diplomacy and war.

A more difficult task will be to impinge directly on the collective unconscious by propagating the archetypal patterns described in the *Apocryphon*. To create Zion is one thing—it is, or will be, a nation much like other nations. But how are we to create a world in which

> the beasts lay butchered in the fields,
> the grain encrypts itself in mad designs,
> and the skies are alight with specters.

It's a tall order but not, I think, an impossible one. We developed a technique in the OSS called psy-ops. (Suggest you leave this to me.)

Allen

Dunphy read the words a second time, and then a third: *The beasts lay butchered in the fields*—and so they did. And he remembered something Gene Brading had said: "Near the end of my hitch, we started making these designs. . . . The Agency called them agriglyphs. . . ." *The grain encrypts itself . . .* And something else, something he'd said about Optical Magick: *"They did Medjugorje, too. Roswell. Tremonton. Gulf Breeze."*

Which meant that Dunphy had been right. The twentieth century was a light show—a conglomeration of special effects masquerading, first, as reality, then as history. And all of it contrived by a handful of powerful men with very peculiar ideas. But why? he wondered, looking out across the mountains toward Africa. For what?

They flew into London on the first of June, using the forged documents they'd acquired from Max Setyaev in Prague. Dunphy was used to traveling with false ID, but Clem—who wouldn't even jaywalk—was nervous. And the immigration line was a long and serpentine one that took fifteen minutes to navigate so that by the time they arrived at the front, Clem was using her new identity as a fan.

"Number eight, Miss."

An elderly Sikh immigration officer waved her over to one of a dozen podiums, where a much younger man sat, fiddling with his stamps. Dunphy marveled at the transformation in the man as Clem materialized in front of him, laughing and pressing her passport in his hands. Dunphy couldn't hear what was said, but it didn't matter. It only took a second, then they were old pals, him beaming, she giggling—*wink, wink, On-yer-way-then!* Soon, she was riding the escalator down to the baggage carousels inside the Customs area. Then it was Dunphy's turn.

The immigration officer was a thin young man with cold blue eyes and a dark beard that formed a shield around his mouth, then followed his jawline to where it met with his sideburns. After a bored glance at Dunphy's broken nose, he leafed through the passport's immaculate pages, looking for stamps.

"Mr. Pitt," he said, pronouncing the name as if he were spitting out a seed.

"Yes."

"Coming from? . . . "

"Tenerife," Dunphy replied.

"Holiday or business?"

"Bit of both."

"And what business would that be?"

Nothing too interesting, Dunphy thought. "Accountancy."

The immigration man glanced over Dunphy's shoulder. "Just yourself?" he asked, sounding doubtful.

Dunphy nodded. "For now. I'm meeting friends in London."

"I see." The immigration officer frowned and gestured at Dunphy's nose. "Fight?"

Dunphy shifted uncomfortably on his feet. "No. I was mugged."

The immigration man grimaced. "Las Americas?"

Dunphy nodded. It seemed to be what the man wanted.

The immigration officer shook his head. "Spanish bastards," he muttered, and brought his stamp crashing down on the passport. Then he handed it back and smiled. "Welcome to the British Isles, Mr. Pitt!"

Finding Van Worden was not hard. The dialing tones on the tape recording indicated that Schidlof's call had been a local one. It was a simple matter, then, for Dunphy and Clem to find an Internet café in the Strand, where they looked him up on the Web. To Dunphy's surprise, the professor was living on

Cheyne Walk in Chelsea. He must have jogged past the place a hundred times.

"Are you coming with me?" Dunphy asked.

"Of course," Clem said. "But shouldn't we call ahead?"

"No."

"Why not?"

Why not, indeed? While Dunphy had no way of knowing if Schidlof had actually met with Van Worden, one thing was certain: Van Worden would know of the professor's demise soon after calling him. And knowing that, he might be cautious about meeting strangers. "Let's just surprise him," Dunphy told her.

As it turned out, Van Worden was the sole occupant of the *Faery Queene*, a rusting houseboat moored in the lea of the Battersea Bridge. Uncertain of the protocols for boarding vessels in the middle of a city, and unable to bring himself to shout "Ahoy," Dunphy led Clem up the gangplank and onto the boat. Coming upon a door, he knocked tentatively and waited. When no one answered, he knocked again—louder, this time.

"Hang on!"

A moment later, the door was wrenched open by a distinguished-looking man in his late forties, holding a glass of red wine and a clove cigarette. "Help you?" he asked, swinging his head from Dunphy to Clem, and back again.

"I'm looking for an Al Van Worden?"

"Ye-esss?"

"My name's Jack Dunphy," he said. "Are you . . ."

"Ye-esss?"

"Well, I was wondering if we could . . . have a chat. It wouldn't take long."

Van Worden looked them up and down. "You're not Jehovah's Witnesses, are you?"

Clem giggled.

"No," Dunphy said. "Nothing like that. We're friends of Professor Schidlof."

Van Worden blinked. Took a sip of wine. "Chap who died."

"Right."

"And you say you're friends of his?"

"Only in a sense. We're following up on an inquiry that he made."

Van Worden nodded, more to himself than to Dunphy or Clem. "Can't help, I'm afraid." And with that, he began to close the door.

"Actually," Dunphy said, pressing his toe against the bottom of the door, "I think you can. Schidlof thought so, too."

Van Worden glanced at Dunphy's foot and grimaced. "Don't want to be involved, really."

"I can understand that, but—"

"Waste of time, in any case."

"Why is that?" Dunphy asked.

"Spoke to the man once. Never really *met* him."

"I know."

Van Worden seemed taken aback. "*Do* you?" he asked. "And how do you know?"

Dunphy thought better of it, then told the truth. "I was bugging him."

Van Worden took a long drag on his cigarette and let the smoke eddy from his nostrils. Sipped his wine. "But you're not the police," he said.

"No," Dunphy replied. "We're not."

Van Worden nodded, appreciative of Dunphy's candor. Then he frowned. "Give me one good reason I should talk to you," he said.

Dunphy thought about it and drew a blank. Finally, Clem stepped up to the door and gave him a soft look. "It would be so nice of you," she said.

Van Worden cleared his throat. "Done," he said, and held open the door for them.

They followed Van Worden down a narrow corridor hung with black-and-white photographs of medieval churches and cathedrals. Passing a galley that smelled of baking bread, they continued on their way through a sort of drawing room crammed with books, then out to the deck, where chairs were clustered around a wrought-iron table topped with glass.

"Port?"

"Thanks," Dunphy said. "I'd love some."

"Clocktower. Not bad. Best I can do, in any case." Van Worden poured each of them a glass and gestured to a plate of cheese. "Damned good Stilton, though. Have some."

Clem was standing at the rail, looking upriver toward the Battersea Bridge. "What a wonderful place," she enthused, as the waves from a passing boat lapped against the hull.

"Want to buy it?"

Dunphy laughed. "We're not really in the market—"

"I'd give you a good price."

"Sorry."

Van Worden shrugged. "Don't blame you. Damned nuisance, really."

"Then . . . you don't like it here?" Clem asked.

"No."

"Why not?"

"Well," Van Worden said, "to begin with, I'm an Arsenal supporter. Worth my life to go out for a pint on a weekend."

"Then . . . why did you buy it?"

"Albert Hofmann," Van Worden answered.

Dunphy laughed, but Clem gave her head a quick little shake and frowned.

"Chap who discovered LSD," Van Worden explained. Then he turned to Dunphy. "Know anything about engines?" he asked.

"No," Dunphy replied.

"Neither do I—so I suppose we'll just stay where we are." The older man fell into a lime-colored Adirondack chair and gestured for Dunphy and Clem to do the same in seats across from him. "Now, then," he said, "what's this all about?"

Dunphy wasn't sure how much to tell him, so he came directly to the point. "It's like Schidlof said. We're interested in the Magdalene Society."

"Because? . . . "

"Well, for one thing, because we're not at all sure it's a thing of the past."

Van Worden grunted. "Well, you're right about that," he said. "It's not."

The answer was unexpected and brought a puzzled frown to Dunphy's face. He was trying to remember the tape he'd listened to. "When you spoke with Schidlof on the phone," he said, "you seemed surprised when he suggested the Society might still be around."

"I *was* surprised."

"But now you're not."

Van Worden shook his head. "Until Dr. Schidlof was killed, there were only rumors."

"And his death changed that?"

"Of course!"

"Why?" Clem asked.

"Because of the *way* he died."

"What do you mean?" Dunphy asked.

Van Worden shifted in his seat and seemed to change the subject. "How much do you know about the Magdalene Society?" he asked.

"Not much," Dunphy said.

"But something, surely."

"Yeah."

"Then tell me something I don't know," Van Worden insisted, "as a way of establishing your bona fides."

Dunphy thought about it. Finally he said, "The one who runs it is called the Helmsman."

"That's hardly a secret."

"In the thirties and forties, the Helmsman was Ezra Pound."

Van Worden gaped. "The poet?"

Dunphy nodded.

"Good lord," Van Worden exclaimed. And then he remembered. "But wasn't Pound the one who . . . "

Dunphy nodded. "Went to the bin? Yeah, he was. But it

didn't get in the way of things. He held court in the asylum—saw whoever he wanted to see, did whatever he wanted to do."

"Really?! Well, I'm not surprised," Van Worden remarked. "They've had a number of *Nautonniers* who've been poets. Madmen, too, for that matter."

Warming to the subject, Van Worden told them that he first became interested in the Lodge of Munsalvaesche (as the Magdalene Society had formerly been known) while writing an introductory essay to an anthology of gnostic literature.

"Hang on," he said, "I've got it right here." Getting to his feet, he went inside and came back a few seconds later with a copy of a book entitled *Gnostica*. It was as thick as Dunphy's forearm. "Some of the most interesting documents," Van Worden explained, "were the pseudepigrapha. And the most interesting of those was the *Apocryphon of the Magdalene*."

Dunphy looked puzzled. "What was that word you used?"

"Which one?" Van Warden asked.

"Pseudo-something."

"Pseudepigrapha?" Van Worden asked.

Dunphy nodded.

"It refers to gospels that were supposedly written by Biblical figures," the professor said. "The one in question—the *Apocryphon of the Magdalene*—was found in the ruins of an Irish monastery about a thousand years ago." He opened the book to the appropriate page and handed it to Dunphy.

Dunphy read a few lines and looked up. "And the original was written by Mary Magdalene?"

"Allegedly." Van Worden went on to explain that while there were a great many gaps in the narrative, the *Apocryphon* was at once a diary and an almanac of prophecies and portents. As a diary, it purported to record the secret wedding of Christ to Mary Magdalene.

Dunphy made a skeptical sound.

"It's not as strange as it sounds," Van Worden insisted. "In many of the Gospels, Jesus is referred to as a rabbi or teacher—and, as it happens, that says a lot about his marital status."

"I thought he was supposed to be a carpenter," Dunphy said.

Van Worden shook his head. "It's a popular misconception. The word that's used to describe him actually means *scholar*. A person with formal training—like a rabbi. And it makes sense. Everyone knows that Christ was a Jew, and that he gave religious instruction. What's less well known is that Mishnaic law demands that a rabbi should take a wife—because 'an unmarried man may not be a teacher.' So the idea that Christ may have wed—and as a husband, sired children—isn't as controversial as it sounds."

"But what about his wife?" Clem asked. "Wouldn't the *Bible* have mentioned her, if he'd had one?"

Van Worden rocked his head from side to side. "If he'd preached without having wed, it would have been scandalous—and we'd have heard about it. Otherwise, the subject would probably not have come up. After all, we're talking about the Middle East, two thousand years ago. Wives didn't have a public role, really. And we don't hear much about the apostles' wives, do we? Even so, it seems unlikely that none of them were married—wouldn't you say?"

Dunphy hadn't thought about it, but now that he did . . .

After the Crucifixion, Van Worden continued, and while pregnant with Christ's child, Magdalene was put to sea in a boat without sails or oars. "According to various accounts—and there *are* various accounts—she was accompanied by Martha, Lazarus, and Joseph of Arimathea. There seems to have been a storm of some duration, and the implication is that it was caused by angels doing battle with the demons that pursued her. In the event, she landed safely at Marseille. And there, gave birth to Mérovée. A son." Van Worden smiled and refilled each of their glasses. "Interesting story, no?"

Clem's eyes were huge. "Then what?" she asked.

"Well, *then* there's rather a lot of prophecy—if you've read *Revelation*, you'll know the sort of thing I mean."

"But what about Mérovée?" Clem insisted. "What happened to *him*?"

"Oh, he did quite well for himself. Founded the Merovingian dynasty." Van Worden's forefingers curled into quotation marks. "Dynasty of the Long-Haired Kings."

"Why did they call them that?" Clem asked.

"Apparently because they never cut their hair."

"Why not?" Dunphy wondered.

"There was magic in it—in their hair, in their breath, in their blood." Van Worden paused. "Look," he said, "we're talking about legends. This was the age of Arthur . . . and the age of the Grail, which, depending on whom you talk to, was either a cup—or a bloodline."

"What do you mean, a bloodline?" Dunphy asked.

"Just what I said: a bloodline. *The* bloodline. The bloodline of Christ. The *sang réel*. The stories we have of the Merovingians suggest that they were as much sorcerers as kings. Magical beings."

"How so?" Clem asked.

Van Worden smiled and lighted a cigarette. "Well, it was said they could heal the sick by laying on their hands. And that they could bring the dead to life with a kiss. They talked with the birds, flew with the bees, and hunted with bears and wolves. The weather was theirs to command, and—well, who's to say? It was a very mysterious period." Van Worden paused, then added, "Some would say, a *deliberately* mysterious period."

"What do you mean?" Dunphy asked.

Van Worden seemed uncomfortable. "Well . . . there are some—I wouldn't call them historians—but there are some who feel that the Dark Ages didn't just happen. They say it was a golden age, and that it only seems dark to us today because our knowledge of the period has been eclipsed. The age faded into darkness because . . . well, because certain institutions wanted it that way."

Dunphy remembered reading something about this in *Archaeus*. "Who are you talking about?" he asked.

"*Rome*. Rome was the custodian of Western history. The Church fathers wrote it, preserved it—and when it fit their agenda, they erased it entirely."

Clementine stared at him. "You mean . . . like the Soviet Union? The way they made people disappear from photographs?"

Van Worden shrugged.

"So you're telling me the Church blacked out three hundred years of European history?" Dunphy demanded.

Van Worden shook his head. "It's a conspiracy theory, that's all. I'm just telling you what others have said. But it isn't that surprising, really. Look at what the Jesuits did to Mayan history."

"*What* Mayan history?" Dunphy asked.

"My point exactly."

"But why would the Church *do* that?" Clem asked.

"According to the theory?"

"Yes."

"To erase the memory of a golden age to which it had no connection, and to conceal the 'dirty war' that brought the age to an end." Seeing Dunphy's puzzlement, Van Worden elaborated. "The Merovingians were a walking, talking heresy, in and of themselves. By claiming to be the children of God—literally, His sons and daughters—they rendered every other throne and secular authority irrelevant or illegitimate. Who needs a pope in Rome if God's own son (or grandson) is sitting on a throne in Paris? It was the most dangerous heresy in history. And because it was, the Merovingians were kidnapped, assassinated, and betrayed until, in the end, nearly every vestige of their rule had been erased. In effect, they disappeared from history—"

"Until the *Apocryphon* surfaced," Dunphy said.

"Precisely. And, of course, when the same heresy was brought to light in the *Apocryphon*, that light had to be extinguished, as well—and so it was. The cult was ruthlessly suppressed until, in the end, it was no more than a secret society, a conspiracy on the run."

"But a conspiracy to do what?" Dunphy asked.

"Bring on the millennium," Van Worden replied. "What else?"

"And how did they expect to do that?" Dunphy asked.

"Once the prophecies were fulfilled, it would be a fait accompli."

"And these are the prophecies—"

"—in the *Apocryphon*," Van Worden replied.

"You mean, about the grain encrypting itself," Dunphy said. "And the skies—"

"So you know them!" Van Worden exclaimed.

Dunphy shrugged. "I've seen references to them."

"Of course, not all of the prophecies were so . . . poetic. Some were quite specific."

"Like what?"

Van Worden shrugged. " 'These lands will then be one,' " he said.

"That's specific?"

"As specific as these things get. It refers to a time when the European nations will be united—a single country, as it were. And there's the business about Israel, as well: 'Zion reborn in the aftermath of the ovens.' Pretty remarkable, wouldn't you say?"

Dunphy nodded.

"Inasmuch as the prophecies are also prescriptions," Van Worden added, "the Magdalene Society would seem to have been one of the first Zionist organizations in Europe. Maybe *the* first."

Dunphy nibbled a bit of Stilton, then washed it down with the Clocktower. "So what happened to it?"

"Until I heard how Schidlof died, I'd thought its only remnants were the black Virgins that you see in churches like Montserrat."

Dunphy and Clem looked at each other. "What do you mean?" Clem asked.

Van Worden shrugged. "They're statues of a black Madonna, sometimes with an infant—who's also black. The Church won't talk about them, but they're everywhere in Europe."

"So why is she black?" Dunphy asked.

Van Worden laughed. "Her blackness was like a code. Because it's not the Virgin Mary holding Jesus—it's the Magdalene, with Mérovée in her arms. It's one of the last vestiges of a secret church—the Merovingian church that the Vatican tried to destroy."

Dunphy got up from his chair and walked to the railing. The sun was off to the right, setting behind plumes of smoke that rose from a factory's stacks on the Thames's north shore.

"You said something about the way Schidlof died," Dunphy asked. "What did you mean?"

"Just that when Schidlof called to ask about the Magdalene Society, I told him they'd gone out of business long ago. He suggested that they hadn't, and I agreed to meet with him— but only as an academic courtesy. I was sure he was wrong. But when I read about the way he died, and where he was found—in the Inner Temple—I realized I'd been wrong."

"How? What was it about his death that made you think—"

"It was a ritual murder. It's the way the Lodge has always dealt with its enemies. I could name a dozen men who've died that way, going back to the fourteenth century, and every one of them was a threat to what you call the Magdalene Society."

"But why?" Clem asked. "What are they after? What could they possibly want *today*?"

"A European throne for Mérovée's descendants."

"Descendants?!" Dunphy exclaimed. "How is anyone supposed to know—"

"There are genealogies," Van Worden told them. "Napoléon commissioned one. For all I know, there may be others."

"Napoléon?!"

Van Worden made a gesture. "He was overthrowing the Bourbons, and I think he found it useful to paint them as the usurpers of an older dynasty. Certainly, it was convenient: Bonaparte's second wife was a Merovingian in her own right."

"But that was two hundred years ago," Dunphy said. "Are there any Merovingians left?"

Van Worden frowned. "Dunno," he said. "For that, I think you'd have to ask Watkin."

"Watkin? Who the hell is Watkin?"

"Genealogist. Lives in Paris. Knows who's who."

"Really!" Dunphy said.

"Mmmm . . . hang on. I may have something for you." Van Worden got to his feet and went inside. Dunphy and Clem could hear him rummaging around in what sounded like a filing cabinet. Finally, he came back out, holding a magazine that was open to a story. "That's the chap," he said, handing him the magazine.

Dunphy looked at the byline—*Georges Watkin*—and then at the article's title: "The Magdalene Cultivar: Old Wine from Palestine." "Fucking hell," Dunphy said. "It's *Archaeus*."

Van Worden looked surprised. "You've seen it before, then?"

"I had a copy for a while," Dunphy told him. "But I lost it."

"Well, old Watkin might be the answer to your prayers," Van Worden told them. "Then again, knowing Watkin—he might be praying in a different church entirely. If you go to see him, you'll want to tread carefully. . . ."

27

They spent the evening on the train, traveling aboard the Eurostar from Waterloo station to the Gare du Nord. Arriving a little after nine that night, they took a cab to the Latin Quarter, then walked a few blocks to the Île St. Louis. There, they found an elegant small hotel on the Quai de Bethune. The reservations clerk turned a skeptical eye on Dunphy, whose broken nose suggested trouble—but the clerk was at least as smitten with Clem as he was suspicious of her lover. Over the muttered grousing of the concierge, an emaciated woman whose rouged cheeks made Dunphy think of the circus, a suite was found for them on the third floor.

And why not? It cost five hundred dollars a night.

"We'll take it," Dunphy said, and paid in advance with cash.

It was a surprisingly large suite for Paris, with ocher walls, Berber carpeting, and black-and-white photographs of jazz musicians hanging from the walls. Clem drew a bath for herself, while Dunphy stood at the open windows, sipping from a bottle of 33, gazing across the Seine at the Left Bank. It seemed to him that he was at eye level with half the rooftops in Paris.

Before long, clouds of steam were billowing through the doorway to the bath, and the air filled with the fragrance of Badedas. In the background, Dunphy could hear the water running in the tub and, just over it, Clem's voice humming an old Stealers Wheel tune. He remembered the words from the movie:

Clowns to the left of me,
Jokers to the right.

Crossing the room to the bath, Dunphy leaned into the doorway. By now, Clem was fully reclined in the tub, manipulating the hot- and cold-water faucets with her toes. Blissed out.

"Clem, darlin'," Dunphy said.

"Hmmm?"

"I have to go out for a while."

Her eyes snapped open. "What?!" Her feet dropped into the water, and she sat up amid the bubbles.

"I have to call Max. And I don't want to do it from here."

"But—"

"It may take a while, so . . . don't wait up."

Before she could argue, he turned on his heel and left.

It took him almost an hour to find a newsagent who sold international phone cards. Dunphy bought one for a hundred francs, and walked a block until he found a pay phone next to a shuttered *boulangerie*. It was a quarter after eleven when the call went through.

Max answered on the third ring with an exhausted mumble. "Unh?!"

"Max!"

"Yeah, okay . . ." The Russian sounded sleepy. "Who is it?"

"It's Harrison Pitt, Max!" Dunphy said. "Your old pal."

There was a short silence in which Dunphy could hear the wheels turning in the Russian's head. Then: "Yeah, sure, Harry! How are you?"

"I'm fine—"

"You're fine?"

"Yeah, but . . . I don't want to stay on the phone too long, okay?"

"Yes, of course—I know how busy you are!"

"Good. So, has anyone been to see you about me?"

"Just that once. I told you—"

"I don't mean that," Dunphy said. "I mean after the last business we did."

The Russian's reply was instantaneous. "No. There is nothing."

If Max had hesitated, even for an instant, Dunphy would have hung up. Instead, he said, "Good."

"What you need?"

It went against the grain to say it on the phone, but, "I want to buy a gun."

"But, I don't have guns. I can make *license* for gun—any country—the Vatican, even—no problem—"

"I know that, Max. But what I mean is, I need a name. Do you know anyone in Paris—"

"Hang on." There was a low clatter as Max laid the phone down on a hard table. Then the noise of wooden drawers opening and closing. A muffled curse. The same clatter. And then, "Okay, is good guy. Ukrainian, like me. But fruitcake, okay?"

"What?"

"He's fruitcake!"

"You mean, he's crazy?"

"No. Gay. This is problem?"

Dunphy shook his head, forgetting he was on the phone. "No, it's not a problem. What's his name?"

"Azamov. Sergei Azamov. He is towel boy—"

"What?"

"Towel boy," Max insisted. "You can find him at Chaud le Thermos. You know the place?"

"No," Dunphy said. "I don't know the place."

Max cackled. "Just checking," he said. "It's on the Rue Poissonnière, around corner from subway stop. I think they call it Bonne Nouvelle."

"So this guy—what? He works nights?"

Max laughed. "What you think? At this place, is *only* nights."

It took Dunphy a while to find a cab, and when he did, he couldn't bring himself to say exactly where he wanted to go. So he told the driver to take him to the Métro at Bonne Nouvelle.

It was almost midnight when the cab left him off, but he found the bathhouse right away, led to it by a trail of discarded latex gloves. The building was a dilapidated brownstone with blackened windows and a crumbling cement stoop that led up from the sidewalk to a crude iron door. Beside the door was a sign, like the ones you see outside rural churches, with little white plastic letters spelling out the day's homily against a black background. The sign read:

CHAUD LE THERMOS
SAUNAS ET BAINS
CLUB PRIVÉ

A middle-aged man with too much hair, wearing boots, jeans, and a canvas tank top, sat outside, smoking a cigarette in conversation with an Algerian boy who didn't look old enough to drive. They glanced at Dunphy as he passed, but said nothing.

As Dunphy entered the building, he was met by a wave of humidity and the not unpleasant smell of steam. Just inside the door, an old man sat behind a battered wooden desk, reading a W. H. Hudson novel in translation.

"C'est privé," he said.

"I'm looking for someone," Dunphy told him.

The old man flashed his dentures. "Isn't everyone?" he asked.

Dunphy acknowledged the jest with a smile. "Sergei Azamov."

The old man nodded. "You aren't the police," he said.

"No," Dunphy replied.

"Because you don't look like the police."

"Thank you."

"He's downstairs, but first you must become a member." He pushed a ledger toward Dunphy. "One hundred francs."

Dunphy counted out the bills and signed the ledger.

Eddie Piper Great Falls—USA

The old man slid the money into his desk drawer, took out a stack of membership cards, and filled one in with a ballpoint pen. When he was done, he handed the card to Dunphy and gave him a couple of folded white towels. "Locks are extra," he told him. "You should get one."

"What for?" Dunphy asked.

"Your clothes."

"That's okay," Dunphy replied. "I'll try to keep my pants on." Then he turned and walked slowly downstairs. As he did, the air thickened even more, so that after a few steps, he was beginning to feel claustrophobic. It was hotter here, as well, and badly lighted, and it didn't take a minute for the sweat to break out on his forehead. Reaching the ground floor, he paused at the bottom of the steps and squinted into the gloaming.

It took a moment for his eyes to adjust, and when they did, he found himself standing in a small locker room. There were a couple of dozen lockers against one wall, some benches, and a bank of individual showers with cruddy plastic curtains. Past the showers was a sauna and, beyond that, a large steam room.

A short man with a perfectly sculpted body emerged from the steam room with a towel around his shoulders and padded softly into the sauna. A naked man in his fifties, with a sizable paunch, walked past with his hand on the nape of a Clark Kent lookalike, replete with tortoise-rimmed glasses.

Now what? Dunphy wondered, feeling hugely overdressed. Then a sigh rose up behind him, and turning, Dunphy saw a man lying prone upon the wooden bench, his only accoutrement the towel under his head. On the floor beside him was a can of Crisco and a copy of *Blue Boy*.

"Yo, Sergei!" Dunphy bellowed at the top of his voice. "Sergei Azamov! I'm looking for Sergei 'the Ukrainian' Azamov! Has anyone . . ."

It took about three seconds for Azamov to appear. He came

out of a room from somewhere in the back, looking as if Dunphy had just pissed on his tires. *"Qu'est-ce que tu fous?"* he demanded, striding up to Dunphy like a bouncer in a bad mood—which, in fact, he was.

Dunphy raised his hands. "Friend of Max's," he said.

Azamov stopped about six inches from Dunphy's nose. He had stringy long hair, glittering blue eyes, and a diamond earring. "Who's Max?" he asked.

"Setyaev. I was told he was a friend of yours."

Azamov looked him up and down. "What happened to your nose?" he asked.

Dunphy shrugged. "A guy hit me."

Azamov smiled. "You should take karate. Learn how to defend yourself."

"Good idea," Dunphy said. "I'll do that."

"You know, Max owes me a lot of money," Azamov told him.

Dunphy turned his palms toward the ceiling. "Maybe I can help with that."

Azamov stepped back. Then he turned, leaned down, and smacked Crisco man on the butt. *"Dégagez,"* he ordered. With an irritated look, the man got to his feet, picked up the can of grease, and shuffled off into the next room. "What are you looking for?" Azamov asked in a quiet voice.

"I need a gun," Dunphy told him.

The Ukrainian winced. "A gun could get me in trouble. Why don't you get stoned instead?"

"I can pay what it costs," Dunphy assured him.

Azamov cocked his head one way, then the other. "What kind of gun?" he asked.

"Something I can carry around," Dunphy told him. "But big enough to knock a guy down the first time."

Azamov nodded thoughtfully.

"You got something like that?" Dunphy asked.

"Maybe. When do you need it?"

"Right away."

Azamov shrugged. "You know I'm gonna call Max, don't you?"

"I don't have a problem with that," Dunphy replied. "You want his number?"

Azamov shook his head. "Where you staying?" he asked.

Dunphy told him.

"Okay. If I can get something, I'll come by tomorrow. Early afternoon."

The Ukrainian was as good as his word. He got to the hotel at one o'clock, carrying a new leather briefcase. Clem was out, looking at a Matisse exhibition in the Pompidou Center. Zipping open the briefcase, Azamov took out three bundles of cheesecloth, one of which was larger than the others, and laid them on the coffee table in front of Dunphy. "I need two grand for it," he said. "Briefcase included."

"Is that francs?" Dunphy asked.

Azamov smiled. "What do you think?"

"I don't know," Dunphy answered. "It depends on what's in here. Could be a starter's pistol."

"It's not," Azamov told him.

Dunphy picked up the largest bundle, which was remarkably light, and slowly unwrapped it. Inside was the opposite of a starter's pistol: a Glock-17 with a four-inch barrel. He worked the slide, sighted in on a picture of Dizzy Gillespie, and squeezed the trigger three times in rapid succession. *Click! Click! Click!*

"What's with the trigger?" he asked.

"It's only got a three-pound pull," Azamov explained. "A woman had it. She wasn't very strong. You want me to adjust it?"

"No, it's okay," Dunphy replied, removing the cheesecloth from the other bundles. Inside each was a fifteen-round clip of nine-millimeter cartridges.

"I know it's expensive, but—you can see, it's not crap. It's a good tool."

Dunphy nodded and got to his feet. Walking over to the

dresser, he took a wad of bills from the top drawer and counted out two thousand pounds in one-hundred-pound notes. Then he handed them to Azamov.

The Ukrainian took the money without counting and shoved it into the pocket of his leather jacket, as if the bills were so much Kleenex. Then he got up to leave.

"Did you talk to Max?" Dunphy asked.

Azamov nodded. "Yeah," he said. "I woke him up. He was pissed."

"And what did he say?" Dunphy asked.

"He told me to tell you, 'Be gentle.'"

That night, Clem lay in bed, working the crossword in the *Herald Tribune*, while Dunphy stood at the window, watching the lights on the river.

"What are you thinking?" Clementine asked as she penciled a word into the upper right-hand corner of the puzzle.

Dunphy shook his head.

"Come on," she said. "You can't *not* think."

Dunphy glanced at her, then returned his eyes to the water. "I was thinking . . . how lucky we've been."

Clem peered up at him without raising her head from the puzzle. "Is that supposed to be a joke?"

"No."

"Because it seems to me that you've had a hard time of it. I mean, they really *nailed* you."

"Ohhh—"

"I'm sorry, I couldn't resist."

"The point is, we're still here. The Agency hasn't found us."

"They found *me*."

"Yeah, but that was then. We got loose. They haven't found us *again*."

"That's because we've been careful."

"Or lucky," Dunphy said. "They have resources . . . you can't even imagine."

"Like what?"

"I don't know . . . like Echelon."

"What's Echelon?" she asked.

Dunphy hesitated. Echelon was one of the most closely held secrets in the intelligence community. It wasn't something you discussed aloud, outside headquarters. Then he laughed to himself. *They're trying to kill me, and I'm worried about OpSec?* "It's a collection system," he told her. "The Agency gives a list of words to the NSA—"

"I don't know what that is, either."

"The National Security Agency. It's the biggest component of the intelligence community. And what the NSA does is, it intercepts every electronic communication in the world—*every one*. No lie."

"That's impossible."

"No, it's not," Dunphy said. "Every phone call, fax, and e-mail is filtered through the system. Every wire transfer and airline reservation, every satellite feed and radio broadcast. They're all picked up and run through this gigantic filter—Echelon."

"And what does it do?"

"There's a watch list of words and terms and Boolean operators like *and, or,* and *not*. When the words on the list show up—"

"Which words? Where do they come from?"

"They come from lots of places. The Operations Division at CIA, the embargos office at Commerce, the bank-surveillance unit in the DEA, the counterterrorism center at the FBI. And that's just us. Then, there's the allies. The Brits, the French, the Turks—each of them has their own little list. That's how they grabbed Ocalan—and Carlos."

"And you think—"

"I think we're on the list. And the Magdalene Society, too. When the words come up, Echelon kicks out the message they're in, and the message is copied and sent to whoever gave them the words in the first place. But that's not the end of it. Echelon is just one system. There are others. So, all in all, I'm amazed we're still out here."

Clem pulled the sheet up to her nose. "Scary," she mumbled.

"I'm serious."

"So am I! Sometimes, I think I liked you better as an Irish accountant, or whatever you were supposed to be."

Dunphy turned away from the window. Crossing the room to the minibar, he opened a bottle of Trois Monts and sat down beside Clem on the bed. "I'm thinking, maybe there isn't any point to this anymore. If we keep asking questions, they're going to find us. And when they do, that's it. So, maybe we should just sort of . . . disappear."

"Where?"

"I don't know. Into the sunset."

"The sunset?"

"Okay, you don't like the sunset. What about Brazil?"

"Brazil?!"

Her tone made him defensive. "We could get married."

The idea seemed to alarm her. "Is this a proposal?"

Dunphy wasn't sure. "I don't know. I guess so. I mean—it's a suggestion, anyway."

"You mean, like, 'Do you want to see *Cats*?' "

"No—"

"Of course," she said, "if we were married, then we'd be Mr. and Mrs. *Pitt*!" She thought about that, then tested the sound aloud. *"Hola! Yo soy Señora Peeet!"*

"They don't speak Spanish in Brazil," Dunphy told her.

"I know, but I don't speak Portuguese, so Spanish will have to do." Suddenly, a daft smile played across her lips, and her voice sank to a silky, bedroom timbre. "Hello, my name is Veroushka Pitt, and *I* pay cash for everything." Looking directly at Dunphy, she lowered her voice even further. "This is Veroushka *Bell*-Pitt, hiding out in Florianópolis!" She wrinkled her nose.

"So, what you're saying is, no," Dunphy said.

She shook her head. "What I'm saying is, we have this problem where everyone's trying to kill you all the time, and I just think we ought to solve *that* before I go shopping for a trousseau."

"And what if there isn't any solution?" Dunphy asked. "Sometimes, you just have to walk away. And this is looking like one of those times. I mean, look at who we're dealing with. These guys have been in business for a thousand years. They *own* the CIA. And what it looks like is, no matter how much we find out, there isn't anything we can *do*. We can't go to the police—"

"Why not?"

"Because this isn't the kind of thing they do well. They write tickets. They look for car thieves. Sometimes they solve murders. But they never, *ever,* assign a special detail to the collective unconscious."

Clem rolled her eyes. "We could go to the press."

Dunphy shook his head. "No."

"Why not?"

"I told you on the plane down to Tenerife. Whatever this is, it isn't 'fit to print.' There's no bad guy—no lone assassin. We're up against a secret church, for Chrissake! And the more we find out about that church, the harder it gets for me to even *imagine* a way out. So you tell me. Where does that leave us?"

"In Paris," Clem replied, and patted the bed. "Now come to mother."

Dunphy frowned. "It's *momma*," he said.

"What?"

"It's *come to momma*," he replied. "Not *come to mother*. Only a Brit would think it's *come to mother*."

"Whatever," she told him, and patted the bed a second time.

Georges Watkin worked out of an apartment on the second floor of an Art Nouveau duplex in the ninth arrondissement. Van Worden's warning that Watkin "might be praying in a different church entirely" made Dunphy especially wary. Concocting a pretext, he telephoned the Frenchman to say that he was in Paris on behalf of the Church of Latter-day Saints, which was interested in retaining Watkin as a consultant on genealogical matters. Was Watkin interested? Would it be possible to meet?

Eh, bien! By all means! Watkin was free that very afternoon. Dunphy was not surprised. The Mormon Church is to genealogy as Hollywood is to film. Even if Watkin were independently wealthy, it was unlikely that he'd dismiss the prospect of such a meeting.

And Watkin was not wealthy. According to Van Worden, he was a lowly hack with aristocratic pretensions. He wrote articles about the Royals—everyone's Royals—for the tabloid press in France and England. An authority on the Windsors, Hapsburgs, and Grimaldis, he supplemented his income by doing genealogical studies for private clients.

With the Glock resting in the bottom of his new briefcase, Dunphy arrived at Watkin's office, accompanied by Clem. Buzzed in, they climbed the stairs to the second floor, where the genealogist stood outside the door to his apartment, beaming.

He was a short and overweight man with a childlike face. He wore a threadbare, but respectable, black suit whose shoulders glowed with wear. Beneath the jacket was a white shirt and regimental tie, the stripes of which betrayed the genealogist's enthusiasm for soup. Scuffed shoes and a whiff of sweat completed Dunphy's first impression of the man.

"Raymond Shaw," Dunphy said, protecting his alias even as he shook hands. "And this is my assistant, Veronica . . . Flexx."

Somehow, her double take went unnoticed.

The office itself was large and comfortable, if overheated, its walls lined with bookshelves filled to overflowing. Stacks of documents and rolls of parchment rested on heavy wooden library tables at either end of the room. Along the north wall, a bank of grimy windows glowed with the gray light of an afternoon that couldn't wait to rain.

"Armagnac?" Watkin asked, pouring himself a glass.

"No thanks," Dunphy said, dropping into a battered leather club chair. "We don't drink, actually."

Watkin gritted his teeth and sighed. "Of course! How stupid of me. I'm . . . " The genealogist's voice dwindled to nothing, as if he'd lost track of what he'd been about to say, even as his smile segued into a look of surprise—or perhaps it was alarm. Whatever it was, it lasted only a second, and then he found his voice and was smiling again. "I'm terribly sorry," he said.

"No need to apologize," Dunphy replied, wondering if he'd just hallucinated. "Why don't you enjoy your drink, and I'll explain what we're after?"

The Frenchman sat down in the chair behind his desk, glanced at some papers, and nodded to his visitors to begin.

Dunphy had spent the morning in an Internet café not far from the Sorbonne. He'd run a search on Mormonism, made some notes, and composed a smarmy little speech that he hoped would be ingratiating. "It's Peter that brings us here," he said. "I don't know if you're a religious man, but Peter tells us that the Gospel was 'preached also to them that are dead, that they might be judged according to men in the flesh, but live according to God in the spirit.' At the Church of Latter-day Saints, we believe that Christ suffered and died—not only for the sins of the living, but also for those of the dead. As you can imagine, this places upon us a very special obligation: to redeem the souls of those who have died—our ancestors in the spirit world. And as I think you know, we do this by means of a sacrament that is popularly known as baptism by proxy. Of course, before we can do that, we must first identify the ancestors in question—which is something we do using traditional genealogical methods."

A complacent smirk from Dunphy. A beatific smile from Clem. A respectful, if distracted, nod from Watkin.

"We've been at this for quite a while," Dunphy continued, "with each family working backward, one generation after another. We like to think that millions of souls have been saved. But as you can imagine—"

"The further back one goes," Watkin suggested, "the harder it gets."

"Exactly. And this is particularly so for Americans, whose generational roots—and records—are almost always on the other side of the Atlantic."

Watkin nodded sympathetically.

"And that's why Ms. Flexx and I are here. We've been asked to set up a research institute in Paris to facilitate genealogical requests made by Church members in the United States."

"I see," Watkin said. "And you thought—"

"We thought you might be able to help. Yes."

Watkin nodded slowly and, Dunphy thought, a bit regretfully—which was not what he'd expected. Finally the Frenchman asked, "How did you get my name?"

It was a question that Dunphy had anticipated. Reaching inside his jacket, he removed a photocopy of the article that had appeared in *Archaeus*: "The Magdalene Cultivar." "We were very impressed with an article you wrote," Dunphy said, handing it to Watkin.

The Frenchman took a pair of reading glasses from his jacket pocket and adjusted them on his nose. Then he cleared his throat and looked at the papers in his hand. There was no obvious reaction. If anything, he seemed, somehow, *stuck*. His face slackened as he stared at the story he'd written, lips moving over the words in the first paragraph. Finally he looked up. "Where did you get this?" he asked.

Dunphy had been waiting for that question, as well. "It was sent to one of our genealogists in Salt Lake City—he passed it on. I'm not sure what magazine it was in. . . ."

"Everyone said the work was first-rate," Clem remarked, sensing Watkin's discomfiture.

"Oh, no question," Dunphy agreed.

Watkin looked from one to the other. "It wasn't widely circulated," he mumbled.

"Oh?"

"No," Watkin replied. "There were very few copies

printed. It was a . . . special-interest publication. Written for a very special audience. Not the public. So . . . it was quite rare."

"Well, then, I think we should count ourselves lucky to have seen it!" Dunphy told him. "And lucky to have found the man who wrote it!"

Watkin nodded slightly, still obviously distracted.

"It was so cleverly done," Dunphy remarked.

"*What* was?" Watkin asked.

"The article," Dunphy replied.

"So witty," Clem added, crossing her legs with a zip of nylon. "The way you wrote about the Merovingian line—"

"As if it were an exercise in viticulture!" Dunphy finished. "Wherever did you get the *idea*?"

Watkin's distraction was now gone. His eyes snapped from Dunphy to Clem, and back again. Then, he seemed to relax—and began to play along.

"I don't know," he said. "It was just an idea. I wrote it as an amusement." He paused and then plunged on. "So! You're interested in the Merovingians?"

"Absolutely," Dunphy replied.

"Who wouldn't be?" Clem exclaimed.

"I wonder if there are any of them still around," Dunphy mused.

"You're not alone," Watkin said with a smile. "Would you like to see the genealogies Napoléon commissioned? Not the originals, of course, but—"

"Hell, yes!" Dunphy exclaimed, and instantly regretted it. "Sorry. Sometimes, I get . . . overexcited."

Watkin shrugged. "They're in the next room," he said. "I'll just go get them. . . ."

When he'd left, Dunphy grimaced, and Clem leaned in. "I think you fucked up, your holiness."

Dunphy agreed, but there was nothing to be done. Getting to his feet, he walked to the window and glanced outside. A light rain had begun to fall, and the street was slicked and glistening. "It's raining," he said as he made his way around the room, studying the shelves of books for clues to Watkin's strange demeanor.

Newsletter of the International Society for British Genealogy and Family History.

Manuscripts Catalog of the Franco-Judaic Archives.

Documents Relating to the History and Settlement of Towns along the Dadou and Agout Rivers (with the Exception of Réalmont), 1330–82.

UFOs over Biarritz!

"Uh-oh," Dunphy muttered, but continued with his stroll around the room, arriving finally at Watkin's desk. There, two things caught his eye. The first was a red diode glowing on Watkin's telephone, indicating that someone (almost certainly Watkin) was using line one in another room. The second thing to catch his attention was a photograph of himself.

This was a passport-sized picture attached to a memorandum from the director of the Security Research Staff, Harold Matta. Aghast, Dunphy read the memo, which identified the man in the photograph as John Dunphy, aka Kerry Thornley, aka Jack. The memo described Dunphy/Thornley as

armed and extremely dangerous. Mr. Dunphy is believed to be traveling with a female companion, using false identification. Subject impersonated a federal official in Kansas, wounded a federal agent in London, and breached security at a SAP facility in Switzerland, where Andromeda-sensitive MK-IMAGE documents were stolen after two members of the archival staff were viciously assaulted. SRS safari teams are TDY to our embassies in London, Paris, and Zürich. If sighted, notify the team closest to you.

Oh, shit, Dunphy thought. What the hell is a safari team? And the answer came back: It's just what you think. Removing the picture from the memo to which it had been attached, Dunphy took the photo back to his chair. Sitting down, he flashed the picture to Clem and whispered, "We're fucked."

"What?!"

"We can give it maybe ten minutes," he said, shoving the picture into his jacket pocket. "Then we have to get out—he's already on the phone."

A moment later, a nervous-looking Watkin emerged with a bundle of charts under his arm. Spreading them out on one of the library tables, he weighted them down at their corners, using books. Dunphy and Clem joined him at his side.

"You're looking at the ancestral charts of the Merovingians," Watkin told them, "as prepared by genealogists working for Napoléon in the first three years of the nineteenth century."

"The Long-Haired Kings," Dunphy muttered.

Watkin put his lips together in a moue. "They've also been called the Grail Kings."

"They're like illuminated manuscripts," Clem observed, pointing to the delicate traceries that crowded the margins of the charts. There were lions and cherubim, flowers and magi. And, in the middle, a latticework of relations, tracing a direct line back from the Napoleonic era to the Crusades, and from the Crusades to the Dark Ages, and finally, to Mérovée himself.

"It's beautiful," Dunphy remarked.

"You have no idea," Watkin commented.

Dunphy scrutinized the names and was somewhat disappointed to see that none of them was particularly recognizable. *Dagobert II. Sigisbert IV.* Those, at least, had been cross-referenced in the Andromeda files—though he had no idea who they were, or might have been.

"Who's Dagbert?" he asked.

Watkin winced. "Dah-go-*bear*. His father was king of Austrasia—"

"Which was what?"

"Northern France and parts of Germany. It's an interesting story," Watkin confided. "Like a fairy tale. When Dagobert's father was killed, Dagobert himself was kidnapped by the mayor of the palace and hidden away in a monastery in Ireland. Apparently, they didn't have the heart to murder him. After some years, the mayor's own son became king, and Dagobert grew to manhood."

"When was this?" Clementine asked.

"In 651. He retook the throne when he was twenty-three."

"Then what?" Dunphy asked, thinking he had maybe five minutes left.

Watkin shrugged. "He died."

"How?" Clem wondered.

"They slaughtered him while he slept—a lance through the eye."

"Who did?" Dunphy asked.

"According to the histories? The henchmen of Pépin the Fat."

"And in fact?"

A dismissive puff from Watkin. "The Vatican, of course."

"What about this one?" Clem asked. "Who's he?"

"Sigisbert," Watkin replied. "The line continued through him."

"For how long?" Dunphy asked, bringing the conversation around to the reason for his visit.

Watkin looked uncomfortable. "What do you mean?"

"Where are they now? Are any of them still around?"

Watkin shrugged.

"Oh, come on," Dunphy chided. "Don't tell me nobody's taken a peek since Napoléon!"

Watkin smiled bleakly. "Well," he said, "it doesn't matter. The last was here, actually. In Paris."

"No kidding," Dunphy said. "Who was he?"

"A banker," Watkin replied. "Bernardin something-or-other."

Dunphy figured he didn't have anything to lose. "Gomelez?" he asked.

The genealogist stared at him.

"I'm right, aren't I?" Dunphy exclaimed. He turned to Clem. "I knew I was right."

"How do you know this name?" Watkin demanded.

Dunphy shrugged. "Internet. I surf a lot."

"What happened to him?" Clem asked.

"To who?"

"Mr. Gomelez," she said, and as she spoke, a car backfired on the street outside. Watkin jumped as if he'd been given a shock. Averting his eyes from his guests, he began to roll up the charts. "I think he was wounded in the war," he said.

"Which war?" Dunphy asked.

"In Spain. He was a volunteer."

Clem walked over to the window, pushed the curtain aside, and gazed out at the street. "He must be very old now," she said.

Watkin shook his head and lied. "I think he must be dead," he said. "This was a very sick man. And not just the war. He had—how is it called? *Pernicieuse anémie?*"

"Pernicious anemia?" Clem suggested.

"Exactly! And in the big war, when the Germans came, they make his house—a mansion in the Rue de Mogador—a hospital. No one sees him after that."

"Even after the war?" Dunphy asked.

"As I said, he disappeared."

"And the house—"

Watkin dismissed the question. "It changed hands. I think, now, this is a museum. For the archaeologists."

Dunphy watched Watkin closely. He seemed to be unusually alert. Indeed, if the genealogist were a dog, his ears would have been standing at attention. It was then that Clem jumped back from the window.

"Uh-oh," she said.

Dunphy went to her side and, looking out, saw five men in black suits and string ties climb from the back of a gray van whose front wheels were on the sidewalk. One of the men was punching buttons on a cell phone as he walked briskly toward Watkin's building.

On the desk, the phone began to ring. Watkin moved to answer it.

"Stay!" Dunphy ordered, as if the genealogist were a large and very excitable dog. Then he reached down for his briefcase and, opening it, pulled out the Glock. "Now, listen to me," he said. "Tell 'em we just left, say we're on our way to the Bibliothèque nationale, tell 'em we're driving an old Deux Chevaux. Tell 'em whatever the fuck you want, Georges, but you'd better be convincing—or it's the end of the line for the Watkin family. Y'know what I mean?"

The genealogist nodded, looking terrified, and slowly picked up the phone. He spoke too fast for Dunphy to understand exactly what he said, but he heard the words Deux Chevaux and Bibliothèque—so he figured Watkin had taken his instructions literally.

Moving to the window, Dunphy glanced outside. He saw three of the men jump into the van, slamming the doors behind them. With a screech, the car backed into the street, came halfway around, stopped, and shot forward, heading for what Dunphy guessed was the library. Meanwhile, two men ran up the sidewalk toward the building. One of them was limping badly, and for a second, Dunphy thought it might be Jesse Curry—but, no, Curry was a bigger guy, and besides, it was too soon for him to be walking around.

"Did they leave?" Clem asked, her voice cracking like a young boy's.

"Some of them," Dunphy said.

The doorbell rang. And rang again.

Dunphy turned to Watkin. "Let 'em in."

Watkin walked to the intercom and pressed a button. Then he turned to Dunphy. "What are you going to do?" he asked.

It occurred to Dunphy that this was a question that Watkin might have asked *before* he pressed the buzzer. But he didn't say anything. He just shook his head. The truth was, he didn't know what he was going to do.

"Jack?"

Dunphy turned to her.

"What's going to happen?" she asked.

He shook his head. "I don't know. I'll try to talk to them," he said. Two men were coming up the stairs—he could hear them now—who, if given the chance, would happily kill them. But, of course, they wouldn't get that chance. Dunphy would have them in his sights by the time they realized he was in the room—and not on the way to the library.

But he couldn't just kill them. Not like that. He couldn't just shoot them coming through the door. They were people. Then again . . .

They were also a *safari team*. That was the Agency's term, and while Dunphy had never heard it before, it seemed to suggest that some poor, dumb, dangerous animal was being hunted—and he was it. Bambi with a Glock.

Then again . . .

A knock at the door. *Rap rap rap rap rap!* Like they were repo men, come to get the TV.

Dunphy motioned Clem into the next room, then stepped behind the door and nodded to Watkin. The genealogist took a deep breath, as if he were going onstage, turned the door-knob, and—

Dunphy had the Glock in both hands, pointed at the floor, when the men came into the room as if the building were on fire. He opened his mouth—perhaps to yell *Freeze*—when he saw, first, the clubfoot, and then the guns.

You wouldn't have thought they'd have been so indiscreet, coming in that way when Dunphy wasn't even supposed to be there. Maybe it was just good training—always be prepared, or something like that. But it didn't serve them well. At all.

Freeze came out, not as a word, but as a bellow of angry surprise—because here was Roscoe's killer, turning toward him with an automatic in his hand. And the man next to him, turning, too, but slower to react—the Suit, with the bags under his eyes even bigger now than they were in McLean.

Dunphy's first shot went through the window behind them, but the next two caught the clubfooted man in the shoulder, spinning him around and down. The Suit got off the next shot, but missed, then lost his legs when a bullet tunneled into him through the navel. Dunphy was firing like a madman with his back to the wall, pulling the trigger as fast as he could, not really thinking to aim, just spraying the room with as much lead as the Glock could throw—until, quite suddenly, it went *click click click*. And Dunphy thought, Now I'm dead. Ohhh, Clem . . .

For a moment, it seemed as if the very possibility of sound had been sucked from the room. Wisps of blue smoke hung in the air, and a weird, almost electrical, smell was everywhere. Then Dunphy heard the Suit whimpering on the floor, holding his stomach in his hands, rocking from side to side, keening. A few feet away, Watkin wept in terror beside the door, squatting on the Chinese carpet, hands clasped behind his head, as if he were expecting a nuclear attack. Closer to Dunphy, the club-footed man lay on his back with a scowl on his face, blood pumping slowly from a hole in his eyebrow.

Dunphy took a deep breath—his first in thirty seconds—and let the empty clip drop from the Glock to the floor. Inserting a new one, he worked the slide, then shoved the gun into the waistband under his jacket.

Finally he cleared his throat. "Clem? Clem?!"

She came out of the other room looking like a raccoon, with black circles under her eyes from where the mascara had run. She took in the smoke and the dead man, Watkin sobbing and the other guy shivering with pain. She saw the blood and staggered. Finally, she rose up on her tiptoes and moved toward the door, trying not to get her shoes wet.

"Clem." He went to her and put his arm around her shoulders.

"There was so much shooting," she muttered, tears streaming. "So much!"

"Don't let him kill us!" Watkin begged.

"Stay out of this," Dunphy told him, then turned back to Clem. "They came in like the DEA," he explained. "Everything went off at once."

"Just don't hurt them anymore, okay?" she asked

"I won't. I didn't. I mean, they did it to themselves. All I did was shoot them!"

He didn't know if she believed him or not, and when he thought of it, what he said didn't make any sense, anyway. So he did what he had to do.

Grabbing Watkin by the collar, he shoved him toward the couch. "Sit!" Then he went to the desk and jerked the phone out of the wall. Remembering the cell phone, he glanced around and saw it on the floor. Picking it up, he laid it on the desk and smashed it with the butt of the Glock. Finally, he collected the other men's guns and dropped them in his brief-case. Snapped the locks and turned to leave.

"I need an ambulance," the Suit remarked.

Dunphy nodded. "Yeah, I can see that." Then he started for the door.

"For Chrissake, man—*look* at me! I'm—I'm an *American*!" The Suit drew his hand back from the mess around his stomach and, as he did, Dunphy saw the blood pulse, as if a part of the guy had come unplugged. Then he clapped his hand over the burble and said, "I think I'm dyin'. " There wasn't any rebuke in his voice. If anything, it was filled with wonder.

Dunphy nodded. Thought back to McLean. The Suit, stand-ing there with that strange little smile. Cop lights flashing out-side. Roscoe dead in a pair of fishnet stockings that the Suit had helped to put him in. "Yeah, well," Dunphy said, "it happens to the best of 'em."

28

They found a cab a few blocks away and took it to Sainte-Clothilde, which was the first place that occurred to Dunphy, and nowhere near their hotel. With barely a glance at the church's spires, they sought out the Métro a few blocks away and descended into its womb. Half an hour later, they emerged in the rain at Mutualité and crossed the river to their hotel.

Clem was surprisingly cool. She opened a Campari soda and dropped to the sofa beside the telephone.

"Clem," Dunphy began.

She shook her head. "You don't have to explain."

"They came through the door—"

"I know. You said. Like DNA."

"No. Not like DNA—"

"It doesn't matter," she told him. "I still love you. I just have to get used to the fact that I'm sleeping with the Grim Reaper."

He didn't push it, perhaps because he knew she didn't really blame him—not after Tenerife. He opened a bottle of 33 and fell into a chair.

After a while, Clem said, "Now what?"

Dunphy shook his head. "I don't know." He sipped his beer and thought about it. "I think we know as much, right now, as we'll ever know and—it's not enough. It doesn't buy us a way out. It just gets us in deeper. So . . ."

She watched him for a long moment, and when he didn't finish the sentence, she asked, "What?"

"I think we ought to forget about it. Just turn around and

331

walk away. We've got some money, good ID. We'd be all right."

"But if we do that—" Clem began.

"I know. They win. So what?"

She didn't say anything for a while, just closed her eyes and sipped her Campari soda. Finally, she looked at him and said, "Well, that's not right. We're not going to do that."

She found the address in the telephone directory, listed under the "Museums" entry for the City of Paris. Watkin had said that Gomelez had lived in a mansion on the Boulevard des Capucines, and that his house had become an archaeological museum after the war.

There was only one such museum in the Rue de Mogador, and it was listed as the Musée de l'Archaeologie du Roi Childeric Ier.

They took a taxi to the address, which was around the corner from the Place de l'Opéra. The museum was housed in a four-story Belle Epoque mansion whose massive iron doors were held open by large brass rings anchored to the granite walls on either side. Floor-to-ceiling windows ran the length of the building in both directions, their wavy glass streaked with rain. Gargoyles leered. Drains gurgled.

In the entranceway, a small sign memorialized the museum's hours. Dunphy checked his watch. They had about an hour.

A gray-haired pensioner with a drooping mustache sat behind a carved wooden table, just inside the door. He was wearing a faded blue uniform and reading a Simenon paperback that was falling apart at the spine. Dunphy gave him twenty francs and waited while the man tore off a pair of ticket stubs, which he handed ceremoniously, and with a smile, to Clem.

They weren't the only visitors. A clutch of schoolgirls moved through the rooms in a sort of giggling scrum, listening not at all to their teacher's lecture.

It was really a quite remarkable museum, with an idiosyn-

cratic collection that became progressively older as one
moved from the lowest to the highest floor. The ground floor
held fifteenth-, sixteenth-, and seventeenth-century paintings,
as well as heraldic devices, blazons, and coats of arms from
half a dozen countries. Most of the canvases were of a pastoral kind, with moony shepherds crouched outside the tomb
of Jesus, and knights at prayer upon a field of flowers.

The first floor was devoted almost entirely to sacred buildings and, in particular, to those that housed statues of black
Virgins. A translucent plastic box was affixed to the wall beside
an architectural drawing of the great church at Glastonbury.
The box held a sheaf of badly printed flyers that explained, in
six languages, that statues of the black Virgin can be found
throughout Europe and Latin America, with France alone
having more than three hundred of them.

"She is known to the Gypsies as Sara-la-Kali," Clem read,
"and to others as Cybele, Diana, Isis, and the Magdalene."

Dunphy peered at the drawing and photographs. Besides
Glastonbury, there were pictures of the Jasna Gora monastery in Poland; the cathedral at Chartres; the abbey church at
Einsiedeln; and other temples and sanctuaries in Clermont-
Ferrand, Limoux, and Marseille. There were sacramental objects, as well: stone reliquaries and marble reliefs, tapestries
and robes.

"Let's go up," Clem said. "We only have twenty minutes."

The second floor was devoted entirely to the Crusades and
Knights Templar. There were fourteenth-century woodcuts of
Jerusalem, a box of Templar regalia, lances, and swords, a
Gnostic funeral stele, a triptych, and a diorama. The triptych's first panel showed Godfroi de Bouillon setting off upon
the first crusade in 1098. Its second panel depicted the Cru-
sader knights triumphant in Jerusalem a year later. The last
panel showed those same knights digging beneath the Temple
of Solomon.

The diorama was less complex. It showed Jacques de
Molay, grand master of the Knights Templar, being slowly
roasted to death on the Île de la Cité in 1314.

"That's where our hotel is!" Clem said.

Clem wanted to read more about Molay and the Knights Templar, but there wasn't time. The museum would close soon.

So they made their way to the fourth floor, where they were startled on the stairs to see what looked like a bear's head forged of gold, floating in the air above them. The metalwork, or whatever it was, was exquisite: you could count the hairs on its neck, Dunphy thought.

"How do they do that?" Clem gasped.

"It's a hologram," Dunphy guessed, "or maybe it's done with mirrors. I don't know." Reaching the top of the stairs, he waved his hand through the image, which seemed to ripple, and as it did, a door slid open to their left.

Dunphy turned to his girlfriend. Most of the exhibits seemed to be off to the right in a sort of gallery that ran the length of the house. But the room to their left waited, and obviously, it was special. "Go ahead," he said, nudging her toward the door. "You first."

"No, that won't happen," she replied. "And, anyway, you're the one with the gun. Have at it."

Feeling like a little boy in a haunted house, Dunphy stepped inside the room, while Clem stood in the doorway, ready to bolt should he be decapitated or set upon by things with wings. After a moment, he called to her. "C'mon in," he said. "It's neat."

In fact, it took her breath away. In the center of the room was a dramatically lighted stone sarcophagus. Casks of wine and piles of grain were heaped against the limestone coffin, while pedestals of various sizes were ranged around it, reminding Dunphy of the standing stones he'd seen in the English countryside. Atop each pedestal was a lighted glass case in which ancient coins and gold and silver jewelry were displayed.

A simple flyer, retrieved from a plastic box attached to one of the display cases, provided a potted history of the display. According to it, the sarcophagus was that of Childeric I, a Merovingian king whose tomb was found in the Pyrenees in

1789—the year of the French Revolution. According to the flyer, the sarcophagus was discovered in a cave beside a severed horse's head and a bear's head wrought from gold. A wreath of eagles' wings were mingled with the bones—which had lain undisturbed for more than a thousand years.

In addition to these things, the room held one other. This was a verdigris-tinted crystal ball, about nine inches in diameter, which rested in a glass case on a golden stand. The stand had been fashioned in the shape of a hand, with the crystal balanced upon the fingertips. Drawn to the globe, Dunphy and Clem did what everyone does when confronted with a crystal ball: they gazed into it. And as they did, the tremulous image of an old man welled up within the glass, but upside down, so that he was at first unrecognizable. Dunphy cocked his head. The old man cleared his throat. Clem yelped.

"Hurry up, please, it's time!" the man said, his voice soft and coaxing.

Clem's nails were dug into Dunphy's arm—until they realized who it was: the old building guard, come to chase them out. He was smiling and out of breath from the long climb up to the fourth floor.

Clem's fingers relaxed. She took a deep breath and bathed the guard in her sweetest smile. "Is it really five?" she asked.

He shrugged. "Almost, mademoiselle."

"But there's so much to see," she entreated.

The guard nodded sympathetically. "And I think you have not yet seen the bees, eh?"

"What bees?" Clem asked.

The guard nodded once again in his courtly way and beckoned them to his side. *"Ici."* He was standing next to an old armoire. *"Regardez."* Taking out a ring of keys, he selected one of the larger ones and, with it, turned the lock on the armoire. Slowly, he pulled open the doors, and as he did, a set of lights came on within. And then the guard stepped back.

Before them was a floor-length coronation robe that glittered with the light refracted from the wings of a thousand bees, handcrafted in gold. "Napoléon's coat," the guard explained. "For when he becomes emperor."

"The bees—"

"Yes! Of course, the bees! The bear! They are sacred, eh? For the Merovingians!"

Dunphy and Clem nodded.

"So Napoléon puts them on his coat—and people think, 'Ah, he is a Merovingian!' " The guard paused and smiled. "But, no, he is not. And I know what you think—one tiny bee? Who would notice? No one! And she is worth more than my pension, this little bee. So, I hear the voice—"

"What voice?" Clem asked.

The old man tapped a finger against his temple. "And she says, 'Luc, you are a poor man, why do you not take one little insect for your family?' But if I do that?" He shook his head and laughed to himself. "Luc is no fool."

"How long have you worked here?" Dunphy asked.

The guard reached down with his palm flat, until it was about two feet above the floor. "Since I am a child. Even before the house was a museum."

"You mean . . . "

"It was a house," the guard told him. "And all these things were . . . *privé.*"

"Whose house?" Clem asked, knowing the answer.

"Monsieur Gomelez. It is his foundation that pays for this. L'Institut Mérovée."

"And did you know Gomelez?" Dunphy asks.

"Of course," the guard replied. "My father was his valet."

"What happened to him?" Dunphy asks.

The old man shrugged. "The war came. He is not well. So he is taken to a safe place. But . . . he does not come back." With a smile to Clem, he closed the doors to the armoire and locked them. Together, they made their way out of the room and began to descend the stairs.

"When you say he was *taken* to a safe place?" Dunphy asked.

"He had friends. Powerful friends."

"But where did he go?" Clem asked.

The guard paused on the stair and thought for a moment. "Well, to Switzerland, of course. Somewhere in Switzerland."

Flying was out. And trains, too. After what had happened at Watkin's apartment, the French police would be looking for him, the border guards alert. Which put them in a bind. They couldn't stay, and they couldn't go.

They drank espressos under the awning of a tourist trap on the Champs-Elysées, while Dunphy considered their options. The problem was the border. Clem could rent a car and take them to it, but they'd never get across. Dunphy's picture would be nailed to the gate at every border crossing in France. Briefly, then, he considered a disguise, but dismissed the notion. There was something about wearing a disguise that, no matter what the circumstances, made you guilty of whatever it was that you were hiding from. And there was also the clean-underwear factor. If someone was going to kill him, he wasn't going to die in an ill-fitting wig or, worse, dressed as a Muslim woman. Which left only one way to get across the border.

It was a long drive, almost 350 miles on the A6, south to Mâcon, then east toward Annecy. They left just after midnight in a rented Audi and drove through the night, arriving in the Haute-Savoie shortly after dawn. The sky was the color of flames, and they didn't need to see the mountains to know that they were in the Alps: every breath told them as much. The air was crisp, cold, and bright; washed down with strong coffee and crunchy croissants at a workmen's café on the fringes of Annecy, it was about as refreshing as a good night's sleep.

After breakfast, they drove through the mountains to Évian-les-Bains, a legendary spa on the south shore of Lake Geneva. There, Dunphy rented a small suite with a large terrace that looked out across a broad expanse of lawn toward the lake below and, in the distance, on the lake's other side, Lausanne.

They were in the Hotel Royal (more expensive than which

it does not get), and Dunphy suggested that Clem might like to "take the waters or whatever they do around here" while he went into town. She agreed enthusiastically and soon found herself naked, prone, and covered from head to toe with gobbets of mud from the Dead Sea.

Meanwhile, Dunphy found himself in the port, looking to rent a sailboat. He wanted something with a cabin, in case the weather kicked up, as it was threatening to do. Even now, cumulus clouds were piling up on the backs of the Alps, like so many cotton balls.

The difficulty lay in finding a sailboat that was more than a day-sailer and less than a yacht. He needed something stable that he could handle by himself. As he explained to the salesman at the marina, he was no Vasco da Gama and would not last long in a J-24. On the other hand, neither did he want any of the fourteen-foot Limousins that the marina was renting. He needed something bigger, something that would stand up to the wind.

In the end, the salesman made a couple of telephone calls and got permission for Dunphy to rent a twenty-three-foot Sonar that its owner hoped to sell. The fee was steep—one thousand francs a day, plus a five-thousand-franc security deposit—but the boat was ideal. It was just the right size, had a cuddy cabin with two bunks, a full complement of sails, and a self-bailing cockpit. The salesman asked when he needed it, and Dunphy told him right away.

The man looked skeptical. It was 4 P.M., there were clouds on the horizon, and the sun would set in a couple of hours.

"We want to take it down to Thonon," Dunphy told him, naming a town about ten miles away. "Our friends have a house on the lake. My wife thinks it would be an amusing way to arrive. And I think she's right. They haven't seen us in years."

Hurrying back to the hotel, he found Clementine in the spa, wrapped in a heated plastic sheet, looking remarkably like a corn dog dipped in chocolate. He persuaded the attendant to hose her down with what turned out to be ice water, then led her back to the room.

"Where are we going? What's the rush?" she demanded. "I was about to get a pedicure. And I've already charged it to the room!"

"We're going sailing," Dunphy told her.

"What?"

"I rented a sailboat."

She looked at him as if he were insane. "But I don't want to go sailing."

"We have to."

"It's almost night," she complained. And when it was obvious he wouldn't relent, she asked: "Do you even *know* how to sail?"

"Sure," he told her. "I'm a great sailor." *Well . . .*

It wasn't rain, exactly. Just drops of water that fell, one by one, to the surface of the lake—a gray mass, quilted with concentric circles that increasingly overlapped. Dunphy pulled in the jib line and cleated it off. Then he pushed the tiller away from him and loosened the mainsail.

And Clem watched with a skeptical eye. "It's going to pour," she said.

"That's why we have a cabin," Dunphy told her. "Not to mention some bread, a little cheese, a bottle of wine. We'll be okay. It'll be fun."

"It's going to *pour*."

"You mentioned that," he said.

"Yes, but I think you should know it's also going to blow." She paused and added, "Like a banshee."

Sitting in the cockpit with his back to the coaming, Dunphy hoped that she was wrong. He was really quite comfortable. "What makes you say that?" he asked.

" 'Red sky in morning?' "

"Ye-aah?" What was *that* supposed to mean?

Clem shook her head disbelievingly. " 'Sailors take warning.' "

Dunphy acknowledged the saying with a grunt and took her point. She was thinking of the spectacular dawn they'd seen outside Annecy.

"It goes on," Clem continued.

"Jesus," Dunphy muttered.

" 'When the wind is in the north, the fisherman goes not forth.' Hmmmnn," she said, and licking a finger, held it in the air—though that was hardly necessary. The wind had begun to kick up, and there was no doubt about the direction from which it was coming. It was blowing off the far shore, straight out of Lausanne. "Which way is north?" she asked coyly.

"Very funny," Dunphy said as the boat picked up speed and began to heel—just a bit. "Whooaaa," he said, surprised.

Clem giggled. "I'll just get the life jackets," she said, crabbing down to the cuddy cabin. "We really should wear them. It's a big lake."

She emerged from the cabin a minute later, wearing an orange vest and carrying another. She tossed it to Dunphy.

Who frowned. He didn't want to seem like a wimp, but—*whoaaaa*, the boat was turbocharged now as it sliced through the water, foam curling at the edge of the coaming. A shuddering sound came from under their feet as the boat began to tremble. Maybe the jackets aren't such a bad idea, Dunphy thought. Anyway, they can't hurt. Giving the tiller to Clem, he struggled into one that seemed a little too small.

"Where are we heading?" Clem asked, raising her voice above the wind, which was now gusting from ten to twenty knots.

"The other side," Dunphy replied.

"Of what?"

"The lake! I don't want to go through Customs. They'll probably have my picture."

"So you're going to sail there—at night?"

Dunphy nodded. "Yeah. That's the idea."

"It's a long sail," she said. "Where do you expect to land?"

"Near Lausanne," Dunphy answered. "Which is right over there . . ."

"Where the wind's coming from."

"Right."

"Well, that will make it harder."

It was dark now. The temperature was dropping, and the rain was falling in long, sweeping lines across the water. They could see the lights of Lausanne on the far shore, but getting there was another matter. The wind seemed to be blowing straight out of city hall, forcing Dunphy to head so far up that the boat repeatedly stalled, going into irons again and again.

It was annoying, at first, and then it began to seem dangerous. The once-black lake was covered with whitecaps now, and the waves were getting larger. It was becoming harder and harder to hold the course that he wanted, and when he did, the ride was like a roller coaster, lifting them gently into the air, then slamming them back down. At other times—when he sailed too close to the wind—the sails emptied, and soon the boat was broadside to the waves. When that happened, it was like the spinning-teacups ride at Disney World—except the lake was cold and dark, the ride was never-ending, and it would not have been hard to drown.

"It's getting rough," Clem said in a voice that surprised Dunphy with its coolness. She was hunkered down across from him, smiling even as the water poured across the coaming. Dunphy himself was seated across from her, high on the side of the boat, using his weight to keep the keel as even as possible.

He wasn't sure where they were. It was hard to see. The rain was flying into his face, and with one hand on the tiller and the other holding the jib line, it was difficult to brush it away. Meanwhile, the boat was pitching and yawing, except in those moments when it began to roll.

Clem shivered. "The water's freezing!" she said.

Dunphy nodded regretfully. "It's from the mountains," he said. "Snowmelt."

"Well, I don't think we'd last long in it," Clem told him, beginning to bail with a plastic Clorox bottle whose bottom had been cut away.

"It's got a self-bailing feature," Dunphy said. "I checked."

"Well, the feature needs help," Clem replied. After a few minutes, she looked up at the sails, which seemed ready to explode, and turned to Dunphy. "Do you mind if I make a suggestion?" she yelled, tossing half a gallon of water over the side, then scooping another from the deck. "Before we lose the rigging?"

"What?!" The wind was even stronger now, howling in tune with the vibrating stays.

"Reef the mainsail, let out the jib, and fall off to starboard," she ordered.

He gaped at her. "What?" The wind tore the word from his mouth.

"I said, reef the mainsail—"

"All right! Okay! I heard you the first time." Clamping the jib line between his teeth, he untied the figure-eight knot that tied the halyard to a cleat on the mast, and let the mainsail drop. Then he reefed the sail until there was only a rag showing, and tied it off. Finally, he let the jib out and turned to her, abashed. Already, the boat was on an even keel. "Which way is starboard?" he asked, knowing she'd never let him forget it.

A radiant smile from Clementine. "That way," she said, still bailing, her hair whipping back and forth in the wind.

As he pushed the tiller away from him, the jib filled with air. The boat turned gracefully away from Lausanne and began to sail more smoothly with the wind. Even the rain seemed to abate.

After a while, when his heart rate was closer to normal, Dunphy asked her, "Where did you learn so much about sailing?"

Clem smiled and put the Clorox bottle down. "My parents had a cottage in Kinsale," she told him. "We went there every summer. I crewed a lot."

"You what?"

"Crewed," she said. "Like you."

"Just checking."

"I got quite good at it," she added.

"I'm sure you did."

"If you'll let the jib out a little more," she said, "I think we may be able to run with the wind—almost. Do you have a chart?"

"No."

"Clever lad. No need for charts." She frowned. "I think that's Rolle over there," she said. "Switzerland, anyway. I suppose we could head for it . . ."

Dunphy gave her the tiller.

They beached the boat a little after ten on the lawn of a large and darkened house about fifteen miles southwest of Rolle, just past Coppet. A truck driver gave them a ride into Geneva, where they checked into the first hotel they found, telling the desk clerk that their car had broken down.

In the morning, Dunphy found his way to the *Handelsregister* in the Old Town and, with the help of a friendly clerk, looked up the Institut Mérovée. There wasn't much.

According to the paperwork, the Institut had been founded in 1936 with a gift from Bernardin Gomelez, a resident of Paris. Its purposes were "charitable, educational, and religious." In 1999, the Institut declared assets of ">SF1 billion." This was, by quick calculation, more than $700 million. But how much more? What did the > really mean? *More than.* Well, Dunphy thought, two billion Swiss Francs was *more than* one billion Swiss Francs. And ten billion was more than that. And so on. And so forth.

There was no way to know, in other words, just how rich the Institut was—though it was certainly very, very rich. Its president appeared to be Gomelez's son or grandson. At least, they had the same name: Bernardin Gomelez. The address of both the Institut and its president was given as the Villa Munsalvaesche in the town of Zernez.

Dunphy asked the clerk, a sixtyish blonde with deep laugh lines around her eyes and teddy bear earrings, where Zernez was. She laughed.

"This is in Graubünden," she exclaimed, as if the canton

was somewhere off the coast of Fiji. "It is very remote, this town. I think, mostly, they are speaking Romansch—not German. Not Italian."

"But where is it?" Dunphy asked.

She rolled her eyes. "East. Below Austria. Past Saint-Moritz." She thought about it for a moment. "But, of course," she said, determined to clarify the matter, "this is where Heidi lives!"

It was impossible to fly into or anywhere near Zernez, so they rented a car at the Zürich airport and set off the next morning on their own. It was a two-hundred-mile drive, more or less, traversing Switzerland west to east, and they hoped to make it in seven or eight hours. In any event, they lost track of the time, because it was so beautiful. The road wound its way through one spectacular vista after another, clinging to the sides of mountains, then racing through valleys next to ivory-colored rivers foaming with glacial melt. Clearly, Dunphy thought, we're in paradise. The mountains were as green as Donegal and fizzing with wildflowers. There were no cities to distract them—just glaciers, lakes, and cowbells.

At Chur—with a population of thirty-three thousand, the Gotham of the Alps—they turned south to Zuoz, then followed a narrow little road through the Inn Valley to Zernez, arriving just as the sun was going down behind the mountains.

Zernez was a very small town, but a lively one that served as a staging area for hikers' forays into the nearby Swiss National Park. This was Switzerland's only federal wilderness, sixty-four square miles of coniferous forest inhabited only by herds of ibex, chamois, and red deer. Unlike American parks, the Parc Naziunal Svizzer was completely undeveloped, with the exception of a single restaurant and the hiking trails that were ubiquitous in Switzerland.

In Zernez itself, the grocery stores were thronged with Japanese tourists and hikers dressed in what Clem described as "Graubünden chic": climbing boots and woolen socks, shorts and work shirts. Expensive sunglasses, backpacks, and book bags completed the ensemble. The atmosphere was festive, and a little frenetic, as the shoppers rushed around in a desperate effort to buy what they wanted before the shops closed at six. Beer and bottled water, Landjäger, bread and cheese. The perfect walking stick, and stronger sun block.

Finding a room was harder than Dunphy had expected. The few hotels in town were full, but they got lucky off the main drag when they saw a traditional chalet with a sign in its window, advertising *Zimmer*. For fifty dollars they were given the key to a two-room apartment with a couple of single beds and a living room that featured a glass case crowded with knick-knacks, a nine-foot-long alpenhorn, and the largest cuckoo clock either of them had ever seen. Otherwise, the furniture was right out of an IKEA catalog.

They had dinner in a pine-and-stucco restaurant that specialized in raclette and cheese fondue. There were candles and flowers on the table, and the food was delicious. After they'd eaten, they went into the Stübli next door for a glass of wine and sat down at a table beside the fireplace.

It was an intimate bar, and Dunphy struck up a conversation with the waitress, kidding her about her traditional costume. Then he told her, "We're looking for a house, here in Zernez."

"A house?" she asked. "You mean, to rent?"

"No," Dunphy told her. "We're looking for a particular house."

"Oh? What is the address?" she asked.

Dunphy shrugged. "There isn't a number, or anything. All I have is the Villa Munsalvaesche. Do you know it?"

"No."

"A Mr. Gomelez lives there."

"He's Spanish?"

Dunphy shook his head. "French."

"I don't think he lives here," the waitress said. "Not in Zernez—or I would know. I was born here." At Dunphy's suggestion, she asked the bartender if he knew a man named Gomelez, or a house called Munsalvaesche. He shook his head and went next door to ask the maître d'—who was also the mayor. Two minutes later, he returned with a suggestion.

"Ask at the post office in the morning. They are sure to know."

And they did.

They went to the post office as soon as it opened, and inquired about Mr. Gomelez and the Villa Munsalvaesche. The clerk behind the counter knew immediately whom they meant.

"Yes, sure—Gomelez, he gets his mail here—since I'm a child. Magazines, mostly."

"Then you know him?" Dunphy asked.

The man shook his head. "No."

"But—"

"He has people who work for him. They come twice a week. Always the same car. You like cars?"

Dunphy shrugged. "Sure."

"Then you'll like this one. It's a classic. A Cabriolet C— like Hitler's."

"Do you know where his house is? The Villa—"

"Mun-sal-vaesche!" the clerk declared, laughing. Then he became serious. "I've never seen the place, but one of the rangers told me the park folds around it—so it's *in* the park, but not *of* the park, you know? A rich man's scheme . . ."

Dunphy nodded. "When do they pick up the mail?" he asked. "Maybe I could talk to them."

The clerk shrugged. "Tuesdays and Fridays."

"Today?"

The clerk nodded. "If you look for them this afternoon . . . maybe you'll see them."

There was a small café across the street, with tables and chairs on the terrace. They drank coffee and read the *Herald Tribune*, keeping one eye on the post office. The air was brisk and sharp, the sun strong, so that when a cloud passed overhead, the temperature seemed to drop about twenty degrees. At noon, they ordered sandwiches and beer, which came in towering pilsner glasses, ringed with frost. At one, Clem went for a walk, leaving Dunphy to work the crossword puzzle in the *Herald Tribune*. If the Mercedes showed up, he said, he'd dash for their rental car and hit the horn—a very un-Swiss thing to do, but she'd hear it. Only, it didn't show up.

Clem returned to the table about half an hour later, bringing a topo map of the park. They spread it out on the table between them and looked for an opening where Gomelez might have his villa, but there was nothing to be seen.

Then, when the post office was just about to close, Dunphy noticed heads turning in the street, and shot straight up to see an antique Mercedes-Benz driven by a dark-haired man in a black suit and string tie. Grabbing Clem by the wrist, he threw a one-hundred-franc note on the table and ran to the car that they'd rented. It was a block away, and by the time they got back, the Mercedes was already on its way out of town, heading east.

They followed at a discreet distance, the map in Clementine's lap. "There aren't any roads into the park," she said, "just equestrian trails and paths for hiking. So I don't know where he thinks *he's* going." A gray and fast-moving river ran beside the road, its waters roaring with gravel.

They were in a deep glacial valley now, with the sun behind them, and the day's shadows getting longer. The river began to twist and turn, and so did the road, mirroring the water's path. A hundred yards ahead, the Mercedes entered a hairpin turn, and Dunphy touched the brakes. Then he followed the other car's path through the turn, pulling out of it onto a straightaway. A sign on the shoulder announced IL FUORN 8 KM.

He began to accelerate.

"Where's the Mercedes?" Clem asked.

Dunphy blinked. There was nothing and no one ahead of them. Applying the brakes, he pulled off the road and shut off the engine. "Where did he go?" he asked. It was as if they'd been following a hallucination.

Clem turned around in her seat and craned her neck. After

a moment, she said, "Look," and pointed back the way they'd
come. A gently arched stone bridge, no wider than a car and
of uncertain strength, spanned the river just behind the point
at which the road came out of the last turn. The bridge was behind a low hill on the passenger's side of the car, and coming,
as they were, from the north, it couldn't have been seen until
they'd passed it—and then in the rearview mirror. To reach
the bridge, the Mercedes's driver would have had to have
pulled off the road and backed up. Which, undoubtedly, is
what he'd done.

Dunphy squinted. Next to the bridge was a small sign:
PRIVÉ.

"It isn't on the map," Clem said, pointing to where the
bridge should have been. "Everything else is. Fire towers,
hiking trails, picnic tables, resting places, ranger huts . . . And
bridges. Lots of bridges. But not this one."

"And not that road," Dunphy said, pointing to a dirt track
that began on the other side of the bridge and disappeared
into the forest. "Wait here," he said, opening the car door. "I'll
be back—"

She was already out the other side and putting on her coat.
"I'm not waiting anywhere," she told him. "Certainly not by
the side of the road. Not this road."

They crossed the bridge together, hand in hand. Knowing
he had the Glock made Dunphy more confident, perhaps,
than the situation merited—but there was nothing obvious to
be afraid of. And the road actually improved as it went deeper
and deeper into the forest. After a kilometer or so, the rough
surface turned to gravel and, a little farther on, to asphalt.
Walking faster now, they saw a light flickering in the distance
and headed for it.

This turned out to be a gas lamp that hung from a post in
front of a towering set of wrought-iron gates. Flung open, the
gates were at least twenty feet tall and spanned the road from
one side to the other. Dunphy squinted at the ironwork, which
was covered in moss and lichens.

VILLA MUNSALVAESCHE
1483

Dunphy looked at Clem, whose almond-shaped eyes were round as billiard balls. "You wanta?" he whispered. She nodded, and together they stepped through the gateway. It was dark now and very difficult to see, but there were lights up ahead, glittering in the trees. They made their way along the road for almost half a mile until, quite suddenly, they found themselves standing upon a broad expanse of lawn.

In the distance, the castlelike Villa Munsalvaesche could be seen, riding the swell of a hill. A sprinkling of stars overhead, and—

"Look," Clem said, tugging Dunphy by the sleeve.

An old man sat in a wheelchair, silhouetted against a black pond that glowed in the moonlight. There was a blanket over his knees, and he was feeding crusts of bread to swans. Though they couldn't see his face, a mane of white hair hung down to his shoulders.

"It's Gomelez," Dunphy guessed, and took a step toward him—only to freeze at the sound of a low and very authoritative growl. Turning slowly, Dunphy and Clem found themselves face to muzzle with a brace of Rhodesian Ridgebacks. Blond and muscular, the shortest of the two dogs was as tall as Dunphy's waist—and without knowing how he knew it, Dunphy realized that the dogs had been following them ever since they'd stepped through the gates.

The old man tossed a handful of bread crumbs at the swans and, without turning, said, "Welcome to the Villa Munsalvaesche, Mr. Dunphy. 'You can check out any time you like, but you'll find it hard to leave.' "

29

"You're an Eagles fan?" Dunphy asked.

"Just the one song," Gomelez replied, spraying an orchid with a crystal mister. "It makes a lot of sense to me."

They were standing with Clem in the Villa's conservatory, repotting and fertilizing the old man's Dendrobium orchids. The flowers had a raspberry-citrus fragrance that was subtle and seductive. Gomelez said that he had been growing them for nearly fifty years.

"I got into it after the war," he explained. "One of my hobbies. I have lots of hobbies."

Among them, it seemed, was the study of languages, of which he professed (half-jokingly, Dunphy thought) to speak every one. Obviously, this was an exaggeration, but how much of one neither Dunphy nor Clem was in a position to say.

One of the largest rooms in the Villa was the wood-paneled library, a vaulted great room filled floor to ceiling with books, most of which could be reached only with the help of sliding ladders. Most of the books appeared to have been written in one or another of the European languages, but there were whole sections of the library devoted to more arcane scripts at whose identity Dunphy could only guess: Hebrew, Chinese, Japanese, Sanskrit, Urdu, Hindi, Arabic, and . . . Euzkadi?

It was possible, Dunphy thought, that Gomelez was more of a bibliophile than a linguist—but he didn't think so. He had seen the old man's mail, and it consisted almost entirely of subscriptions to scientific and medical journals in the native languages of countries as far apart as Denmark and Indonesia.

By any standard, though, the library was a magnificent room. About thirty meters long, it accommodated displays as well as books. There were antique telescopes and ancient astrolabes, chronometers and violins. Etruscan coins and terracotta pottery vied for space with a Honus Wagner baseball card and a collection of Byzantine and Roman oil lamps.

But it wasn't the library that seemed to delight Gomelez the most. It was a small workshop reached through an alcove between two standing shelves of books on Japan and Judaica. In the room was a medium-sized desk that supported an array of electronics equipment. On the wall behind the desk was a poster with the words, *La vérité est dehors là!*

Gomelez watched with a look of bemused curiosity as Dunphy and Clem took a closer look at the equipment on the desk. Two machines were hooked in tandem to a printer, which even as they watched generated a continuous paper feed on which a penlike instrument described a wave of spikes and oscillations. "What is it?" Dunphy asked, squinting at the lighted dials and knobs.

"It's a spectrum analyzer," Gomelez told him, "hooked up to a digital-to-analog converter. And the printer, of course."

"But what's it *for*?" Clem wondered.

"Well," the old man replied, "what it's actually *doing*— what it's doing right *now*—is examining radio signals from space, paying particular attention to frequencies in the 'water hole' between hydrogen and hydroxyl."

"Oh," Clem said. And after a moment, added, "Why is it doing *that*?"

"Well," Gomelez said with a chuckle, "it's doing *that* because I'm part of an amateur effort to help professional astronomers look for signs of intelligent life in deep space."

"You mean—"

"There's a radio telescope on the roof. It's small, but it works."

"This interests you?" Dunphy asked.

Gomelez shrugged. "Not really."

Dunphy started to ask another question. "Then why—"

Gomelez put a finger to his lips. "You'll understand later."

Dunphy hated to stay in other people's houses (even when they were palaces). He was a hotel guy all the way. But Gomelez had the answers he needed and, although Dunphy pressed his questions (Did you know Dulles and Jung? What was the Society after?), the old man had his own timetable for revelation, and it was clear that he would not be hurried. So Dunphy was patient. As patient as he could be.

After a week in the Villa Munsalvaesche, they'd come to know Gomelez rather well. The old man—and he *was* an old man, having just celebrated his ninety-second birthday the week before—was the perfect, gentle host, attentive to his guests' every need, intelligent and good-natured. He had a way about him, a mixture of gravity and sweetness, that made Dunphy wish that his father had been more like him. As for Clem, she was head-over-heels for the guy, spending each morning with him in the conservatory, then wheeling him outside to feed the swans in the late afternoon.

Not that Gomelez lived alone. There were a dozen people on staff at the Villa—some on the outside, some in. These included two gardeners and a chauffeur, a nurse and four housekeepers, a secretary who doubled as a valet, two cooks and some seldom-seen security guards who patrolled the estate's perimeter, riding golf carts.

"I can't talk to any of them," Gomelez said. "They're idiots."

Dunphy scoffed. "They're worse than idiots," he said. "They're slackers. I don't know where they were the other night, but they weren't watching the gate. We *walked* in—on the road—in the moonlight. We could have been the Russian army."

"Well, of course you did," Gomelez exclaimed. "That was the idea."

"What do you mean?" Clem asked.

"They wanted you here. In fact, we both did."

"But why?"

"Because they couldn't find you. It seems you kept finding *them*—first in London, then in Zug. And then, again, in Paris. So I think your friend, Matta, had a brainstorm. And they decided to let the mountain come to Muhammed."

"So we're trapped," Dunphy said.

Gomelez shrugged. "There's never been any violence in the Villa, Mr. Dunphy. There never will be."

"And if . . . I mean, *when*—we try to leave?" Dunphy asked.

"They'll kill you as soon as you step off the grounds."

Dunphy thought about it. "Before . . . you said, 'They wanted you here. In fact, we *both* did.' What did you mean?"

"Ah," Gomelez said. "Now you've hit upon the question. What I meant was that I'm as much a prisoner as you are. And, while I can walk, I can't walk far. I'm old, and the motorized wheelchair is a great convenience. So, as you can imagine, it would be very hard for me to leave on my own. . . . "

Dunphy saw immediately what he was saying. "But you've given some thought to *how*. . . . "

Gomelez nodded. "I haven't thought of anything else—not since I was a child of fifty." Then he sized Dunphy up from head to foot. "How strong is your back?" he asked.

Dunphy shrugged. "Pretty strong, I guess. Why?"

"Just wondering." And, with that, the old man did a sort of wheelie in his chair and beckoned for them to follow. "Let me show you something," he said, and pressing a button on the wheelchair's arm, shot forward.

They passed through the library to the great hall, where a turn-of-the-century elevator awaited them. Dunphy saw that the wrought-iron doors had been forged into a scene recreating the fall of Lucifer and his angels. Dunphy held the doors open for Gomelez and Clem, then stepped inside himself. The doors rattled closed as Gomelez inserted a key in the control panel. Slowly, the elevator began its descent.

After what seemed a very long time, they arrived in the

Villa's subbasement, where the scene took Dunphy by surprise. He had expected a wine cellar, or perhaps a block of dungeons, but found instead a sleek corridor outside a suite of ultramodern offices. Telephones rang. Keyboards clicked. Copiers hummed. Men and women in dark suits went about their business with only the most furtive glances at Gomelez.

"It's like they're afraid to look at you," Clem told him.

Gomelez shrugged. "They think I'm God," he said. "It makes for a complicated relationship." Then he wheeled a little way down the corridor, stopped, and nodded at a wall of glass. "Look."

Inside the dimly lighted room, men in dark suits sat before a bank of green-glowing monitors, manipulating toggle switches on a brushed-aluminum control panel. On the wall beside them was a map of the surrounding forest, crisscrossed by fiber-optic threads.

"What are the blue lights?" Clem asked.

"Trails through the park," Gomelez replied.

"And the red one?" Dunphy asked.

"That's the perimeter of the Villa's grounds. It's constantly monitored by cameras."

"Even at night?" Clem asked.

Gomelez nodded. "They've synchronized image intensifiers with thermal-imaging equipment," he explained. "So they have the best of both worlds. Light from above, light from within."

Clem frowned, not understanding.

"Starlight and body heat," Dunphy muttered.

"That's another way of putting it," Gomelez agreed.

"How come you know so much about this stuff?" Dunphy asked.

"I've had a lot of time on my hands," Gomelez replied. "In fact, I've had my whole life on my hands."

Rolling a little farther down the corridor, Gomelez gestured over his shoulder for the two of them to follow. After he'd gone about twenty feet, he stopped outside a darkened room whose corridor wall was mostly glass. The glass wall reminded Clem of a hospital's nursery, and looking through it, she almost expected to see a row of incubators. Instead, there was a single man seated in front of a computer monitor, reading a book. On the monitor, a cartoon character walked in a circle with a beatific smile on his face.

"Who's that supposed to be?" Dunphy asked. "Mr. Natural?"

Gomelez shook his head. "No," he said. "That's me." Then he rapped on the window, and the man in the chair looked up. Gomelez waved and smiled. The man dropped his head in a deferential nod, then returned to his book.

"I don't get it," Dunphy said. "What's the point?"

Gomelez reached down and lifted the cuff of his right pants leg. "This is the point." A black strap encircled the old man's ankle. Attached to the strap was a small plastic box.

Clem peered at it. "What's that?"

Dunphy shook his head in disbelief. "It's a monitoring bracelet."

"Very good!" Gomelez remarked.

"It sends out a weak radio signal," Dunphy told her. "The signal's picked up by a transponder, somewhere on the grounds. The transponder rebroadcasts it to the receiving station. Am I right?"

Gomelez nodded, obviously impressed. "Absolutely."

"So long as he stays in range of the transponder—which is what that guy's monitoring—everything's jake. But once he moves out of range . . . " He turned to Gomelez. "How far can you go?"

"About a hundred meters from the house—around the pond, if I like."

"But why don't you just take it off?" Clem asked.

"Because I'd have to cut it off," Gomelez said, "and then I'd break the circuit. No circuit, no signal. No signal—big trouble." Suddenly he smiled. "C'mon," he said, "I'll show you something else."

Steering his wheelchair farther down the corridor, Gomelez

came to a stop, then opened the door to another room and flicked on the lights. Dunphy and Clem peered in.

The room appeared to be a state-of-the-art surgical suite, replete with X-ray and other diagnostic equipment, and a recovery bay with life-support machines. Gomelez snapped off the light and shivered. "I wanted you to see that," he said.

That night, they dined off TV trays in the armory and watched a *Seinfeld* rerun under the protective gaze of the old man's Rhodesian Ridgebacks, Emina and Zubeida. The dogs followed Gomelez wherever he went, padding silently behind him, in and out of the house. Occasionally, he'd reach out blindly from his wheelchair, and one of the dogs would lope up to him, cocking an ear to be scratched.

When the show was over, Gomelez led them to a little study overlooking the lake. There was a fire in the fireplace and, above it, a painting so powerful it took their breath away. Clementine read the brass plaque affixed to the gold frame:

DE MOLAY AT THE STAKE
TITIAN (1576?)

"I don't know this picture," she said. "Which is strange, because I took a first in art history."

Gomelez shrugged and poured each of them a glass of Calvados. "That's because it's only a rumor," he said. "It's never been photographed, never loaned."

"You mean—"

"I mean it has always been here."

They were quiet for a moment, and then Dunphy said, "Unlike yourself."

Gomelez gave him a quizzical look.

"We visited the museum on the Rue de Mogador," Clem explained.

Gomelez closed his eyes and nodded thoughtfully.

"What happened?" Dunphy asked.

"Happened?" the old man replied.

"To you. When the Germans came . . ."

Gomelez shook his head ruefully. "Everything that happened, happened *before* the Germans came."

Clem settled herself in the seat by his side. "What do you mean?" she asked.

Gomelez stared into the fire and began talking. "When I was a boy in Paris, I was taken by my father to meet with a group of men who, I was told, were powerful in the worlds of business, politics, and the arts. At that meeting, it was explained to me that my family was 'different'—*I* was different—and that we had special responsibilities. I was told that I would one day learn more of this, as indeed I have, but that they were there to swear allegiance to my cause."

Gomelez took a sip of Calvados.

"My cause? You can appreciate my reaction. I was ten!" he exclaimed. "What 'cause' was this? I asked my father. And he explained the cause was *me*. And why? I asked. Because while their veins ran with blood, salvation ran through mine. They said I was a prince who must become a king—or if not me, then my son. And if not him, then his." Gomelez shook his head. "You can imagine how I felt. I was a child. And so, of course, what they had to say was less than a surprise. Like any child, I had always known—or, at least, suspected—that I was in some sense a magical being. And truth to tell, it seemed both natural and right that I should be the center of a secret universe, a dark sun orbited by swarms of faithful followers. And yet, as I grew older, I came to understand that there was a price to be paid for this, and that price was a terrible one: my life was not mine to live. It was simply to be waited out."

Gomelez scratched Zubeida behind the ear and poured a second Calvados for himself. Dunphy grabbed an andiron and stirred the fire.

"So I left—in '36. I went out the door for a pack of cigarettes—and kept going, looking for adventure, good friends, a just war—whatever. I was 'political' then—everyone was political in the thirties. So it didn't take me long to find the headquarters of the Franco-Belgian Commune de Paris. Two days later, I was on a train to Albacete and the Spanish Civil War. A week after that, I was lying in a field hospital, gut-shot with shrapnel."

Dunphy blinked. "When was this?"

"November 4, 1936."

"So that's what he meant," Dunphy said.

"Who?"

"Allen Dulles. In a letter to Jung. He said there had been a catastrophe. I guess that was it."

Gomelez nodded. "*Catastrophe* is the right word. My father's friends found me, and I was taken back to Paris. But the damage was done. Because of my wounds, I could never father a child—at least not directly. And the horror of this was that, as the end of the line, I became all the more precious to those whose cause I had become. The result was . . . this entombment."

Neither Dunphy nor Clem knew quite what to say.

"And, strangely enough, this injury seemed to galvanize my father's friends who saw in it the fulfillment of a prophecy."

" 'His kingdom comes and goes,' " Dunphy recited, " 'then comes again . . . ' " He couldn't remember the rest, but Gomelez knew it as well as his own hand.

" 'Then comes again when, wounded to the root, he is the last, yet not the last, emblazoned and alone. These many lands will then be one and he their king till, past, he sires sons down all the days, while deathly still and celibate.' You know the *Apocryphon*?"

Dunphy nodded. "I've seen it. But it seems to me it missed the boat with that last bit."

"What do you mean?"

"The part about having kids and being celibate. How are you supposed to pull that off?"

Gomelez frowned. "That's the easy part," he said.

"How so?"

"I gave a sperm sample to the Eugenics Institute in Küsnacht.

That was sixty years ago. It's been cryogenically preserved ever since."

"You're *sure*?"

Gomelez smiled. "Trust me. They never throw anything away."

"Then why do they need you? The Society, I mean. Why can't they just—"

"The prophecy is explicit. The kingdom can only be restored to a lineal descendant who's wounded and emblazoned."

"Emblazoned?" Clem asked.

Gomelez shifted in his chair. "I have a birthmark on my chest," he explained. "But that's not all. The restoration must take place in the lifetime of the one who is the last—"

"—'yet not the last,'" Dunphy added.

"Exactly," Gomelez said. "In light of which, you can imagine their enthusiasm for my candidature."

Dunphy smiled despite himself.

"What worries me," Gomelez went on, "is that I'll live forever. Don't laugh! You've seen the hospital. It's fully staffed. They can keep me breathing until the end of time. And they intend to." Gomelez paused and looked up. "Which brings us to the mystery of your coming here. Why *did* you?"

Dunphy glanced at Clem and shrugged. "There was nowhere else to go. I'd come from Langley. We'd been to Zug. And I got the feeling they'd follow us wherever we went. So I thought I'd go to the source."

Gomelez nodded. "And did it occur to you that you might have to kill me?"

Dunphy shifted uncomfortably in his seat, as Clem protested. "It crossed my mind," Dunphy said.

Gomelez smiled. "Well, in that case, I have a proposition for you."

Once again, Dunphy and Clem exchanged glances. "Look, Bernard—I'm not Dr. Kevorkian," Dunphy said. "And, anyway, you don't look that bad."

Gomelez laughed. "That isn't what I mean," he said.

"Though, if I said to you that I was tired of London, would you understand?"

Clem nodded. "It means you're tired of life."

Gomelez agreed. "Though, actually, I've never really been to London." He paused and thought about that. "Even so, I *would* like to let nature take its course. So, what I'm suggesting is simply this: if I show you a way out, will you take me with you?"

"Of course," Clem said.

"But what good will it do?" Dunphy asked. "They'll find us eventually, and then what?"

Gomelez shook his head. "You'll be safe when I'm dead," he said. "When I'm gone, this comes to an end."

"This?" Dunphy asked.

"The Society," Gomelez explained. "I'm its only raison d'être."

Dunphy thought about it. "I see what you mean," he said, "but—don't get me wrong—I don't mean to be insensitive, but, uhhh . . . that could take a while."

"Jack!"

Gomelez laughed. "No," he said, "once we leave here, I won't have long. I think you know, I suffer from anemia. Without the B12 shots . . . "

"And in the meantime?" Dunphy asked. "Where would we go? They'll look for us in every country on earth."

"Oh, of course, they will," Gomelez told him. "But that's exactly where we *won't* be."

"What?!"

"I said we won't *be* in any country on earth."

It was two in the morning when the old man came into their bedroom, trailed by the dogs. "It's time to leave," he whispered.

Together, they went into the hall and down the spiral staircase to the library. Turning left at Judaica, they entered the little room where Gomelez was monitoring signals from outer space. Flicking on a light, he rolled up to the desk and switched the printer off. Then he flicked a couple of toggle switches and slowly turned a series of dials on the spectrum analyzer. In front of him, an oscilloscope's green light began to tremble and spike.

"What are you looking for?" Dunphy asked.

"The bracelet's frequency and amplitude," he said. "I think it's around eight hundred fifty kilohertz, but they change it every so often, and it would be—well, it would be murder if I got it wrong."

Dunphy and Clem watched as the old man tuned through the spectrum. Every so often, the oscilloscope would spike and Dunphy would think, That's it! But it wasn't.

"There's a pirate radio station in Zuoz," Gomelez said, "and the rangers have radios, as well. There's a couple of hams in the area, and some military sources—There! That's it! Got it." Removing a small notebook from the top desk drawer, he checked the frequency against the digital readout on the machine. "It's the same as it was last week," he said, reaching into the bottom drawer of the desk.

When his hand returned into view, it held a cigar box. Inside the box was an object wrapped in tissue. Gomelez removed the tissue.

"What is it?" Clem asked.

"A transmitter," Dunphy told her. "I think he's going to try to duplicate the signal on the monitoring device. Then he'll substitute it for the one he's wearing—so it will look like he's here when he's gone."

"Excellent," Gomelez remarked, "only I've already done the work. The hard part wasn't so much identifying the carrier, but demodulating it. There's an encoded signal built into it—"

"Which is why you needed the converter," Dunphy said.

"Right," Gomelez said.

"So this whole thing of yours with the telescope—"

"—was an excuse to buy a spectrum analyzer," Gomelez replied. Then he attached a pair of batteries to the little transmitter on his desk. "They last about six or seven hours," he said. "By then, we'll be to hell and gone."

Dunphy and Clem looked at him.

"Joke," he said, connecting the transmitter to the batteries. Then he took a pair of scissors from the top drawer and, reaching down, cut the bracelet in half and let it fall to the floor.

Gomelez showed them an underground passage that was reached through a false door on the ground floor of a turret in the Villa's west wing. The passage took them down to the sub-basement, where a four-person subway car waited on a set of narrow-gauge tracks. At the old man's direction, they ignored the car and followed the tracks into a dimly lighted tunnel.

"Know anything about subterranean military architecture?" Gomelez asked.

Dunphy shook his head. "Another hobby?"

"The Swiss are crazy about it," Gomelez explained, slowing his wheelchair so that Dunphy and Clem could more easily keep up. "The entire country is honeycombed with secret installations. Whole mountains have been hollowed out to accommodate tanks, missiles, and fighter planes. This particular tunnel was built by the Air Force. If there is ever an invasion, the Villa Munsalvaesche will be the emergency headquarters of the Swiss general staff."

"And where does it lead?" Dunphy asked.

Gomelez shrugged. "There's a chalet in Il Fuorn. At least, it looks like a chalet. The tunnel comes out there."

Dunphy winced. "They'll be waiting for us," he said. "They wouldn't leave something like that unguarded."

"Of course they wouldn't," Gomelez replied. "But we're not going there, so it doesn't matter."

They continued walking for another twenty minutes until Gomelez put the brakes on his wheelchair. "There," he said, pointing to an iron ladder that climbed the smooth concrete walls to an air shaft. "If you'll carry me," he said, "we can get out that way. They don't watch the air shafts—there are too many of them, and there has never been a problem, in any case."

Hoisting Gomelez onto his back, Dunphy began to mount the ladder, one rung at a time. Behind him, he could hear Clem muttering under her breath. "What's the matter?" he whispered.

"Heights," she gasped. "Not good at them."

And, indeed, the air shaft was much longer than Dunphy would have expected. He asked Gomelez about it. "How far did you say it was to the top?"

"Thirty feet," he answered. And then, in a lower voice, added, "Maybe it was meters."

Right the second time.

When they reached the top, Dunphy was trembling with muscle fatigue and fearful that the grill would prove impossible to move. But there was no need to worry about the grill. As he soon discovered, it had been made with typical Swiss efficiency. Three compression locks were all that held it in place, and they were easily opened with the thumbs alone. Pushing the grill aside, he rolled, exhausted, out of the hole. Clem emerged a minute later, white as paper.

Dunphy looked around. It was three in the morning, and pitch-black.

"Where are we?" Dunphy asked.

"Next to a trail," Gomelez told him. "We can follow it out to the road, and perhaps find a ride. Otherwise, Il Fuorn is only a few miles from here. You could get a car there, and come back for me."

And so they walked out, with Dunphy carrying Gomelez the last two hundred yards. When they finally reached the road, the sun was up behind the mountains, lightening the darkness without actually dispelling it. Dunphy stood beside the road with his briefcase in one hand and his thumb out in the other, soliciting rides from the handful of cars and trucks that passed at this hour. He was cold and tired and worried that one of the people who worked at the Villa would pass that way and recognize him—in which case there would be a lot of shooting. Finally, Clem told him to sit down with Gomelez, whose back was up against a tree. "Let me try," she suggested, and cocking her hip, stuck out her thumb.

A minute later, a truck slammed on its air-brakes and came to a halt about fifty yards away. The driver was visibly disappointed to learn that Clem was one of three, but one hundred francs from Dunphy took the edge off.

"Benvenuto al bordo!" the driver exclaimed, and putting the truck into gear, lurched off in the general direction of Italy. Dunphy's worry that Gomelez might not be able to cross the border proved unfounded. The fact that he was ninety-two years old, and that his passport had expired fifty-seven years earlier, was a source of concern to the lone border guard at Glorenza, but that concern quickly turned to amusement when Dunphy helped him to a hundred-franc note. Moments later, they were on their way to Bolzano.

In Bolzano, they bought a couple of suitcases and some clothes, then took the first train they could get to Trieste. Seated in the first-class sleeping compartment that he shared with Gomelez and Clem, Dunphy wondered aloud what the Magdalene Society was *"really* after."

Gomelez gazed out the window at what seemed like an endless field of sunflowers. "They've changed," he said. "There was a time when its goals were . . ."

"Noble?" Clem suggested.

Gomelez nodded. "I think so, yes. They opposed the Inquisition. They fought the Terror. But, something happened, and what had begun as a religious struggle became a struggle for power. Which isn't surprising. The assets of the Magdalene Society are enormous."

"What I don't understand," Clem said, "is how they hoped to establish a monarchy. I mean, a *monarchy*? They're a bit passé, aren't they?"

Gomelez chuckled ruefully and shook his head. "I'm not sure they are, really, or ever will be. It's a powerful attraction. Look at what happened when Diana died. Europe lurched. So I don't think it would have been so very difficult—far less difficult, in fact, than uniting Europe in the first place. On the few occasions when I spoke to them about it, they took the position that it was, or would be, just another electoral campaign. Advertisements would be launched, lobbyists retained, and testimonials secured. And, in the end, a referendum would be held in every country of the European Union. It's a Christian continent for the most part, and the monarchy was supposed to be symbolic—a 'constitutional monarchy' that would serve as a rallying point for the EU."

"And you think they'd have succeeded?" Clem asked.

Gomelez shrugged. "Their assets are tremendous, and they'd have used them all—including those they used to make the prophecies come true."

"But what's their agenda?" Dunphy asked. "What do they really want?"

Gomelez looked at him. "They imagine the millennium arriving when the prophecies are met. Most of them haven't given a thought to the day after—just as no one ever really asks what they'll do once they get to Heaven. They'll be there. And that will be enough. But in the absence of the Rapture, or some such event, I think the Magdalene Society would turn Europe into a theocratic state—a pilgrimized version of Khomeini land, if you see what I mean. I think the Society would then take it upon itself to expand its authority to include all of the Americas, and that it would then act to purge the Merovingian dominion of sinners. In fact, I've heard them discuss it. They call it the Cauterization. No one would be spared."

The train reached Trieste an hour later. And it was there, in a seaside hotel, that Dunphy learned what Gomelez had meant when he told them they would not be in any country on earth.

The *Stencil* was a forty-five-foot wooden ketch whose red sails were questionable and whose hull badly needed paint. It was Chilean-built in the late '70s, with cabins fore and aft, and boasted an elegant salon trimmed in mahogany and teak. While its deficits were many, its advantages were two: it was wood, and it was for sale. They bought her for £60,000, cash, with Clem grumping that fiberglass would have been more practical. But Gomelez wouldn't have that: he insisted on wood.

They sailed the same night on a broad reach into the Gulf of Venice, then came about at the end of the Istrian Peninsula. Turning to the southeast, they headed for the Dalmatian coast, where there were hundreds of islands and thousands of inlets that would hide them.

There was no doubt in Dunphy's mind that the Agency would find them. The border guard at Glorenza would be questioned, and word would get around about the old guy in Trieste, and the young couple who were with him, who'd paid all that cash for the *Stencil*. And then they'd look for them, tasking the overhead spy satellites for saturation coverage of the Adriatic.

Which meant that most of their sailing was done by night, with layovers in crowded marinas and sheltered bays. And in the course of this, something strange began to happen.

Gomelez found happiness.

For what may have been the first time in his life, the old man experienced joy, the pure joy that a dog feels running free. "The last time I felt this way," he told Clem, "was in '36—and then they blew me up!"

With Clem as captain, they sailed a zigzag route past hundreds of islands with strange-sounding names: Krk, Pag, Vis, and Brač. In a fishing village on the island of Hvar, they painted the hull black, but Dunphy knew that wouldn't be enough. The ship's silhouette and rigging were distinctive, and so were its sails. It was just a matter of time before someone in the Washington Navy Yard found the boat in a satellite photograph. Dunphy could see it: a nerdy image analyst who'd been told the Agency was looking for a terrorist, sitting behind a Fresnel screen at a long table in a warehouse with blacked-out windows, staring at pictures. And then: a photo of the Split marina, its waters carpeted with sailboats, and there—in the lower right-hand corner—a ketch whose red mainsail, while reefed, runs like a capillary down the boat's centerline. Bingo! An intelligence medal for the analyst, black helicopters for Dunphy and his friends.

But there was nothing to be done about it. They were as safe at sea as anywhere else, and probably safer. The only other thing they might do was split up, and Dunphy wasn't about to suggest that. Gomelez needed them, and Clem wouldn't have heard of it.

By now, she loved him like a father. And it was hard not to feel that way about him. He had a sly sense of humor and, for a man whose life had been a prison, an astonishing repertoire of stories. Night after night, as the *Stencil* slid across the waves, Gomelez kept them spellbound with a narrative that tacked through his life as if every person and event had brought with them a change in the wind.

They might have gone on this way for quite a while. Dunphy was even becoming a decent sailor. But soon, the old man's anemia began to bring him down. Clem repeatedly urged him to let them put in to shore, so that she could get him the B12 injections he so badly needed.

Gomelez shook off the idea. "I'll admit, I was just beginning to get interested in London again—thanks to you, my dear. But that's a very subversive development. And it's not why we're here."

Dunphy disputed this with the old man as he helped him down to his cabin. "You can't be the last of them," he said. "A line like that—there must be dozens of people who can claim Merovingian descent. Even if it *is* far removed, they're still—"

Gomelez shook his head. "There's only one line that matters," he said, taking off his shirt in preparation for bed. "And it's by this sign that you'll know it." Slowly, he turned toward Dunphy, so that the younger man could see the mark upon his chest—a red splash about the size of a hand, in the shape of a Maltese cross. "My birthmark," Gomelez explained. "All of us have had it, going back . . . forever. So you see, it's not just a question of paperwork. And that brings me to something else, Jack. When I go, there's something I want you to do for me. Something I *need* you to do."

In the days that followed, Gomelez became progressively weaker, and as he did, the weather turned. A damp and unseasonable cold settled upon the coast. The sky grew overcast. And it began to rain.

Dunphy welcomed the change. Cloudy skies would neutralize overhead surveillance and give them a chance to slip farther down the coast. Despite the forecasts, then, it was agreed that they should head out to sea as soon as night fell. And so they did, running parallel to the mountainous coast on a broad reach.

The *Stencil* was moving faster than it ever had, heeling well to port, with the wind filling its sails from the west. Dunphy was at the tiller, holding a course for Dubrovnik, while Gomelez remained below, sleeping. Clem moved about the deck, with the confidence of one who'd grown up on boats, adjusting the rigging.

The seas were high, but not so high as to seem dangerous. A bigger worry was the lack of visibility brought on by the darkness and the rain. While there were no rocks or spindles in their path, they knew they weren't the only ship at sea, and a collision could be disastrous.

So they kept a close watch on the shifting darkness, screwing up their eyes to slits, blinking furiously against the rain. There was lightning, now, and more lightning, conjuring images that burned on the backs of their eyes, long after the light had gone. Again and again, the tumbling coast of Dalmatia flashed in front of them until, quite suddenly, Clem's voice rang out and Dunphy saw her pointing dead ahead.

He squeezed up his eyes against the rain, but there was nothing to be seen—until a thread of lightning tore a hole in the sky and left it sizzling. It was then, with the ozone all around him, that he saw it—a pitch-black squall coming at them like a bowling ball the size of Manhattan. There was nothing to do but keep the bow of the boat heading into the wind, and Dunphy did this as well as he could. But the squall was pregnant with a wave that had no business in the Adriatic. Seeing it approach, growing taller and darker against the night, watching it assume a mortal inevitability, Dunphy shouted to Clem to tie herself off—but it was too late. The sea lifted them in its arms, dragging them out of the trough of the wave, pulling them higher and higher until, it seemed, they were higher than any wave could possibly be. And for a long moment, they balanced there, with the *Stencil*'s bowsprit pointing toward heaven like a lance. Then the wave rolled out from beneath them, and the little boat fell back into the sea and pitchpoled.

It seemed as if everything had happened in a single second. One moment, Dunphy had been straining to see what lay ahead, then he was soaring toward heaven—then he was cast back down to drown. The water was so cold it ripped the air out of his lungs, and then he was under it, drowning in the darkness, his legs hopelessly tangled in the rigging. He swung his arms this way and that, as much to find Clem as to free himself, but there was no up, no down—and no way out. He was drowning. He was dying.

And then, as suddenly as it had pitchpoled, the *Stencil* righted itself, so that its hull was once again in the water. In an instant, Gomelez came staggering out of the cabin, coughing, growling, the blazon on his chest bared to the wind. Rushing to Dunphy's side, he dragged the younger man on board and helped to free him from the ruined rigging.

"Where's Clementine?" Gomelez shouted.

Dunphy scrambled to his feet and looked wildly around. The air and the sea were at war with each other, and the boat's mast was in splinters, the mainsail hanging overboard. Dunphy took this in at a glance as he rushed from one side of the boat to the other, searching the water desperately for his Clementine. But there was nothing, and no one. Just the night and the angry air, and the limitless Adriatic. She was gone.

And then he saw her, maybe twenty yards away, facedown in the water, rising and falling on the swells. He didn't think about it. He didn't even kick off his shoes. He just threw himself into the water and began windmilling through the waves as if they were enemy soldiers who stood between him and the woman he loved.

The boat was in irons now, heading up into the wind, halyards clattering against the deck, slashing the air, but the boat was going nowhere. Even so, the seas were so bad it took Dunphy almost five minutes to get to her and bring her back.

And by then she wasn't breathing. Gomelez dragged her aboard, and Dunphy clambered onto the deck. At a glance, Dunphy saw that she'd been struck on the head, by the boom or the bow, and that she was bleeding. But there was nothing to be done about that.

Dropping to her side, he brushed the blood away with his hand and tried to remember how the drowned might be brought back to life. Laying her on her back, he lifted her chin and pushed back on her forehead in an effort to clear the airway through her throat. Then he pinched her nostrils closed with his fingers and, putting his mouth over hers to form a seal, delivered two slow breaths. He could feel her chest rise, and fall back. But there was no other movement. And then it seemed her heart was still.

So he tried again, and again, alternating rescue breathing with CPR, compressing her chest with the palms of his hands, pumping rhythmically, desperately trying to kick-start her heart. And breathing for her, too, until twenty minutes had passed and Dunphy, exhausted, rolled away, unable to do any more.

She was gone. And with her, the fulcrum of his world.

"Let me try," Gomelez said, and sinking to the deck on his old man's knees, he lowered his face to hers and exhaled, then drew back . . . and again, and again, his long hair mingling with hers and fanning out over her cheeks.

Dunphy was sitting, stunned with despair, on the smashed cabin top when he heard her cough, and cough again. And then her voice, bewildered, asking, "What happened? Where was I?"

* * *

In the morning, Gomelez was gone. His frail body lay in the bunk with his eyes closed, as if he were asleep. But there was no breath left in him. With tears streaming down her cheeks, Clementine drew the sheet over the old Merovingian's face.

It was a moment that all of them had known would come, and they were prepared for it. That the boat was a wreck did not matter.

They sat for hours in the open sea, a hundred yards offshore, flaunting the *Stencil*'s position during the very time that satellite surveillance was likely to be the most intensive. Then they put in to a nearby cove, and while Clem gathered pine boughs from the shore, Dunphy laid Gomelez out upon the deck and carried out the promise that he'd made.

With only a hammer and screwdriver to hand, he performed a crude trepanation on the old man's skull, releasing his soul in a Merovingian rite as ancient as the bloodline itself. "Free at last," Dunphy whispered.

When Clem returned, they banked the old man's body with branches of pine and soaked it all in gasoline. Then they fashioned a slow fuse, using candle wax and string, and lit it.

"They'll have seen us by now," Dunphy said. "The whole coast is under surveillance, so they'll be on their way by now. And when they get here, they'll see what's happened, and they'll know it's all over for them."

Moving forward, Dunphy raised the little boat's jib and tied it off. Then he set the self-steering gear on a course for Jerusalem and, with Clem by his side, slipped into the water. Together, they swam for shore as the smoke began to rise from the floating funeral pyre behind them. Within a minute or two, they were standing on the beach, watching the boat as the rigging caught fire and the ruined mainsail burst into flames. Even so, it continued sailing, heading out to sea— when, suddenly, a dark shadow swept silently across the beach, and looking up, Dunphy and Clem saw an unmarked black helicopter race silently toward the burning sailboat, only to hover haplessly in the smoke above it.

"It's over," Dunphy said, and taking her hand, started walking toward a fishing village down the beach.

Clementine shook her head. "I don't think it's over," she said.

Dunphy looked at her.

"I think it's just beginning," she told him.

He wasn't sure what she meant. But, for a moment—when their eyes locked—he could have sworn he saw something in them that didn't belong there. A reflection, perhaps, of the *Stencil*'s jib, or a trace of blood from the blow she'd suffered the night before. Whatever it was, the mote had a shape, and in the instant he beheld it, he could have sworn that it was neither of the things that he'd imagined, but something else. Something that wasn't there before. Something of Gomelez.

With his wife Carolyn, Jim Hougan is part of
the writing team of John Case

Don't miss these bestselling novels of suspense
by John Case!

THE GENESIS CODE

Joe Lassiter awakens to the ring of the phone in the
dead of night. His sister and her young son have
been brutally murdered and their house set afire.
Determined to uncover why an innocent mother and
her child—his last living relatives—were targeted
for death, Lassiter is drawn into an international
conspiracy of unholy proportions. At its center is a
secret so powerful, so cataclysmic that it could alter
the course of Western civilization. . . .

**"A spellbinding biomedical thriller. . .
Terrifying."**
—*San Francisco Examiner*

**"[A] taut thriller. . .Razor-sharp dialogue,
Byzantine story twists, and several
harrowing encounters."**
—*Chicago Tribune*

THE FIRST HORSEMAN

In the Arctic, a scientific team hopes to unearth the bodies of long-dead miners. Reporter Frank Daly has the story of a lifetime. But his plan to join the scientists on their historic mission is ruined by a ferocious storm. When he meets up with the ship upon its return to port in Norway, it is clear that something has gone terribly wrong. No one will talk. But the more Daly uncovers, the more dangerous the stakes become. Until at last he comes face-to-face with a shocking secret, a secret that pitches him into a harrowing race to prevent nothing less than. . .apocalypse.

"Gripping . . . [A] tense thriller."
—*Publishers Weekly*

"Highly recommended. . .
[A] page-turning scientific thriller. . .
Unnerving and compelling."
—*Library Journal*

Published by Ballantine Books.
Available at bookstores everywhere.

THE SYNDROME

A promising research fellow for a venerable think tank in Zurich has just filed his last report, as he is forced into a grisly experiment....A seductive young woman travels to Florida on a shocking mission that she might not even be aware of.... A psychologist who helps patients confront and dispel past trauma through hypnosis battles his own silent demons.... In *The Syndrome*, John Case combines these intriguing elements into a pulse-pounding, mind-twisting new thriller....

"A GLASS-SHATTERING, DIESEL-FUELED, HARD-CHARGING THRILL RIDE OF A READ. The pages are filled with characters rich in detail and nuance forced to swim the murky waters of silence and secrecy. The plot zooms along at Formula One speed."
—Lorenzo Carcaterra,
Author of *Gangster* and *Sleepers*

Published by Ballantine Books.
Available at bookstores everywhere.